BUNKER 13

ANIRUDDHA
BAHAL

FARRAR
STRAUS
GIROUX

NEW YORK

Farrar, Straus and Giroux
19 Union Square West, New York 10003

Library of Congress Cataloging-in-Publication Data
Bahal, Aniruddha, 1967–
    Bunker 13 / Aniruddha Bahal.—1st ed.
     p. cm.
    ISBN 0-374-11730-6 (hc : alk. paper)
     1. Jammu and Kashmir (India)—Fiction.   2. Journalists—Fiction.   I. Title: Bunker
Thirteen.   II. Title.

PR9499.3.B175 B8 2003
823'.914—dc21   2002192521

www.fsgbooks.com

10   9   8   7   6   5   4   3   2   1

WILDERMUTH

FOR HIS HOLINESS

JAGADGURU SHANKARACHARYA BHARATI

TEERTHA MAHASWAMIJI OF

SHARADA PEETHAM, SRINGERI

BUNKER 13

You have soldiering boots stuck between your teeth so you don't maul your tongue. Major (Dr.) Sandy is lancing a blister on your toe at the turning point of your twelve-mile tab. The others have overtaken you. After fixing you up, even Sandy goes on ahead. You are left alone to pull up your boots, and you tense with pain as you dig your toes in and put some weight on them. You are increasingly feeling that you needn't have got into the shit you find yourself in right now, tabbing twelve miles with a forty-five-pound rucksack burning your back.

But out of the many ways that a *Homo sapiens* with an IQ of 130 can fuck himself at the flagging end of the twentieth century is by writing the following to his country's army chief: "Dear sir, With reference to our telephone conversation of a few days back, I am hereby forwarding a written proposal for your perusal. We at the *Post* would like to do a photo feature on the making of an Indian paratrooper: to put one of our writers through the course and see whether he can make it. In the competitive news environment we face, the treatment that we give to our feature sto-ries is important, hence the rather offbeat request. But it's our sincere be-lief that the piece would be a great image-building exercise for the army and do much to bolster its own efforts to draw top-notch talent through its gates. Yours sincerely, MM."

The request was granted in February 1999, after you pushed hard and greased the army's public relations officer, who, an ex–9 Para himself but now an army headquarters memorandum expert, kept looking at you weirdly all three times you met him and asked each time, "Are you sure of this?" Of course you were then. If he had spelled out in vivid terms what you were getting into, you might have been a little less sure.

But now that your sorry ass is in, you plan to stick it out to the end, make your jumps even if you have a pound of blisters on each foot. You have your reasons.

Sergeant Major Islamuddin is really enjoying putting you through the paces. He thinks of guys like you as soft ass to regulate, show what a tough guy he is. Do some show-off. He is now coming back through the run-ners to see what's with you. He thinks you are regular army grade four.

"What's up?" he asks. "Running out of gas? You want to go back a week, repeat the whole fucking thing with the next batch coming in?" It's in Sergeant Major Islamuddin's interest to kick your ass through the fit-ness course before the army lets you even touch a parachute. Maybe that gives him some career motion. But the talk is, he likes only new faces in his basic fitness program. He doesn't like leftovers to fill in the new guys in advance about what a bastard he is. He likes them to discover for themselves.

You are not part of the regular 9 Para course, but the one they run for officers from other regiments, a kind of contingency reserve they have a policy of building up. That saves you all the 9 Para advanced hocus-pocus that you are convinced would send you straight to sick bay in two days flat. But even though they have condensed their drills and tabs into a diluted version of the big fuck routine they run on their own lads, it's still enough to screw your biocycle, give you a high-fatigue RPM.

What no one wants to do is have a second crack of Sergeant Major Islamuddin's fitness regimen, give him the opportunity to tinker with your biorhythm, reprogram it permanently with his 5:00 A.M. PT.

You get up and wobble along on the one and a half legs at your disposal, but then you say, What the hell, fuck the toe. You pick up speed and find you can move into higher gear because the pain isn't as bad as before. Major (Dr.) Sandy has worked some magic.

It's a different point altogether that none of this blister shit would have happened if Sergeant Major Islamuddin hadn't told you to stuff your Nike power joggers in your locker the first day of your hitting base. The army likes its boys in leather boots. Likes to give them a shot at stress fracture in their first fortnight of marching and tabs. The guys in your batch have been wearing them for years. You haven't.

"Watch out for tendinitis," one of your batch mates from 9 Jat Regiment warns you. "That's even worse than a stress fracture."

"What's that?" you ask him. "It sounds like a cow disease."

He looks at you with pity. "The muscles at the back of your ankles flame up from stretching too much. You be careful. I got it at the Academy. Got it in both legs. Couldn't walk for a week."

You don't know how to be careful to avoid tendinitis, but it's at the back of your head, so you try some fancy running steps that you think will keep you free from tendinitis. Then you get blisters instead. That's not as bad as all four of you, who are packed into this L-shaped army-hostel accommodation, taking off your boots at one go after a tab. Dogs, you read somewhere, pack a sense of smell that's a thousand times more sensitive than a human's. You are sure if a dog came sniffing in at that time, it would die.

For the last week, you have to attend theory plus practical. A two-day dose of airborne history precedes the technical stuff. You learn about the airborne brotherhood, the International Standard Organization one thousand mark that is the Red Beret.

The instructor reads out from his notes: "The Italians raised the first para force in 1928. In 1930, the Soviet Union formed its first battalion. In April 1940, however, it was the Germans who first opened the eyes of the world to the successful use of paratroops. Germany used her para-troops force, the Fallschirmjaeger, on Norway and then, a month later, in the Netherlands, with spectacular success.

"The Allied forces, particularly Britain, were quick to realize the po-tential of the paratrooper. The British set up their parachute training school in Manchester in 1940, after Winston Churchill called for the immediate creation of a five-thousand-strong para force. Within a year, an Indian parachute battalion was approved, and soon other Common-wealth countries followed. The Canadians followed suit in 1942. Al-though many of these para forces were started and trained independently, the unifying trait was the Red Beret emblem of the forces in Common-wealth countries. But this was just the outward sign of the bond that formed between paratroops of different countries as a result of combined operations during World War Two. The two most famous are the June sixth landings in 1944, part of the Allied invasion force, and Operation Market Garden later that year."

Here, Instructor Bhaumik hangs his reading spectacles around his neck and throttles his memory. He narrates for us the street battle of Arn-hem, where the British 1st Airborne Division was ordered to capture and hold the road bridge over the lower Rhine for forty-eight hours. First, the British fucked up by air-dropping just half the task force on the first day, while chuting the rest too late in the battle. But they landed and found that intelligence fucked up even worse and that the forces whose de-fenses they had to smash through included an elite SS panzer corps. But in spite of having the SS nuts right up their asses, about seven hundred–odd men made it to the bridge and took on German tank and infantry attacks for three days and nights. Until finally the SS decided that enough was enough and that you couldn't let so few men keep bothering you for so long. So they chased the 1st Airborne from the burning houses they were holed up in. Instead of surrendering, the paras dispersed. After nine days of fighting, the 1st Airborne finally pulled back across the Rhine, 2,163 survivors out of 10,095 men.

The British parachute regiment, however, you hear, established its Red Devil lore in North Africa as part of the Allied 1942 offensive in Morocco and Algeria, where battalions were air-dropped to capture runways and road networks ahead of the ground forces, which were supposed to come later and relieve them. This, you learn, is vintage Airborne initiative.

But on one occasion at least, the ground forces forgot to link up with 2 Para, and the poor guys found themselves fifty miles inside Rommel territory and had to make a two-day march to join their own forces. Only a quarter made it.

The regiment also established an early reputation for botching up its drops. For instance, in an operation in Sicily in 1943, just three hundred–odd men out of more than eighteen hundred who jumped off planes landed in the drop zone. This allowed the three hundred–odd guys an opportunity to become heroes by defending the Primosole Bridge for one whole day. Instructor Bhaumik's historical erudition regarding the paras doesn't include telling you why the bridge was important for the Allies to hold for a day. Maybe they couldn't find enough whores around the bridge for their officers to bounce before retreating.

While the British have just an airborne brigade, the U.S. airborne freaks have an order of battle that contains the 82nd Airborne Division, the mechanized infantry division, an armored brigade, an antitank air cavalry brigade, and the 101st Air Assault Division.

The 82nd Airborne Division, of course, are the designated out-of-area motherfuckers who first took on this role on D day at Normandy. With about seventeen thousand nuts on its rolls, the 82nd also packs enough wing power in C-130s, C-5 Galaxies, and C-141 Star Lifters to lift and

deliver their load of nuts at any point on an atlas. They train at Fort Ben-
ning, Georgia, and take up their dates on AH-1S Huey Cobras, which
you can mount TOWs on.

But if the U.S. parachute forces dwarf the British, the Russians are in a
league of their own. They are quantum motherfuckers. The Vozdushno-
Desantnyye Voyska is more than 100,000 strong. If NATO does something really pissy, the guys are going to chute down in Western Europe
behind enemy lines and riddle French and German ass with 73-mm
hardware, the AT-4 Spigot antitank missiles, the 120-mm self-propelled
2S9 guns, and whatever thing handy they can mount on some turretless
shit called the BMD M1979.

The reason they will be running into the French early on is because
part of the brief of the French paras is to go save German ass if the Russians come paying a visit. The French airborne strength in the 11th Parachute Division is about fourteen thousand strong and is based at Tarbes.
That includes the 2 REP from the French Foreign Legion, which carried
out the assault on Kolwezi in 1978. These elite motherfuckers have
about four companies of elite assault paratroopers. They are so elite, they
don't talk to civilians.

The unique aspect of the French paras is that they have undertaken
more operational jumps than any other para force in the world. They
have seen action in Indochina, the Suez, and Africa, particularly Algeria.
The French campaign in Indochina saw them make 156 operational
drops, culminating in the historic jump in the valley near Dien Bien
Phu, where General Giap's Vietminh took the French out of the battle
and eventually out of the region in 1955.

In 1957, the French paras returned to combat. This time, the 10th
Parachute Division took over the city of Algiers and restored order within
a month. But the force received a setback by involving itself in the attempted overthrow of General Charles de Gaulle in 1960 and has been
looked upon with suspicion ever since. Yet it produced two very striking
generals in Jacques Massu and Marcel Bigeard. The latter's appearance

at Dien Bien Phu did much to raise morale in the beleaguered garrison. The trademark that distinguished him from other generals was his habit of arriving to inspect units by parachute, his hand at the salute as he landed in front of the honor guard.

The Indian para strength is modest by comparison: a token force of nine battalions, with a total strength of 5,500 men. Of the nine para battalions, 1, 9, and 10 are para commandos and have most recently seen action in Sri Lanka and the Maldives, but the 50th Indian Parachute Brigade was formed way back in 1941 and saw action mostly in Burma and the North East. The Gurkhas were the first Indian troops to wear the para wings. When para forces were still in development, the British found it easiest to sucker the Gurkhas into jumping.

The 152nd and 153rd Gurkha parachute battalions saw magnificent action against the Japanese at Sangshak when they were on their way to Imphal. Bearing the brunt of the flanking attacks by the Japanese on the retreating 14th Army, the batallions gained time for the garrison at Imphal to reorganize its defenses.

Later, the brigade distinguished itself in the British efforts to recapture Rangoon from the Japanese. The paras jumped over Tawhai, south of Rangoon, to clear Japanese coastal defenses on the Rangoon River to make way for the Indian 26th Division, which headed upriver under the amphibious operation code Dracula.

After you are through with theory (an area in which you intend to take an unassailable lead over Major Rodriguez, with whom you have a bet to top the course), they herd you into landing practice. You learn to touch ground in a dozen different ways. The standard position—elbows tucked in, feet and knees together, and legs loose like box springs—has the potential to save you from all but the heaviest of landings. But since army-issue chutes are nonsteerable, giving you scant control over the direction of your approach, you have to learn how to land forward, sideways, and backward, bucking with the way the wind brings you down. You are told never to break your S position. The army has even developed laid-down procedures for fuckups you can see coming, like hitting a church wall. It wants you injury-free for the screwball mission it sends you on. It teaches you how to reduce impact. It teaches you to avoid frontal collisions with stationary objects. It's better, they tell you, to bust your ribs than to smack your face on concrete.

For two hours, the parachute-jumping instructor (PJI) makes you do about forty parachute rolls from any angle he hollers out. Next to you, Major Rodriguez whispers, "Hey, MM, what about a dick landing? Do they teach that, too? What could happen to a guy like Islamuddin on an emergency dick landing?" That, you agree, is a tremendous theoretical point of concern. Islamuddin has an organ the size of a forty-pound dumbbell. Your stick of ten men saw it once when Islamuddin put you through compulsory showers to build comradeship.

But you refrain from responding to Major Rodriguez for fear of attracting the PJI's attention. You are familiar with the major's unscrupulous tactics. For Major Rodriguez, there are just two categories of the living—players and fucked-up eggheads. Major Rodriguez fancies himself a player. While you don't begrudge him that status or doubt the merits of his claim, what you have strong reservations about is sliding into the fucked-up classification that the major's social theory will shove you into should you lose the bet with him. You have observed the major at close quarters when you were together at Siachen in December 1998. He'll do anything to come out on top. So you want to make him sweat till the last moment. Your only chance lies in squeezing an error out of him by cramping his style, throwing him off his game.

What immediately follows your landing period is an introduction to canopy, the special nylon that stops your falling like a stone from up above. The main chute of the Indian paras, you learn, is the paratrooper main (PTRM), a nonsteerable parachute with a destiny you cannot control except by lifting the webbing on one side to allow air to hiss through so you don't crash into other jumpers on the way down. The PTRM is modeled on the American T-5, but the cords play out before the canopy locks, so you don't get that body jerk that the American T-10 gives you. On the other hand, the American T-10 is fully steerable, with the canopy opening out even before your cords tauten up.

"But," throws in Major Rodriguez during one of your stick drinking sessions, "the T-10 is actually a military disadvantage in certain situations." None in your stick can figure out any obvious disadvantage in T-10. Better to steer to a DZ of your choice than land on electric wires and have yourself barbecued. The major, however, has been putting in extra time in the library, getting some solid purchase over you in theory.

He explains: "It could create problems when you have sim sticks on both port and starboard sides of the aircraft. Every steerable chute has a bias. It doesn't drop you straight down the way a PTRM or a PX4 does."

The rest of you nod intelligently.

Right now, your batch is simulating aircraft-door sim launches. You drop through a door slowed by a giant fan. You have to indulge in skillful manipulation to avoid having the major right after you in your stick of six, or you might find yourself catapulted out with more force than necessary, an unnerving contingency, even if the drop is only thirty feet.

But you flow through the fan trainer with ease, and the next step in your training takes you to the tower, where you hurl yourself down 130 feet on a harness that connects you to two wires, a kind of aerial runway. A bit like a slide, only the ride's a lot more bumpy. You slide a cool 325 feet. It's the nearest you can get to knowing what it's like to jump into an AN-32 slipstream. For three days, you have also been practicing harness release and drag. You are given tips on how to avoid being dragged on the ground by the canopy after landing.

The next day, you are supposed to go up for your first jump. Everybody in your stick is at Major Rodriguez's quarters, taking turns sipping rum from paper cups. Through cigarette smoke and rum fumes, Major Rodriguez is giving you all a blow-by-blow account of an accident that took place yesterday in a simulated runway raid.

"Jumping on an airfield, you have to be quick. But if you are too quick, you could end up like those two guys yesterday. The second guy out got right above the first guy out. He went into an air lock. His chute candled. That's what happened."

"You mean they went into an entanglement?" Major Sandy tries to clear the technical fog in his brain.

"Yeah. Two guys right on top of each other, rigging lines kissing each other," says Major Rodriguez. "The guy on top had an air steal all the way down to two hundred feet, and then the guy below tried to get his lines straight, but then his chute went limp and both of them came down from two hundred feet. They tried pulling their reserves, but all the chutes did was blow up in their faces and get entangled in their rigging."

"Are they dead?" you ask, before you can help it.

"No," says Major Rodriguez. "They're having tea with the base commander. Broken legs, broken pelvises, fractured backs, heads, hands, every fucking bone. DOI case."

"DOI?" asks Sandy.

"Dead on impact," Major Rodriguez says. And the way he rolls the word *impact* over his tongue has everybody silent for a while. "One of the worst incidents these guys have had in a while. The other day, they had this group up on first jump and the last guy on the stick wouldn't jump. He just caught hold of the door frame and wouldn't budge. The PJI whacked him on his wrists and kicked him way the hell out to make him go. The guy got a fractured right wrist, and he doesn't remember how he got it. He's gone blank. You go in shock out there sometimes when you see the ground, and you can't remember shit from then."

"The PJIs are not supposed to force someone out on the first jump, I guess," you say.

"Who the fuck knows what the PJIs are supposed to do or not do?" asks Major Rodriguez. "We got this rookie asshole anyways. We are his first stick. Maybe the guy kicks us all out. Maybe we all go in shock up there. Bring the fucking plane down."

It's para practice to have a full-blown morale-building battalion drop within twenty-four hours of some freak para accident. It's also general para practice not to club first jumpers with veterans. But one of the IL-76s gets a bird hit, a hawk through the jet turbines, and three greenhorn sticks have to crowd in with 5 Para doing a 135-pound-kit jump. The big boys keep lugging these containers all over the aircraft, falling over everybody else. And the joker sitting next to you goes to sleep before the bird starts taxiing. Then you have this dispatcher nearly walking over everybody's heads to check things out.

But all you are thinking of is to stay ahead of Major Rodriguez after the light turns green. Your bet with the major stipulates a significant point bonus for whoever hits the ground first. A little game within a bet. The major's own game, of course, has been to up on Benzedrine. That's his thing. A speed booster to up his confidence level, tone his central nervous system for the high-stress maneuvers ahead.

The way he's done it is to roll the sulfate in a Wills cigarette paper and swallow it. He chases it down his gullet with chilled beer in the mess before arriving at rendezvous point.

The bomber takes hold of him in half an hour, and you can see his eyes light up. You don't like to swallow the stuff. That, you feel, dilutes the hit. You want your rush faster, so you do a few lines on your shaving kit's mirror, chopped fine to reduce the burn and sniffed through a rolled tenner. Of course, you got the stuff from Major Rodriguez. Where he got it from is his business.

All the chatter stops when the green comes on. Your three sticks are right at the back, sweating it out, waiting for the big guys to jump in the wind. The thing about jumping, you remember, is to go out with a thrust. That stops the slipstream from getting a hold over you and banging you against the AN-32 body, loading your face full of aluminum rivets.

Major Rodriguez is the last on your stick. You are two guys ahead of him. The major's giving the works to Sandy, who's behind you.

"Hey, Sandy, you checked your chute? Looks very bad to me. Looks like your cord's stuck in your harness," says Major Rodriguez.

Major Sandy starts sweating like a pig.

"Fuck you, Rodriguez," he says. "You got stones in your nylon."

"Man, this is serious. You ought to have a look. There's this gooey stuff sticking all over your pack," Major Rodriguez says.

He's got Sandy fidgeting like mad. Then there's this other guy on your stick, Capt. Prem Prakash, who's behind Sandy but in front of Rodriguez. Sandy looks up at him for psychological support, but the young captain is having none of that. He's clearly having some kind of quiet freak-out of his own, and he's fully preoccupied with keeping himself sane.

Rodriguez keeps at Sandy. He yells at the PJI to have a look at Sandy's pack. And when your stick gets the go, Major Sandy's so tripped, he starts yelling and unhooks himself from the line.

You, of course, are only too aware of what Rodriguez is up to. Narrowing the numbers between you and him. Reducing the three-second advantage you have over him. But you figure victory is yours. You are still going to have a lead of fifty feet by the time Rodriguez jumps.

But you haven't counted on Sandy blowing all the fuses in his head. He's howling a demented howl, making all sorts of gestures at Rodriguez. It's then you realize fleetingly that maybe Sandy's on a bomber, too. Only he doesn't know it. You see your PJI leave the door and come to Sandy. Keep him in grip. It's then that your turn comes, and you exit the AN-32, pushed out by one of the three PJIs standing at the door with monkey harnesses.

"Go, go, go, go . . ." they all shout.

And as you go past the slipstream and feel the reassuring jerk of canopy, amid all the new sensations that rush in and stall your thinking for a while, you still feel the need to glance up and flash the V sign at Major Rodriguez.

You hear the crack of canopies opening. Rodriguez is forty feet above you. You can see the concentration on his face. You also see him go for his parachute-release mechanism, the two levers on his shoulders. Rodriguez is free-falling now. He goes below you. You can't believe what you are seeing. You see him pull the rip cord on his chest, where the reserve lies, and you wait what seems an interminable moment before the lines deploy and the nylon balloons. His body jerks up 150 feet from impact. The lines pull him taut at his chest. Rodriguez goes horizontal. You see him pull the lines down, stall his chute, go vertical at the moment of impact.

You chew the cud over what you just saw. In the catalog of crazies it has been your fate to meet, Major Rodriguez is in a class of his own, you decide. And then the ground comes at you much faster than expected and you are concerned about your own fate. You tense your limbs. You go into the S formation. What you have to avoid is falling like a bag of shit. That's what they have taught you. They have also taught you about harness release and drag. What they haven't taught you is what to do if there's no wind and the son of a bitch of a canopy falls right over you. It takes you about a million minutes to come out of that.

Kudos come Rodriguez's way after the news of his presence of mind during his first descent filters through. Surviving a reserve-chute landing on first jump is unprecedented in Indian para history and ensures Rodriguez's name in the battalion hall of fame. The major, of course, is smart enough to locate his released main chute immediately after landing and knife through five compartments. The blowing of panels on the main canopy is a well-documented hazard. The hard-boiled 5 Para nuts came and shook his hand and congratulated him on his narrow escape. Major Rodriguez took these things in stride.

He couldn't duck an inquiry because of the thing with Sandy. But nobody except Rodriguez himself, Sandy, and you quite knows what took place, and so the major's version goes uncontested. You have your reasons for sealing up on Rodriguez, and they aren't the ones that Rodriguez thinks they are.

Most important, nobody got hurt, and if anyone came close to squeezing the ghost out of his frame, it was Major Rodriguez himself. There is
no reason not to believe what he says, especially since Sandy didn't crack,
though he knew what it was all about. He just packed his stuff and went
back to the 9 Rajput Rifles like nothing had happened.

The good thing about army training, you discover, is that it's geared for
eventualities like Sandy's. There was nothing fishy in chickening out at
first jump. Para drops are scary, and there is nothing wrong in getting
scared. Fear management is essential para drill. The only surprise was
that Sandy had made it so far. The army is good at filtering out the scum
at first stage. They pick guys who can piss high. Where it's weak in tackle
is when it has to deal with fringe bastards of the Rodriguez variety.

The major's testimony was a lot of horseshit, but it sank well. He
claimed he thought Sandy's pack looked kind of funny from behind and
all he did was warn him about it. Strangely, since Sandy flung his pack
aside and diddled with it while in flight, the pin cracked and burst his
chute in the fuselage. He was lucky he wasn't anywhere near the door.
He got his chute so messed up, nobody really doubted Major Rodriguez's version of events. That left just the question of Major Rodriguez's
shoving the PJI at the door in order to leap into the slipstream. Not an or-
dinary shove, but one that cracked his ribs against the fuselage and
yanked his collarbone right out of the socket. This, Rodriguez did to gain
some vital fractions of a second in his pursuit of you.

Major Rodriguez's deposition was electric: "From the moment the
green light went, I wanted to go. I sat crouched during jump run, my
eyes locked on to the light, and nobody could stop me from jumping. I
was in an aggressive, relaxed, concentrated state of mind. That really
helps me on with things. I don't remember the incident with the PJI. After all that waiting, the fear and the apprehension, I just needed to go. I
went into a kind of blackout after the jump. I didn't know what was happening. Then I felt the jerks on my shoulders, and when I looked up, I

saw the panels begin to rip. That's when my training took over. I am thankful to all my PJIs for the innumerable drill sessions. I am alive because of them."

That is what he said, or thereabouts. You got it from the garrison commandant, whom you met just before you left and who was so impressed by Rodriguez's wordage, he'd jotted it down in his diary. He planned to recommend Rodriguez for a Republic Day medal. He was the one who got the base psychiatrist off Rodriguez's back. The doc was poking at Rodriguez for a while, getting his fun. But Rodriguez came out flying from all the psychological traps he'd sprung on him. If you don't know what you are looking for, chances are you won't find anything interesting. He ranked him top beef. What the medics didn't do was check his blood after the jump. Or yours or Sandy's, for that matter. That might have shaken up the set a bit.

Of course, you lost your bet with Major Rodriguez. He did top your batch. He took a hundred bucks off you. But you know it wasn't the money Rodriguez was after.

Four jumps later, Rodriguez volunteers for Pathfinder Company, the military free fallers—a club so elite, it's an active force of just a hundred people. While your basic para course took you twenty-one grueling days, military free falling, you learn, is a place for the truly mad. A full-length course strings you up for three months. But the para forces are raising a show jump team on the line of Britain's Red Devils and are prospecting for talent a little further afield than the regular para battalions.

You aren't keen on continuing at the Agra para base, four hours from New Delhi, but your business is to bait Major Rodriguez, so you are left with no choice but to tap your own sources and let the army trim you a vacancy in the free fallers. You sell the army chief the idea of a glossy book this time. To sound convincing, you make your editor and publishers fax him a bogus contract letter, including a clause for all royalties to go to the Army Women's Welfare Association. You know people who can push the army chief's hand, but you prefer to play it this way. You want to pull zero fucking confrontation. A war on two fronts is not your way to conduct business.

As a professional, you have already broken rules. You are neck-deep with Rodriguez into pumping your veins with all kinds of mind-blowing pharmaceuticals. Bumping into each other again ten years after the Academy, you recognized this common weakness in each other. It let you strike up an instantaneous rapport. Just because one day in the near future you may feel the need to shut him up permanently, speed-post him to Goa to lie in his family burial yard, it doesn't take the pleasure out of your dealings with him. Instead, it introduces a sense of contrast. It's a tussle that you enjoy.

You are back to the drawing board again. Free falling, the PJI explains, is all about oxygen, thermal wear, air pressure, and flying. If you don't get your basics right, you might end up in a bullet drop, a 120-mph base hit, but at 120 miles per hour, the air rush is full of convertible energy. And if you learn to direct this airflow, you do not fall: you fly.

"You need to have a feel for the air," PJI Malhotra tells you as he puts you through the wires to post you on the basic positions.

Your bread-and-butter position on the way down is the spread eagle, legs and hands in a V, your face down, your back arched in a hollow to maintain equilibrium. Lose this position and you might drop through space in involuntary loops, somersaults, barrel rolls, or a vicious flat spin, which would centrifuge the blood out of your brain and whip you unconscious.

This is where you are taught the principle of controlled bypass from your symmetrical poise, which is possible through a rearrangement of airflow against your body surface.

"You can initiate movement by bending one or both legs, your hands, arching your body, even angling your palms," says Malhotra. For four days, Malhotra hangs each one of you on suspension wires and you learn various body geometries. A head-down or a no-lift dive, for instance, increases vertical speed by reducing the area of body surface presented to airflow. In sky divers' jargon, it's known as a delta, track, or max-track approach. Or you can fly horizontally by sloping your body at an angle to the air. Or if you are one for show-jumping positions, you could take the Canarrozzo position, a head-down dive with legs apart and hands folded across the chest.

To come out of delta dives, you practice the reverse arch: body balanced on fingertips and toes, cupping your body to catch the air full-on.

"This is a dangerous position, though," warns Malhotra. "If you don't have enough feel for the air, you could end up on your back all the way down." To flip out of this position, you have to arch your back upward and let the air do the rest. If you fail and pull the rip cord in panic, you are likely to wrap the main chute around your body, with little chance of firing your reserve.

The way the army starts you off on free-fall jumps is by dropping you on static lines for the first five jumps from twelve thousand feet. Canopy control is what you have to master before getting high on ground rush. The Pathfinders' steerable rectangular canopy is a revelation, a flying machine with a forward speed of twenty-nine nautical miles in zero wind conditions and a ratio of 3:1. It imparts a forward thrust of three feet for every foot it takes you down. What is impressive is the degree of maneuverability you can exercise at this speed. The toggles serve as your brakes and accelerators as well as your steering wheel. Because of them, Pathfinder platoons can be dropped miles away from the DZ and from great heights.

Malhotra builds up your mentality. "You don't have to know everything about physics, Newton's law of action or reaction, or your dive angles. The important thing is to think flying rather than falling. That goes for landing, too. You have to drive toward touchdown on a downwind approach, your toggles at shoulder level. If you are overshooting, you press the levers further. If you are falling short, you let them loose. Piece of cake."

But stalling, you are told, is the main killing statistic for free fallers. Braking the toggles beyond a certain point takes the air out of your chute, and you go down like a stone from that point.

The history of parachuting is, however, more colorful than that of the paratroopers alone. The para school occasionally invites veteran sports enthusiasts to fill you in on the trial-and-error methods of early pioneers, some even going back all the way to the eighteenth century. The whole of the nineteenth century and the early half of the twentieth were crammed with great aeronautical expectation. People launched themselves from balloons, off bridges and spires, anything that let them fly. The current safety levels in the descents, lecturers tell you, owe much to trendsetters who risked cracking their skulls and backs and losing their lives in experimental jumps.

You are particularly enthralled by the era of show jumpers and the trailblazing free fallers, who got the hang of controlled free fall simply by climbing out of cockpits and letting go. These are people after your own heart.

Two mammoth jumps stand out for you: first, Joe Kittinger's in Operation Excelsior, which was launched to test endurance at the frontiers of the atmosphere. In 1960, on his second jump, strapping on his Beaupre multistage stabilization parachute, Kittinger stepped from an open gondola 103,000 feet above New Mexico, twenty miles above earth. He reached a speed of 615 miles per hour at ninety thousand feet, slowing down as the air became thicker, and opened his chute after four and a half minutes of free fall. He landed safely in the desert thirteen and a half minutes after stepping down from the gondola. No man has jumped from those heights since.

But there have been attempts. A crazy bloke by the name of Nick Piantanida tried in 1966. The New Jersey truck driver had big ambitions. He wanted to be the first sky diver in history to crack through the sound barrier. For this, he had to attempt his jump from 120,000 feet above sea level, which would take him to Mach 1 speed before he hit thick air. The attempt ended with tragedy at 57,000 feet, when his face shield blew out of his pressure suit. Piantanida died four months later, without ever coming out of a coma.

Rodriguez has been a quiet participant in the training and lecture sessions. It's like the calm before a storm. He hasn't picked up your bait yet, and it's making you nervous. People like Rodriguez are fast movers. His patience gives you cause for alarm, although you are careful not to bring up matters yourself. From what you know of Rodriguez, he can sniff a trap in his sleep, and you don't want the scent to lead to you.

Instead, you have left letters and invitations on your bed that should indicate to him your presence at international seminars involving issues like defense and environment: the fixer journalist with heavy connections. Even clinchers like inducements from the U.S. Institute of Peace and the Carnegie Foundation to accept yearlong fellowships. You have been heedful not to flaunt these personally. And Rodriguez has been careful not to let on if he has snooped through your documents, and he's far too cautious to let you catch him in the act.

Your strategy has been three-pronged. Besides your document display, you have shown significant willingness to dilute your moral standards. In fact, you have taken pains to indicate none at all. You know he has appreciated your silence in the matter with Major Sandy. Complicity in minor intrigues is a great bond with sizable rogues like Rodriguez. So, too, are drugs. There, you are as degenerate as Rodriguez. You need no special preparation for shooting and snorting yourself to high altitudes. You feel a solidarity there that levers you free from your long-term plans.

Third, you have given him evidence of your criminal genes. The bogus NGO that you floated to siphon off a Swedish grant committed enough foreign-exchange violations to put you behind bars for five years, not even counting forging checks. You left the fake clearance certificates lying unattended in the hostel you shared with him. Rodriguez quizzed you on the procedure, but he stopped at that. It was enough; you'd given him his edge. You want Rodriguez to get heady on that. Let him get an uppity feeling.

You have also let it be known you're looking for a big score. A tally large enough to set up in a mansion in the English countryside. You've drawn the line at this, however. Any more perfume in the air, and warning bells might ring in Rodriguez's ears.

But the closest connection between you comes from the game of danger you are involved in and the new dimensions that Rodriguez brings to it. You discover that the airborne brotherhood is a place for togetherness of a high order. It brings you especially close to play this new game, waiting to see who will drop lowest before pulling the cord. This came a little later, after you first started snorting on Lady H at ten thousand feet. (Actually, even this was a little ahead in the sequence of things.)

First came the death of Captain Prakash. You have numerous hypotheses concerning Prakash's death. But start with the facts. The timer on Prakash's chute activated at eight thousand feet in a Cessna when he was standing near the door. The pilot chute dragged Prakash out of the exit, and his head banged on the side before he was plucked into thin air. At that height, Prakash had forty-five seconds before impact. Captain Prakash's main chute wrapped itself around his spinning body, and since reserves have no timers and he was unconscious, he hit the earth at terminal velocity, a small matter of 120 miles per hour.

To Rodriguez's credit, he displayed great presence of mind, fast reactions, and supreme courage. He deltaed after Prakash, in the vain hope of catching up with him at a sufficient height to pull his reserve cord. Rodriguez was nearest to the door, in jumping gear, and one whose responsive hands Prakash desperately lunged for but failed to meet when he saw that his life's plug had just been pulled. Rodriguez came within sixty-five feet of Prakash, but the creep of the altimeter reminded him at eight hundred feet that he had better leave Prakash to his own fate. There was nothing anybody could do to save his skin.

Your first hypothesis regarding Prakash's death is that he forgot to switch off the timer on his chute after the pilot was forced to turn around from launching point by a murderous-looking cumulonimbus with enough water to outweigh a couple of aircraft carriers. A single wind from the cloud-swept mass could have cracked the Cessna like a tin box. In a hurry to get away, the pilot neglected to issue the compulsory warning when the plane descended. Timers operate on the barometric principle and activate at the air pressure you have set. It is part of procedure to deactivate your timer in the case of an aborted run, but this seemed to have slipped Prakash's mind.

Or the timer malfunctioned. But they are reliable gadgets. Your third hypothesis, and the most troubling one, is that somebody else activated Prakash's timer after he had switched it off. Somebody who stayed focused while the rest of you gazed through the Cessna's portholes at the ready distraction provided by the swirling black mass.

In spite of Rodriguez's gallant act, something that even PJIs with over a thousand jumps to their name are scared to attempt, the needle of your suspicion swings to him. Prakash's rag-doll death doesn't have the look of a technology fuckup, or human error. Somebody wanted him out of action. And you figure Captain Prakash had something on him that made Rodriguez desperate enough to go after it. Also, all you have is Rodriguez's version of Captain Prakash's fall. By the time the Cessna turned around and swung below the cloud cover, everything was over. Maybe Prakash's reserve did open and Rodriguez jumped to ensure that he stayed dead even if he survived the drop.

You don't discount such ominous possibilities. Especially when you take into account Captain Prakash's background. Captain Prakash was an officer from the 7 Sikh, which right now is based in Kashmir's Kupwara sector, the same area as Major Rodriguez's 5 Kumaon.

A week before, you heard a heated argument of some sort between the two as you entered Captain Prakash's room, a discussion that terminated abruptly as soon as you made your appearance. You never bought Rodriguez's explanation that Prakash was upset because he (that is, Rodriguez) was mainlining in his room. He had all the toking paraphernalia spread in front of him. Whatever else Captain Prakash might have been, he was pretty cool about high octane levels in somebody else's bloodstream. He wasn't a snitch, either.

He knew what you and Rodriguez were up to when you chose to be the last to jump into the slipstream of the AN-32. Snorting H at terminal velocity is hardly an efficient way to get your rush. Since there is no way you can nose in an appreciable quantity the regular way, you have to smear your thumb and forefinger with powder before you jump and stick them up your nostrils after you've cleared the air cushion from the plane.

There are a few drawbacks inherent in the method. You have never taken to the taste of heroin. It's bitter, and you have to drag it one nostril at a time. Besides, though the powder hits in a minute, you get none of the blinding buzz that comes when you mainline. You also have to take into account the waste of material that occurs with lots of it remaining in your nostrils, plus the amount that you lose in the wind. And H is gold dust, as far as you are concerned.

The injecting rush is intrinsic to your pharma-diving plans. Though the rush is something that veteran users are immune to, you have not let the drug run away with you, and you don't fall under the addict classification. You want to let the wooziness hit you even as the air is blowing past. You want to run with life-and-death forces before you pull your cord. Of course, mainlining at ground level is a sufficiently complex procedure. It depends upon the purity of the heroin you can corner from retail. If it's prime-grade stuff, you spread it on a spoon with a small amount of water. Your next step is to flame the solution so that the particles dissolve easily. Then you suck it up through a syringe and hit a vein in your forearm. Of course, if all you can get hold of on street corners is brown, your kit will have to include citric acid or ascorbic acid to ensure powder assimilation. To sift the impurities further, you have to syringe the solution through a cigarette filter.

An attempt to go through these steps during sixty seconds of free fall is fraught with various unknowns. But that is hardly a deterrent for you and Rodriguez. You test a few breezeproof lighters in flight, but they aren't designed with free fall in mind. You go for a battery-operated wire lighter, souped up by Rodriguez to include an additional pair of pencil batteries.

"It's cold as a morgue up there. We need some supplementary power heating to get us by," says Major Rodriguez.

You have to dig your glucose disposable into a forearm vein before taking flight, and keep it in place with a smartly wound Velcro strap. You have the syringe taped right next to the tube opening, which is capped. You take the precaution of corking the needle tip. You carry your premixed ammunition in a small bottle and attach a paper clip to use as a handle. Theoretically, all you have to do is get on your back, heat the bottle, detach the syringe from its holster, suck the solution through, unhinge the syringe, and depress the plunger in your tube.

Because of the precarious nature of your circumstances, you have to keep glancing at the altimeter strapped to your midriff. Altitude has a way of creeping up on you unawares. It also teaches you in unambiguous terms the direct relation between cause and effect. Your head elevates more than is necessary and the spin works on you; you go into uninvited somersaults, losing the tenuous hold over your kit.

You try streamlining your procedure at ground level. Rehearse after dinner on the suspension wires. Pick up Formula 1 pit-stop speeds in your routine. For all of Rodriguez's automated bluster, at heart he's a risk-management expert. He accepts the hazards involved, but he works at blunting the luck factor. That's the way you operate, too. You believe in giving yourself sufficient chances to pull things off.

You come up with the idea of falling together, have just one man go for the needle. This way, you have a watchdog to pull your cord should the hit take you too deep into the game to bother. Heroin puts the troubles of the world at a great distance; you fall in a beautiful bubble of stupefaction. And one of the uncorrectable things it can do to you at two thousand feet, the recommended safe height for pulling your cord, is sink in you the belief that life is too complicated to manage and the best way out is the free ticket to oblivion.

You spin a coin to decide who's going to take first shot. You call right. The first time you do it, Providence smiles your way. You are not on a regular training run but are doing an unofficial exit from an IL-76, on a pilot-training sortie. It's only the two of you in the whole wide bay of the

160-seater. You bend your routine a bit. You take your shot at the door it-self before yahooing into space. The major goes nonnuclear. You lacked the foresight to keep some spare ammunition.

At moderate doses of H, your brain retains its distinctness and dy-namism. You go into sharp focus, and the warm feeling that emanates from your belly steers you clear without any effort from the everyday clut-ter that ping-pongs in your head. You gravitate to a spiritual exactness. You are like a seer soaring and swooping in heaven. You are into NOW. You are into nothing. You see the ground rush into you, and when you pull the cord, it's an afterthought, with none of the urgency and fear that categorized this action for you in the past. When the nylon jerks you vi-olently into deceleration, you hardly feel the cords bite into the bruises on your shoulders.

The only luck that comes Rodriguez's way is that you manage another training-sortie ride, but this time the seats are full with veteran Pathfind-ers from the 10 Para commando battalion who are sneaking a joy jump free of military encumbrances. For plus-twelve-thousand-foot jumps, you need thermal suits, oxygen masks and cylinders, and acclimatization rou-tines. You talk in hand signals at these heights, and although you have jumped with all that gear, it makes your dives too technical for you to think of introducing the Afghan soldiers into your bloodstream. Even though you get more time with a mask on your face, you can't see for shit.

The advantage that informal leaps give you is there's no PJI breathing down your neck when you fall a mile away from the drop zone. You can never make it to the designated drop zone and punch your way to God at the same time; your chute opens too low for you to get much glide mo-mentum.

But this time, you're going to drop close to a highway and hitch a ride back to base.

Rodriguez slips in the midair engagements with robotic accuracy and speed. "Nobody goes faceup," he keeps mumbling to himself, his mantra. The two of you jump together.

After mainlining with swift efficiency, he gives you the thumbs-up sign, chucks the syringe into the air, and you can see it sharing the ride with you twenty feet away. Before you split, you check the major one last time, and you see symptoms that you recognize as signs of an overdose. Rodriguez is slipping into a daze, his eyes falling shut and his chin slipping to his chest.

You realize that the H Rodriguez has mixed today is purer than both of you thought. You have been so used to the inferior dimorphine base stepped with glucose, lactose, chalk, and talcum powder that the real thing has put you in a spot. Brown has purity levels ranging from 20 to 40 percent. The same quantum with weapons-grade heroin can steer you into some serious side effects, all perfectly visible in Rodriguez's case. His head begins to roll uncontrollably.

You realize that if you don't do something for Rodriguez, and quickly, he'll go the way of Captain Prakash. A part of you sees justice in such a scheme of things, but you also understand that Rodriguez is your only overpass to more sinister happenings in Kashmir, and he is worth more to you alive than dead. Still, there's only so much you can do, since even after you pulled his cord and split, his chute would launch from a faceup position and tangle him hopelessly in its lines.

But people like Rodriguez aren't what they are without residual survival syndromes. Even as you pull the cord and before the pilot chute comes flapping out, some aboriginal instinct tunes Rodriguez to the danger he is in and you see him bend in a reverse arch and flip over as his main chute surges up. You take a look at your altimeter as you open up. You have dipped five hundred feet below expedient altitude.

Rodriguez survives the landing with his bones intact, though he is in and out when you reach him in a tomato field. The experience of the fall makes the two of you abort future heroin skydiving. Instead, you go on speed, which you snort in the loo next to the briefing hall. It fortifies in you your resolve to pull your lifeline at heights below one thousand feet or whoever cracks up first. It is here in the loo that the two of you first shoot methedrine, and you discover that the hit is much more powerful than H, doesn't last long, and won't put you to sleep in midair.

But you don't want to push your luck with methedrine. One of its potent effects is that it makes you feel omnipotent. Unlike H, it doesn't give you an insight into things; it becomes the insight. You become God. And flying with that fiery brand of philosophy in your head is, you decide, a prelude to dangerous consequences.

But after bailing him out, you command an emotion from Rodriguez that you thought lay outside his repertoire. He occasionally flashes you a look of something like gratitude, even respect.

And one day, he feels the need to confide, his way of handing you his balls. A motherfucker's reciprocative gesture.

"Hey, MM," he says. "You know why Prakash died?"

"Because the timer fucked on him," you offer with a poker face.

He looks straight into your eyes. A bastard's piercing gaze. "Because if you play out of your depth, and you don't pack what it takes to get you out of a hole, you just sign up for what's headed your way."

This is as far as he goes in his confession. But it is easy to take things from there. For you, the shark had sunk its teeth on the bait. Now it is a question of giving a lot of slack and reeling in at a propitious moment. Rodriguez taps you on your intents, tempts you with the big score, and you, in turn, nibble on the enticement offered your way.

The two of you don't stick around at para school after this. There's no need to. For one, you aren't part of the para crowd and are pissing off the regular bunch with your fucked-up attitude toward free falling. Also, sticking around would mean falling eventually to another bout of pharma-diving sessions, which might well lead you in the footsteps of Captain Prakash.

You give them reason to tick you out of base. You botch three consecutive DZs, and PJI Malhotra decides that he isn't in the mood for another casualty so soon after the Prakash incident. Even if the Army Women's Welfare Association could use the royalties.

When you next meet him, two months down the line, it's in a very different locale. You are in Kashmir partly to shoot a documentary on the line of control at Kupwara, where the 5 Kumaon and Major Rodriguez are posted, but you haven't sought him out just yet. Although there is a lot of pressure on you to whip up the pace in your dealings with him, you want things to develop naturally.

It's late April 1999, and you have come a few days ahead with half your crew, a sound engineer called Siddy. You have to push paper with the 15th Corps at Srinagar, part of the Northern Command at Udhampur, get them to sort out the logistics.

Siddy is the son of a veteran with a distinguished record of service in the 1971 East Pakistan war. Right now, he has with him a manual that he pinched from Major General Mahalingam's office at 15th Corps, *Standard Operational Procedure in Low-Intensity Conflict Areas*, volume 1.

"We have fucked it up from the start," he says.

"Fucked what up?" you ask, alarmed. In your life, you have fucked up many things, often with painful results, and you like to stitch up the loose ends in your control.

You realize after Siddy hands you the SOPLICA manual that your beginning in Kashmir has been both illiterate and dangerous.

Rule 1 of SOPLICA warns you not to arrive in low-intensity conflict areas in military aircraft. That might single you out as part of a Special Forces group. You and Siddy hopped a ride in an army Avro. Siddy's red London Fog jacket must have been visible for miles around. You learn that airports in LIC areas are usually where the Mossies sponge for tips on arrivals. Rule 2 of SOPLICA warns you not to stay in street-level hotel rooms, as they are easier to get into, and it's easier to throw something through your windows. Right now, you are freezing your ass in room 101, ground level, soft target for loony Mossies.

You have assiduously refused army guest house accommodation. You are in the mood for some luxury, and even though the hotel you have pitched camp in, bordering the Dal Lake, isn't luxurious, it is better than the squatter mess settlements that the Western Command is most likely to put at your disposal. You also learn in detail about soft and hard targets. Soft targets don't stay alert, aren't aware of what is happening around them, are predictable, don't blend with the environment, are high-key jerks, and don't stay informed. Conversely, hard targets are inaccessible, unpredictable, aware, low-key, and own a dog.

This is knowledge. All you have to do to become a hard target is start acting like a low-key jerk, buy a dachshund, and adhere to individual protective measures. Two of these being not opening doors to strangers and wedging a one-inch screw betwcen the doorjamb and the door. So you tell Siddy to go hunt for a screw and jam the door up. You tell him to find a screw, and what he does is use the tin top of your black Cherry Blossom boot polish. That's Siddy for you. You can't get him to do a thing straight.

If you delay entry of the terrorist, SOPLICA explains, you have time to rush to alternative exits or lock yourself in the bathroom, where you can get into the bathtub and start raising hell. That's if the tub's not made of porcelain or something akin to it, in which case it wouldn't be enough protection against gunfire. The bathroom in 101 doesn't have a tub.

You are also supposed to learn sentences like "Help me," "I need a doctor," and "Where is the police station?" in the local language. The best way, however, to keep from being selected as a target is—and here you quote—"not to say, do, wear, display, or drive anything that will help the terrorists identify you as non-Kashmiri. Wearing military uniform, for example, will identify you as an Indian. When a uniform is required at work, wear civilian clothes while traveling to and from work."

Even if you do blend in with the locals this way, not observing local customs and habits will give you away.

You have started reading the manual aloud, and Siddy, who's dusting the lenses of his Panavision video camera, is getting more and more agitated. Part of the reason for his perturbation is, of course, your own put-on about the whole thing. The main reason, however, is that after a binge last night on Tibetan temple balls, nuggets of hash he periodically gets from Dharmshala, he is a little edgy. He has run out of the stuff.

If you are locked in a hotel room six hundred miles from home with a guy like Siddy, one of the ways of entertaining yourself would be to read documents like SOPLICA.

You may also, just for the hell of it, try following some of the less bizarre recommendations. For instance, when room service knocks on your door to clear your American breakfast, you tell the guy (through the door) to come back later. Meanwhile, you have Siddy wrench the Cherry Blossom tin top out from under the door, which takes him ten times longer than it did to insert the stupid thing and renders it useless as a tin top in the process.

Out in the lobby, where you hang around for a while with Siddy, you bump into Sally Jennings of the *Times*, London. Sally seems hugely interested in what Siddy and you are up to in Kashmir. She's chasing the story of the four foreign hostages taken by militants. Nobody is quite sure whether they are alive or dead. You, of course, know the fate that befell them and when and at whose behest, but this is not the time to spread any free enlightenment. When you tell her you are here on a film project, she gets even nosier. At first, it strikes you as suspicious when Sally says she's heard of you, but you have learned that the big reason journalists talk to other journalists is to get story ideas, and Kashmir in April is a bit silent, and Sally from London seems more than a little desperate.

So you spread some bait. You mention a survey you would like to show her later, after she has spent her seventh day chasing army and police bureaucracy. There's this unpublished sex survey that *The Post* commissioned. You have been carrying it around in your leather satchel for well over a month. A sneak preview in a London paper would give the magazine some welcome publicity, besides forcing Digs, your editor, to slot the survey and your lead essay on a priority form. It's one of your weaknesses to want to see yourself in print every now and then.

Besides, there is always sex. Your strike rate in alien territory is something you are proud of. It beats reading the *SOPLICA* manual in the hotel room and watching Siddy jam doors with Cherry Blossom tin tops. So you exchange some more pleasantries with Sally before heading out with Siddy to pick up tomorrow's itinerary at Northern Command's local HQ and lobby for a chopper ride to the Kupwara sector. Going by road would be time-consuming and uncomfortable. More important, you want to sound out military top brass on your editor's questionnaire.

Srinagar, when you are high on acid and *SOPLICA*, isn't much fun. Especially when you remember that one of the *SOPLICA* clauses relates to inspecting your car, even if it's a taxi, for telltale signs of a bomb. You have to look underneath as you approach, walk around the outside and examine for smudges, marks, and fingerprints at the doors, the hood, and the trunk. A careless Mossie might have dropped something on the ground—electrical tape, a broken circuit board, or a detonator. There may even be wires hanging out that weren't there earlier.

Hard targets are also supposed to look around the interior of the car and not dump their personal stuff on the backseat. That makes it easier for some Mossie to conceal his explosive mechanism. Try explaining that to Siddy. You are even supposed to look under the front seat and the dashboard before you sit in the car.

It's a tedious routine, and since you went through all the initial maneuvers without noticing that your driver was watching you all the while from inside the taxi, you feel like a fool once you and Siddy get in. It's only the 250 micrograms that's holding your shit together.

But *SOPLICA* is on you like a demon. There are these bold clauses about keeping your windows rolled up when coming to checkpoints and just rolling down the one on the driver's side about four inches to show the pass. But the van you are riding in has no air-conditioning, and this is Srinagar in April. Siddy has his face hanging out his side of the Ambassador like a dog.

But your paranoia levels are revving up. Acid sometimes does funny things to you. You try checking on other *SOPLICA* transit desirables. You are supposed to have a first-aid kit and a fire extinguisher stashed within the vehicle. Zero. The gas tank has to be topped off to minimize explosive effects. Condition unknown. Have two good side-view mirrors outside and one long rearview mirror inside. The van, you observe in a psychedelic haze, has no side-view mirrors, and the one inside is cracked.

On roads, drive in the center to avoid being boxed in. The officials at the checkpoints wouldn't let anyone do that. You count ten that you have to cross before you reach HQ, a grim reminder of the war zone you are in.

You leave Siddy in the magazine-filled cubicle that Maj. Gen. Suresh Mahalingam's personal staff passes off as the waiting room. Siddy, at best, is unpresentable in delicate situations like the one you are about to negotiate.

When you last met Major General Mahalingam, he was running the National Security Guard in Delhi. Your persistent image of him is when he tried opening a 747's wing emergency door from the outside in front of the minister of defense, who had, at Mahalingam's insistence, made a courtesy appearance to watch a quick-reaction team make a dummy run on the plane. Mahalingam yanked the handle so hard, his hand slipped, and the momentum swept his heels from under him, sprawling him on the wing, from where he had to take a ride on a stretcher.

Clearly, it had been decided that inherent potential for fuckups would have less impact on national security in a FUBAR area like Kashmir than in the nation's premier special force. You interviewed him once for a documentary on the NSG. To get clearance, you showed him rushes that included a long, uninterrupted sequence of his talking mug, which pleased him no end. But since you snipped all of that in the version that finally aired, Major General Mahalingam has nursed a silent grudge against you for not propping his career curve.

And right now as you discuss your editor's questionnaire with him, the only ammunition you have at your disposal is a letter from the Defense Research and Development Organization certifying the psychological methodology you have adapted to anagram the souls of the people running the army's line-of-control patrols. Yes, and a letter from the vice chief of the army requesting cooperation with personnel from *The Post*.

It was part of Digs's editorial brain wave, based on your subtle input, to peg a defense cover for the magazine on a morale poll of the army, with special focus in LIC areas like Kashmir. Give the readers souped-up psychological statistics that would tell them something. Needless to say, in a scheme as grandiose as this, a lot depends upon army cooperation. Or your ingeniousness in slipping it in through their bureaucratic setup, an act equivalent to passing RDX through airport security.

But you have plans. You have a two-part questionnaire. The first, which is Digs's creation, is essentially your smoke screen. You explain the intricacies of this open-ended questionnaire to Major General Mahalingam.

"Sir," you begin, "the good part about this questionnaire is that it can be administered individually or in groups. It's the first time that military psychologists have devised such an analytical and psychological tool."

"I didn't know we had military psychologists," comments Major General Mahalingam.

"They just started the wing at the DRDO. It's a small one. In fact, our editor, Ashok Mehra, helped them manufacture this open-ended structure appraisal and coping-assessment technique. He's got a degree in psychology from Cornell University," you say.

"What's 'open-ended'?" asks Mahalingam suspiciously.

"It's a questionnaire that opens and ends," you say rather lamely.

"Doesn't every questionnaire do that?"

"I guess not, sir. Or they wouldn't have called it that. Most of the assessing techniques developed so far start midway. Not this one. Also, you can't go on listing thousands of factors, or there would be no end. The subjects are asked to write down just twelve factors that are most characteristic of the war situation. There is also a time limit. Most psychological tools don't have that. This is a new-generation psy ops. Please, have a look at it, sir," you say, and push Digs's questionnaire right up Mahalingam's nose.

Major General Mahalingam looks at the three sheets of paper the way a cobra stares at a snake charmer's stationary gourd stem.

"What are these segments?" he asks at last.

"Those, sir, are for the factors that the subject will address in the questionnaire, elements that he thinks are typical war characteristics. There are twelve of them," you say.

"But there's no war?"

"The psychologists maintain that a LIC situation is sometimes even more stressful than a regular field war, sir," you say. But Mahalingam is not listening to you right now. He's intrigued by certain details.

"What are these numbers here?"

"Those are the rankings, sir. The soldiers are supposed to rank the factors in order of importance. Two or more factors can have the same rankings. For instance, a soldier might say that fear of death has the same order of importance for him as the fear of maiming himself."

"What are these plus and minus signs here? What do they mean?" Major General Mahalingam was getting inquisitive.

"They, sir, are the negative or positive evaluation of the factor itself by the subject. For instance, if he listed not letting his comrades down as a factor in a war situation, he might cite that as a positive factor and fear of death as a negative factor. So he might rank the positive factor as four plus signs on a five-point scale and the negative as four minus signs," you say.

"What good is it going to do?" asks Major General Mahalingam. His eyes don't blink as he peers at you.

"Sir, the test is designed to index the motivational, coping, emotional balance, and ambiguity levels in the subject," you say.

"Ambiguity levels. What does that mean?"

"That's the effectiveness of differentiation, sir. The degree to which perceived elements are distinct and unique," you say. You have learned in your experience with army brass that one sure-shot method to freeze hostility levels is to become unintelligible.

"What's this?" asks Major General Mahalingam, looking at the second part of the questionnaire, the toxic one.

"That's the backgrounder, sir," you explain. "Its purpose is to glean over the fault levels of the questionnaire. See whether the subject is answering questions truthfully or not. It's for the psychologists' own use."

But among the questions that you have listed, there are many that could embarrass the military. One, which you have hidden somewhere in the middle, reads: "Have you ever indulged in self-mutilation to duck the border patrol?" Your sources report high levels of self-mutilation as yet undeclared and unaccepted by army authorities as fact.

Another is a set of three variously dispersed questions about drugs: "Have you ever taken drugs on the border or seen other military personnel take them? If so, how frequently do you take them or see other personnel take them? How do you finance your drug habit? Do you sell captured arms or loot in cordon-and-search operations?"

But before this set of questions come the more generic ones: "What for you is the most frightening aspect of battle—letting dependents down, death, injury, letting the unit down, being a coward? Are you happy with your officer, or do you think he should be replaced?"

Midway, Major General Mahalingam's brows knit a little and you think you have fucked up—but you needn't have worried.

"MM, do you think we could add an extra question?" asks Mahalingam.

"Certainly, sir, anything you suggest."

"Something about whether the soldiers would feel better if they had on 9-millimeter body armor when doing cordon-and-search operations," he says. "We have had ten deaths in the past month. All close-range shots."

One of the most satisfying moments in Major General Mahalingam's career was when he designed shock pads and shrapnel glue for the "Tiger Steel" 9-mm bulletproof vests developed by the DRDO. He gave you a demonstration of the vest for the documentary, then he took the shock pads and shrapnel glue out of the vest and had a dummy shot. The dummy went back five yards and had a head full of shrapnel.

You remember him saying, "Vests are no fun if they stop slugs but still can't keep metal out of your face. You also have to keep your balance; a bullet hitting you is like five mule kicks. The shock pads spread the force of the slug over your whole torso, and the glue on the steel grabs the lead." It's been Mahalingam's constant lament that the value of his inventions has been given short shrift by the DRDO. It's also been his relentless endeavor to publicize himself as the chief designer of the vest.

"I guess that's an excellent idea, sir. It would establish the degree of fear psychosis present in cordon-and-search operations," you say. "If you are in agreement, sir, we could also toss in a question about whether the soldiers would like to wear the Tiger Steel 9-millimeter vest during border patrols, too. It would make the job tough for snipers on the other side."

"Yes. It would reduce casualties, too. Besides, if they had to make so many vests, they might put some money into research and come up with a lighter variety of steel," says Major General Mahalingam. His eyes sparkle.

"Yes, sir. Twenty pounds is a little heavy right now. They might come up with something as light as a Gore-Tex jacket," you say.

"What kind of a jacket?" asks Mahalingam.

"It's a brand name, sir. The company specializes in mountain gear."

"Oh."

"Another thing, sir," you begin. You like to strike the iron while it's hot. "One of the statistical components of the test is to administer a few of them in battlefield-like conditions. Like a little before, after, or during a cordon-and-search operation, or even after a Special Forces operation. I was wondering if you could have something organized in the Kupwara sector in the next two days, sir."

"Why do you want to do that?" asks a perplexed Mahalingam. His idea of a psychology test slickly administered would be to herd his unit into battalion HQ and hand out test sheets to the men to fill in, squatting in the open field—military-style.

"Well, you see, sir, soldiers are in different mood frames in battlefield conditions. They answer questions in a different manner when the action's all under their nose, rather than far away. We want to map the fluctuation levels, sir," you say.

"Well, MM," says Major General Mahalingam, "I wouldn't mind letting you do that, but frankly, as you will understand, it's all somewhat out of my hands. I mean, you don't know what's going to happen." Then, a little wickedly, he adds, "But maybe I will go through last evening's sitreps and see what can be done. If anything's possible, I will have my aide contact you."

"Yes, sir," you say. "That would be just perfect. By the way, sir, we are also planning a documentary on the twenty best inventions in India in the last five years. Even the BBC is interested. We were thinking of putting the Tiger Steel vest in the top ten. I hope you don't have any objection to that, sir?"

"BBC? When is this?" asks Mahalingam. You can actually see his nostrils quiver.

"As soon as we get back from Kashmir, sir," you say. "We would like to send a crew up to shoot you with the vest and all, sir. It would be very impactful."

"Certainly," says Major General Mahalingam. His chest swells and he twirls his mustache.

Then you decide to fuck with the general a bit for a little parting entertainment.

"Actually, sir, what the producer of our documentary wants is for each inventor to use his invention in front of the camera," you say. "I hope you are okay with that, sir."

"With *what*?" asks Major General Mahalingam nervously. You notice about half the blood disappear from his face.

"Like we would want you to wear the vest and have a soldier shoot at you from an AK-47 or something. Makes the whole thing dramatic. Like, in your case, the inventor putting his life on the line to support his invention," you say.

"I am too old for that kind of thing, MM," says Major General Mahalingam, and he gives a sickly kind of laugh.

Your face falls. You behave as if this attitude he has might cause you some major problems with the BBC.

"It's part of the film format, sir. And it's kind of approved by the BBC, which has bought first airing rights for the documentary. You can't change the grid of the thing. The BBC would throw a fit. Like we have this guy in Bangalore who's featuring in the show, who's developed this special putty for making bricks that are stronger and cheaper than the regular ones. We have him making the bricks himself. And he has to step up to his neck in mud to mix the bloody thing," you say.

You wait for this to sink in. Watch the clash between opportunity and fear in Major General Mahalingam before you decide to bail him out.

"But I will see what I can do, sir," you say. "I might get them to agree to a wooden dummy, or even a volunteer from one of your battalions."

Siddy is rather upset with you. If your limited range of emotions included empathy, you might be tempted to feel more charitable.

Siddy spent the day in Major General Mahalingam's outer office, working the Tiger Steel vest question into the questionnaire. After he typed the whole goddamn thing in (and Siddy types with about half a finger and takes two minutes to search for a letter), there was still the logistics of rolling a thousand-odd printouts. Mahalingam's laser printer had just enough toner to reel out a hundred copies. The rest, Siddy had to photostat, and it took him all evening to get to four figures, because the power kept tripping on him and the machine kept heating up, spitting out copies that looked as if they'd been distorted by magic mirrors. All this you got to know via Siddy's periodic abusive telephone updates.

Then Siddy's return to civilization wasn't much better. You poked your head out of room 101 just long enough to tell him to buzz off. One thing you dislike with intensity is someone watching you turn the smile for half a chick. Sally Jennings just about makes it to the halfway mark:

Her thin upper lip gives her a flat, stupid grin, as if she smiles by stretching and clenching her upper lip in her mouth.

That is the reason you aren't giving her a reason to smile. You couldn't take that smile even on LSD. Instead, you are discussing the sex survey, the first and only one of its kind to be conducted in India, you tell her.

The survey itself, you have discussed ad infinitum in its many intriguing details. Starting with the multiplicity of sex partners, you have reeled off the figures on premarital sex. Of course, you never let her read the survey herself. That would be giving away the mystery. But you let her absorb the occasional pie chart, throw enough numbers at her to keep her scribbling madly.

"Don't you think it's amazing that Calcutta is India's sex capital? I mean, all the numbers are so high out there," says Sally.

"Yes," you say. "You never would have thought the Bengalis had it in them. Actually, I think it's just the women who are more into it." Yours is a subjective opinion.

"But women are only into it with men," clarifies Sally rather wickedly.

You begin to notice her break into the preparations for a grin. You forestall that with a grim recitation of statistics.

"Our respondent base in the survey has been close to three thousand. We spread them over twenty cities. Even in the cities, we had a minimum of twenty clusters from which we selected them," you inform her. You begin to feel rather inappropriate to the task. You have never done it before—played a seduction game with this taxing parameter of not having the woman smile.

But her lithe form is rather setting you off, and what you do is get your sunglasses out from your suitcase and put them on so if she does grin, it won't grab you that bad. "I have this problem with my eyes," you tell her. "It's a kind of allergy. They start to water without notice. Would you like some Kashmiri tea?"

"No thanks," says Sally.

You get up to go to the loo for a chemical infusion. The acid in your bloodstream is weakening. Acid lowers your threshold, lets you distract yourself with almost any woman. You have been in love just once, but that was way back during your Academy days. Afterward, there were some in college.

Then you got into drugs. Grass first, acid later. Mercifully, you could register enough control not to reach escape velocity, and you didn't quite graduate into heroin. Instead, you took up interests like mountaineering and soon realized that you had to cut down on the chemicals to keep your muscles trim and nourished. But you never lost the taste for the rush. For you, it isn't just a chemical wonder. It's what happens to you when you are in the game with an adversary like Major Rodriguez. When you are free-falling from ten thousand feet or holding on to life from a slender crevice at twenty thousand feet on the Nuptse face.

Your quality of life is defined by the rushes you can generate without short-circuiting your system. You have yet to reach optimum levels of efficiency. This is one of the reasons you live the way you do. A hole, a vacuum, that sucks your life in between two rushes—this is where you sense the danger lies.

Right now, for instance, it lies in your search for sex without intimacy. Though it's nothing new for you, the various permutations and combinations of danger this lifestyle can generate aren't beyond your capacity to grasp. For one, you could get AIDS, since you are out of raincoats for your apparatus. Two, and here lies the real danger, you are prone to indiscretions when you lie in bed with a warm body wrapped around you. It does things to your head. It makes you talk about Shomali, your sweetheart many years before. Perhaps one of the reasons you go to bed with women you don't love is to talk about what happened. It happens only after the temporary cleansing that sex brings about, after you ride a woman.

Sally is jotting masturbation statistics from your survey when you come back from the loo chemically invigorated.

"It's funny," she says, "how forty percent of the woman left this question unanswered. Why is it that much of a taboo?"

This is the kind of opening you look forward to in order to give a crank to the proceedings.

"I thought even the Kinsey report had a low response to this question," you say. "Would you answer this question?"

"Yes, of course," says Sally. "There's nothing wrong with answering the question."

"Do you masturbate, Sally Jennings? If so, what's your frequency? At what age did you first start masturbating? Do you indulge in clitoral stimulation only, or do you use insertion devices? If insertion devices are unavailable, would you be content with using just your fingers to achieve penetration? Have you ever masturbated in a group? Do you think it's more satisfying than the act of sex? Have you told your boyfriend or husband about this habit of yours? If so, what was his reaction?" you ask.

"You mean it went like *that,* the questionnaire?" Sally asks. You can feel her self-composure thin a bit.

"I am asking you," you say impishly.

For a while, you feel that she isn't up to it. But she rallies, though you never would have thought that she would fall to the obvious bait of answering your series of questions. She takes a deep breath and reels out some very private statistics.

"Yes, I masturbate. My average should work out to something quite above your Indian women's mean average of five times a month. I first started masturbating at the age of thirteen. I indulge in both clitoral as well as penetrative stimulation, but my favorite remains clitoral. I am content to use my fingers for stimulation. I haven't masturbated in a group, though I have had frequent fantasies of doing so with males. There's nothing that can beat the act of sex. I have never talked about this habit of mine with any of my boyfriends," says Sally.

That's how you start up on her. But it takes a while to soften her enough to get her to ride the night in your company. For that, you have to lace the late-night coffee you order with an ampoule, after which you have things running easily and in control.

The key to control, you have worked out, is being in lesser need than the person you seek to control. The way to work on it is not to decrease your own need, for that may or may not be possible, but to increase the need of the other. What you have learned from experience is that while it is possible to induce a physical need, that's not what you are looking for in someone you might happen to fall in love with. For instance, the need that makes someone take you for what you are is something you can always be sure to fail to induce.

The way you like to take your girls is to begin on them slowly. If you are in a freaky mood, you work on giving them the shave. You especially like to lather girls with compressed foam from Gillette canisters. You are armed with a Bentex double-edge razor blade, which you keep in your shaving kit for encounters like these.

Shaving pubic hair is an art in itself. The skill lies in making it an enjoyable experience for the woman. You ease Sally's stiffness and apprehension by spraying on her a liberal dose of foam. Then you start rubbing the foam on her mound till she stops giggling. That's when you know that she has entered the pleasure zone. You have to allow ten minutes for the foam to soften the hair roots. Most shavers don't have the patience to work this time into their schedule, and that makes the razor work tough.

But once you weave that bit of technicality into the proceedings, your razor movements become silky and slice through the hairs as though they were cobwebs. The other trick is to keep on stimulating the girl even as you shave, to swamp any prickly and unsavory sensations your shaving might be giving her.

While generally your shaving posture is ankles under the girl's thighs and knees bent as you crouch over her mound, you try an innovation with Sally. You face the other way, with your knees digging beside her waist and your head bent over the mound the wrong way up. This gives you the deluxe facility of having Sally stroke the base of your dick with her fingers, rub it against her breasts, or take you in her mouth.

Although it upsets your concentration on a couple of occasions, especially when she suckles you in one deep and lasting lip squeeze, it is not enough to shake your shaving hand.

After you are through with shaving, you wipe Sally clean with a towel and uncap the bottle of olive oil you use for postshaving interludes. You sprinkle a few drops on her clitoris and spread the puddle over in smooth strokes. The secret of your olive oil is that it has half a dozen poppers dissolved in it, making it a lethal arousal fluid—the nitroglycerin of pussy.

You stop in between your rhythmic stroking to make her cry for you to continue. The begging acts like an aphrodisiac on you. The more you leave off, the more she begs and the more you feel strong enough to move into your penetration routine without bursting a popper under your nose.

But you haven't taken into account the ghost that roams your mind. The hurt that's there and won't let go for those few brief moments that bring with them the joy of oblivion. But first, you feel a compulsion to make Sally come harder than she ever has before, and as you rub the oil on her smooth mound, you start finger-fucking her. One, two, and then three fingers, and when she is nearly shouting for you to mount and perform the final rites, you burst a popper under her nose with your left hand even as you increase the speed of your lubrication. And now you glimpse firsthand the frightening sexuality of a woman fully aroused and in the act.

What you regret is that the sight hasn't the impetus to move your own drive into top gear. You lie shrunken and handicapped beside Sally as she comes back from her shudders, and when she lets go the tight hug she has you in, you ask, "Have you ever been in love?"

"What?" she asks. The timing of the question produces a little incomprehension. But she rallies. "Yes," she says.

"What was it like?"

"It was like being in perpetual pain," she says.

You think you might have to rethink her philosophical potential. You become curious. "And why was that?"

"I wanted to possess him, and when I couldn't, it turned into pain," says Sally.

"Why did you want to possess him?"

"My love is like that. It doesn't seek a moment or a fuck. It wants all of something. And very few people can give all of theirs to somebody. They want to keep a lot of it for themselves," she says. "What about you? Why didn't you come? Should I work on you?"

Sally tries to blow some air into your limp shooter, but it's got a puncture she doesn't know about.

"Are you still in love with him?" you ask.

"Yes, but I don't think about it. It's over," she says.

"How can you still be in love and say that it's over?" you ask. Such things are always great puzzles for you.

"What I mean is, I still have a soft corner for him, but there hasn't been any motion on the thing for a couple of years now," says Sally.

"So how can you say it's over if you still have a soft corner for him?" you persist.

"Because there's no pain anymore. I don't have to start hating him to get him out of my system."

That's what all emotional recuperation is, you figure, getting the pain out of the nerve cells. "But what if you can't get somebody out of your system and you continue loving that person even though it gives you pain?"

"Then I would say you have a problem," says Sally, and rubs her tits on your side.

"Who's talking about me?"

"So what if it's you? People have to have problems. What would they be without them?" she says, and goes off to sleep, snuggling against your chest.

But in the middle of the night, when you think about Shomali even as you lie with your hand sandwiched within the folds of Sally's freshly shaved crotch, there's a problem you would rather do without. It's Sally. She wakes up and asks you, "Will you stuff ice in my cunt?"

The woman starts howling. Capt. Satish Warrier, aide-de-camp to Major General Mahalingam, who's been eyeing you cagily, finds it difficult to carry on with his insulated composure.

Mahalingam had gone through the various situation reports on his desk and singled out three districts you could take a chopper to—Kupwara, Baramulla, and Poonch. You are interested only in Kupwara, where both the 5 Kumaon and 7 Sikh are based, one hour's drive apart on the line of control. As it happened, Major Rodriguez himself was in Srinagar, on his way back from home leave in Goa. Division HQ at Kupwara immediately assigned him the task of interrogating certain Mossies caught by the 7 Sikh. Though the 5 Kumaon and 7 Sikh report to different brigade headquarters at Kupwara, they are both part of the 27th Division, which, in turn, is part of the 15th Corps. You travel with Rodriguez in the chopper, with Siddy and Captain Warrier for company.

You try including Warrier in the conversation you are having with the others, but Warrier is still smarting from the *SOPLICA* doctrine you sprang on him when he knocked at your door with two packets under his arms.

"Thanks a lot, Captain Warrier," you said. "But don't you think you put yourself in danger bringing these?"

Captain Warrier was perplexed. His scope blinked off. A civilian asshole with some Major General Mahalingam connection was telling him he was in danger bringing in the packets. He found it difficult to shuffle the information in place, get his scope back on alternate power supply.

"It's there in *SOPLICA*," you said, hoping to bail him out. Captain Warrier looked at you from a very military posture. His gaze said a lot of things. His scope hummed back with light and he identified the quarry as a jerk from Mars, whom, unfortunately, he had to humor because he was under orders from his CO to escort him to Kupwara.

"I don't think I understand, Mr. Mehta," he said.

"Oh, it's your own guys who made up the stuff," you said, going to the table and picking up the manual. "Section B. 'Do not load yourself with packages in civilian areas, so you can react with speed in case you are attacked.'"

Here, you chucked the *SOPLICA* manual right at Warrier's chest. He dropped your two packets, which contained photostat copies of your questionnaire, in panic. He couldn't latch on to the manual, either.

"There, Captain," you said. "The manual's right. It could have been a knife coming your way. You shouldn't burden yourself with such things when there's a war going on. Do you know that human beings can't react faster than one-thirtieth of a second? A *second*. I mean, that's the fucking fastest they can react to anything happening around them. And even guys like Billy the Kid didn't have those reflexes. Not carrying that packet might have meant the difference between life and death to you. You roger?"

Captain Warrier was pretty shaken.

The arrival of Major Rodriguez spared him further embarrassment.

He begins to think you are from military intelligence. He asks Major Rodriguez that over the rotors when he thinks you can't hear, and the major has such a laugh that he nearly rips off his seat harness. The major doesn't tell him anything, and Warrier's dilemma continues.

Of course, now he is standing right beside you and you are watching soldiers from the 7 Sikh search a household in the village of Nunkar. The Mossies Major Rodriguez interrogated have squealed on the village. The Rodriguez preliminary interrogation chemotherapy involves the use of pliers and bandages, hot and cold stuff to get the assholes on the information highway. Prior to this, the emphasis is on psychological stress to break down a prisoner's resistance. If the major has time on his side, conditioning of the prisoner starts under solitary confinement, where the prisoner's conception of place and time slowly begins to dissipate. According to the Rodriguez doctrine, removal from reality can be further advanced by applying the technique of total immersion of the prisoner in warm, black, and neutral water. The tank is designed for total sensory deprivation. It's easily portable in a truck as well. You can also increase the level of noise, followed by periods of silence to heighten a prisoner's sense of danger.

Of course, the advanced Rodriguez pyrotechnics involve Soviet techniques. This hyperaccelerates the whole process and is right up the major's sleeve. It means using drugs. Hallucinogens and tranquilizers deepen a prisoner's disorientation and begin the onset of phobias that break his mental resistance. Rodriguez's speciality is the use of tubocurarine, a muscle relaxant that in increased doses results in a paralysis of the diaphragm. Hooked to artificial ventilation, the prisoner becomes beholden to his interrogator for every life-giving breath.

You haven't yet seen the major's skills with tubocurarine firsthand. But you don't doubt them. He acquired his expertise in a training program in Moscow. That's the reason HQ called him in to help the 7 Sikh. HQ doesn't care about turf.

There is a significant cache of arms somewhere in the village and the

7 Sikh has gone through every single one of the fifty houses with a fine-tooth comb and come up with nothing more than a used truck battery, which, try as they may, they cannot link to the cache.

And now there is this motherly woman howling the village down and soldiers from the 7 Sikh coming out of her house with their faces sheepish and the search half done. This is when Captain Warrier is provoked enough to come up to you and gesticulate.

"Jesus, she's like my mother. These guys can't behave like that with her," he says.

Warrier is as green as they come. Even you, from the looks of it, are inclined to give the woman the benefit of doubt. But it's here that Maj. Raunaq Singh makes an entry. Counterpart of Major Rodriguez in 7 Sikh, he has been watching his troops work the ropes.

"Get the woman out, then search the fucking place down. Break anything you want," barks Major Singh.

Even Rodriguez, who himself has been straggling, a mercenary working in hostile command, perks up. The two majors are reading something in the situation that is escaping the others. Rodriguez, too, goes into command mode.

He takes the safety off his Glock. "Be careful. We might have company," he barks.

Captain Warrier is a little taken aback. The woman is silent now, but you recognize a new fear in her eyes. You can almost hear her heartbeat. Then there comes the moment that shapes Captain Warrier's destiny. He goes up to Major Rodriguez and inquires in a soft tone, "Don't you think you might be making a mistake here? Overreacting a bit?"

Rodriguez blushes. You don't know whether it is because Warrier omits the word *sir* or because a few 7 Sikh soldiers are glancing his way. Then Maj. Raunaq Singh smirks at Rodriguez, who has no option after that. Rodriguez hands over his Glock to Warrier, who was unarmed, and orders him to lead the way. Major Singh relinquishes territory, a little puzzled.

"It's for you to find out," says Major Rodriguez, and Warrier, who wasn't expecting this turn of events, leads four soldiers of the 7 Sikh into the house. He does it with attitude, too. And you see a smirk on his face through one of the windows right till a dumdum knocks his head off.

It happens like this. One of the soldiers inside drags a chest of drawers some way and Warrier notices something and bends down. Right then, you notice the woman turn deathly pale, and Major Rodriguez, who's been watching her all the while, is about to bark something, but it's too late. The first bullet of the Mossie, who's hiding beneath the trapdoor under the chest of drawers, takes Warrier smack on his face.

You see him spin and hit the floor with a thud. The rest turn around and start emptying their AK-47 magazines into the trapdoor till Major Rodriguez goes inside at a gallop and pulls them out. He doesn't want them blowing up the dump. They drag the Mossie out from the trapdoor, and though he might have taken about thirty slugs, he's still got a pulse.

"Afghan *gandu hai,*" says one of the soldiers.

They search in the alcove behind the trapdoor and come up with radio control sets—the kind that are used to explode mines, detonators, fuses, grenades—five AK-47 rifles, four boxes of ammunition, and two RPG-7V rocket launchers with ten projectiles. Enough stuff to take out an entire convoy.

Major Rodriguez is hunched over Warrier's body. One of the men has to tie his bandanna around Warrier's head to keep his brains from dropping out. They take the woman into custody. Nobody talks to her. As a parting gift, they shoot the place up—furniture, walls, beds, cupboards, even the cutlery.

"How did *you* know, Major?" you ask. You are stuck with the 7 Sikh for the night. Sometime in the early morning, you will be moving with Rodriguez to the 5 Kumaon camp. Rodriguez himself is tense at having to give up a five-minute chopper ride to his base, but it can't be helped. The chopper is flying in the bodies to Srinagar. His place has been taken up by Siddy, who wants some aerial shots of the village. On the army field telephone, Major General Mahalingam is livid that Rodriguez hadn't taken better care of his aide. But Rodriguez's tension has more to do with having to be in 7 Sikh environs, even though on division work.

"Seen it a couple of times. A woman crying loudly means there's a dump nearby," says Major Rodriguez.

"You should have gone yourself," you say.

"I was going. But you can't stop someone who wants to get his head blown off," says Major Rodriguez. You can't really pick holes in Rodriguez's reasoning. "First fucking commandment of life. Live and observe. Don't make a play if you don't know the moves."

But in the night, you break Major Rodriguez's first commandment. You go out on a patrol with him. Even this has come about because of the departure of 7 Sikh from the area. The two of you will be spending the night at a nearby Border Security Force camp. You realize that for the major, going on patrol is a fundamental necessity, as vital as the morning shit. But you are greener than grass. It's a new rush for you, and what you sense is that Rodriguez's rush in the thing lies in going out with someone green. Or, to put it more accurately, someone he thinks is green.

Major Rodriguez has hold of some intelligence that certain Mossies might come for the cache the 7 Sikh just cracked, and he's plotted an intercept course. The 7 Sikh had the same intelligence but disregarded it. Why put yourself in danger when the booty is already yours? This, you surmise, could have been their line of thinking. A philosophy at distinct variance with that of the major from 5 Kumaon.

Rodriguez is packing an AK-47 and two knives. The major is a man who believes in very basic hardware. No fancy technology for him when he moves in the night. What you have is the Glock Rodriguez loaned Warrier. You try not to look superstitious as the major watches you wipe the muck off the gray handle. You are familiar with the weapon. You have checked the magazine. Its big grip fits your palm size. The major makes you change your shoes, too.

"We don't want your Woodland sole patterns in the woods," he says.

You remind him that it's night, but the major is firm. He wants to be sound on patrol basics. So you have to do with Siddy's plimsoll trainers. They have flat soles and nearly no patterns. Because of the irregular nature of what you are doing, you have to slip out unobserved from the BSF camp.

In the woods, Major Rodriguez tries to get you up-to-date on patrol psychology.

"It's not enough to gawk around. You have to train yourself to look right through the static," says Major Rodriguez. Static for him means the trees, the shrubbery, the grass, the noise. There's not much of a jungle in Kashmir. "Once you get the hang of looking through it all, your eyes will go down that extra dozen yards. Mossie camps here are not in the open. So you don't have to sniff the air for their socks. What you have to do is listen for static that doesn't fit in. That's the odd guy out for you."

Major Rodriguez picks a place by a stream where he thinks the Mossies might cross. He knows the topography well. The 5 Kumaon has been here before. Grass, thick shrubs, and trees conceal you from the stream, and even though it's a moonlit night, the place scores nine out of ten for an ambush site.

Just to be with the major is an education. It's business, too. You are also the kind for whom the nearness of death doesn't matter. Warrier's death hasn't put a damper on your plans for the evening. It isn't that you don't know fear. But the way it hits you is like a popper in your veins. Amyl fucking nitrite. Arousal and fear, you think, go together.

In the night, Major Rodriguez talks about insurgency in Kashmir. You have never before heard him exercise his tongue so much. He starts in a whisper.

"When it all started in 1989, it would take, on an average, five hundred hours of patrolling for a soldier to have his first encounter with the assholes. For the normal regimental unit, the figure's come down to three hundred hours. With 5 Kumaon, it's seventy-five hours. If you haven't had your first taste of live fire by then, you start getting an inferiority complex."

"And your first kill?" you ask.

"Usually about the same time. But we were the first guys who started going after the Mossies, instead of waiting for them to bump into us. That was new to them. We brought down our firing initiation average to one hundred and fifty hours by organizing our patrols better. The more erratic and disorganized our second- and third-tier patrols were, the more chances we had of running into the Mossies, getting to fry the bastards. Then HQ sent us these five ground-surveillance radars for trial evaluation. The LMT RB12A, a solid-state radio transmitter you can fit in your rucksack and move on. It can be operated by remote, and it picks moving targets a mile away. It gives you bearing and range, and if you want, it even plots an intercept graph for you. Five are too few for the border, but we started having excellent results. They cut down on our casualties. Understandably, we posted a negative on the equipment to HQ. We said we needed more time to assess them. We didn't want other units getting the same edge. It would mess with the flow of inventory we were piling up. Later, we reported them as damaged beyond repair in a bomb blast."

"What about the stress, the people around here? The minimum-force army doctrine?" you ask.

"That's something for assholes at the LIC school at Udhampur to work out in their textbooks. For us . . . we try to find the bullets before they find us. The problem starts after the first few weeks that you come in fresh. You are all psyched up to fight terrorists, and all you get to do is knock civilians on the head. The locals look on you like an occupation force.

"So you don't know who's the enemy. First thing one learns is that each civilian is a potential asshole. Some try to worm their way into our hearts. But they could be friends today and throw a bomb at you tomorrow. A twelve-year-old could be playing cricket with you in the morning; in the night, he could be burying you with cutter slugs. Sometimes they use special ammunition, which at exit makes holes the size of fists. But even with all this, there comes a time when you're not sure of the rightness of your actions."

"What happens then?" you ask. "When you're not sure of the rightness of your actions?"

"You heard about the Bell rat experiment?" asks Major Rodriguez. He takes out one of his knives and starts working his nails.

"No."

"They keep rats on one of these plates they run a voltage on. The rats run on to the next plate, but that, too, gives them a shock. They keep going to the next plate but can't find one that's normal. Once they come to understand that moving to another plate isn't going to help, they accept the situation. They learn to live with the shock. So once your morality gets the right hook, your values become more fluid and malleable. Even at command level. Your reaction toward unacceptable behavior becomes softer and more understanding."

"You turn beast."

"That's too harsh, MM. What you start doing is latching on to anything that dehumanizes the enemy and dilutes your sense of responsibility," says Major Rodriguez. "You also become cruel. That comes with the feeling of power. You feel mighty with respect to the civilian. You realize how easy it would be to misuse that power. You start destroying property at the first excuse. Since there's not one particular direction the Mossies are supposed to come from, you are forced to have a light trigger finger. You need to have lightning responses, which, of course, increase your chances of hitting innocents. And once you hit them, you go into that trap. You dehumanize them."

"And that makes your job easier?" you ask.

"If you get a justification for anything, your job turns easier," explains Major Rodriguez. He raises a finger to his lips.

This is when you hear the *swish swash* sound coming from the opposite end of the stream. A big hulk emerges from the trees on the other side. He comes cautiously to the edge of the water and swings his Kalashnikov over his shoulders so the barrel doesn't get in the way of his drinking from the stream.

Four dark forms follow him. They are too far away for you to catch the white in their eyes, but you file the fact that they all pack Kalashnikovs. You remember with alarm that you haven't cocked your Glock. Silence, as you well know, is the essence of a successful ambush, and though mathematics has never been one of your strong points, it doesn't take you long to calculate that the two seconds you'd need to cock your personal weapon would give enough time to a single AK-47–packing Mossie to push twelve rounds into your rib cage at 2,330 feet per second. You figure that would be mortal, even if the Mossie pressed the trigger at a thousand feet. One of the AK-47's highlights is its low recoil, which allows for the weapon to be controllable at auto.

Your memory also retrieves for you the fact that Mossies have sometimes been known to fire at every bit of shrubbery that looks like a potential ambush site and falls on their trail. This you had picked up in an apparently erudite article on Kashmiri militant training camps across the border.

The only thing you are reasonably content about is that you aren't on acid. That would have amplified the series of horrors unfolding before you. You might have given the game away by hollering at them. Also, you have a proven Mossie decimator in Major Rodriguez.

You hope that the Mossie squad doesn't cross where you are. When two of them proceed downstream to check the water flow, you start easing up. But it's a short-lived relief, for you observe the group making preparations to cross right under your nose. Three of the five hang back at the edge of the trees on the other side, prepared to give covering fire for the advance party of two. This creates battlefield complications. Do you take out the two up front, which would be the easiest thing to do, or do you wait for the entire party to come across? If you plug the two advance Mossies, there is every chance the rest will escape. You realize you would, too.

But Major Rodriguez, you know by now, isn't a bits-and-pieces man. He's a wholesale connoisseur, the all-or-nothing man. You look at him for strategy confirmation, and it's a shock to discover that the major is no longer where you thought he was. While you have been busy watching the progress of the Mossie squad, you haven't noticed the major disappear, leaving you to your own resources.

This unexpected twist in proceedings puts a crimp in your mental equilibrium. You go through your list of alternatives. Your escape route at the rear is clean as a whistle, and you still have time to crawl away to safety. If you don't, you may slowly get sucked into a situation known as "isolated individual fighting with his back to the wall," or "hero fights to the last bullet" syndrome. But you have serious doubts whether you will get to fire anywhere near your last bullet.

Naturally, you harbor no animosity toward the Mossie squad. Your work is with the major and those he represents. And even though you think you cracked the major at Agra in your sky-diving sessions, it is proving harder than expected. You want to win Rodriguez over by deeds he appreciates, even though it makes you commit acts that don't, in the longer run, help your cause.

You strain against the darkness to get a bearing on Rodriguez's position, but all you can see is a lot of bark. You look back at the squad just in time to see one of the front men chuck something right where you are. Even as you try to figure what it could be, you fail to pick up on the downward curve of the object, and it lands right on your face. Grenade, you think. What saves you from pressing the panic button is the smell of the thing. It is the Mossie's pair of sneakers tied together, with his socks right in them. He wants to keep them from getting wet. Son of a bitch. He could have hung them around his neck.

Your last and most dangerous alternative is to hope they won't see you. That would be risking your neck for nothing at all, and unless you plan to take out the guys, the better option is to slime out of the whole thing, retreat while you still have time. Besides, there is the business of the sneakers. Lying low doesn't sound like too healthy a possibility with one of the Mossies flashing his hooded pencil light in your direction to hunt for his footwear.

But what, you wonder, is the major's game? Your guess is that Major Rodriguez is throwing you into the deep end to see the balls you pack. Trust is an important factor in the kind of business you and he are involved in. Maybe he's testing you. Or so you think.

It could also be that the major is indulging his perverse sense of humor. Watching you sweat till the last possible moment.

Either way, you don't want to give the major the mental edge, confirm his role as chief chemist in a laboratory situation he's cooked up. Even though you are outgunned and outnumbered, you plan to stick it out. Observe the way the Zen flows out of the next few moments. You are beginning to get the rush.

And you are banking on an instinct that the major hasn't deserted you but is around somewhere, waiting for his moment. According to Major Rodriguez, things turn out for the best only when you recognize which moment to seize on and turn to your advantage. For the major, the play doesn't work unless it's at the ripe instant. If there is to be a skirmish, it will begin at the moment of the major's choosing. When it begins will also depend on what Rodriguez wants. Right now, you don't know what he wants. But when the forward party of two crosses the stream with their AK-47s held over their heads and the major doesn't make his play, you know that he's going to stretch the game right till the end. All you can do is tense yourself for the moment or let it come and grab you.

The Mossie who chucked his shoes is in no hurry to come and get them. He's covering up for his buddies at the other end, whose turn it is to cross. The other goes behind a tree and takes a pee.

While you have maneuvered away from the shoes, you are still only three yards from the Mossie taking a leak. He has the barrel of his rifle pointed right where he is aiming his pee, and as the vapors hit you in the night, you think how easily you could take him and the other guy, but you wait patiently for the major's move.

What you don't want to do at any cost is start your play before the major starts his, let the Mossies see you, and blow whatever the major was planning. You don't have any affinity with moments. The ripe one could pass and you wouldn't know it.

Soon the two become five, and while four have crossed with their shoes hung around their necks, the single Mossie comes looking for his sneakers. He spits once, about five feet, before he comes by his sneakers, and the spray from it hits your forehead. It creates prickly sensations on your face. Ambushing, you figure, is full of the unexpected. It rains things from above that you can do nothing about.

As the spray starts making your nose itch, you also see for the first time the major's knife, still on the stone where he was trimming his nails. The discovery is something that is shared by the Mossie as he drags on his socks. He lets out a whisper of surprise. As he does that and the other Mossies perk up, you feel the moment coming, even though it's your first patrol and you have the antennae of an amateur.

You don't hear the roar of the AK-47 in auto. The major's rifle is on single fire. You hug the ground. You see four Mossies folding up and falling on the grass. You cock your Glock, aim at the Mossie who was dragging his socks, and lift yourself from the ditch you were in. His eyes turn wide with terror; his mouth yawns open. Gritting your teeth, you fire a round from your hip. You don't intend to hit him, but you suddenly realize that firing has a calming effect on you after the sustained rush you have had. You empty your magazine at his feet, around his face, at the Mossie's sneaker. What you don't do is fire to kill. You fire to overcome and control your fear. Or perhaps you fire to give the major the impression that you do so to administer your fear.

As you fire like a maniac, you also see Major Rodriguez eyeing you from your right. He has a look of unconcern on his face. All he says once you have run out of rounds is "What a waste, what a fucking waste." Then he straightens his arm, and before you can gear up to what he is about to do, he fires his fifth into the Mossie's head and fluid comes spraying onto your face once again.

You are somewhere in Kupwara, Kashmir, guests of the 5 Kumaon. You are progressing toward your target in steady bounds. Quarry like Major Rodriguez and his confederates is to be stalked over months. The snow has started melting, and the reason you are here with two of your colleagues is ostensibly to finish your border patrol documentary on the line of control. That and the thing with the questionnaire, which has yielded rich dividends. A camerawoman has flown in for the mission, a troop increase, a girl called Teresa. Siddy, your main cameraman, who also doubles as sound recordist, is still with you.

Right now, you are working yourself up to be pissed with him. You can't do anything except glare, because if you so much as took a deep breath, you might get your head blown all the way to Rangoon. There are four of you in the bushes, and ringed around you and converging at top speed in a semicircular arc are about a dozen, or maybe a few less, Mossies from the Islamic side of things.

It's night, and that's what saves you, for your two armed escorts pack Panavision night viewers, gizmos that give them all-weather data in magnified green blurs. You and Siddy were doing a cursory terrain scout to pick an advantageous position for your forty-five-pound remote-operated video camera. What, in fact, saves you from running smack into the Mossies is your having borrowed the night viewer from one of your escorts, who had it slung on his left shoulder. You indulge in a private peek, and when you see an assortment of green blurs that could be carbon-based life-forms similar to your own, you raise a quiet alarm.

Advantageously, all of you are in army greens and have complexions that can do without black camouflage paint. And you have enough time to huddle into a four-by-six-foot ditch that no Kashmiri, Mossie or otherwise, should have reason to cut across. It's out of the way and surrounded by pines.

They go past you and beyond in a silent but fast flurry of feet. You lie low for a further three minutes to keep out of the way of any slow tail; then you hear one of the escorts use his walkie-talkie to warn the inner-perimeter patrol about the baggage coming its way. You tell Siddy what a jerk you think he is for not loading the battery in the control handset.

"We could have had all the shots we wanted the first day if you had just done what you have been brought here to do," you tell him. "And now we don't know whether we will bump into another bunch."

"We can stay here for a few more days," says Siddy.

"That says nothing. You could be here the whole year and never be closer than this," you say.

"Jesus, we weren't expecting anything like this, MM. It wasn't even a dry run."

"That's the point," you say, backing him into a tree. "Each time you hold a camera, remember you are on. If you spot the heat around the corner, there's nothing that should take you more than fifteen seconds to get fixed."

"Be glad you are alive," says Siddy.

He's still shaking and sweating. He's never been in anything this tight. He's so traumatized, he can't carry the camera straight from where he left it on the trail back to our bunker. You carry it for him. Digs wouldn't like to hear a probationer jerk went and screwed a rented, uninsured $150,000 camera. For your part, you are smug in the knowledge that you voiced your objection in distinct, unambiguous terms about being saddled with two greenhorns on a run like this.

But Digs pulled rank on this one. "There's always the first one. You had yours. It's time for the others now," he said. And you didn't really push all that hard, since you didn't want to provoke him into knocking you off the list. Your plans are too important to let Digs foul them up. You meet Major Rodriguez and seven men from 5 Kumaon halfway to Bunker 13, the name 5 Kumaon has given to the underground shelter they have built for officers to duck in if shelling becomes incessant. They are going to be sealing off the retreat of the Mossies you just watched go past. They are the men you are here to watch.

"I hear you had flying guests," says Major Rodriguez. "Got any on film?"

"Junior here fucked it up, Major. Forgot some batteries back at the bunker," you say.

Then the major turns around to one of your escorts and slings on his AK-47. The major now packs two. "Hey, MM," he says as he pokes the butt of the spare AK-47 in your abdomen, "you got the stomach for this?"

It's easy once you get the direction the game is taking. "You bet," you say, smiling as you hand over the camera to one of your escorts with explicit instructions to drop it by Teresa in the bunker. You ignore Siddy.

The run is nothing like you have ever done before. It's part of the major's ploy, you guess, to soften you up and gain the upper deck in the negotiations that will follow. A little dose to bean you, numb your intelligence.

But you can feel he didn't expect this calf-and-thigh response, this fast twelve miles per hour through Kupwara geology, matching pace for pace and stealth for stealth. You have the capacity to outgun them, steal a march on pure gas. But you are unfamiliar with the play. The desperation of cornered Kashmiri Mossies might not be to your liking. Nobody's briefed you on the cute little tactics they might employ, the little tricks that might trip you up on your life expectancy. So you run with your pack but bring up the rear. You don't want the first burst of lead to kiss your anatomy. Your bones and flesh are something you like to strut, and they work out for you even when your mind is in low gear, doing its best to screw things up yet again.

Among the things that come high on the list is misplaced initiative. You know from experience what high energy levels, erroneously directed, can do. You found that out one fine summer in 1985, during your first semester in the National Defense Academy at Khadakvasla, when you decided to form a cadets' union after the excesses of a drill sergeant led to the death of a roommate. Nothing more avant-garde had ever happened at the Academy. You lasted four long weeks because the commander of the Academy, in the note he had forwarded to the general in command, had added a few lines in the margins: "Though recommend dismissal, would like your permission to let things be for a while because the subject in question offers immense research richness that could come in handy, keeping in mind long-term army-training procedures. We would also get to know the names of some of the other ringleaders, if any do exist."

So, in fact, the fogies were on to you long before you ever imagined. You suspect the only reason they gave you a long rope was to determine the toxity coefficient of a single cadet preaching mutiny.

Of course, when two whole semesters you did not turn up for drill, one fine Monday morning the general thought enough was enough and handed you your letter of discharge. At that point, you remember talking of the orders as "such a sham," because even though you, in your teenage perspicacity, had set the ball rolling, new faces had taken over—cadets who were your classmates or a little senior. Some of them in Kashmir and now in positions to strike some lucrative alignments with you.

You have been running for a full forty-five minutes. For the past fifteen minutes, you could hear sporadic automatic fire. Major Rodriguez calls for a halt.

"MM," he asks, "what's your fear gradient? Does it hang low?"

You get your breath back, balance your ass on a stub of pine root. "As low as it can get, Major. I got a high chassis. You make me turn tight and you got a peacetime statistic to deal with."

"Peacetime! It's so hot in here, you get blisters while dreaming," hisses Major Rodriguez.

"So, tell your lads not to dream, Major. Dreaming's bad for soul mechanics. REM upsets your biorhythm," you say.

"What also upsets it is trying to dodge AK-47 lead that's bent on drilling you a backup asshole each time you take your compulsory shit," says Major Rodriguez.

"Bunker politics. Part of the game," you say.

"Maybe," says Major Rodriguez. "But try shitting in polyethylene for a week, and you'll evolve a new worldview. You will forge new insights into geopolitics and your own survival schemes in the sea of shit around you."

"The shit could be your own making," you say, checking your magazine. These are things you learned to do a long time ago.

"We didn't go load these Kashmiris with independence doctrine. Some people have some half-assed abstract notions, they deserve the half-assed state knee-jerkers coming their way. It's physics. Seventh grade. First law of Newton and our first rule of survival."

"What's the second?"

There's a crackle on the radio being carried by one of the lads on his back. A squeaky voice comes on the air: "Delta calling Dhatak Company. We are under attack. Need reinforcements quickly. Over and out."

You can hear the fireworks shift to higher gear half a mile up ahead. You and your pals need to speed up your act, or the plan to trap the Mossies in a pincer might fall through. The major, though, maintains radio silence. He takes a packet of Wills Classic out of his dungarees, and one of the men lights his stick for him. You didn't know smoking had the green at night. Give some trigger-happy two-legged mammal the chance to know where you're at. But the major covers the lighted portion with his palm.

You fidget. You want to rush in, help the crowd in trouble. More important, to appear to want to do so. You wait with interest to see the course of action that Rodriguez will embark on. Whether he will indulge in some mutual regimental-level back-scratching. You are trying to figure out the major's game plan when the message is repeated. This time, the voice is desperate. There are gunshots close to the radio and then continuous high-pitched static.

"Funeral time," says one of Major Rodriguez's sidekicks. He has a four-inch scar on his forehead, and a scowl that shows some satisfaction at what is going on.

"Shouldn't you be helping, Major?" you ask. "Use some of the skills you draw your pay for? The 7 Sikh is calling for help."

Major Rodriguez takes a drag on his cancer stick. "This is our second rule of survival, MM. Newton's first law in reverse. For every action, there's an equal and opposite inaction. You don't shoot, you don't get shot at, because the Mossies wouldn't know where you are."

Your adrenaline level is undergoing a metamorphosis. "Are you a genetic asshole, Major, or do you feel the need to be one on specific occasions?" The firing comes closer to you. "It's your side out there, Major. They need help."

"My side's here, MM. That's a Sikh outfit," the major says quietly.

"What's the difference? What is this, regimental politics? Today, it's their ass. Tomorrow, it could be yours and they could be in smoking standby."

"Our ass has been taken and gone, MM. This is judgment time. The equalizing hand of fate," says Major Rodriguez.

"I am going in, Major, with or without you. You want to send any of your sidekicks with me?" Of course, your wanting to join the action has much deeper implications than anybody out there with you, including Rodriguez, can fathom. It's not the rush or patriotic affinity with the 7 Sikh that's molding your actions, the way you make out. In time, if the major is astute enough, he might know. But in the job you are in, it will be your business to ensure that it's too late for him to do anything about it, if and when he does manage to put two and two together.

The major hadn't seen this coming. A journalist with mad responses is not what he has been trained to handle in pressure situations. Especially when there's more to the journalist than profession dictates.

"Trying to be a hero, MM," he says, smiling. He doesn't look all that confident. "You know what? Sometimes it's better to be an asshole than to try to be a hero. You stay alive. But be my guest."

You have no option after that. You don't particularly relish what you are about to do—on the face of it, a solo run to save a Sikh patrol platoon—but one talent that you pride yourself on is concentrating on the job at hand. And when you are doing that, there's no time for rumination.

"Fuck you, Rodriguez," you say, and head for the danger zone. You hear some rustling behind you, but for all you care, the major could be collecting leaves, toilet paper substitutes to smooth the rough ends of bunker politics.

You hit the turf running full tilt. You hear cries, shouts of pain. Sensory information, from which you can deduce the mortality of human affairs, the agenda of death that's the permanent milestone beyond all other individual manifestos.

Suddenly, you're in the shooting, you are shooting, and you trip over a body (dead or wounded, you don't know—except it's the still remains of one of the cross-border Mossies) and go headfirst into a tank-size ditch, which, even as you crash, you see is manned by a turbaned life-form of the 7 Sikh, bleeding but still there. At least you have the consolation of knowing, as you phase out, the side you have managed to sling your hero's ass into.

When you regain consciousness, you feel the poke of metal in your ribs. Unfriendly jabs, which swell the panic in your arteries, bringing you alive to the fate that is likely to be yours.

"Indian army dog," says a Mossie, and thumps his rifle butt on your ribs. You find that such minor pain-relieving options as squirming and twisting are denied you because of two Mossies holding you down by your arms. "Seven of my friends you dogs killed. The time is not far off when you dogs will have to give up Kashmir."

Kashmir. You are too fused out to counter a Mossie's political science predictions. All you can lock to is visual ground realities. A rifle butt going up comes down. Law of gravity. You tense your abdomen, beef your ribs for the blow. But the butt is moving in semantics you can't hang a pulse to. What is up, for instance, you learn quite late in life, can cruise down in unpredictable trajectories. Your left temple, in this case. And then a little combination therapy of ISI-issue boots, a blur of fists, and the butts of rifles.

Finally, time for the climax. A barrel is slanted and you can run your tongue over hot iron as you tense for the high-velocity lead that's going to tear you a ticket for heaven or hell or your next life as the Panchen Lama. You close your eyes and prepare for what is coming. But then you feel a body slump on your chest and gunfire that keeps reverberating in your tympanum. You know some miracle has happened. You open your eyes. You see Major Rodriguez glaring at you with strong disapproval.

Kashmir in May has a strong smell of something you can't put a name to. Teresa is tending to your bruises in Bunker 13, aghast that you could possibly have crossed the line from recorder of events to participant, even if the breach was on the patriotic side of things.

"Some things you just don't do as a journalist," she says. "You don't take sides. You don't erode your status as an independent player."

You keep quiet. You don't have the time for crunching ethics with amateurs in the game, people who have little clue to the many factors cooking the broth.

Right now, you are soaking in the few luxuries that Bunker 13 affords you. A rickety watercooler whirs eight feet from you, powered by a clump of batteries. Illuminated by weak bulbs, the rooms in the bunker also have a permanent odor of sweat and curry. The organizational acumen of 5 Kumaon hasn't extended yet to converting their officers' bunker into an underground resort. The enormous kitchen tent above ground has an

unstoppable ability to waft down the smells of spices, charcoal, condi-
ments, and other cooking paraphernalia.

A flight of forty steps leads into the bunker. The first time you entered
the concrete fixture, it took you many minutes to adjust to the dim light.
The bunker is like a military barracks underground. Four rooms lead
into one another. Two are bedrooms; the two others have feeble preten-
sions toward being an officers' mess. A makeshift bar, a carom board, and
a reading table, adorned with two-month-old magazines, are the sum total of recreational embellishments.

The USP of Bunker 13 is that somebody has to point out its existence
for you. Or nobody would notice. A column of men could march past it
and not know of the facility underground. At ground level, it's covered
with thick vegetation. From the air, you would just see the trees. To the
trained eye, there would be telltale signs of shelling—trees split in half,
enormous holes in the ground, shattered wood, and, farther afield, local
village houses smashed by shelling, lying abandoned.

After a while, you walk up the steps and proceed to Major Rodriguez's
tent, one of the five below and behind the concrete bulwark that faces
down on the stream separating you from the neighboring nation of the
Mossies.

You raise the flap and go in. The major has company.

"Ah, who do we have here? Our hero from the forest. So eager to have
his head blown off in the face of some higher calling, a one-man rescue army trying to save the hide of three leftover Sikhs," says Major
Rodriguez.

You give him a thumbs-up sign, gratuity for pulling the cord on someone about to hole you.

On the way back, the major took the lead with a vengeance, and
though you were giddy from the beating you had survived, you could still
muster the reserve not to ask for limb support. That was one of the ways
to salvage your respect. The 5 Kumaon squad, you learned fast, didn't
give a hoot for misplaced initiative, particularly if they had to come and

bail you out of the hole, which, according to them, you had no business digging in the first place. You also wonder if you had come out with your gun blazing, piling the Mossies in a bloody, tattered heap at your feet, what then? Denied the major the chance to tool his "I told you so" sneer. But maybe it's better this way, better to have a crazy reputation than one that makes the others fear you as an independent player.

"They were on your side, Major. I hate the fact that some Mossies managed to kill a few of our soldiers," you say, observing the uniformed colonel in the shadows. You have counted the stripes.

"Are you accusing me of anything, MM?" asks Major Rodriguez. He's spinning this stirrer he has in a martini he has fixed himself. The colonel's loaded with a glass of scotch. The 5 Kumaon seems well stocked in the spirits department.

"Not offering an injured guest a drink?"

"My apologies," says Major Rodriguez. "Shall it be scotch or a dash of vodka?"

"If you could spare some Old Monk, it would be perfect," you say. Nobody's offered you a chair yet, so you lift the only one remaining away from the gas lantern in the tent. You don't particularly relish these pump lights. They have a built-in destruction mechanism, and you don't want your face to be the only casualty in the vicinity. And you want your features to be in the shadows, away from the sharp eyes of the major and his accomplice, whoever he may be.

"Ah, Old Monk. The favorite brand of the soldiers. Your taste is a trifle too close to earth, MM. It goes with your labor-leader image. But you shall have what you want," says Major Rodriguez, pouring the liquid in a steel cup. "I hope you don't mind the steel. We can't keep you in city comfort."

You ignore this dig. "You haven't introduced me to the colonel yet."

"Ah, what's happening to my sense of propriety?" queries Major Rodriguez as he turns around with your drink. "Colonel Sangma, light of 5 Kumaon, and Minty Mehta, journalist at *The Post*."

You shake hands with a reluctant Colonel Sangma. You understand why. He has two fingers missing from his right hand. You know this man. The powder pusher in Assam and Mizoram. The colonel was transferred from a Madras regiment posted in the North East to the 5 Kumaon six years back after developing a reputation for being involved in the drug trade. The colonel, then a rank below, had carved a retail market for heroin in Mizoram with the help of thugs from his unit. So you have been told. Of course, Sangma soon infected Rodriguez and other officers from his new unit with his brand of criminality.

But Colonel Sangma is a minor-league player. His ambitions don't extend beyond retail. Rodriguez, on the other hand, doesn't look the type to even consider running a loose-change dealership. He's a major-league bastard.

"A toast," Major Rodriguez proposes, and as he lets the words hang in there a few seconds too long, you fill in the blanks.

"To mutual gain and long-term association," you say.

"Cheers," says Major Rodriguez.

"Cheers," says Colonel Sangma.

"Cheers," you say, but you don't like the taste of rum coursing through your gullet. You pour in some more water. What you observe is that even though the 5 Kumaon is tanked on liquor, they have no supply of ice.

The major switches moods. He drops his patronizing air, shifts smoothly into speech mode, 5 Kumaon philosophy and peacetime economics, a development of decade-long low-intensity conflict. You, at last, are about to get your reward for many months on Rodriguez's trail.

"MM," says Major Rodriguez, "let's get one thing straight. The war's not of our making. The 5 Kumaon is but one of many deluxe strike arms of the northern command keeping its claws sharp by engaging Mossies with numerous agendas. Our one and only mandate is to keep the Mossies plugged on their side of the fence and issue shoot-and-search warrants for those who manage to spill over, trying to upset the delicate power equilibrium in the valley. Of course, as you have discovered, we are just not any other army unit on the border. We have been here eighteen months, and along the way we have hooked ourselves to gun economics, white-dust mobility, and other such unlawful distractions, which, apart from keeping us sane, exhilarate us with the profit motive. And as our returns are linked to the number of Mossies we bust, our energy isn't an evil force to the nation to which we belong. The 5 Kumaon has the distinc-tion of having hauled in twenty-five hundred armed mercenaries so far, twenty times more than any other unit in this part of the world. Officially, that is. We have busted about two thousand more that nobody knows about, save our parallel-economy bookkeeper. Our contribution to the Indian nation's long-term stability is perhaps right there at the top, and—"

"What we want is a slice of the GNP commensurate with the toil we put in," you say, finishing for him.

"Well said," says Colonel Sangma. You were starting to think the colonel couldn't talk, but the major's speech is like a syringe of steroids straight in his larynx. "What we have faced here, we alone know. All of us have lost buddies. The army, MM, fights at the company level on per-sonal bonds. Flimsy constructs like nationalism mean nothing to us. You hit at that bond and you have a bunch of angry men to deal with, who suddenly go about asking themselves what all this rigmarole is about. Why do they have to risk their lives for a nation that's insulated to their hardships? Who's skimming the milk and where's their share of the cream? It's certainly more than the basic two thousand rupees take-home plus C-grade rations that include eight eggs a week. Would you risk even a single finger for that, MM?"

"No, Colonel," you say. You don't want to embark on any impertinent digressions or disagreements, especially when what is on tap is a prime-grade peep into the motives of the 5 Kumaon brain trust.

"Well, this is the premium I paid a little more than a year back," con-tinues Colonel Sangma, waving his three-digit hand. "For a policy that's going to retire me four years from now and dispatch me, at age fifty-four, to quiet civilian repose, when I shall no longer have the shelter of a uniform to hide my low social mobility from the Nokia asshole next door. It's not a fact of life we are content to live with. The major here lost his wife and kid recently. Casualty of 5 Kumaon overconfidence, but a casualty nevertheless. Family is never permitted to travel in convoy. But ours was the first to be taken on by the Mossies. They took out the jeep with a rocket. We didn't find enough flesh to fill an envelope. We have lost a hundred men so far, figures that don't make their way into newspaper ink, and no reporter has ever had the initiative to lever out any such statistics from the Central Defense pension office at Allahabad. We don't matter is the message we get. The 5 Kumaon could lose a trained patriot once every two days and the nation wouldn't pause in its stride. We are sick of being expendables, peacetime attrition arithmetic. The scars of hate run deep and long in us, too, and we don't know the fate that may be ours when all this will be over, when we no longer will have the license to hate. We don't want the millennium to glide by us and our children. What we want is minimum grease to stay afloat with some dignity, and you know where you plug in so we can all make the leap."

"Colonel, with due apologies," you begin, "could we bypass the motives? We might lose focus. Could we have some idea of the quantum we are talking about? The booty we seek to peddle so we can all upholster our lifestyle. You don't need to sell me your ideology. I am a convert. What's the game?"

You know of Rodriguez's personal loss. You have sometimes broached the topic, but the major hasn't encouraged you. You attribute the recent spurt in the major's drug habits to that. So, too, his buccaneering spirit, which almost borders on suicide.

"We will come to that when the time's ripe," intervenes Major Rodriguez. "First we would like to know the kind of collateral you can toss our way to make us breathe easy six hundred miles away."

"How about a few snaps you can circulate within the police forces to help track me better if I fly off with your retirement cache?" you say.

"Come on, MM, you can offer better than that. We would rest easy if we had a fix on you. It's safety dynamics. Circus-net routine. You wouldn't like to do a two and a half without the netting, would you?" asks Major Rodriguez.

"Major, I do things for the ride. The bigger the spin, the better."

"Is that why you slipped in your solo today? A fix to keep your chemicals in shape?" asks Major Rodriguez. You notice he isn't smiling. The motives of your solo run have eluded him.

"I don't like people on our side dying without my extending a helping hand. Especially if I can influence the pattern of things," you say, looking him straight in the eye.

"Not even if the guys asking for help did in one of your officers and a *jawan* in a joint patrol? Slimed out of a mission and the guys didn't know till very late. So late that they had their epidermis taken off as trophy, little Mossie knickknack for drawing room exhibition," says Major Rodriguez.

"You have a brother, MM?" asks Colonel Sangma.

"No."

"Would you go to help some people if you knew for a fact that they had delivered your brother to guys who skinned him alive? Would you?" asks Colonel Sangma.

"No," you say.

"You remember the guy with the scar today in our chase? On his forehead?" asks Major Rodriguez. "His name's Indramani. The *jawan* was his brother."

"Why did you venture out at all, Major?" you ask.

"You have to play by the rules, MM. But if you're late on the draw, it's not bayonet time," says Major Rodriguez.

"And there's the booty, of course," you say.

"That wasn't the case here. But that, too," says Major Rodriguez with a smile.

"And all yours. You wouldn't have to share it with some parallel Sikh operation," you say. Sometimes you have to hit blind to get the ball where you want.

"We can handle competition, MM. Not that there is any. All you need bother yourself about is whether you can handle bulk. Or do your skills and ambitions lie in retail? We don't want to piecemeal our inventory, increase our overheads," says Major Rodriguez.

"Which again brings us to the load factor, Major. Even genius has to know what's coming. You have to give advance warning or the system overloads," you say.

"All we can tell you right now is that we are talking big. Very big. So sleep well tonight. At dawn, we are raiding the village of Ur. We like to provide some entertainment for guests. Memories they can chew on back home," says Major Rodriguez.

And as the major's dismissal is timed with the end of your drink, you nod and step out in the chill of a starry night.

Major Kohli of 5 Kumaon comes to deliver your next day's itinerary before the three of you turn in for the night. Little dos and don'ts to brighten your perspective, enlighten your ignorance.

"You all know where the shit pits are. There, behind the mound. It's beyond sniper range. We don't usually mortar each other's pits. It's a mutual agreement. Earlier, it wasn't so, and all of us used to have a tough time. It used to get so hot sometimes, you had to stay holed up for days. Same on the other side. But then we thrashed out a pact with the guys at a border meeting. We call it our 'shit truce.' We have a meeting every month. Of course, if we have something pressing to discuss, we use mirrors. We can have no radio contacts with the enemy," says Major Kohli.

"Something pressing?" asks Teresa.

"Yes. You see, if the major's birthday comes up or something, we organize a little celebration. Or if somebody becomes a father," says Major

Kohli. "We wouldn't like to be chasing Mossies on a night like that. So the pact is that they don't push anything on mutually agreed dates."

"And they don't?" asks Siddy. He has a four-cylinder incredulity quotient.

"Well, except for once. But we taught them a lesson for that on Id, the Mossie festival. You see, they had their goats stashed in this tent for the big day. But we put four snipers on twenty-four-hour alert on the tent, and they couldn't get to their fucking goats. Then we knocked the tent off and picked out the goats. That taught them an important lesson. Violence is a game two can play at," says Major Kohli.

"A very basic lesson," says Siddy.

"Yes. But, you see, units keep in rotation. The guy you are dealing with might not be there tomorrow. And it takes the new guys some time to learn the law of the region," says Major Kohli.

"And what's the law?" you ask.

"The law is what you agree upon. The rest is a game of chess," says Major Kohli.

"How do you win?" Siddy asks.

"By being ahead. Using deception to kill deception," says Major Kohli.

"How do you do that?" Kupwara has been the biggest fucking thing that's happened to Siddy's career. The bold lettering on his CV.

"You see, for a long time the jerks would shell point X and then slip the Mossies in at point Y. It took us some time to figure out that the shelling was a red herring, a whore dance to make you look in the wrong place. They used to wait for us to go on our wild-goose chase before moving in, so that even if we wised up, we would be too scattered to crack some muscle. Of course, once we understood the game, we started moving small decoy parties toward the shelling, while the bulk of us lay in wait at the right place. For a long time, they didn't know what was going wrong. Now, of course, they just try to figure out where the 5 Kumaon patrols are and avoid them at all costs, even if it means taking other units head-on. We have really botched up the Mossie slippage schedule. Sometimes they have to cool it on their side for two to three weeks, trying to work out what patrol timings we are keeping. But Rodriguez thought up these random patrol runs. We would pick chits out from a helmet with a time written on them. That keeps them on a real hop. Confuses their reconnaissance. That's what increased our take," says Major Kohli.

"*Take?*" asks Teresa. You have to be sharp around that girl. Siddy, he's got a Stone Age IQ. Just knows what hole's for what.

"Yes," says Major Kohli, eyeballing you steadily, "the Mossie capture tally."

"Oh," says Teresa. "What do you do with the captured men?"

"We post some in big black plastic sheets to Mother Earth. No one wants to buy stiffs around this place. The hospitals are far off. The hardcore parcels, we kick ass all the way to Srinagar. The dopeys, we chase back where they came from after relieving them of their hardware. You see, there's no place we have to pin them down, and it would weigh too heavy on our souls if we put a hole apiece in their heads all the time. Besides, we would have to dig graves, and we like to avoid unnecessary labor, to keep our fatigue levels low."

"So you let them go?" asks Siddy.

"What, you want us to mail them to you? Bunny boys for the night. Handsome, hairy cuties to keep your mean temperature going," says Major Kohli. He smiles to keep us guessing.

"No, I mean they might come back," argues Siddy.

"We want them to. They are the soft ones. You can nail them with your eyes closed," explains Major Kohli.

"But what moves these guys? Why do they keep coming? What's their problem in life?" asks Teresa.

"You mean the Mossies?" clarifies Major Kohli.

"Yes," says Teresa. You can see she is getting a little sheepish with the word *Mossie*.

"Rationality is not one of their strong points. Certain races are born without logic. Or maybe the DNA has a kink that boots their logic in deep freeze. Like that gay gene they're talking about these days. But in the long run, I think, some people just like getting fucked. They don't know it, but they do."

"That's absurd," decides Teresa.

"That's a fact of life," defends Major Kohli.

"Nobody likes being tortured," says Teresa.

"Who's torturing anybody?" asks Major Kohli, looking at you for moral support. "We kill some dumb-asses who are shooting at us, because if we don't get them first, they are going to get us. We pack some off to Srinagar, the state capital, where the government can do anything they want with them, make them members of Parliament or anything. And we chase some back. That's what we are doing to keep you guys down south in good health. So you can sleep easy in the night."

"What about the interrogations and torture?" persists Teresa with embarrassing obstinacy. But Major Kohli has had his training.

"Who's got time for interrogation? You interrogate only when you know the answers are going to help you," he says.

"But how do you know what answers you are going to get if you don't interrogate?" asks Siddy. He's confused.

"Because we are psychic. We know all we want to know to run the border. The locals coming back after three months of Mossie mumbo jumbo and basic arms training know no secrets that we can squeeze out of them. We just ask them their names. They don't want to tell us, we don't waste our calories kicking their balls. We cook some name up. Exercise our imagination. Shift our workload to Srinagar, where the guys are trained for sorting out confusion. They have procedures. They open a file in the name we have given the Mossie. Maybe it happens to be his real name, or he likes it so much that he takes it on. Then they interrogate the fucker twice a day for three months, sponge him of all he knows, and transcribe what he says on white sheets of paper and run these through their encryption machines or whatever the fuck they have there. But the basic problem remains: The guy knows nothing. So he has to invent stuff to keep the interrogators off his back. And when you're tossing data out of the blue, you don't often remember it the same way the second time around, so you end up contradicting yourself. That's the opening the interrogator is looking for to prove to himself that you are hiding something, and so he extends your interrogation schedule by another month. At the end of it, your average Mossie goes dumb; he has a problem getting even the alphabet right. When you reach that stage, the interrogators at Papa 2 jump you to the list of hard-core nuts. Once you get that status, you have fat fucks coming from the Ministry of Home Affairs to Delhi to talk elections and strategies with you. Some would like to delete their hard-core status, but their newfound privileges are too tempting to give up. Your new status fetches you extra dietary supplements, pieces of animal protein to boost your immune system, give you enough calories to thumb through a week-old *Times of India*, your factual update on national-level horseshit," says Major Kohli. At some level, even he's riled.

"You are nuts," says Teresa. Such candid spelling out of policy is more than she is equipped to handle.

"That's why I am still alive and a hundred of my unit are dead. They weren't nuts. They took life seriously. It isn't worth it. Your line of duty is what keeps you breathing," says Kohli.

"So chasing Mossies through Kupwara is your key to being alive?" you ask.

"My way. I chase them my fucking way," emphasizes Major Kohli.

"What's the difference?" you ask.

"Difference is I know where they play hide-and-seek," says Major Kohli.

Intelligence is that forty-odd Mossies are playing hide-and-seek in the three-hundred-house village that is Ur, five miles from Bunker 13.

Chased a long way by the 7 Sikh, the Mossies splintered and recollected at Ur.

A cordon-and-search operation involving the dimensions of Ur calls for major logistical planning. You have to congregate the different 5 Kumaon companies, some in dispersed locations. You have to post sentries round the clock to keep an eye on the village so that you know if the Mossies try to make a break for it before dawn. They all want to reach a big town, where they can merge and start payback time. But the army's job is to prevent them from doing that. Plus, 5 Kumaon likes an even flow of inventory increase. No highs and slumps for them. They want to reel in the hardware at a steady trot.

Speed is essential. You want to swoop before the Mossies get any advance warning of what's coming and zip their flies and run for the woods. Things even out in the woods. It's difficult to chase splintered groups. And there's always the fear you could catch some stray bullet, have your photograph printed in the biannual regimental signpost column that housewives use to wrap their kids' lunches in.

An operation starts at 4:00 A.M. in the summer. A little later in the winter, but there's not much loot in that season and things are lax. Summers are makeup time and business booms.

The danger, of course, in these gestapo-style maneuvers is that if a trigger-happy Mossie decides to open up in front of civilians, the casualties are the innocents, victims caught in the cross fire. Since the Mossies never stay bunched together in one house but are scattered in twos and threes in houses all over the village, the trick is to not give them time to regroup. Achieving isolation, the army has learned through experience, fucks the morale of the Mossies. Springs a leak in their adrenaline reservoir. Makes them amenable to surrender and forces them to put their faith in army amnesty.

So speed is the key. For if you are slow, things start happening in reverse. The Mossies bunch up. Try punching a hole through the net the army has woven around them. While some escape, the rest come back to the village and take civvies hostage. They are scared of army retaliation, because the group that got through has inflicted some terminal statistics on the predator. It's even worse if one in the unit is only wounded, because helicopter evacuations take time and the soldier's out there howling away for his buddies to hear. And then hell breaks loose in the village. Hostage or no hostage, an SLR slug can take out three guys standing head-to-head.

Among the memories you will carry is that of 5 Kumaon fucking up on Operation Ur. If your success rate touches the sky, a fuckup's around the corner. That's established morphology. But nobody could really anticipate the direction from which the heavy shit would come.

First, Bravo Company, whose job it is to cordon the village, is late in coming. They had to take a detour because of unforeseen landslides. So instead of hitting at four in the morning, Colonel Sangma, who is commandeering the operation, finds himself digging the village ninety minutes too late. Shit-taking time for Kashmiri shepherds, who raise such a racket before the troops get into position that the Mossies have time for a five-minute assembly bang in the middle of the village. And this time, the Mossies whom the major's men are trying to outsmart aren't all local Baramulla, misguided Mossies, but have a dozen-odd share of Afghan mercenaries, Islamic muscle export to aid jihad at trouble spots around the globe where Mossie fortunes have taken a nosedive.

The first move to break through the cordon comes right where you are. Next to the command center, five yards from Major Rodriguez, who's on the walkie-talkie, getting his troops to move door-to-door. Tighten the lid. You have positioned Siddy and Teresa two hundred yards away from the village to get shots of peaceful surrender, images to make Indians sleep easy at night. The major has detailed four soldiers to look after the security concerns of your two colleagues.

But the opening salvo here is a rocket that takes out Major Rodriguez's jeep, with his driver still in it. Casualty number 101 for 5 Kumaon. Then the automatics start sending buzzers around your head, and you and the major have to hug the grass. The major drags his driver's body around the bend to feel his pulse without having a Harkat ul Ansar asshole line him in his sights. You help the major as your support group gives you covering fire.

At the other end of the village, where the 5 Kumaon presence is in diffused numbers, the Harkat ul Ansar strives to gain its freedom. A small but potent rear guard keeps the troops engaged toward the south. You watch the mayhem with the awe of a kid in a museum.

A rocket misfires, blowing the roof off a house fifty yards from you. People come scurrying out. Scared women, children, and men howling and running for cover.

A Mossie emerges from a burning house. His skin's hanging from his face, but with his right hand, he's emptying his AK-47 magazine into the troops taking him on. You watch; the major watches. The guy keeps taking bullets, but the mule kicks don't slow the momentum he has developed in his running. His left hand rips off his body. Just like that, a piece of wool in the wind. Blood rushes out like a spring, but his leg muscles keep pounding. The whoof of battle and the hate give him unknown sources of energy. Then his head, suddenly, is no longer there. It's rolling backward, two pieces of it. But the legs still have it for two more paces as the automatic goes silent and clatters to the ground.

"Holy shit," you say. This is beyond anything you have ever seen. You feel like puking.

The major looks transfixed. It's clear he hasn't seen anything like this, either. You wonder whether Teresa got the action on Beta cam.

For a moment, things stand still. Clearly, a surreal episode makes for a pause on both sides. But the fire is spreading and the roofs are catching it all at once. People thrown out of their wooden doors are of two minds—to run for water or to save their bodies from lead. The women have no choice. They run with little girls and boys into fields. The men take stock, crowd around a well, watch the conflagration. This is war.

Colonel Sangma is fazed, out of his depth with the ferocity of the events. Major Rodriguez has more or less taken over. He is barking orders in his wireless.

"Stop firing," he's shouting.

Civilian casualties are something he would like to avoid. That's a black mark in your confidential report. It might also signal the end of the road for 5 Kumaon's stay in the neighborhood. Get army brass to move them to the North East or something, where they might learn that messing with the Naga rebels is a different piece of cake. Also the terrain, a pound of leeches sticking in your boots if you take ten paces.

The Harkat ul Ansar seize on this window of opportunity, this lull in the proceedings. They ram a corridor northwest in the welter of confusion of women, children, shrieks, and cries, sprinting for the woods before the major can lower the gates on the leak.

More bad news. While the troops are busy plugging the gap, a splinter group of radical Mossies sneaks up southeast, undetected, half a mile down to the metaled road, where 5 Kumaon have a few of their trucks parked. They make off with one after suitably incapacitating four others by tossing grenades in their gas tanks, standard guerrilla policy, practiced to good effect on retreating Russians. Hit-and-run, using the enemy's own wheels, ancient Shaktiman six-tonners that bounce you like Ping-Pong balls in back. But better to toss around like a white ball than have the troops break your bones for pleasure, or worse, have five dozen 5 Kumaon veteran motherfuckers, led by Major Kohli, chase you through the woods, determined to plug lead two times your body weight into your frame, give you a heavy send-off.

Meanwhile, things get sad and ugly at Ur. The troops have knocked two houses out with mortars to stop the whole village from torching up. Knots of brave civilians try salvaging stuff from ashes, inferno, and smoke.

In the midst of the confusion, Major Rodriguez remains resolute. He starts rounding up villagers, trying to grind out information about the arms and ammunition dump belonging to the Mossies the 5 Kumaon just flushed from Ur. Apart from wanting to increase the 5 Kumaon inventory, the major doesn't want it blown up in the fire. A profit smashed to bits under his nose. A percentage decrease in the cut for all the dealers.

But the people feign ignorance. The major follows unwritten army procedure for civil disobedience in disturbed territories adjacent to the national border. Step one: Separate the population by sex. It's easier for rape.

You see troops put a ring around the women, who cling to one another in fear of the wave of lust around them, cutting off escape routes. Your superior vantage point allows you to monitor facial signals, subtleties that you have to be alert to tune in to. What you see is the major jog his jaw about two inches in the way of the noncommissioned officer in charge of hustling the women, and two burly 5 Kumaon veterans tear two teenage girls from the swirling mass and push them into the nearest unburned interior of a single-story building.

The movement is fast, too fast to register on the retina unless you were looking for it, and it's escaped most of the frightened villagers. But it's locked on the mother—you assume the relation because she's the solitary one pushing and screeching at the cordon even as the troops switch modes to automatic and let loose bursts in the air to add to the confusion.

You look inward to see how you feel, but of all the images in your head, there's only one turbocharged visual, the memory of the one-handed and headless assault of a nameless Mossie. As a general rule, when you are numbed by blood and mayhem, rape shifts to low gear, a sour taste that you can brush away with Colgate.

Major Rodriguez now switches to step two, in normal circumstances the first step, but now, in action mode, in tandem behind step one. Get the civvies in formation and run them single file in front of an army *jonga* with black-tinted windows, inside which sits an informant, a village dickhead in army pay, to spot your leftover Mossies for you. The smartest don't go for the break but stick on, try to pass as harmless locals.

Step two pays off handsomely. A catch of three prize Mossies, pointed out with little hesitation by the informant. Of course, the danger here is that the informant could be settling personal scores. But the test is to see whether some howling mothers come to snatch their wards away from custody. Then you might be on the wrong track and would have to further exercise your judgment. Basically, it's no skin off the 5 Kumaon. Sometimes a Mossie or a local is all the same. You just need a butt for your toe to sink into.

The village of Ur is relieved when the cache is found. It's stacked in the attic of one of the houses. Enough hardware to take on Mauritius— two hundred AK-47 rifles, twenty thousand rounds of ammunition, four hundred grenades, one hundred antipersonnel mines, walkie-talkie sets, detonators, IEDs, RDX, and, for the first time, an item long suspected, five Stinger missiles, shoulder-fired surface-to-air motherfuckers with an operational range of six miles.

The major is a happy man. As happy as a man can be whose driver has taken a rocket hit. The day's not a complete snafu, though three in the major's unit have been killed. The Mossies have taken a heavy knock: eight in the village, and the rest being chased through the woods.

The blips on the radar, though, are the civilian casualties. Fourteen villagers have died in the cross fire and twenty are wounded. The army doctors are stuffing plasma and glucose into the injured, trying to keep the Ur casualties from spilling over into a human rights fiasco. This in addition to the rape victims. You count six, but there could have been more.

By eight in the morning, Operation Ur is history. You return to Bunker 13, hitching a ride on one of the returning trucks, where two sulking colleagues confront you.

"They didn't let us shoot after the jeep got knocked off. Did you see that?" asks Siddy.

"They just herded us off, didn't even let us stay, watch the fun," says Teresa.

"It wasn't any fun. It was dangerous," you say.

"What happened?" asks Teresa.

"Usual stuff," you say. "Some died; some lived."

Your socializing instincts are below ignition level. There's something new biting you. The eyes of the mother who saw her daughter dragged in. What you are wondering is which one of the two the daughter was. Or were they both.

You are with Major Kohli. You have volunteered to be part of a reinforcement team, saying you want to experience the thrill of the chase. Although Major Rodriguez was initially disinclined to accede to your request (for the very convincing reason that to lose you would be to lose the sole conduit he trusts to peddle his inventory), he shows the green after assigning a section with the specific duty of getting you back alive.

Major Kohli knows where his quarry's headed, and he plans to outsmart them by being the first one there. You yourself are there as a field academic. To observe, at close quarters, the Indian army's Mossie-capturing techniques. You plan to write a book someday.

"MM, what do you think is the main ingredient in the LIC situation we have right now?" asks Major Kohli. The major, you feel, is trying to assess your jargon compatibility.

"To prepare a threat-situation template of the LIC situation," you say.

"Wrong. That's for the armchair guys at the Academy. You have to get your terrain analysis right. What do you think the Mossies need most?"

"Shelter," you say.

"Shelter, yes. But for what?"

You duck the question. Major Kohli enlightens you.

"For food and medical supplies," he says. "Sometimes terrain that has no tactical importance becomes important for a Mossie force's key logistical needs."

"Okay," you say. "So what are we going to do about it?"

"We are going to get a little ahead in the game. Integrate our terrain analysis with our anticipation template."

"What does that mean?"

"It means you might be the first civilian in history to be part of an army ambush force," says Major Kohli as he twists his disruptive combat material combat cap from front to back. "That's my personal code, you see. My men now know what's up."

You hope so. For your furious clip through Kupwara to reach Rajor, the town that Major Kohli insists the Mossies are heading for, is like nothing you have ever done before. First you go on a slight detour, confusion tactics for any Mossie rear recce teams, and then cut northwest again, a diagonal that should get you there ninety minutes ahead of the Mossies to prepare for their reception.

You arrive at seven in the evening, and it's time again for you to receive an enlightening discourse from Major Kohli, beef up your theory firsthand.

"Where do you think you are standing, MM?" asks Major Kohli.

"On a streambed," you say.

"No. You are standing in the central ambush zone. Our principal 'hello' area for the Mossies, where our ambush will be initiated with a maximum-personnel-casualty-producing device. In short, claymore mines," says Major Kohli.

"What's this, an area ambush or a point ambush?" you ask, a lame effort on your part to beef up your end of the exchange.

"Ah, I am impressed. This is going to be an area ambush, but with a high technical rating. In keeping with the superior nature of our Mossie threat, this time we are planning very fluid assault formations, a 5 Kumaon speciality," says Major Kohli.

"What, a line formation?" you ask.

"No, MM. We will begin with a line formation and then switch to an L assault on the west side and then L and Y again at the bend in the streambed, and then the Y and Z formation, nail the Mossies on the riverbed," says Major Kohli.

"Why the Z?" you ask.

"No point taking chances. The Mossies might have high-frequency radios and could have called for reinforcements or other help. We need the additional side of the Z to keep off a reinforcement force and seal the end of the kill zone," explains Major Kohli.

"What about a chopper? Why don't you just pick them up from the air?" you ask.

"Too risky. You never know when they might be packing a Stinger. Also, the air force is always on a frequency that doesn't match the army's. You have to knife through a lot of red tape to requisition one," says Major Kohli.

You nod. Then you watch the *jawans* lay the streambed with water-proof mines. Swiftly, two pits are dug for placing machine guns, one on each side of the stream, but with a limited arc of functioning, so that the *jawans* coming in through the three access lanes are not caught in the cross fire.

"Every properly prepared ambush should have three elements, MM. The assault force, the backup group, and the perimeter party. The backup group functions as the secondary assault force, and the perimeter party secures outlying ambush zones, where leftover Mossies dispersing from the central ambush zone are mopped up," says Major Kohli.

"What if outlying ambushes are discovered by the Mossies before they walk into the main killing area?"

"Good question, MM. The *jawans* are under orders to open fire if discovered but not to yell or shout," says Major Kohli. "But, of course, the whole purpose is to lure the Mossies into the main killing area and draw any relieving forces into our multiple ambush points. Get the fuckers from all sides. Zap them with our hardware."

"We aren't supposed to capture them alive? Make them surrender or something?"

"Frankly, MM, that's not an option. It only increases your casualties. Also, I am not in the mood. They got three of our men. We are out to get their ass," says Major Kohli. Then he does a bit of landscape survey. "Besides, for that we would have to have a harassing kind of ambush, but the terrain here is not suited for an L-formation assault, where the attack element is deployed at a right angle to the movement of the Mossies so that the attack element and the Mossies form the letter *L*. With this formation, a small platoon can skew and harass a much larger force without at any moment becoming decisively engaged and suffering losses."

"There might be more casualties on your side."

"No. Even though it's night, we know the direction they are going to come from. If we hadn't known that, we would have deployed the triangle formation, a small unit strong point to counter night movement of Mossies when the Mossie approach route is unknown. A general-purpose machine gun placed at each point of the triangle with a 30-degree arc-of-fire so that it can be shifted quickly to form crisscrossing fields of fire with the two other GPMGs. And then alternate-flank firing, just before you break into the T, subject them to interlocking fire. Fry their flesh for them," says Major Kohli.

Well, the Mossies come, but from the wrong direction. And though Major Kohli's command to his men to take their safeties off is given at eight o'clock, it isn't till nine that the moonlight shines off the first of them. Major Kohli has you placed in sniper position. Away from the approach or assault zones but on the left bank of the stream, on the top of an embankment, sixty-five feet high. There, with the knowledge that mines guard the escape route up the embankment, along with the presence of a multidirectional machine gun, a certified widow-maker, you eye the Mossies through your AK-47 sights, flanked by your bodyguards, waiting for the major to signal the shit to start.

But what happens is that one of the Mossies trips on the green nylon cord that connects lead members of assault teams on the right bank of the stream to coordinate timing for the blowing up of the mines. This much, Major Kohli will piece together for you in the aftermath.

So, the soldier in charge of blowing up the mines blows the whistle prematurely, thinking the tug on the cord came from Major Kohli. What this does is starts the game before barely 20 percent of the Mossies are in the central ambush zone.

It's the first time you see what a personnel mine bursting under the groins of a group of three Mossies can do. It blows them about fifteen feet in the air. Each comes down with either one leg on or no face at all, depending upon his body angle at the time he was negotiating the stream — that is, whether he was looking downward or at the moon or someplace else.

In case he was looking anywhere else but down and his face is still intact once he comes down, he has it in him to start screaming a very special kind of scream, which makes even his Mossie buddies stick him one in the head to take him out of his pain. If no one's around, he keeps screaming till he goes unconscious and then bleeds to death. Yes, he also gets splattered remnants of his balls popped up in a shower, which could land anywhere within a radius of 325 feet. You say that with confidence because you are somewhere at the 195-foot mark and your cheek gets some of it from the sky.

Now, with the mines going up, the GPMGs start their slaughter, and because the Mossies are coming the opposite way from the one expected, they could, if they had the presence of mind, run to the end of the stream, for this isn't as efficiently bottled up as the one they passed coming in, when nobody was firing.

But with guys screaming that special scream, something happens to your head, and the Mossies who are at the perimeter, still with remote chances of giving the whole thing the slip, keep getting drawn in, an example of suicidal comradeship.

You let loose a couple of shots in the air, your contribution not to Mossie mortality but to the confusion. You get more from the scene by lying low and watching, benefits of the geophysics of your location.

But these soon alter.

The Mossies organize amid the slaughter and go for a counterassault along the right bank. They try to beat lead with lead, following the access lanes the assault teams were using. They cant their battle hymns. You can hear them over the din of the automatics, though they keep getting feebler and feebler. You have been too busy following the massacre below to notice two Mossies climbing the bank on your side. Your bodyguards are busy giving covering fire to the line formation on your side of the bank and are too far to your left to have intercepted them even if they had noticed.

The first time you notice their presence is when soldiers on the right bank start picking the dust on the embankment below you.

You see a turban and then a face red with blood. Then you see the brown eyes, and they belong to someone very young, maybe eighteen, perhaps younger.

You feel like helping him up, a solitary jab of sanity in the murder around you, but then you see the terror in his eyes. You realize what you look like. The threat you represent. And even as the Mossie is trying to raise the barrel of his automatic from down below and level it at your chest, you see what you have to do, for there is no time to explain to him the ridiculousness of your position. You have no option but to pull the trigger, and then you see a big empty hole where you once saw a pair of brown eyes.

Your bodyguards pick off the Mossie below him.

The next day, in the evening, Major Rodriguez summons you to his tent. Business time. He is alone and his feet are stuck up on his desk.

"Ah, MM," he says, "things are grim."

You have gotten a bit of your starch back.

"War is grim," you say.

"This is not war. This is battalion headquarters. They don't like what happened at Ur," says Major Rodriguez, clicking his heels.

"Neither do the people of Ur," you point out.

"We didn't ask them to give bed and board to forty Mossies," argues Major Rodriguez.

"You don't say no to men with guns," you enlighten the major.

"You have to make your choice. Us or them," explains the major.

"That's not much to go by, Major," you say.

"It's enough. You have to understand who can fuck you more. Play your game in that light."

"You don't need to burn half a village down to show who's boss. The army's got some cannons, somebody breathing down their neck in battalion HQ."

"We didn't burn the village down, MM. Asshole equipment error. Maybe the rocket was aimed at your ribs. You should go bury the Mossie personally, thank him for letting you be."

"Maybe somebody let things get out of hand on the women's side," you say. That catches the major a bit off guard. The rhythms of lust are not something he thought you picked up in the din.

"Maybe they ought to let you run a unit in this area on Saint Paul's precepts. Get you started with ideas to baptize the Mossies, convert them if you can't catch them. MM, tit for tat is the only Tao principle that plugs with the blood groups down here. What you say you saw is an old weapon of war. They have done us worse. It's good to have them fear us. Make them reorganize their priorities for next time," says Major Rodriguez.

"Hate you is more likely," you say.

"That's good enough for me. When you hate, you slip up. Keeps my men out of the barracks to straighten you up," says Major Rodriguez.

"And levitate the inventory," you add.

"That's one of the perks," admits a smiling Major Rodriguez.

"So what's grim?" you ask.

"Battalion HQ doesn't like burned-up places. They set up inquiry committees that go around asking embarrassing questions. It's bad PR for them. Loses them brownie points with the state government. And these human rights assholes," says Major Rodriguez.

"I thought the state government was on your side," you say.

"The government is on nobody's side but its own. Besides, they have a balancing act to do. Give no reason for Amnesty International to make some noise. Or worse, invite the New Delhi diplomats down their throats. Make them shift their offices from Chanakyapuri to Kashmir."

"Nobody should know anything, Major. Ur's nowhere from anywhere."

"News travels, MM. You can't brush the fire and the civilian casualties under the carpet. I would love to, but it's not going to happen. This is our first fuckup, and it looks like it's going to be our last in this region."

"You shouldn't have forced your way in. Just laid a long-term siege."

"What? And get the media at my door? Lose control of my operation? Have everybody know we've got Stingers? No way."

"You're going to swallow them up, too?" you ask, a little taken aback at this daring.

"What do you think? Give it up to the warehouse guys?"

"Sometimes there might be more gain in giving something up. Deflect attention from what happened. Create a scare that makes you a hero and has the Ministry of Home Affairs people shitting in their pants. Stingers can take out planes flying the hotshots into Srinagar. It will make them stay put in Delhi, keep their ideas to themselves."

The major muses on this awhile.

"Won't do," he concludes. "It's tempting, but it won't help the unit stay on beyond normal schedule, get us some more time."

"There's no harm trying," you say.

"And lose the cash due from the Stingers in the bargain? No way. A bird in the hand is worth two in the bush. But we will play the Pathans up. The Taliban from Kabul looking for a kick in this part of the world. That may suit our purpose. We wouldn't mind losing them," says Major Rodriguez.

"But you have only stiffs. You have none alive. Major Kohli saw to that," you say.

"Yes. Twenty stiffs. But the problem is, they don't speak. If only you guys had flushed a few alive, we might have had a good TV talk show," says Major Rodriguez. "I hear you knocked one out yourself, MM?"

"You heard right," you say. You have locked that scene right out of your mind. You may get back to it one day when the world isn't looking, but you aren't doing it now.

"You okay?" asks Major Rodriguez. You sense that what you may say now is crucial for whatever the major has called you about.

"Mossie's about to poke his AK-47 in your face. You blow his face off. Nothing in it that should make you feel the need to ask whether things were okay or not," you say. "Cause and effect. Cause: Mossie lines his gun. Effect: You blow his brains into the stream. As long as you got the effect all sewn up on your side of the game, everything's okay."

The major sizes you up for a good thirty seconds, as if he's making up his mind one final time.

"Now to the point, MM. Ur was sad and unforeseen. It's expedited certain decisions that we had hoped wouldn't have to be taken so soon."

"Who's 'we'?" You don't like the knowledge of faceless players.

"That's something you needn't concern yourself with. You were concerned about bulk yesterday. You can chew on some of the numbers before you leave. We are talking big. We are talking thirty thousand AK-47s, one million rounds of ammunition, two hundred and twenty pounds of RDX, detonators, five thousand grenades, a hundred Uzis, twenty automatic grenade launchers, fifty state-of-the-art mortars, five Stingers, and, the big cake, four hundred kilograms of heroin that we captured from the Mossies over a period of nearly two years. You ready for this?" asks Major Rodriguez.

"Major," you say after you whistle, "you are talking big league. You are talking my language. We could take over Africa with that kind of stuff."

Your job brief as executive producer of Putman Offshore involves working for Digs's television company, Media Vision. Here, you are directly in charge of the documentary division. For complex tax reasons, which you could never quite figure out, Digs doesn't use his TV company to hire staff, preferring instead to wire your salary through Putman, an arrangement that often leads people to think you are working for a finance company.

As part of the special deal you have cut with Digs, you also hold the post of Features editor for his weekly news magazine, *The Post*, which he started a year ago. You are primarily a print man, but you started flirting with television a few years back because of the profile it brought you. You needed that profile to stay ahead in the information game.

After many years, you met Major Rodriguez in December 1998 at Siachen glacier in Jammu and Kashmir, where you were crafting the first-ever documentary on the region. That is, after the National Defense Academy in Khadakvasla in 1985. You knew him there, but you weren't friends.

Siachen was one of the ideas you had sold Digs, before you got in, to get him interested in you. Your expertise in defense and environmental reporting made you ideal for the job. High-altitude mountain warfare has lately become an Indian speciality. The Yanks have been wanting joint exercises in the region to cut in on what's happening, but the chiefs have been reluctant, so you figured it was a bright commercial idea to feed Yank curiosity, have them know what it takes to hold on to a barren piece of land 21,000 feet above sea level, stop the Mossies from building the highest piece of mosque in human history.

You got to sit next to the major on the chopper from Leh to base camp, the training area for the troops moving up, the place where the first thing they teach you is how to walk on ice and how not to fall in a crevasse. You, of course, were familiar with this rigmarole: You had been as high as Camp 1 with a U.S. team on Mount Everest.

The major was on the advisory committee to the glacier think tank, which meets annually to reassess the long-term glacier situation. He was too junior to be on it, but he was a special case. He had honed some warfare techniques that busted five Islamic choppers, one with a brigadier on it. The 5 Kumaon had seen action at Siachen. It was the major's first posting as a raw second lieutenant straight out of the Academy.

You hadn't any pleasant memories of Rodriguez from your revolutionary days at the Academy, but at Siachen the vibes between you were good. Those were the days, only six months back, when the major's family was still intact. He showed you a snap of his wife, a honeymoon shot at Lakshadweep. The major came in handy. Your stay permit for your crew at the glacier was just five days, this after all the strings you had pulled at the ministry. But you were thankful you got in at all. The major saw your point of view. He sympathized with your concerns for quality. He had the chopper pilot pull out a flight due to technical reasons the day you were booked for return. And that extended your stay for five days, by which time the weather screwed up and you got another five days. You ended up owing Rodriguez for ten days.

Of course, the major had his reasons for slowing you down. You were bunkered with him and he did his sonar booms on your personality, listening for shallow reefs and sandbars he should steer clear of. The general message he got, you guess, was that you were open to new ideas, exciting rides to punctuate the monotony of life.

That's when he baited you on pushing certain hardware, a sample run to test the market and see the depth you packed. In that deal, you netted the 5 Kumaon $500,000. Your share was a cool 10 percent.

You used to be a guy with scruples, but in your early thirties, you started hitching on to things for the ride. Illicit gunrunning simply came your way.

What made you up to this enterprise was your international mobility, the contacts you had nurtured overseas in seminars by spreading half-truths about the nuclear position in South Asia, the subject of your dissertation and later of your articles when you were defense correspondent at *News Today*. You were the first to break news about your country's ambitions in the field of nuclear submarines—a news report that had put you under the surveillance of the Research and Analysis Wing for a month, until one day you walked in the RAW chief's office and cleared things up, gave him reason to believe in your innocence. So much for India's premier foreign intelligence agency.

Along the way, when you ran out of stories on defense, you widened your scope of operations to include the environment, specifically toxic waste, climate conventions, and ozone. Toxic waste you developed as your forte, your tag to establish journalistic currency. India is huge, and who knows who is dumping what? You made it your business to find out. Not everybody wanted to depend upon Greenpeace alone to give them estimates of Indian scrap-metal imports, the trading lacunae companies abroad were using to dump a lot of stuff they couldn't cram into their neighborhood landfills.

You also expanded your brief a bit by including your concerns about indigenous poison generated in places like Gujarat and Maharashtra. You realized that foreign expertise was needed to teach Indians what not to do with their industrial excreta. So, accordingly, you submitted a proposal to the Swiss Development Authority to help you understand the holistic approach to inorganic and organic waste disposal in developed countries, specifically Switzerland. The Swiss were only too happy, since they had been agonizing for months over how to spend their aid grant, and here was this guy walking in with a concrete proposal, even if it was not a part of their charter. You got a grant of twenty thousand dollars, a four-month stay in Europe.

It was then that you developed your acquaintance with Dinesh Patel, at the time a diamond merchant. You interviewed him for a story about Indian diamond dealers in Antwerp, written for *News Today*, to let everyone back home know you were still alive. Patel, his moneymaking schemes in diamonds exhausted, soon rose to become the second-largest arms dealer in Bosnia and, later, Kosovo. Nobody knew about this development then; nobody knows about it now — the Indian connection in the Serbian wars. For your own reasons, you never got around to doing a profile on Patel. Perhaps you intended to store the intelligence for future encashment. Stories didn't give you a fix anymore unless they served your larger agenda.

It was Patel who took your first consignment of five hundred AK-47s and other knickknacks. The advantage of dealing with Patel was that he picked up your merchandise in Delhi. You didn't have to work out the sea route or bother your head about the end user. Your stuff went 30 percent cheaper, but you liked it this low-risk way. It didn't push you into unfamiliar territory.

But now you are getting into high-risk maneuvers. Major Rodriguez has the first heroin shipment delivered to your apartment by 5 Kumaon personnel on leave. Wooden crates with red outer markings saying they are government of India disaster relief, medical consignments, glucose powder for the dehydrated.

Your immediate problem is to hunt for a safe hibernation zone for your white packets. They have given you two sleepless nights and you can't take two more.

You sort your shit at work, rack your brain, and decide to stash the packets in the air-conditioning vents of Digs's Media Vision office, neutral, unexploited space, where the H can't be traced back to you. You can crawl into the vents from the mezzanine floor. The aluminum is thick and strong enough to bear the weight of a man on hands and knees. You know this because you have seen the electrician do it. Yes, as part of your preparation, you plan to indispose him for a couple of months and, in his place, recruit one of the two muscle men Major Rodriguez has provided you as backup—Indramani, with the scar, and Gulab Chand. Both from 5 Kumaon's Alpha Company, they are eating their annual two-month army leave to earn their part of the cut.

It's Chand you have in mind as designated temporary electrician. He knows his circuits, and when you have Brandish, the electrician, knocked off his Suzuki Samurai at night by a speeding army *jonga* with Indramani at the wheel, you create the opening for Chand to come the next day and flash his fake CV, which lists work experience in your friend Jumbo's fictional air-conditioner dealership. The guy knows everything about air-conditioning; he can keep your ass cool through an Indian summer, provided the power's available. He's hired on the spot.

Once you have your man on the mezzanine, guarding the ducts, it's easy work getting the packets in piecemeal, an inch-thick white carpet over sixty-five feet of aluminum. You hope media premises would be the last place the Narcotics Control Bureau would poke their nose. At night, the doors are double-locked, and nobody has the keys except Chand. You have a copy made, in case of emergencies.

A few days after your return from Bunker 13, Digs takes a walk upstairs to your cabin. As a rule, he stays clear off the TV floor; the logistics confound him. He feels out of sync. But today, he has things on his mind.

"MM," says Digs, "I want you to hire some new staff. Features has the highest turnover. This time, no experienced staff. Just trainees you can run around and get some honest work from. And what's happening to the border thing? I hear you got some good rushes for the documentary."

"Plenty," you say, but before you can elaborate, Digs nods and walks off. Digs's attention span is shorter than a pigeon's. He can't switch it on for longer than fifteen seconds. If you pitch a story to him, you have to run the whole knickerless cancan routine in ten seconds flat. Grab his attention and get him to sign whatever you want in that period. Or he is going to shelve your proposal. Sit on it for two months, till you forget what it was.

He drives the regular *Post* guys nuts. He fancies himself an editor. He is because he owns the damn thing, but he has ambitions to leave his mark on Indian journalism. The kind of editing he does is to snoop around the place with his neck lowered. If you didn't know him, you would think he was the floor inspector or something. It always takes the news guys a while to get used to him. He gives them the creeps. He stares over their shoulders at their computer screens, and half the time when they look up, he is there grinning at them. It cracks them up so fast, they keep looking over their shoulders. In the end, they get kind of addicted to his presence.

He doesn't do this much with the senior guys. Instead, he keeps them off balance when he brushes shoulders with them in the loo. He asks what they are doing. Most of the guys are doing nothing, naturally, and start to hem and haw, waving their big whales over their trousers, making interesting patterns. Then he pushes them into his office and assigns them some update on the whore district or crime nonsense, and there goes their week. Even the reporters who are doing something forget what it is until Digs has just slapped them with some shitty assignment. They end up having to do both Digs's stuff and theirs.

The trick is to burst into an answer. Say you're doing a story on floriculture exports. That kind of thing cuts him dead in midsentence. He loses his vowels. "Yeah, okay," he says, and walks off. His memory's shorter than his attention span. He's never going to come up to you and ask how the floriculture thing is going. In case he does, you tell him your section editor put you on this or that. The thing is, once you start talking, he isn't interested in listening.

But you like Digs. He got his nickname because he digs his nose in public. That's second only to his burping in your face when you are talking. But Burps didn't sound as good.

While you are contemplating your hiring methodology, Digs comes by once again for a twenty-second verbal burst.

"Oh, I forgot to tell you. My daughter Karnam's back from the States.

She wants to see how this place works. See if you can take her in Features. Show her around," he says.

"Okay," you say. She won't be picking a hole in your salary is how you console yourself. But you find it odd that Digs can't do his own hiring. He does all the sacking. Recruitment doesn't contribute to his blood pressure. It wouldn't fray his hypertension.

You place calls to journos on the circuit, leave word around that you need a couple of trainees to beef up your Features division. (You don't want to run an advertisement and get a million CVs to read.)

You tip your chair back, gazing up at your safe, invisible stash. Kashmir feels a million miles away. And that's when the call comes from RAW, the call you always knew would come.

"Hello," says Col. Ray Chowdhary, your RAW Godfather, who thinks he runs you. You have run for him and RAW on occasion. These days, your loyalty could only be called sporadic.

"Yes," you say.

"What's the news, pal? You remember your friends?"

"Always."

"What's the score? You have anything to help us nab the bastards?"

"Not yet."

"What the fuck have you been doing up there? We've been hearing things."

"Ears are for hearing. That's what God made them for."

"I am in no mood for your cockiness. You get to go where you want; we dropped you a line to Bunker 13. We want to know what the weather is up there."

"I told you. Nothing. The place is clean as a whistle. Just the usual army bullshit. They went and razed that village, Ur. But you don't need that from me. That's everywhere. Even the media's got it."

"You sure?"

"About what?"

"About the weather up there?"

"You couldn't fry an omelette."

"We've been hearing talk about some Stingers they found on the raid."

"Not that I know of. They shooed us off when it started getting shirty."

"It's not your business to shoo off."

"It's also not in my interest to have a Mossie tear holes in my chest."

"Is that why they bounced off all the Afghans? Stop them singing about the Stingers under interrogation?"

"Doesn't make sense. They took a few local Mossies in, alive and kicking. They, too, must have seen what was going on."

"Those are the guys who told us," he says.

"You guys pump Mossies so bad, they start inventing stuff. You see, if, as you say, they had found Stingers, they wouldn't have left any Mossies alive to tell the tale."

"Maybe. Maybe they slipped. You got anything at all?"

"They haven't taken my bait yet. Give me some more time."

"Time is running out, my friend. It's time for you to press their hand. You stay wired." Colonel Chowdhary hangs up.

For all your bluster, you take a long breath and mop your face.

Later in the day, Digs's daughter comes by. She isn't what you have been expecting. You have been imagining someone with Digs's porky looks, a pest you would have to put up with. But it looks as if Digs had someone else turn in the rod, squirt some prime-time genetic fluid.

"My dad said to come and see you," Karnam says.

"Yes, I was planning to call you. He says you want to have a look around, see the levers."

"Actually, I was planning a bit more than that. I was hoping I could pitch in somewhere, get some work experience."

"What have you been up to? I hear you've been chasing some piece of paper back in Texas."

"Yes, I just finished my MBA."

You feel the first shiver of need seep into your veins.

"M fucking BA. You could be barking up the wrong tree, you know. You should be sharing the latest you have in circulation technique with our marketing guys. They can't seem to be able to push it beyond the five-digit barrier. Make them go sonic."

"No. Actually, I hate marketing. I don't want to whip up soap or something like that. I want to be a journalist. I want to make a difference."

"You, too? Another member of the caring brigade. Maybe somebody ought to tell you there's not enough foam you can hose in out there."

"You are so cynical. Are all of you like this?" she asks. "Journalists, I mean."

"No. I haven't progressed to the point where it's just another job for me. If you are only cut out for doing some particular chore in life, it makes the choice easy."

"They should put you in career counseling," comments Karnam.

"That's my in-house specialty. The crowd comes to me for straightening out their change-the-world kinks. Change yourself, I say; save the world your brand of revolution."

"Would Features be a good place to start off?" asks Karnam.

"Well, actually, no. The Desk would be ideal, but that would be grade-four, Third World pay. We'll start you off in Features, and then maybe you can move to Business once you get the hang of things," you say.

"Marketing sounds so boring," she comments.

"Boring is as boring does. You could pack some action there if you got the right ideas," you say.

"What's the basic tip?" she asks. "I mean the Zen of journalism. No ten-minute speech."

"Well, it's like any other job. Just don't fuck up. Get your *w*'s right— the why, what, where, when, and who—and you should chip along fine," you say.

"That's it?"

"What did you expect, a warden's monologue? It's more than I got."

"What did you get?"

"A test trial, the first day I walk in for this interview at *The Statesman*. The editor asks, 'So you want to write?' 'Yes, sir,' I say. 'What's the time right now?' he asks me. 'Nine-ten, sir,' I say. 'Well, writer boy,' he says, 'get me three exclusives by five in the evening and you have your job.' 'Yes, sir,' I say, and walk out of his office. I didn't even know what he meant by 'exclusives.' I checked it out with some blokes who seemed to know. This was in Calcutta. I hang around the Esplanade for a while, figuring what to do. I can't figure out shit. I walk in the sun, hoping to bump into something. And bump I did. I find myself kicking a packet of something by Ho Chi Minh along this side street they have by Tata Center. It's a packet of letters some postman chucked into the drain; they had four-month-old postmarks. That's my first story.

"I hang around a bit, hoping to latch on to something else, but it's all fucking dead around there, and so I call this friend of mine for some help. He gives me a lead on this guy who can light electric bulbs anywhere on his body. Nobody's ever done him in press, he tells me. So I go all the way to Jadavpur to meet this man and plead with him to get into the mood to show some of his stuff. And right there he takes a bulb out of a socket and presses the slim end on his nipples. Then he sits like that for five minutes with his eyes closed, and the filament glows up. I mean, it isn't bright or anything, but it's heated up. He shifts it to his tummy, and bingo. He does it about five different places. When I ask him whether he can do it on his dick, he chases me out. I try to get an explanation on the phenomenon from a physics professor, who thinks I am wasting his time. But I have two stories, and when I am going down in the lift from meeting the professor, this guy next to me gets his hand jammed into the gate grille. It rips his wrist off before I can push the stop button on the lift. I and some others take him to hospital, and when I am free from all that, it's late afternoon and I don't even have time to change my shirt before returning to office. 'So what do you have for me, trainee boy?' the editor asks me. I give him my two stories. 'Where's the third?' he asks. I tell him I don't have a third. 'I didn't get the time after taking this guy to hospital,' I tell him. 'That's your bloody third,' he tells me. 'The best human interest shit you have.' Then he packs me off to get a quote from the guy's wife. How she felt seeing her husband's wrist knocked off? That's how my interview went. You want something like that?" you ask her.

"Jesus!" she says. "Who was the editor?"

"His name was Suman Sinha. One of the maddest I ever worked with. He was fifty-seven then. He drank himself to death," you say.

You're cooking the stuff as you go along. Sinha was indeed your first boss, but the way you got your first footing was through a sedate copy test that the man gave you. A thing to gauge your precise writing skills and whether you could locate the state of Mizoram on the atlas.

"How old were you?"

"Eighteen," you say to sustain the myth, though you were hitting twenty. "That's how we started off in those days."

"When can I start?" asks Karnam.

"Anytime. Now," you say. You shrug your shoulders. "It's up to you."

"Okay, now," she says, smiling.

"Fine, I want you to give me four story ideas, first thing tomorrow morning. Let's see what's in you," you say.

"Could you show me around a bit?" she asks. "Like what happens where. A conducted tour. I am kind of nervous."

So you take her for a three-floor spin. You start with the Desk.

"This is the Desk. The last net. You don't have it, you end up looking stupid in print. Basic job function—cleaning copy, giving headlines, in-tros, captions, and cutting copy to length. If you have copy that needs fix-ing, they may or may not end up running the story. They may reassign it to one of the staff writers."

"Sounds like a lot of dull work," says Karnam.

"It is. But if you go through the grind for a year, it will fill the holes in your system, make you a better journalist," you say.

With such penetrating insights, you begin the tour.

You are out drinking with the lads at Moets, in Defense Colony: Karim, Matthew, Dravid, and Jolly. You aren't so pally with your crowd up at Documentary, Siddy, Teresa, and the others, as you are with the Features gang. Dilip from Systems hops on your gang. He has some news for you. But first Karim has to do some takedown.

"Hey, MM, boss, hear you're hiring a million-volt broad for Features. You have to develop a two-guy recruitment panel for these tasks, boss. Get yourself a second opinion," advises Karim.

Karim's a cunt you have to tolerate. He hails from Bihar. But the thing is, he's a workhorse. He's also plugged in to the corporate world. And, on occasions, it's in your scheme of things to organize sponsorship for events. That's where Karim fits in.

"She is Digs's daughter," you inform your crowd. Your thousand-dollar chip for the evening.

"You're kidding!" says Karim.

"Serious?" asks Jolly, her turf as sole belle of the department threatened.

"No jokes. Ask Dilip," you say.

"Yeah. I had to give her a password for the system," says Dilip. "She couldn't make up her mind for ten minutes."

"What did she choose?" asks Dravid.

"'What did she choose?'" mimics Dilip. "What are you going to do? Look up her files for sexual preferences? She hasn't any yet."

"What, files or preferences?" you ask. The others laugh.

"Give me a break, MM," says Dilip.

"Okay, tell me how many letters," says Dravid, persistent now.

"Fuck off," says Dilip.

"Letters, for Christ's sake. It would still take me a million years," says Dravid.

"Four," says Dilip.

"What's her ID?" asks Matthew.

"Karnam," says Dilip. "The same as her name."

Soon they forget her, and Dravid starts complaining about the Desk.

"Hey, MM, you got to prune their hormones a bit. Give them some reality programming. There's this new bitch they have who's called me at *two* in the morning, asking whether this quote I have from Perreira on this Zakir guy was *on the record* or not. It went, 'Zakir scalps his clients out for the ten minutes he spends thinking about them on his shit pot. It's shit thought, something the companies can well do without.' She asks me whether I was sure he said it. I mean, *I* am the reporter. I filed the stuff five days ago."

"I had this other guy—what's his name? The guy with hair down to his balls," says Karim.

"Aiyar," says Matthew.

"Yes, this Tamil Nadu fuck. The hard-metal asshole plays the drums in this chakra band. He calls me up on this real estate story I filed. He says editorial policy is to have all measurements in square meters, not yards. I tell him the whole North Indian market ticks on yards. You say meters and everybody's going to have calculators out to understand the story. He says no, he has to have his meters. He showers me stuff about *The Economist* and their metric style sheet. Then he branches off into pounds and kilograms and prepositions and God knows what else, till I tell him to do what he wants, double-decker the fucking masthead, bring in a design revolution. But he says no, he doesn't have to do the conversion, *I* have to do it. I say sorry, I thought that was the Desk's load of shit. He says even if it was, though it wasn't, he couldn't find any conversion table and he was most likely to botch it all up. I said the software was all there on the system. All he had to do was enter *Calculate* on Advance, but he said if he could do that, he would be working with Bill Gates, not *The Post*," complains Karim.

"Guy's got a point," you say.

"He didn't, boss," says Karim. "He was just playing hockey, trimming his workload."

"How's Nonita doing these days?" you ask. You have been out of office gossip for a while on the copyeditor. "Is she still humping Digs?"

"As far as I can see. One of the drivers dropped them at the Imperial at ten at night, after the political snapshot pages went to bed," says Karim.

"God, he's so hooked on her. You should have seen him last Monday when the Atex started playing funny," says Dilip. "She was fixing this Momin special report on the fodder scam in Bihar and, swoosh, the system goes down and she can't recall her file. She does a search on it and system says there's no such file. I mean, you guys know how the Atex behaves sometimes. You need some time to coax things out of it after it trips. In the first place, they have thirty terminals going when the mainframe's built for twenty-two. Then they have this news coordinator asshole doing H and J's on files as big as *Middlemarch*. The system can only take that much load at one go. Anyways, the Atex trips about three times during the evening, and twice Digs is affected because he's writing his comment piece. But he doesn't flap. He sits in his own office, corrupting his lungs with his Marlboros. But Nonita goes running to him the third time, saying the system administrator should be sacked, that she's lost her file and all that crap. And Digs comes running out of his office like somebody's keyed his buttocks up. He just lights into me, gives me hell. The bitch. Somebody'd lend her a spare tit, loan her some silicone, she might give Digs something to hold on to."

"She lost the little she had, rubbed this pimple cleanser on them," bitches Matthew.

"Yeah, Reinhold Messner would find it tough to climb on those nipple holds," says Karim.

"No, now these silicone babes have this new scare. They can't go Concorde," you say.

"How's that?" asks Matthew.

"The silicone explodes the moment you break the sound barrier," you say.

"Serious?" asks Jolly.

"As hell. Straight out of *New Scientist*. You get a silicone job on your boobs and you get a job as an air hostess on the Concorde, you could end up serving nipple pie," you say. Everybody laughs. Your contribution to the evening's humor.

"Now look at Minnie; that's where all the action in the office is now. A woman has to have tits like hers to shoot her stock up, get her beyond competition," says Dravid. Minnie's this designer beauty at the *The Post* whom Karim has been zoning in on for about two months, but without much apparent success.

"I think this is getting sick," says Jolly.

"How are things with you, Karim? You make any progress?" you ask.

"No progress, boss. Biggest luck I have had so far is taking her out for a pizza. I had to eat half of hers as well. She wouldn't leave unless I had the whole thing mopped up," says Karim.

"You should have ordered the dump down. Monopolized the call numbers, hogged all the trays. Made Slice of Italy work overtime. Taken yourself a year to finish the stuff," advises Matthew.

"And pay off by washing their dishes," Karim adds with sarcasm. "What I get out of that luck is this business fuck we have, this Jain asshole, needling me all afternoon because he has seen us coming back together. He goes into this ankle-biting routine, and Minnie happens to pass by and hears some of the stuff. The next thing she says to me when I call her is 'So you have been bragging that you took me out.' It takes me a week to explain Jain psychology to her."

"The problem with you, Karim, is that your strategy is outdated. Fucking *pizzas*. You got your brain scrambled. Take her out for some of this band stuff. Like the Ricky Martin show that happened some time back. Take her to see Ricky fucking Martin," you say.

"That Jain asshole's been giving me a headache, too. He gets me to input on this story, how the white skins are squeezing out Indian managers, and I slog my ass for two days, get the dope on the thing, file him a thousand words, no fluff, and he doesn't even give me a joint byline. He stuffs my name at the bottom, takes his own above in Helvetica bold. He uses all my stuff; it's better than he could fish out himself in one week. I do it for him as a favor because he comes whining to me. He says his own crowd's on leave. Slime," says Matthew.

"You should have told me," you say.

"Well, I didn't want to blow things of proportion," says Matthew.

"Hey, MM, you got any load on this new design thing? The guys are going nuts. Leaving about an inch for copy. Some gag these marketing guys are playing on Digs about the reading habits of Indians. They have had some survey done that shows the letters are too much for the readers to absorb. The picture's all they can take, color their time in the loo. I mean, if somebody doesn't play the right song, Digs's going to buy it all, make us take our golden handshake," complains Jolly.

"Digs's too cautious to innovate in a hurry, whatever that dope Leslie might sell him," you explain.

Leslie's *The Post's* art director and chief in-house bull-goose loony. You got him in, but the career motion he engineered, once he got in, took him way beyond all reasonable expectation. You remember how you took Digs out to lunch to check on Leslie, somebody you got friendly with in the press club. You remember, with admiration, the kind of wholesale shit Leslie sprayed all over Digs, stuff about design, type size, typeface, grids, and other incomprehensible designer lingo that you'd think was some pig disease. But seeing Digs in solid listener mode, the kind of attention that he gave to people about twice a year, you had to alter your thinking. Leslie got hired on the spot. You got a lesson in bullshitting.

"He can't make a decision, either," comments Karim. "I tossed up this idea at the meeting about *breaking* into a prison illegally, taking photographs, and coming out, just to prove the kind of shit that goes around in jails here. How prisoners are committing crimes and using jail as an alibi. He's put that on hold."

It isn't till the second round of beer is gone and the crowd splits up, leaving you alone with Dilip and Jolly, that you get to know what's on their mind.

"MM, boss," says Jolly. "We have this scoop."

"What?" you ask. You have known many hot stories start this way. But this, you get the feeling, is different. Dilip is your resident Kevin Mitnick. Mitnick, of course, was for years the world's most notorious cybercriminal. Dilip, though not in that league, started off as a ham enthusiast but eventually fleshed his skills in cellular-phone eavesdropping. The gizmos had come home, and Dilip had already busted Airtel phone software, giving him unlimited free-time access to the airwaves. Right now, however, he's been giving an unofficial helping hand to Jolly, trying to bust her man for her and get some pussy in the bargain.

You have put Jolly onto doing this investigative piece on the 120 MiG-21 Bis avionics and armament upgrade deal that has gone to Russia. This after three other countries, Israel included, slogged their ass off trying to swing it. But the Russians get the nod because, as Jolly's sources have tipped her, the Price Negotiation Committee got an all-expenses-paid tour of Russia, with their fair quota of ballerinas and Saint Petersburg whores. Which happens all the time, but this time with a difference: The Russian Mafia tailed the contingent across the whole place, taking photographs of air marshals and additional secretaries from the Ministry of Defense snorting powder and feeling ass. All of which were given to them as souvenirs to admire in the choked Aeroflot loo on the flight back home, color prints to remind them of their promises.

What Jolly got hold of was a few of the prints from one of the air marshals, who came clean. Howling the story out, risking his pension. The only catch was that the Russians were the lowest bidders—so why, Jolly wanted to know, had they thrown in all the perks, not to mention blackmail?

But here the story really hotted up. What Jolly found out was that the Ministry of External Affairs had taken the matter up with the Russian ambassador and the latter was due for dinner at Defense Minister Suresh Yadav's house, to clear the static in the air, reaffirm commitment to the Indo-Soviet friendship treaty, notwithstanding the damage done by some hired Chechens.

So what Jolly does is park her car fifty yards from the minister's house, hoping to sandbag the Russian ambassador for a comment right on Yadav's doorstep. Dilip's with her, tagging along for fun. He has all his eavesdropping truffle cart in place from yesterday, because he was doing some test runs in Vasant Vihar, fine-tuning his technique. But for the heck of it, he switches on his stuff and starts playing with his antenna outside the window. And bang, they are on to this power conversation between Suresh Yadav, who also holds the power portfolio, and some Korean fuck, deal coordinator of a Seoul power conglomerate, whose voice Jolly recognizes. The company just struck a power deal with Uttar Pradesh to throw a plant in the Terai region, bordering Nepal.

Jolly plays portions of the tape for you, gets it somewhere in the middle.

"We regret the mistake," the Korean is saying. You can feel him bowing in the phone, lifting his ass. "We confuse between bank. I get information you call, I call you immediately. We rectify mistake tomorrow. We will pay you the whole amount. Okay, sir. *Gam sa nida.*"

You can feel the minister getting edgy on the phone; he didn't expect it on this number.

"Yes, yes," he says, but he forgets caution for a brief while. "Could you repeat the number, please?"

"Seven eight nine one oh one two three," says the Korean.

"That's right. Please do the needful. I need two million dollars immediately," says Yadav.

"Okay, sir. *Gam sa nida*," says the Korean, and the line goes dead.

"Well," says Jolly. "What do you say to that? You recognize Suresh Yadav's voice or not? I think it's him."

"I don't know. It's too brief a conversation to go by," you say. In fact, you recognize the minister's audio from the moment he says, "Yes, yes," but you don't commit yourself to anything.

"I will talk with Digs," you say. "Let me keep the tape. You got copies?" You look at Dilip.

"No," says Dilip.

"Okay, I will get one made," you say.

"The thing is, can I go ahead with my MiG story, or should I wait a bit, coattail an angle on this tape, rake mud at two places, and reel the minister in?" asks Jolly.

"No, you go ahead with the MiG thing. The tape, let's think about it. I will get the legal angle. Besides, we can't just honk the tape. We would have to show how it dropped in our lap, and that would lynch us, get both your asses, too," you say. "Just be careful where you wave your antenna next time around. You could come on the radar of the Special Protection Group the next time you use your equipment. They could antenna your shit hole, get the friction in your mucus, if you aren't careful."

"They wouldn't know a computer from a TV," says Dilip.

"You think too much of that and you'll be the first Indian arrested on cellular-eavesdropping charges," Jolly says.

"You, too," you say to Jolly, getting up. "Don't lead him on. This is no backseat ambassador power fuck."

"You are gross, MM," says Jolly. Dilip grins.

"Tell me something I don't know," you say.

Outside, you get in your Defender, a power chip in your pocket. A fucking bonanza. A tool to soften the minister should the game heat up. You feel the tape with pleasure.

A van tails you all the way home. You don't floor your pedal. This isn't the time for lane-dog fights. You don't spill your cards so early in the game.

Saturdays, you usually spend with Jumbo, go swimming at the Sheraton or dig Djinn's, if you feel like it. Or the Dragonball, where you can do any one of Jumbo's girls who takes your fancy.

You don't like taking your prey home. It clouds your neighborhood image, messes up the sheets as well, and you do your own laundry. Your help is limited to a Nepali cook-cum-housecleaner, who comes in the morning, does his stuff while you are around, and packs up for the day after he polishes your Defender. You love vehicles from the Land Rover family. You bought it secondhand from a British diplomat.

Today, you find yourself making small talk with Jaspreet in the backseat of Jumbo's Mercedes. She is in a sleeveless something that could be doing wonders for her figure, but you are too fucked up to give her points for that. You have done today what you never did before. You snorted some of the stuff that Jumbo does about four times a day. He said there had to be a phase in everybody's life that they could turn to and say,

"That's when we popped the Burmese talc." "Especially you," he said, "when you are holding some of the stuff." You hadn't told him how much yet. Jumbo's generally into the Orient, except for things like transportation and the Russian Mafia, whom he has to keep in good humor because he's also the boss of the company that handles the Russian plane charters into Delhi, carting in the hordes for shopping and holidays.

You feel things happening to you. You watch your hair standing on end. You want to rip the leather off the front seat, but Jaspreet's reading your palms, mumbling prophecies about your sexual affairs, playing seduction games that have the firepower of BB guns.

You want the wind to hit your frame, loosen you up. You can't push the right button for the glass, so you say what the hell and open the door and stand on the rim where the door fits, the way you have seen the American Secret Service do—in which movie, you can't remember. Your brain doesn't want to tell you that right now. But the Mercedes is doing 120. You don't remember the presidential limousine going that fast. You think maybe they were, but the producers had to slow it down using digital cinematic make-believe. This new stuff that can have Tom Cruise shake his digits with Hitler or anybody.

Jaspreet is tugging at your trousers, trying to pull you in. Jumbo hits on the road to the airport, where Dragonball is, but he doesn't slow down. You yell at a 747 lining up for final approach. "Hey, Jumbo," you shout, "your twin brother's up in the air."

You feel like you're being funny. You retreat next to Jaspreet to laugh. She's looking at you in a very startled way, as if you are wriggling your ears. The ushers at the invitational discotheque check you in. Jumbo's partner so far, on this Saturday expedition, is a striking Russian girl, angular features, all legs, no English. You get her to repeat her name about three times. It's Catherine or Rina or Tsarina or something. You are too fucked up to listen properly. Jaspreet is tugging at your sleeves, urging you to take on a bhangra sizzler, but your movements on the floor are painfully arthritic unless rum's raiding your circulatory network. And now there's this something new that you have tried and your footsteps on the stairs to the bar echo like gongs in your head.

The trapezium shape of the bar appeals to your sense of post–Burmese talc aesthetics, but you remember distinctly running it down about a month back in a learned geometric exposition in front of female models who didn't understand what a protractor was. You remember telling them something, but you can't remember what. Heroin, you get the feeling, is all about not being able to remember things. Though the word *protractor* sticks in your head, you can't figure out what to connect it with. It sounds to you like a dinosaur species.

You try to bounce it off on Jaspreet, but you have oddly lost her in the maze. You are in the bar, sitting next to a miniskirted mammal on the lap of a son of a bitch in a silk shirt. A sweaty silk shirt. He's massaging her thighs with one hand and the other holds something red, maybe a Bloody Mary, which he gazes at when he's finished ogling the multitudinous shapes and forms down on the dance floor while the DJ launches into "Cotton-Eye Joe" by Rednex.

To your right, gazing philosophically at something very whiskeyish in a glass, sits what you could get away with calling a *Homo sapiens* of indistinct sex, who's contemplating some big fuckup that happened, or is about to happen and could be countered by an urgency in gaze.

You wonder how you got here and how others are gauging you, when Jaspreet rejoins you from wherever she was roving. You ask her if she knows what a tractor is. She looks puzzled. You know you have got the word wrong, but you don't know how or where. She nods her head. Maybe she thinks it's some new game you are playing. Something she's been too dumb to pick up. But you take comfort in the knowledge that at least she knows whatever it is you have asked her.

You start looking around for Jumbo. You suddenly need insulation, for a while, from this girl.

But her nonheroin status is making her restless in a different way. She's tapping her feet to the music, and soon she pulls you, even as you try to hold your rum aloft, to the floor, where you spot Jumbo in full swing with the Russian, whose height, you notice, clears Jumbo's by six inches.

The Russian's throwing some fancy footwork that you infer could be a major new dance step that still hadn't diffused in your part of the world. You try to match her for a while, which amuses her, but you can't copy the rhythm and you step on about four toes.

You grin at the aggrieved faces you see, soothing their fears by renouncing your flamboyance. You jerk about in your own space, consumed by the braless tits of your partner in motion. The Burmese talc should have made you lethargic by now, but you figure it's acting slowly.

But denied an uninterrupted supply of photo images because of her habit of spinning around and disappearing for vital seconds into adjacent medley, you gravitate consciously toward the perimeters of the dance floor, where, on a waist-level ledge, you set down your half-full glass of rum a few moments ago. Expectedly, some asshole's discovered it and the glass is now empty. But there's a full one next to it of something that you take a big gulp of anyway, hoping to boost your morale for the evening, which, you feel, could have reached its apogee.

The DJ, in his own way, is trying his best to get you into the spirit of it all. Jumbo beckons you. He is doing a threesome with the Russian and Jaspreet. Dick to ass and cunt to ass and, when you join, another dick to ass. A foursome now, swaying like an independent entity to some guitar pyrotechnic that has scores of eyes glancing enviously at the massing of flesh and bone that isn't their own.

Then some dickhead takes it in his head to join the movement by pressing his dick in your ass, and there's a scramble, and soon there's a chug-chug train around the perimeter, which you do once and then disengage, because that's the rule, you have learned, of any temporary innovation.

When the train loses momentum and the people merge and you can't locate your partners anymore, you split to get some fresh air outside, and you spot someone who you think resembles in left-side profile the brief image you had of the guy trailing you in a van a few days back. It bothers you enough to go back to the action you jettisoned. And the music suddenly is such that you don't want to waste time looking for Jaspreet. You cut a direct route to the center of the floor and start an exhibition of a solo something, muscle power responding in tandem to something that cuts to 2 Unlimited and then opens in samba country. Others, by now recognizing the wild spirit in you, provide you space for your antics.

The Russian girl emerges at your side. From which direction, you don't know, because you have your eyes closed. But she gets you into a pelvic-grinding number, front to front in circular vectors, and from the way her flesh rubs you in the chest, you, for the first time this evening, feel the emergence of an erection.

And then by some strange, unargued, silent hedonistic compliance, Jumbo and you switch partners. You suddenly discover increased compatibility, even though you can't figure out what Tsarina or Catherina is saying. But it's the language of the heart and body, which doesn't need linguistic embellishments.

Soon, you have had your fill of Dragonball. You ache to see action elsewhere. Jumbo suggests a jump in ethos and character, and five minutes later, this time with you driving and Catherina or Tsarina in front, with her arms around your shoulders, you accelerate to make up about eighteen-odd miles before the action dissipates at the Kamal cabaret joint in West Delhi.

At a traffic light at Naraina, a cop waves you to the curb. It's past midnight and you surmise that he has taken offense at the blaring stereo. But whatever his agenda before he stops your Mercedes, he now switches it for an inspection of your front passenger's passport, whose sensual deportment isn't chiming with his sense of road discipline or personal unfulfillment.

You wave your press card, which dilutes his sense of investigation. You point your finger to the MP sticker on the windshield. He hesitates. You take that as a green, release your clutch slowly, and then, as a passing gift, watch Catherina or Tsarina flash her left breast at the night sentry. He doesn't like it, or thinks he can eye more of it by delaying you a bit longer, but you floor the gas and leave him behind.

At Kamal, you watch as the doorman winks at Jumbo, calls him "Sir," salutes you, and opens a brass door to admit your group to a fifty-by-one-hundred-foot joint that's in full swing, your timing perfect. An unslim Eve, clad skimpily, is in the throes of some daring calisthenics in the middle of the cabaret floor. She walks up to a few individual tables and performs some powerful brand of breast tectonics, which the live band finds hard to keep up with. She gets currency notes stuffed in her mirrory bra.

"Now this is what I call real action," says Jumbo. "You take too much of that Dragonball stuff and it will fuck up your taste."

"It's pathetic," says Jaspreet.

"It's different. It's not sanitized the way you want it," says Jumbo.

You are here for the first time. The two girls, too. You arrange your chair in the dark at the back so you can do things to Tsarina or Catherina that people would have to turn their necks to see. She has a mass of zip slits on her dress that allow you easy access. What you are interested in knowing, the way your dirty mind works, is whether Tsarina or Catherina has panties or not. You suspect not. You are just confirming a hypothesis, ironing out a doubt tinkering your mind. It's as you have guessed. Lingerie either comes too expensive back in the place Tsarina or Catherina comes from or she leaves it in her suitcase at her hotel so that guys like you can give her a little quiz.

On the floor, the girl transfers her currency collection to her panties and then jerks off her bra in one fluid motion. The band marks the event by letting its drums go berserk for a while, reach a crescendo in disorganized sound. Jumbo has Jaspreet's tits cupped and he asks her, "Like that?"

You don't know whether he means the action on the floor or what he is doing to Jaspreet. Jaspreet says, "Yes." You don't know which question she's answering. Such evening ambiguity keeps you from descending to low spirits.

"Do they go any further?" you ask Jumbo about the girl out on the floor.

"Some days they do, if they don't spot any plainclothes cops," says Jumbo.

All of you sit and wait in dim hope as you taste some snacks that Jumbo orders. You wonder how much anticipation you would have if you were biding your time, waiting for a gigolo to kick off his pants, and whether it is the same for the two girls with you. How much are they putting up with? You realize the complexity of explaining your query to Tsarina or Catherina. And Jaspreet is busy with Jumbo.

You try concentrating on the floor, but the sight doesn't excite you. The woman's only interested in going to tables and stuffing currency notes in her undies. The guys who wave five-hundred-buck greens, she allows to do the stuffing themselves. They keep their fingers in there till the girl has to pick them out delicately. Tsarina or Catherina is trying to feel your armament, but today, you have on buttoned Levi's, and that's posing insurmountable problems for her backhand grope. You don't feel like helping out Tsarina or Catherina. Instead, you start nibbling at her ears. She begins giggling. She says something to you. For once, you understand. Tsarina or Catherina wants to dance on the floor. Maybe, you think, she has an act in Moscow.

"Hey, Jumbo, she wants to dance," you inform him. You don't want to have a hand in such advance decisions, help her with something whose chemistry you can't control. For all you know, the in-house girls shoot foreigners who cut in on their take. But you suspect that Tsarina or Catherina wouldn't be interested in the green wads. She might be a show-off instead. Inform you Indians about what you're missing.

"Why not," says Jumbo, and beckons someone who looks to you like the guy who is responsible for the shit on the floor. He's never had so outrageous a request. He doesn't know whether to say yes or no. He's in a bind. Jumbo says something to Jaspreet, and she gives a feel to the guy's trumpet. He jumps about two feet, looks at your crowd like they're the best weirdos he's had in the months or years he's been working in the joint.

Meanwhile, Tsarina or Catherina is under the table, snorting something that Jumbo has passed to her. She snorts it off a mirror in her handbag. She comes up and tells Jumbo to call off the whole thing. She wants to sit in your lap instead, and you worry about what this means in her current state. After you worry some more, you signal to Jumbo that it's time to abort the setting, leave the place intact, even if it means not getting to see the kind of dynamite the girl out on the floor packs below her waist. Some things you can leave to the future.

Outside, it's a question of Where now? Jumbo's suggesting his place, but you want something very neutral. You don't want to use his neighborhood. You suggest this Golf Links guest house you know, which has big rooms and is ideal for the kind of thing that is left in the night to do. Once again, peculiarly, your group compatibility undergoes a metamorphosis. You think it has something to do with the traces of what you can still see on Tsarina's or Catherina's nose. You sit in the rear with Jaspreet, and this time you have your arms interlinked with hers. You feel the heat of her breasts on your elbow. For the second time this evening, you feel your blood surge below your waist. You are not sure whether you have condoms in your wallet. You don't remember a recent refill.

You keep a lookout for some open drugstore as Jumbo knifes through the streets. But it's too late for commerce to cater to your software needs. You hope Jaspreet or your other two companions have some to spare. In this day and age, it's the women who go loaded.

You are still in the hit zone. It's over three hours since you made your heroin hit. There's a strange taste in your mouth; you don't feel like lifting your arms sometimes.

You guide Jumbo through Golf Links to the place you have in mind. There's one vacant room, which means that you have just one room to try out any stuff that you might have planned. It means that for the first time in your life, you find yourself one of the participating cogs in a foursome.

Clothes, you feel, once you have your room secured, are something irritating your state of mind. You feel more relaxed in your BVDs. You look at yourself in the mirror. You want to see whether heroin has done any visible damage to your frame. Your eyes are a little puffy, the way you are accustomed to seeing them after a night that lasts till six in the morning. But otherwise, your systems seem to be pulling on.

Looking in the mirror, you can see Jumbo start on his program, getting Tsarina or Catherina to peel the layers off him. Jaspreet, you sense, is a little unsure of what is about to happen. She, it registers on you, is the only one not on Burmese talc. Which, perhaps, aggravates her nose for suspense.

And Jumbo is in the mood for something really kinky. He's egging Tsarina or Catherina on to something, and she's begun to giggle like mad as she unstraps what's hers to discard, even as she gives Jaspreet some lascivious glances. You can guess what's coming, but Jaspreet is still clueless. But when Tsarina or Catherina starts helping her loosen her stuff, Jaspreet's instinct rings the right bell. And though she is not taking a puritan stand, she does feel a mild panic, which induces her to say, "I haven't done this kind of thing before."

"There's always the first time," Jumbo tells her, and you view the sight that develops within the next few minutes with not a small degree of interest, even though, as things stand, you aren't the one finger-fucking Jaspreet on the king-size double bed, but Tsarina or Catherina, and it is not your hardware that Jaspreet is swallowing and sliding on with immaculate timing and sense of purpose, but Jumbo's.

For two minutes, you stand and watch the scene the way any triple-X director would do, trying to spot the weaknesses in the frame, any loose ends to tie up, and you conclude that even though cinematically you might be missing the camera's acute angle, the daisy chain won't be complete until you accept Tsarina's or Catherina's desperate pleadings to bury your stick in any of the orifices she has offered.

Her body language makes it clear it doesn't matter to her which hole you choose. Still, you take the one you know best.

You do it slowly and rhythmically at first, trying to work out a thrust that squeezes the maximum out of your exertions; then you work up a pace, the likes of which have your end of the chain arching up spasmodically, forgetting all about Jaspreet, who soon complains, until you work out a count that doesn't disrupt the harmony of your group.

But soon you feel the urge to innovate, and you break up the formation to realign in a different combination.

A triple sandwich, with you at the bottom, Jaspreet digging you, and Jumbo working on Jaspreet, while Tsarina or Catherina has you lick her. Then she turns around and fixes her butt between your face and Jaspreet's, offering you the same place but requiring Jaspreet to pay some attention to her other hole.

All of which continues for some bewildering length of minutes. Jaspreet is the first to come, and Jumbo soon follows, which leaves Tsarina or Catherina and you to take your time and prolong your increments of pleasure. For her a shudder and then release, but for you a wave of nausea and a convulsion that sends you straight to the pot. Tsarina or Catherina follows you inside to see you don't choke to death, and from the room, Jumbo shouts, "How's he, Nina?"

This time, the heroin doesn't fuzzy your hearing. At least you vomit in the comfort of the knowledge that you have cracked Tsarina's or Catherina's real goddamn name.

You are in Moscow. Jumbo's with you, but you're worried. Yesterday, you had an evening rendezvous with a Chechen Mafia head, Rustam Akramov, but his henchmen never showed up. You were supposed to be at Dolls, a strip joint on the Krasnya Presnyaul, between seven and eight in the evening. You sat at a corner table, and it took you and Jumbo till half past ten to finish your beef Stroganoff and have a dozen lap dances, but nobody turned up.

Though Jumbo has a liaison office in Moscow to run his air charter deals, you haven't used his contacts to tune in on Akramov. You touched Dinesh Patel. The way you communicate with Patel is through encrypted software on the Internet. You have a decoder on your end. It's costly software, but you cannot do without it.

Akramov is one of Patel's point men in Russia. Nobody's seen him for the past ten years, since he was stabbed by a Belorussian. Even Patel. Or so Patel has told you. But when you are in a foreign land trying to work

out a channel for four hundred kilograms of heroin worth $200 million
retail, you don't easily believe what anybody tells you. Though Major
Rodriguez has delivered just half of that quantity so far, there's no reason
for the future not to be promising. The 5 Kumaon is going to be judging
you by the price you nail for them. And you don't want to disappoint.
They have held half the heroin load back as an insurance policy.

Patel's sent you a file on Akramov. You have done your own research,
too. Talked to a Tambov gang chief from Saint Petersburg, under whose
protection Jumbo runs his office on the Polyarnya UL.

What you know about Akramov is interesting. He made his reputation
and first few million staging traffic accidents against middle-class Mus-
covites owning cars and homes. The modus operandi was simple. It was
so simple, he duplicated the operation in Brighton Beach for three years,
before insurance companies got wise, but not before they had forked out
nearly $8 million.

But while sponging big insurance companies in the United States has
nobody complaining except the companies themselves, in Moscow the
unfortunate victim is made to settle the accident claim with Akramov's
muscle men. The price set is high enough for the victim to have to sign
over his house for sale in Moscow's tight real estate market. Nobody goes
to the police—they are in league with guys like Akramov.

But Akramov's real killing came after perestroika struck roots and Russia boomed with entrepreneurs having their first shot at business. The
starchy Communist bureaucrats looked with disdain at these upstarts,
but it soon turned to unease when they discovered that the change to a
market economy was not only viable but lucrative. Then began the huge
tussle for control of the successful enterprises. The old bureaucrats tried
to muscle in on entrepreneurs, and goons like Akramov stepped in to
stave them off.

Of course, Akramov didn't step in for charity; he got a cut from each
entrepreneur for his services. And in 1988, something wonderful happened that sent Akramov, Inc., through the roof. The government, for

the first time, allowed the export of metals that home industries couldn't process. Akramov was the quickest to seize on the economic opportunity this new export law presented. He became the copper king of Russia. In two years, he, almost single-handedly, was responsible for making Estonia, the Baltic nation where he originated his complex shipping patterns, the sixth-largest copper exporter in the world.

The Russians woke up when their ordnance factories had to halt production because there was no raw material for bullets, but Akramov had shifted to arms and armament by then, which is where, you presume, he first established links with Patel.

It was here that he got into RM 20/20, or "red mercury," the trading metal of the eighties and early nineties, and established his reputation for ruthlessness. Middle East Mossies were willing to pay $400,000 for a single pound. RM 20/20, with the chemical formula $Hg2SB2O7$ and a flare temperature of 180.5 degrees centigrade, has special properties as a neutron reflector. It increases the efficiency of the nuclear-fission process. It allows you to make nuclear grenades the size of apples, which can knock aircraft carriers right out of the sea. Some versions also leave no residual radioactivity. You can move in right after a land blast and find skyscrapers still in place and the lifts working.

But the former KGB officers who shipped Akramov his red mercury, and who had, in turn, obtained it from production bases in Ykaterinburg, stepped on one of his consignments: a 220-pound batch headed, by way of an unknown UK firm, for South Africa, the biggest end user of the product in the world. The $40 million deal fell through when part of the consignment turned out to be red nail polish.

With a forfeit clause in the contract, Akramov was forced to dish out $10 million for his inability to supply the original amount.

Akramov traced the four former KGB officers to Germany, where they met such violent ends that he acquired the title of "the Ruthless." Red mercury dried up after the Gulf War, with governments launching secret clampdowns on traders, and the product disappeared from the world market.

It was then that Akramov switched to drugs. He became the biggest Russian conduit for South American drugs passing through the former Soviet Union on their way to Europe and the United States. What you were about to offer him was another supply source, a pipeline so fresh that the international narcotics trade would take some time to analyze the new push in the market.

Today, you are not at Sputnik. You are at a smoky joint called Mothball, which is on the outskirts of Moscow. You are hoping to be picked out by Akramov's crowd, since the whole day you have been spamming on the Net, posting coded adverts with the names of the four former KGB officers whom Akramov liquidated in Berlin on June 13, 1991. The file Patel sent you had their names in it.

You are not really happy bringing Jumbo in on this. Especially as it could get dangerous and you might end up needing some outside help. But you have taken care of that. What you are a little nervous about right now is carrying two hundred grams of your white powder in the inner pockets of your blue Savile Row suit. In a Russian neighborhood, that's like carrying $100,000 in cash. Very fearful things can happen if a person continues to be so foolish for the second consecutive evening.

You were given an introduction to the fear psychosis the Mafia had built up in the city when you negotiated for a cab to one of the city's Western-style hotels from Moscow's Domodedego Airport. The going Mafia take for one such ride was two hundred dollars, but you paid seventy for a gypsy cab. The cabdriver was too scared to take the money in the open. He pulled curbside and made you part with your cash away from all prying eyes. He showed you the penalty inflicted on him for disobeying an airport shark once. He had just half a little finger on his left hand. Not too horrific by Moscow standards, but the only warning he would get before the Azerbaijani Mafia, whose turf included the international airport, where they did their money changing, decided to pass the death sentence.

All around you in Mothball are members of Mafia families dining on borscht. On the fringes of the room, scar-faced bodyguards keep a close watch and gab on their cell phones.

What you are thinking is that Akramov may not be in town, and that you have to cast a wider net in your search for a pipeline, when the room visibly tenses. A thug straight out of a Martin Scorsese film pulls up the third chair at your table and sits down without an invitation.

"I hope I am not disturbing you gentlemen," he says.

"Depends on who's saying it," you say.

"Let's say Netiquette demands people don't spam or post in the wrong news group," he says. "We like people to check on their FAQ before shouting on the Net."

You had posted your advert in all caps.

"People have their ways. I have mine," you say.

"Sometimes the ways of people take them very close to being flamed," he says. You take notice of the double play in the last word.

"Some people have exaggerated notions of what others could be capable of," you say. "It shows a lack of confidence. It hurts, too, especially if people have contacted you through mutual friends."

"It's a crazy world," he says.

"So am I," you say.

"The corner of Petrovka and Ogareva, beside the fire station, in fifteen minutes. Ask the time from the person in a red coat," he says. Then he looks at Jumbo. "Who's he?"

"A friend," you say.

"We like our friends to come alone," he says, and goes.

"That's cool," you tell him. "How far's the place?" you ask Jumbo.

"How the fuck should I know," says Jumbo.

But your Hertz chauffeur is a local and understands the need for punctuality. You make your corner with a minute to spare, feeling surprisingly calm. Seeing a gangster movie, you feel, is different from acting in one.

You spot your red-coat honcho as you light one of your Marlboros. You go up to him and ask the time. Somewhere a car screeches, wheels leaving their rubber on the road. A Mercedes, its windows tinted black, lines up alongside you, and Red Coat extends the courtesy of opening the back door. You grind your just-lighted cigarette with your leather boot. Red Coat sits next to you. The bearded flunky beside the driver turns and tosses you a balaclava.

"That wasn't mentioned as part of the plan," you protest.

"It's the price for meeting Akramov," he says.

"I would prefer to keep my eyes closed," you say.

"Have it your way," concedes your escort, but he barks something in Russian to Red Coat. "I have given him instructions to blow your brains out if you open your eyes without permission," he explains for your benefit. You hear the cocking of an Uzi, the preferred weapon of the *shabaskniki*.

All that stuff you read about in books about heroes keeping track of where they are headed when they have a cloth over their head is all for nutcases who haven't tried it themselves. The real pro drivers take you once around the block and then take a couple of 180-degree spins on the wheel before they shoot the hood the right way. By the time you hit the second block, you aren't even trying. Working on Akramov's HQ isn't on your immediate agenda. You're busy concentrating on keeping your eyes closed. You don't want to call any bluff, what with your head at stake. The Mercedes slows. You hear some gravel bounce off the chassis. Then the light dims and you figure you could be in some kind of garage or tunnel. The car weaves its way down an incline. A basement, you think. The guy in the front has to gabble at some other guy. You hear a gate clocking open. The Merc comes to a halt. A twenty-minute ride, give or take a few minutes.

"Hey, Mr. Red Coat, you still got your Uzi at my head?" you ask as the door on your side opens. He stays silent. Maybe he doesn't know English, you think. But what he does is sneak the balaclava over your head this time and prod you out.

"Hey, that was sneaky," you say.

"I am sorry, Mr. Mehta," says the voice you recognize as that of the bearded guy up front, "but we can't take chances now. Nobody sees Mr. Akramov. You only hear him."

"I could have kept my eyes closed," you say.

"But you might open them. And if you did and Mr. Akramov didn't like what you had to say, you would take up permanent residence in the Volga," he says.

"I am prepared to take the chance," you say. You have walked into a room with a carpet that sinks you nearly to your ankles.

"You are a courageous man, Mr. Mehta," says a voice. "And you have a strange way of contacting us."

"You didn't keep to the meeting yesterday. I had little choice, Mr. Akramov."

"You must be desperate. What other things did you find out in that little research of yours about the KGB officers?" asks Akramov.

"Nothing you don't already know."

"Do you know, for instance, how they died?"

"No," you say. You hear him draw up a chair. You are hustled into one.

"Do you want to know?" asks Akramov. "How they died?"

"I am listening."

"Ninov Arkady, Dimitri Shubasenko, Rudolf Karenin, and Boris Yegeney. Do you know who was the leader, Mr. Mehta?"

"No."

"Can you tell the name of the leader from the way the names sound? I am told some Hindus are good at this sort of thing."

"I am not one of them," you say.

"That's a pity. Well, the leader was Rudolf Karenin. He was built like an ox. He was a Greco-Roman wrestler. He used to practice in the Nuyayev stadium. How well built do you think I am, Mr. Mehta?"

"I can't see through the hood," you say.

"That's just as well, or you won't live to tell the tale. Now, my deal was with ARMSCOR. Armaments Corporation of South Africa, Ltd. They were to pay for part of the consignment in Swiftarrow missiles. You know what those missiles can do?"

"No."

"They can burn their way through three feet of steel armor. They use red mercury in the nose of the missile. Once it is ignited, it creates a super-high-temperature blowtorch. The Iraqis were willing to pay me three times the market price for them. But the problem was, Rudolf was running this other deal with the Saudi Arabians around the same time, which I didn't know about. You know how red mercury is packed, Mr. Mehta? I hope you haven't come here to sell me red mercury."

"No, Mr. Akramov."

"Just as well. Red mercury is packed in containers weighing four, fifteen, twenty-two, and eighty-eight pounds. It's highly radioactive and carcinogenic. It's got various names, depending on the type of mercury. Burning Rogue comes with a stick of uranium down the middle. Red Glitter is the forty-five/fifty variety, which is much in demand. So Rudolf gets these fucking Arabs to Berlin. You know how these guys travel?"

"On camels," you say.

Akramov ignores you. He is too engrossed in his tale. The chair they have you on is more a stool, about four inches from the ground. Motherfucker strategy to keep you in a low launch position, a gravitational disadvantage. Akramov's voice hits you from the top of an inclined plane. More Mafia psy ops to disorient you.

"These days, they come on Falcons. The guys in Riyadh are the biggest buyers of red mercury. Nobody knows what they do with all the stuff they buy, but they buy like hell. They have this lead-lined laboratory at the back of a Falcon jet. It has fancy metal analysis equipment and even robots for handling radioactive material. They have the jet sitting at Riyadh, ready to fly within two hours anywhere in the world. Rudolf is selling them one hundred and ten pounds of Moulin Rouge, a hundred/hundred type that goes into the making of a clean atomic bomb. A bomb that leaves no residual radioactivity. His initial plan was to con the Arabs. Land them with two twenty-two-pound containers of mercury nail polish. But he didn't know anything about this flying lab that the Arabs had, and they were testing every sample before payment. So he tells Arkady to fly two genuine containers, the ones meant for us, into Berlin. You know how they went in?"

"No."

"Lufthansa. Diplomatic baggage," he says. "A little of this stuff leaks, and your Boeing electronics couldn't run a pocket calculator. Boris flies back this nail polish in lead containers to Moscow, and the German immigration creates a big racket. They hold the thing up for two days. Now you know why Hitler lost the war. Anyway, Boris and Dimitri play a con on Rudolf. They tell him they have contacted some scientists at Nalchik-44 who can refresh some of the out-of-date mercury we had. You know what Nalchik-44 is?"

"No."

"It's a closed military city. It doesn't even exist on the map. That's the place they make their red mercury in," says Akramov. "Do you have any such cities in India, Mr. Mehta?"

"No."

"Then it would be no fun for a guy like me to do business there, would it?"

Patience is in order.

"You need a nuclear reactor to restore red-mercury properties. But what Boris and Dimitri do is pass on the old stock to me. Even the old stock has some value these days, but you can sell it only to governments. Unlike us in Russia, only governments have access to nuclear reactors in other countries. Maybe if they had done that, passed me the old stock, they might still be alive. But I doubt it. In our business, some rules are not made to be broken. It's the only way we can survive. But they don't even do that. Rudolf now plays a con on Boris and Dimitri. He switches the containers that he thinks contain the recharged stock with those containing the nail polish and makes his team deliver the consignment to me. Now, Arkady comes and tells me the whole story. He thinks there will be some reward for him. But he, too, dies. I don't like squealers. Do you?"

"Not particularly," you say.

"What does that mean? That in some situations you like them and in some you don't?"

"How did they die?"

"Have you heard of the Rooivalk attack helicopter? This superchopper that the South Africans have developed? They were giving us a demo at the Angolan border. Do you know that the South Africans have developed a variant of red mercury that's more powerful than the Russian one?"

"No."

"You don't know many things, Mr. Mehta. It would be fun doing business with you. I could teach you a lot. Well, they showed me some of the stuff. They have a membrane separating two chemicals, and that increases the shelf life of their product. They gave me a three-and-a-half-ounce sample after the demo. You know what they did in the demo? They took about a third of an ounce of the stuff and mixed it with a third of an ounce of the other stuff and blew a bulldozer tank away. You understand? Blew it away. It just disappeared. Of course, I brought this sample home to Moscow. And one day, my four friends were playing basketball at Rudolf's house. He had a small court in his house next to the subway at Krasnopresnenskaya. You see, I put about an ounce of my sample inside the ball they were playing with. It came to the size of half a ball bearing, the kind they use in cycle axles. The rest you can guess. . . . So what brings you to Moscow, my friend?"

"Business," you say.

"Buying or selling?"

"Selling."

"What does India have to offer us that we don't already have, Mr. Mehta?"

"Hospitality, for one, Mr. Akramov. When we talk to guests, we look them in the eye," you say.

"In my business, it's better that few people know what you look like," says Akramov.

"Are you that ugly, Mr. Akramov?" you ask. "Did the Belorussian leave a big souvenir on your face?"

"If you don't watch your tongue, it's going to get you into big trouble."

"Story of my life."

"What do you have on offer? My time is valuable. Yours could be running out." You don't miss the sinister tone.

"I have a gift for you," you say.

"Aha," says Akramov. A friendly blip on the radar. All stations hold firing.

"It's in my breast pocket," you say.

"Ninov," barks Akramov, and you smell Red Coat's special cologne as he reaches inside for the packet.

"Heroin," you say. "Ninety-five percent pure. A special token of affection."

You feel the room going silent. Russian motherfuckers getting a toke on the situation. A Hindu asshole doing the overtake, leading the pack. "The people I work for want to know whether you can play big numbers."

"What numbers could you be talking about, Mr. Mehta?" asks Akramov. "Ninov, please take the balaclava off our guest."

"Two hundred kilograms to begin with," you say. "And much more to come." You notice the two stitched-up sutures on Akramov's cheeks. You take note of his eyes. Glassy and small, but with a gaze like a pair of pistols.

"Welcome to Moscow, Mr. Mehta," says Akramov. "Tell me, do Bengal tigers shit in the same place twice?"

You make it back from Moscow in time for the weekly editorial meeting on Monday—the 10:00 A.M. assembly that Digs orchestrates in the conference room. On other weekdays, Digs goes by quorum, a battle of turf limited to section heads. But on Monday, he has an open house, gives all kinds of scumbags an opportunity to punch holes in editorial policy.

Your standard operating procedure at all editorial meetings is to perform a holding operation, ricochet arrowheads winging your way. What you really specialize in is neutering your threat template before the meeting. That way, you have an easy glide on your Marlboros. View all the butchering through the haze of smoke you exhale. You have seen careers go up in smoke in these meetings. What helps you is your reputation for neutrality when the point at issue is not your own turf. You are happy to see the minnows slug it out without taking sides yourself, which could nip at their rudders.

The others realize that your Vatican stance is dependent on them playing by the book, bypassing your territory as they launch their assaults. On occasions when you have your own program, a battle of space with the political badasses, you maintain your observer status by letting your henchmen argue the case.

But today, you walk right into an unexpected combination. A Leslie, Jain motherfucker, and Digs triumvirate, a fucking rear para assault. While Digs's accepted role at these meetings is to stick to his thermostat function, not let temperatures blow the machinery in place, when he does join battle, it's usually a swift annihilation of the opposition. A mosquito kill.

But your battlefield acumen makes you a worthy opponent. Right now, it's not the magazine's interests you are worried about. You are concerned that your ace in the hole, the tape that you hold on the defense minister, is common editorial knowledge. Jolly has fucked up. She has gone and talked to Digs about the tape. Digs gets overexcited when he smells a scoop. It does wonders to his biomechanism. His attention span proliferates and you suspect that the switch on his sex drive flicks to turbo.

You can smell the urgency in his system to get on with it, get the scoop in print. He can't sustain excitement levels, take a course on long-term orgasms, prolong his journalistic stimulation. He likes the sharp thrust, the flood that overcomes the system. Right now, he is arguing that *The Post* should get on with the raw tape and nail Defense Minister Suresh Yadov. There's also economics at work—the timing of the next issue, where Digs wants his scoop in banner headlines. It's the anniversary issue, and with all the hoopla planned for it, plus the ABC media audit coming up, Digs wants a steroid boost in the works, something to take the circulation soaring above the five-digit mark.

What's heating you up on the inside in Leslie throwing his hat in the ring, aligning himself with the troubleshooters. A stab in the back from someone you were responsible for bringing in. Jain is new to the game.

He's swinging along for the fun of it. He's too blind to see the fist you were preparing to shove up his ass to split him in two.

The highest form of generalship, you have read in Sun Tzu's *The Art of War*, is to prevent the junction of the enemy's forces. Along with that, you plan to generate a few allies of your own, try to increase your numbers.

"A problem we will have if we want to run the tape the next issue is what to drop," you say. You consult the printing form in your hand. "We will have to drop four pages of the crime piece. Can you do that, Mukherjee? Condense your story to three pages?"

Mukherjee is a political badass, someone you understand at a very basic level. Nothing hurts anybody more at meetings than a tangle with him. The tape issue was, strictly speaking, a turf squabble that should concern no one except Mukherjee and you. Till the time you drag him in. Mukherjee has been watching the proceedings from the fence, but now, with your special gambit, you hope to convert him to your side in the skirmish.

You know that Mukherjee's crime story is very dear to him. He has been nurturing it for two months, building his file on politicians with Mafia connections. He has had to contend with the frustration of seeing Digs put the story on hold on two occasions, and just when he thought he was past any last-minute hurdles, some tape looms large to screw his seven-page investigative report to three piddling pages.

You, of course, have a few other Machiavellian considerations in drawing Mukherjee into the field of mayhem. You have made allowance for the ethnic ramifications this will have. Having Mukherjee on your side will permit you to pick up the Bengali votes in the conference hall, and there are two in crucial positions to blow some wind in your sail. Saurabh Sen, the news coordinator, and Mahesh Deb, who as production manager is vital to your immediate strategy, which is to attack the triumvirate not on editorial grounds but on the sheer impracticality of their logistics.

The other consideration is simple. On the two occasions when Mukherjee's story was held back, it was because Jain had argued and won his case for some telecom crap. On one of those story holds, you had given the signal to Karim to argue in favor of Mukherjee, but with no success. Now you are simply providing Mukherjee with a target and reminding him of past favors.

"Absolutely not," says Mukherjee. "*News Today* is working on a similar story. I don't want us to come out after them, especially when we have cracked it earlier."

You look at the form with new concentration. "Then I don't see how we can squeeze in the tape unless we drop four advertisements in the first form," you say. Any mention of dropping advertisements hits Digs in the lower guts. The wind gasps out of his frame. You feel you have your flanks covered adroitly. But Jain, the motherfucker, is on a suicide mission.

"I won't mind if you held back four of my pages. You can junk the Bangalore crash," says Jain. He's willing for his pages to be taken out. You figure that either the guy wants your ass bad or he's plain dumb.

"What's it about?" asks Digs. That's Digs's editorial hold. A story's on form and he doesn't know what it's about.

"It's about software companies going bust," explains Jain.

"Oh, yeah," says Digs.

"It would save time, too. The Bangalore courier is running late. We haven't got the slides yet. The tape thing, we can do with stock photos," says Leslie.

You feel the swing in momentum. But Mukherjee provides you some temporary covering fire.

"But I think we should run the software story. The Singapore delegation is coming to town next week. They have invested over a billion dollars in Bangalore's software setup. Besides, did you read Bill Gates's interview, Jain?"

Jain feels the need to take off his glasses. As Business editor he is supposed to know these things, not have a political badass like Mukherjee take him blind.

"Ahm," he goes. "What interview?" He wipes his glasses on his tie. You figure he wouldn't be so prized an asshole if he didn't come wearing a tie. It sets the tone against him.

Mukherjee likes to rub in these things, get the salt in while he can.

"Don't tell me you haven't seen it," he says, shocked. "It was all over the Net. It was this live Internet session he had with some college guys. He mentioned Bangalore as the next destination for the software industry."

Jain wipes his glasses. This is not perhaps as big a goof as it could have been had it come in one of the Indian papers. The Net is something very fringy in Digs's mental framework.

"Oh, that," he says, rallying. But Mukherjee presses his advantage.

"If the facts are right in your piece and you can really show that the software industry might go bust, you have a story, pal. The right time to do it would be when these Chinese are here from Singapore. Make a lot of noise. But I don't know how strong you are on the facts," comments Mukherjee, and lets the thing hang. On your part, you aren't so sure whether there is really a delegation coming, and you think even the interview might be a rapid creation of Mukherjee's imagination. But right now, the triumvirate is ducking under his armor-piercing slugs.

Jain looks like he is about to cry. He backpedals.

"No," he begins, "we are pretty solid on the facts. Real solid." He clenches his fists. He feels like he can hide behind the word *solid*. He wants to regain lost ground. He opens his fists and grabs his chair arms tightly. He modifies his position. "Well, I hadn't thought of it this way. Maybe we could drop the letter pages this time, and the diary as well. That should give us four."

Digs snorts from his chair. Jain realizes too late how dear the diary pages are to Digs. Next only to the advertisements. He lifts himself on one side. You suspect he's so nervous, he's breaking wind.

"No, not the diary," barks Digs.

"I still think we can hold Bangalore. How long is the delegation going to stay, Mukherjee?" asks Leslie.

"A week or so, I guess," says Mukherjee.

"Then there's no problem holding the thing up till the issue after next. It will still be current," says Leslie.

"I think we shouldn't be guided by which delegation is in town or isn't," declares Digs. "If the story holds, it holds even after they have left." Jain gets some starch back into his shoulders. "I don't particularly relish timing the two things." Jain nods in agreement, a trifle early. "But I think the story might act as a demoralizer on India's liberalization efforts. We should avoid doing these negative stories if we can."

Digs's commercial antenna opens up to anything that could cut into his advertisement intake.

"Let's run the tape stuff. We will club it with the air force story. What do you think, MM?" asks Digs.

Mukherjee casts a glance at you. You sense the ball is in your court.

"It's okay by me, except I was thinking on a slightly different line, Mr. Mehra," you say. Mukherjee's covering fire has given you some time to reorganize your editorial geopolitics. "I was thinking instead of running the tape cover, we could go instead with the sex survey in our anniversary issue. It's bound to be a hit, Mr. Mehra, especially with the kind of statistics we have. Also, if we don't run it in this issue, *News Today* would be stumping us to it. They have gotten wind of our survey and are getting MARG to do one for them. Let's drop the Bangalore story and the letters and run a seven-page sex survey as the cover story."

You can see Leslie panicking. You place the missing piece in the jigsaw puzzle. Leslie's reason for coming out into the open to root for the tape becomes clearer every second. He has seen you come into the meeting with the sex survey and he doesn't have his layouts ready—the illustrations that you gave him to do a month back. Digs likes to see all cover layouts the hour after the meeting. You press home your advantage.

"Leslie has some deadly illustrations ready for the thing. I told him to merge the *Kama Sutra* elements into a modern kind of collage with sepia borders. We can be out with the form by noon tomorrow," you say.

Digs chews on this awhile. Leslie sweats.

"I think it's a great anniversary idea," says Mukherjee.

"Yeah, it's going to be a sellout," says Deb.

"When did you get this done, MM?" asks Karim.

"I didn't. It was Mr. Mehra's idea. We had it done three months back," you say. Digs colors. God, you think, he doesn't want to be recognized as the originator of the idea. You know, for instance, that Digs took a whole week over framing questions for the survey. He spit-and-polished them and ran them by you to show off his meticulousness in the matter.

"It would be great timing, MM, but my only concern is that we might not be able to do justice to it in seven pages. We need at least five more to make an impact. Let's not piss off a great spread in a hurry," says Leslie. He still has fight left in him.

"I would love to, Leslie, but we don't want to be 'us, too' journos, do we? What's the point if you let *News Today* steal all the thunder? We have spent five lakh rupees on the poll," you say.

"We can't be 'us, too' journalists," says Mukherjee. "I think we have to keep the importance of the anniversary issue in mind. What do you say, Mr. Mehra?"

You have set Digs's mind in motion. You can see it whirring, deliberating, little weights falling on and off the scale.

"Let's go for both," says Digs. Nobody, to your knowledge, can set different people on the route to a coronary faster than Digs.

"Both?" asks Leslie. There is still fog around.

You feel the need to tap your third Marlboro out. Get a puff of nicotine to boost your brainpower.

"Yes, let's run the sex survey as well as the tape," says Digs.

Deb pales. "We don't have the space for both, sir," he says. "We would have to drop a lot of advertisements."

"Who's talking about dropping advertisements? Let's add more editorial pages," says Digs. In living history, Digs hasn't made such a decision—whacked more newsprint into the issue than he needed to maintain the edit-ad ratio at 60:40. "That takes care of all the problems. After all, it's the anniversary issue. We have to come out with a bang."

You take a long drag on your stick. It's not that you haven't prepared for contingencies like this. But the nuke you have in reserve is the last shot you have to halt Digs in his tracks. You punch in the code, clear your throat. Deb, however, is beefing Digs on the economics. You want him to soften Digs up for the kill.

"That would be a cost overrun of eleven lakh rupees, sir. We could also end up late on the stands," says Deb. "I will have to check whether they have the extra newsprint. We are usually going issue to issue on the imported glaze we are using."

The blood drains from Digs's face. Cost overruns in percentages are things he is used to handling, but a recognizable two-digit hole in his pocket is screwing up his body language. He wipes his palms on his trousers, looks at his belly, sends his forefinger up his nasal cavity, and gets his spine straight. "If it's to be done, it's to be done," he says. He makes a brave face. You figure it's time to bail him out.

"But there's a problem, Mr. Mehra. I hadn't wanted to bring this out in the open, but I think you will need to change your decision," you say.

"What is it?" asks Digs. A lifeboat to the rescue.

"You see, Mr. Mehra, I have dispatched the tape for a VMA. They don't do that kind of stuff here in India. There's a laboratory in Phoenix, Arizona, that does it on a commercial basis. The latest we can have a positive confirmation is within a fortnight. I thought with such a sensitive issue as this, it would be better to have a lab back what we say, give us a certificate we can flash in court in case we get sued for libel. After all, we don't want to demolish somebody's reputation without scientific backup," you say.

"VMA? What's that?" asks Digs.

"Oh, sorry. That's a voice-match analysis. The intelligence agencies do it all the time," you explain.

Nothing this fancy has ever happened in Digs's journalistic career. He is intimidated. The others, too, take time digesting the information.

"How much does it cost?" asks Digs. You, of course, don't want to take any chances with Digs's stinginess. You have it all worked out.

"It's not costing us anything. I have a friend from school days working as a technician there. He's doing it for us free. Otherwise, I think they have a flat fee of fifteen hundred dollars," you say. Digs beams at you.

"What are they matching it with?" asks Digs.

"I got a recording of one of the minister's All India Radio speeches," you say.

"I guess we will have to hold the tape, then," says Digs.

"Yes, Mr. Mehra. I think there's no point in increasing the size of the issue," you say.

Your coup is, however, incomplete. Leslie's just returned from a monthlong stint at *Time*, in New York, where Digs sponsored his stay to see how the design department there works. Digs is planning on a design overhaul a year into the stands.

"When do we get to see the dummy design?" you ask Leslie. The dummy design has become a sore issue with Digs. Leslie is behind on his deadline by a month. He tightens up, gears for the assault.

"Just got a few more pages to crack. We are developing a gutter design for the news pages. It's taking time," says Leslie.

"I was wondering, Mr. Mehra, if Leslie could circulate a paper on the design concept he is working on so that all of us could contribute. I know a few designers at the National Institute of Design who would be eager to pitch in. Even come and give Leslie a helping hand as part of their semester work experience," you say. The two ways to fuck up Leslie big time are to make him write something beyond a margin note and get a couple of eager-to-contribute designers on a summer job loitering in his setup. This drives his blood pressure through the roof.

"That's a good idea," says Digs. "It would speed up things." Digs puts great store by institutions like the NID.

Leslie's aghast, but before he can voice his dissent, Digs breaks up the meeting and says to him, "Could I have a look at the layouts for the sex survey? I will be out of the office for a couple of days."

Nothing like coming out of an editorial meeting with all the blood sticking elsewhere.

A week after you met Karnam, you feel the tremendous urge to know the key to her. Actually, come to think of it, you can also say that it was she who really set the ball rolling, fencing you with this schoolgirl drill on the office stairs. You saw her coming up the steps and she wouldn't let you pass, blocking the way, daring you to detour her. And you played the game her way. You have taken her out to lunch four times in the past week, a record of sorts in your romantic history.

And today, she's your date at Jumbo's birthday bash. You are waiting in Digs's sitting room for Karnam to get ready. You have invited the rest of the Features crowd as well.

You look at the miniature paintings hanging on the walls, the brass fixtures getting at you from all angles—the banisters, doors, planters, candle stands, and even a brass sofa set. Digs is a brass maniac. In his next reincarnation, he might settle for an evolutionary downgrade, come merged in brass, become an electrical frame in a high-class strip joint.

You have a look at Digs's music system: Bose speakers, a tape deck with a silver frame, a collection of CDs ranging from American country music to Nusrat Fateh Ali Khan. A liveried asshole breaks up your inspection. He comes pushing a cart arrayed with tea paraphernalia. "Lemon, Darjeeling, ice, or herbal tea, sir?" he asks. You go for a Darjeeling brew. You have never had tea that sells at $150 a pound. You want to test it for psychotic properties. Check out the motives of the gentry buying the stuff.

Something catches your eye—a shelf of albums, photographic archives of the Digs family tree. You flip through a few. Digs puts great store in pumping the hands of sports celebrities. You see him in a two-paw grab with a reluctant Sunny Gavaskar, a ribbon opportunity with Greg Norman. Digs is divorced. He split eight years back, but the divorce hasn't made him junk his history. His ex looks pretty, but she has no contours that match Karnam's.

You look for early snaps of Karnam, see what she was like as a kid, but you draw a blank. The only photo you see is recent—Digs giving her a hug at the airport. Strange, you think. A significant flaw in memorabilia.

You have finished your tea. It was faintly bitter. Someone walks down the stairs, clutching the curved banister. You see Digs coming toward you.

"Hello, MM," he says. His eyes are cold, as if he's taking the intrusion as a breach of protocol. "There's something I want to talk to you about."

"Yeah," you say. You still have the empty cup in your hand. You place it delicately on one of Digs's brass side tables.

"The army's been up my ears all day. They are getting pretty worked up about the questionnaire. They are saying it was unauthorized. That if we go ahead and publish it, they will bust us with both the Official Secrets Act and the National Security Act," he says.

"The more the merrier," you reply.

At Srinagar and Kupwara, Siddy's career graphics had performed hot-air maneuvers. He had managed to set up sessions with eight hundred soldiers from seven different regiments. *The Post* now has eight hundred pieces of paper telling whoever wants to know the FUBAR status of the personnel in charge of protecting the nation's borders. Among the things that you tabulated, keyed in, and analyzed: 90 percent of the enlisted men outside 5 Kumaon consider their officers to be a bunch of fuckups. Morale is at an all-time low. Seventy percent honestly think they can't win a war against a crowd of worked-up Mossies. Ninety-five percent hate what they are doing. A significant 7 percent are punching holes in their veins. The army is so heavily right-wing, they hate the guts of all civilian Mossies in Kashmir.

"But they wouldn't dare," you add.

"Yes, they will," says Digs. He's in a confrontation mode. He presses charges. "You told me it was authorized."

Digs, you feel, needs a crash course in army psychology.

"Mr. Mehra, no army in the world will ever authorize any civilian to sink shrink probes into the minds of their soldiers. If somebody gets to do it, he slips in unobserved by the top brass," you say. "It has to be civilian sleuthing at its best."

"That's the point. They are calling our tests highly illegal," says Digs.

"We have a piece of paper from the army PRO requesting assistance be given to *The Post* personnel for the poll. It would help in court," you say.

"That's not the point. What we don't need is a toe-on-toe situation. If they think it's sensitive, we should respect their view," says Digs.

A prima facie case by the government would, of course, see that Digs would be the first one charge-sheeted. Lawsuits upset Digs's constitution. And this promises to be much more, a collection of army crooks cracking the NSA in his shit hole. A job many sizes too big for his in-house legal cell to handle.

"You know the way armies think. They call all kinds of junk 'sensitive.' What we aren't going to do is tell the world the force breakdown in Kashmir or the kind of hardware they pack behind their backs. The Pakistanis know it anyway. Our job is to give our readers an honest situation report. We owe it to them. We didn't tool what we found. And right now, they don't know it anyway," you say.

"They want all the test papers back and a written statement saying we haven't made any copies," says Digs.

"Tell them to stuff it," you say.

Digs reddens. "There's something else, too," he says.

"What?"

"They have made complaints against you. Military intelligence wants to have a chat with you about certain killings on the border," says Digs.

"The army ambushes?" you ask.

"From the looks of it, you were where you weren't supposed to be. There's an official complaint from the 7 Sikh," says Digs.

"I was where the army took me. What are they complaining about?" you ask.

"The army vice chief wants you to come by for a chat, sort things out. They are saying they are all for an independent media but that some co-operation is in order," says Digs.

"Why don't you go pay him a visit?" you suggest.

"It's you they want," says Digs. You don't like the tone, the smell of putting distance. "It would be a good idea to junk the Q. The long shot of it is, we are all Indians."

Karnam walks downstairs. "Let's go," she says. She kisses Digs.

"Take care, sweetheart," says Digs. "You, MM. I hope you are taking my daughter to a decent place."

"Don't worry, Mr. Mehra. The army won't be around," you say. Digs looks at you suspiciously.

"What was all that about?" asks Karnam as you turn your Defender around the first bend after Digs's house.

"The army's getting your pop on the hop."

"You, too," says Karnam.

"Me? I am an innocent little motherfucker."

"My father says to watch out. He doesn't trust you."

"Fathers never trust guys who take their daughters out for the evening."

"It's not that."

"Then?"

"He says you might be involved in something big. I mean bad."

Your hand tightens on the wheel. You turn and smile at her.

"And how is that?" you ask.

"You should know," she says. "He said you did some shit while you were at the border."

"What shit?"

"How should I know? You were moving around, carrying guns with patrol units."

"That was my job."

"Your job was to make a documentary."

"The only way you can make your subjects easy in front of the camera is to start behaving like them. Become one with the lads. Merge with them. They don't teach you that at business school."

"They don't teach you to shoot people, either."

So, you think, that's what it's all about. You relax a bit. It's better than her knowing how deep you were in the works.

"Mossies," you say.

"What?"

"Mossies. Not people. Terrorists, if you like to go by official nomenclature."

"You shot some terrorists?"

"One."

"You killed a man?"

"It was me or him."

She stays silent for a while.

"What was it like?" she asks.

"There are some things you just lock in your brain and then throw away the key."

"You know, when I was in high school in Texas, I used to go around with a Syrian—second-generation. We were friendly, and one day he took me on a roller-coaster ride and proposed right when we were going through a dinosaur's belly. I was seventeen. I said yes. I told my mother. She moved me to California the same week. She said she'd had enough trouble with my father to have her daughter start the same way," she says. "I didn't have the guts to stand up to her."

"What happened?"

"He tracked me down three months later. My mother called the cops and had him thrown out. He came back a month later. My mother wasn't in. He said, 'It's me or you. Choose.' I said, 'I choose me. I am sorry, but I don't think it can work. Our religions don't match.' 'What has religion to do with it?' he asked. 'It matters to my parents,' I said. 'If I don't care what my parents have to say on this, why do you?' he asked. 'Well, I am Indian,' I said. 'Well then, choose Indian,' he said. 'Choose me or you.' 'What's all this rubbish about choosing?' I asked him. 'Indian,' he said, 'if you choose me, both of us live. If you choose you, one of us has to die.' 'I choose me,' I said. You know what he did?"

"You are alive. That's all I can go by," you say.

"He shot himself with a pistol right there on our balcony. You could have swum in the blood," she says. There's a mist in her eyes, but no tears trickle down. She hasn't finished.

"Yes," you say.

"You know, you looked the same way when you said, 'It was me or him,' like when Yakub said, 'It's me or you. Choose.' And you choose you."

"We are sailing in the same boat," you say.

"Difference is, you pulled the trigger," she says.

"You pulled it with what you said," you say.

What you know is that every person has a thing. Major Rodriguez's thing is on the patrols, in the woods that he said you could never trace echoes in, and the rush of execution. Your own thing is that you live for rushes and don't care where they come from. The similarity between your thing and the major's is that both of you are addicted to risk. You get high on adrenaline, among other things. The bigger the risk, the bigger your addiction. Life for you and the major is just the rushes. The thing you do in between is a lot of waiting. Akramov's thing is that he provides a code for business in a country where government is still without regulation. Jain the motherfucker's thing is that he is an asshole and doesn't know any better. Karnam's thing right now is to bush you with her past.

What's also true is that sometimes the thing that people strut doesn't give you a hold on the surface underneath, the hand they might be holding, which never comes out in their temporary thing. For you, things are like little acts in movies. Most of the time, you know where the script's headed, but there's always the deal that surprises you in the end. What you are trying to say is that when you poke to find Karnam's deeper thing, all you get is a busy signal.

At Gurgaon, in the farmhouse where Jumbo's throwing his party, the cars are already in rows of twenty and five layers deep. This is Jumbo's fifth experiment in raves. He's teamed up with Cedric, a veteran in setting up raves at Goa's Bagga Beach. Cedric supplies Jumbo with all the ecstasy, speed, and other chemical knickknacks, while Jumbo looks after the logistics of the operation.

He's had the place wired with Bose speakers, his favorite. You can't tell the difference. The music itself is DJ-orchestrated. It patches synthesized percussion tracks with the latest in disco hits, volatile Eurobeat sounds, bleep-teep jungle, and trance-producing om renditions that mix with osho chants. An acid house clone.

The music isn't the only draw. There are laser beams, eleven video monitors, smoke machines, and private rooms on the third floor where you can do your own stuff, buff a girl or mainline into your system. There's even karaoke. And Jumbo plans some videoconferencing in some of the rooms to spin his rave global. As a precaution, there's also a medic in case some shooters mess it up. When it's a mixed bunch of pros and amateurs, you have to look out for the initiates.

You have split with Jumbo on the expenses, taken a silent partnership. Though the main hall's big enough to squeeze in a thousand, the maximum you have taken in so far is about half that. You don't get the London warehouse kind of numbers here. Not even the attitude. Here, guys dress to pull in birds. No headbands, slogan T-shirts, or Day-Glo outfits. You, however, flash an I LOVE GRAVITY T-shirt.

Though Jumbo and you have immediate commercial motives for the place, the setting gives you an ideal location to surreptitiously film important people in compromising situations. Tapes you could then archive for future use.

Your promotion is limited to word of mouth. It's Jumbo's invitations on the phone that bring in most of the crowd, though gate-crashers are not unknown. But the chemicals are available only to the cool heads, the professionals Cedric and his gang think can handle the mood elevation.

For an initiation, the customer has to be known to the main handlers.

Till now, however, seeing the nascent nature of the operation, you aren't charging for the hits. You are farming out friendlies to establish a clientele, build a base. The way you have financed your side of the operation is by selling Cedric five hundred grams of heroin from the load you hold. With him, you are exploring the possibilities of a distributorship in Goa. The Germans and Scandinavians, you are told, can sustain the bottom line in retail, move a dealer's stock at sonic speed.

You have always dreamed of a home in Goa. A place where you can recuperate from sustained chemical abuse, get your bloodstream on keel. In your fantasies, you aren't alone. You have a woman. Sometimes it's Shomali, sometimes someone whose face is a blur. But she always wears white, your favorite color. You also have a couple of kids playing around. Yours or somebody else's—it doesn't matter to you. What mat-

ters right then in the fantasy is that for a while, you are happy with the little concerns of life. A baby on the lap and early-morning swims in the
Arabian Sea. A lunch of rice and prawn curry. A night with your
woman—just lying together, no sex.

But even there, as the fantasy arcs toward exit point, you feel inun-
dated by restlessness. You feel you don't belong there in that coziness.
The hooks in your back, reeling you out of that scene, are big and deep.
For you, it's a place to sit and get your breath back.

As you enter the hall, you spot the ecstasy guys and the blokes on
speed on the dance floor. It's a hidden talent you have. Ecstasy does
something to the face. It eats into your sex appeal. It does that because
when you are on it, you get so freakish that sex somehow recedes to the
background. It has to do with the precise pharmacological thrust the
drug delivers, excessive dance energy and an absurdist view of the world
that makes you empathize and dance the night through.

Speed, on the other hand, is like an additional supply of voltage to
your central nervous system. A six-hour high that starts with a tickle in
your guts and floods you with the confidence of God. You flow with wit-
ticisms and your libido increases in horsepower. You feel you can fuck a
horse and get away with it.

You have to work your way through the floor to get upstairs. But Karnam pulls you into the crowd. The thing with raves is, you have to get
your air-conditioning working overtime or the heat starts flooding the
floor. It's more of a problem than in your normal kick-and-shake discos.
Here, once you are on a trip, you stay in. You don't even feel the need to
empty your bladder.

And Karnam soon discovers basic rave tectonics. You pull her to the
side of the hall, move into a low-density area cordoned off with a wooden
screen. She clings to you, and that triggers in you a question.

"What's your thing, Karnam? I can't get a reading on your pulse," you
say.

Karnam smiles. "I heard you went parachuting with the army," she says. It's difficult to talk above the music. You have to shout.

"I think you are a mystery woman," you say.

"What was it like?" she asks.

"Fun."

"I don't think it was just that."

"It was lots of other things, but *fun*'s the best word."

"What was the first jump like?"

"You don't know what's going to happen, so it's the easiest. You put a lot of faith in your equipment and tell yourself what you need to hear to get yourself out of the AN-32," you say.

"That doesn't sound like fun."

"Fun, my dear, is a lot of things. One of them is fear when you don't know the invariables in a given situation. There are basically two kinds of people—those who can do fun and those who can't," you say.

"Where do I fit in?"

"That's what I would like to know," you say.

"I love fun," says Karnam.

"Prove it," you say.

"How?"

"Kiss me now," you say. That's when you spin her right in the middle of the hall, where the lights hit the strongest and you can have your crowd watch the fun. And she does it, all right. She doesn't go for your cheeks or anything. She sinks it right on your lips and what you feel is like what you felt when you took your first jump without the static. When you forced the hand of destiny and came back in one piece.

Karnam doesn't let go till the end of the song, and when you do break up, you carry with you the sweetness of her mouth as you go upstairs, where the rave is picking up gas.

You find your Features crowd and some others in the room next to the pool table. Journalists, you think, need to be told where the action is. Jolly, Dilip, Matthew, Dravid, and Karim sit on chairs, watching the video monitor. Karim's managed to swing his desk girl, Minnie, over to the place, and she's smoking a menthol. At least she's smoking, you think. Siddy's there, too, and already screwed up on acid. He looks at you dispiritedly.

"What's the action, guys?" you ask. You push Karnam ahead of you and put an arm around her hips.

"Siddy here knows some guys who are throwing ecstasy tabs for free," Jolly informs you. She is in diaphanous black. Her tits, you observe, are more out than in.

"Any of you guys want a trip? Something to smooth your Saturday?" you ask. Your crowd, you figure, hasn't gone beyond prep school where mind-benders are concerned.

"Jesus, MM, it's scary down there. I mean, some of the blokes are dancing like they have four legs or something," says Dravid.

"One dose of MDMA gives you insights into the world that you won't get in twenty years of journalism," you say. "It makes you believe in the oneness of body and spirit."

"I would rather go for old-fashioned sex," says Matthew. "It's proven technology, and it gets you right up there believing in the oneness of body and soul and all that crap."

"Yeah. When was the last time you cracked the whip?" asks Karim.

Matthew blushes. Karim, you deduce, is still a virgin. His question has the agony of expectation.

"Less time than you can even think of or would like to know," says Matthew.

You are the only one who sees Minnie blush. Oh my, you think, what's going on here?

"Ha-ha," goes Siddy. It's an acid laugh, manic and loud. No amount of booze drinking can make a person throw the acid kind of laugh. Or even, for that matter, the peculiar shine that it brings to the eyes.

"Well, let me see," says Karim. You know what's coming next, and before you can glide the moment into neutral by continuing with your discourse on expanding the mind's horizons, Karim puts his foot in. "When was it that you went to Japan?"

A year back, you were responsible for sending Matthew on a Suzuki junket to Japan, where he struck gold as far as pussy was concerned. The very peculiar circumstances rather blow your head even now. Matthew patted the cheeks of a two-year-old girl on a Tokyo subway and the mother threw kidnapping charges at him.

It was the best thing that ever happened to him, in hindsight. The Japanese had to keep him in detention for a week till the charges came up for hearing and Suzuki and the Indian embassy got their act organized. In confinement, he struck up a friendship with a Jap police-woman, who expressed commiseration over his plight. To make amends for his introduction to Japanese culture, she invited him to stay at her flat for the remainder of his stay. Matthew got to do things that blew his mind. His conquest wasn't limited to the Japanese police force. It spread to Suzuki, where he got friendly with the PR assistant assigned to him, and he claims to have given her an introductory course in ancient Indian gymnastics with reference to the *Kama Sutra*. The reason everybody knows the details is that he went around with snaps in his wallet for a while. The strange thing is, his golden run continued after he returned.

"I think you are full of shit, Karim," says Matthew.

"I think it's time to give you guys a course in the recreational use of drugs," you say. You see Cedric passing by. You yell for him. "Hey, Cedric, how about an alphabet course for my friends here? A group lecture in divinity."

Cedric is down to his sleeveless vest. Rivers of sweat are flowing down his steroid-pumped muscles. But from the way his jaws are locked and he's jerking his arms around, you figure he's in the first phase of a 1,500-mg dose of acid and still half an hour away from going on autopilot. The thing about acid is that the first rush takes some time evening out, getting the fin stabilizers in place. And Cedric looks like he's on a real twister.

"Who's this?" asks Cedric, and peers at you closely. "Is it MM?" He's having trouble focusing.

"Relax, Cedric," you say. "Do you have our lecture visuals on you?"

A gleam of intelligence raids Cedric's eyes.

"It's here in this fucking locker," he says.

Strangely, it isn't locked. You locate your drug folio beneath the warranty papers for the video system. You withdraw it.

"Now this, guys, is what I call 'the different aspects of God,'" you say as you unveil your folio. Your crowd creeps up. You kick the door to the room shut. "The first eight letters of the alphabet. What's missing is F, but you leave that blank. Because F's for *fuck* only and the whole world knows it."

Siddy claps. "F's for *fog*, too," he says, and laughs.

"That's when you are funked on acid," you say. "Then it's *float*, too."

"Fly Agaric," says Karnam.

"My, what do we have here. The Narcotics Control Board," you say. Karnam smiles.

"What's Fly Agaric?" asks Minnie. She's smoked her Moore. Karim's carrying around the ashtray for her.

"Mushroom. *Amanita muscaria*. Grows mostly at the bottom of trees. Identifiable by its bright red cap. Eaten for its psychotic properties, but it passes through the body mostly unmetabolized. Makes a good case for siphoning off your urine, which is what Siberian tribesmen do," you say.

"Ugh," says Jolly.

"But let's start with A. Amphetamine sulfate. Commonly known as speed. It's the favorite of all punks and Nazi shitheads. It gives your whole CNS a buzz," you say.

"What's CNS?" asks Dravid.

"Jesus. What are you guys? Nursery school? Central nervous system. *B* here's for *barbiturates*. They're downers. They depress the CNS. One barb that's guaranteed to fuck you up is Seconal. It's a Lilly product. If you resist the inclination to sleep, you become a mean bastard, especially if you chase it down with a dose of Benzedrine," you say.

"C's for *crack*, I presume," says Dilip.

"I don't need to tell you about that, do I? D's for *Diconal*. It's a synthetic opioid. Dangerous, too. It's rich in silicon. You try injecting it and your veins fill up. They get as hard as steel. But if you tab it down, it gives you a rush as good as H. Now E here's for *ecstasy*. It's a rave special. You can dance the night through on this, but you have to see that you don't heat up. You lose fluid fast, and you could end up with blood clotting your lungs. All you have to do is keep standing under the vents every now and then to chill out."

"You also blank out on ecstasy, I read in the papers. You go blind or something," says Karnam.

"Please don't scare my flock like that, Karnam. It's called a 'head rush.' You just go blank for a couple of minutes. But you take Jolly here. She would love ecstasy. It would make her lose all that lard on her hips, because this thing puts you on a diet like nothing else."

"Shut up, MM. I have no lard on my hips," says Jolly.

"Hey, look who's here," says Karim. You turn to the video monitor. You see Leslie and Jain dancing in the hall with two British embassy staffers.

"Who the hell brought those guys here?" you ask.

"None of us did," says Matthew.

"Hey, Cedric, you know those two guys? The white-shirt assholes?" you ask.

But Cedric is busy calling Siddy the mother of twenty bastards, and Siddy's pushing him off his chest.

"Get away, you bat," Siddy's shouting. Two chemical casualties. You don't like to see your main chemical man grounded so early in the gig.

"Are those two married?" asks Karnam.

"Leslie is," says Minnie. "Don't know about Jain."

"He's married all right. He has two kids, the asshole," says Karim.

"Now with G, you can go for either ganja or GBH. Ganja, you all know about. GBH is a powerful anesthetic. Not as dopey as Ketamine, which takes you right up after you start sliding on ecstasy, but nearly there," you say.

"I have smoked ganja a few times," says Dravid.

"Attaboy, Dravid. That's the spirit," you say.

"It just cooled me up for a couple of hours. The thing is, it shrivels your pecker up," says Dravid.

"Shut up," says Jolly.

"You can't get a guy to shut up if he's got his facts right," you say.

"You are a corrupting influence, MM," says Karnam. But she slips her hand in your palm.

"Hey, MM, I want five days off, starting this Monday," says Dravid.

"Crazy fucking Jesus. Here we are, just about to get to the *H* word, and you come up with this leave business."

"My mom will be in town," says Dravid.

"What's up?" asks Jolly. "She's trying to fix you up again?"

"Sort of," says Dravid.

Dravid's mother lands in Delhi from Bangalore every six months, trying to find him a girl to settle down with. She inserts a matrimonial advertisement in the *Hindustan Times* and checks out the responses.

"Hey, Dravid, you done it yet, or you are waiting for your mom to fix you up?" you ask. You really are curious. How can a person remain sane if he's a virgin till the age of twenty-five? What substitute does he have in place?

"Shut up," says Karnam. "It's personal."

"The fuck it's personal," you say. "The guy's either done it or he hasn't. All Features people present raise hands if they have done it."

Everybody raises hands. Dravid half lifts his.

"What's this half-mast thing?" you ask. Everybody laughs. Dravid goes sheepish. But he has the glow that comes from a child suddenly receiving extra attention. He plays to the gallery.

"I did half of it," says Dravid.

"Now, this sounds too interesting to miss. Can anybody do half of it?" you ask generally. Then you look specifically at Matthew. "Can you, Matthew, given your experience on the international scene? Can you do it half?"

"Not me," says Matthew.

"It's some new thing," says Karim. "Dravid's invented some new maneuvers."

"Do you want the girls in on this?" you ask. Dravid takes on a new red hue. It's getting out of hand for him.

"I mean I just didn't go all the way, guys. I could've, but I didn't. I wasn't in the mood," says Dravid.

Minnie giggles. Karnam looks like she wants to empathize with Dravid.

"He could've, but he didn't," echoes Jolly.

"The guy needs some counseling," says Dilip.

"Fuck off," says Dravid. He's getting some color back. Confidence on a rearguard action.

"What you need is some chemical support. A dose of speed that will make you rip it up. Keep your serotonin levels at the red mark, check your mood fluctuations," you say.

"What I need is my own concern," says Dravid. "I am going to get me some dancing."

"You're too hard on him," says Karnam.

"Hard! We were soft as butter."

"Look at Jain and Leslie," says Karim. And all of you look at the closed-circuit monitor. Jain's got his shirt unbuttoned and Leslie is smooching his partner.

"Let's go down and give our friends a welcome," you say.

"Can't we, like, lace their drinks with something?" suggests Karim. "Give them the trip of their lives."

"Good idea," you say. You take out two blotters with a 30-mcg dose of LSD. Acid with alcohol is, you know, a dangerous combination, especially on a first trip. "You guys want to try something? Let's work out a lottery with speed, ecstasy, and acid. Okay?"

"Okay by me," says Karim. "You have to try it sometime. See what it's about."

"Just put it under your tongue," you say as you hand out a blotter to Karim. This is your amateur dose. A two-hour binge. A bit of a laugh, rather than a six-hour escape-velocity thrust. A 100-mcg-plus dose at first shot, you know, is a recipe for sensory battering that not all people can contain. After four years of tutelage, acid has taught you that its best effects depend upon proper mood and setting. A sober and attractive room. No wild bats around. Some introspection about the nature of self before you pop the dose, which acts like a throttling of the system, or you will be in flight without preparation.

Since what the drug is going to shout loud and clear in your mind is that your self is an invention and that you are just part of a whole. Acid has taught you that you have to absorb this constructive lesson graciously, for if you don't, and attempt to go fist-on-fist with a few grains of rye fungus, you get a big puncture in your confidence for your efforts, which it could take a few weeks to recover from.

There's also this little secret that veteran acid trippers are familiar with. The anticipation you carry for the experience controls its effects as much as acid itself. And if you go into it with a sense of fear and hundreds of people around shouting like maniacs and have a run of *The Silence of the Lambs* on the television in front of you, the experience could be traumatic.

"What's happening?" asks Jolly. The rest look at Karim expectantly. But takeoff thrust is still fifteen minutes away for him.

"Nothing's happening right now, guys. Cool it, will you? Tap in one yourself," says Karim. The initiative swings, Jolly's the next to fall in with the mood, and soon you reach critical mass. Your whole herd is into acid, but you abstain. You take the responsibility to shepherd your lot, steer them away from precipes, check their paranoia levels.

"Should I?" Karnam asks you.

"Of course," you say. "I am here. There's nothing to worry about. No one ever got hooked on a single dose of acid."

You go downstairs for a while, greet Jain and Leslie.

"Hi there," you say.

Leslie's jaw drops. You know his wife well. Jain's a little too stoned on Johnnie Walker to look at you straight. Life for him was getting too complicated without getting stoned. A dot of acid in his whiskey, you figure, would take him to a new planet. For Leslie, a source of new visions that would energize his design concepts. Acid makes you evolve visions from almost any background and object, and even some that aren't there.

By the time you usher Leslie and Jain into the pool room, where you have them run *Aliens*, the two are waving their arms like propeller blades, trying to ward off the crazy beasts. There's just one thing good about LSD when you are on a bad trip. It's not an immobilizing drug. You can make use of your legs if you think there are a couple of dozen monsters giving you the chase. You can run out of the room like a bat out of hell.

Choosing ammunition when you have to hop police HQ, where Major Kohli finds himself temporarily locked up for careless driving, can be a tedious process. Kohli has the keys to the warehouse where 5 Kumaon's delivery of inventory has begun. The advance party of the regiment has already come in with half the hardware—crates full of AK-47s, machine guns, assorted ammo, wireless sets, rocket launchers, grenades, explosives, detonators. Though you have solved the problem of the small entrance door at the warehouse by blowing its hinges with Hatton rounds and then having the door refitted with new locks, Kohli is in a rather delicate position. If wind of his location gets around to military intelligence, it could blow the whistle on your operation. With Kohli, you are doubly worried because, through your sources, you know that he is on deputation with an elite agency nobody knows anything about. And even at your last meeting with him at Kupwara, he was basically on leave from the agency and not supposed to be with his parent unit, 5 Kumaon.

Though you don't tell him you know, you are worried about the position he is in.

Breach of discipline by army personnel invites a new kind of wrath from divisional HQ. Especially if you have been yahoo enough to ram into a police wireless van broadside at thirty miles an hour, breaking about thirty bones in three night-beat constables, six hundred miles from where you are supposed to be. It raises all manner of questions.

All of which qualified personnel will try to answer during Kohli's interrogation. The scrutiny will be relentless and revealing. Right now, Kohli is in police custody. Within twenty-four hours, he will have to appear before a judicial magistrate, who could sentence him to remain in police custody for a maximum of two weeks. He could also be given bail. But even though Major Kohli is traveling under the alias of Major Joseph, exposing him to a police interrogation at this delicate stage of your operations is fraught with risk. Different intelligence agencies might start getting wind of things. Especially if they began examining the crates at the back of Major Kohli's truck.

Even though Kohli might be your man to organize ambushes, his skills won't extend to staving off mind probes by the likes of Colonel Chowdhary.

And the colonel, you fear, might be closer to the gig than you gave him credit for. In which case, Kohli will be like a bone to a pack of dingoes.

But time is on your side. It is three hours since Kohli went in, and it's still just five in the morning. If only he hadn't hit the police van right in front of police HQ. On any of the other local beats, things could have been quietly settled with a bit of monetary incentive. You can hit a lot of the locals in this part of the world if you have a little cash to spare. Besides, it was a wireless van, the thing with an antenna on the top. You can't hush one of those. The sound bites were on the air, and HQ preserves a recording for three straight days of talk on the air. This you know from having been on the crime beat as a cub reporter for the *Indian Express*.

But you have to deal with these sorts of unforeseen eventualities if you want to keep up your part of the game.

You view the spread before you. Your personal weapon these days is the Glock that Major Rodriguez gave you when you left Kupwara. It's the same weapon he had handed over to Capt. Satish Warrier, with rather tragic consequences. You were able to fly it out from Srinagar because you didn't use civilian transport. The army doesn't bother frisking you on its runs to Delhi.

You are reviewing your hardware purely as a last option, the nuke on your shoulders if the situation gets unpleasant. The last thing you want is a shoot-out at police HQ. Although you aren't too nervous about the outcome. You have confidence in your superior firepower and the intrinsic motherfucking capabilities of Gulab Chand, Indramani, and yourself. What you would like to be spared is the negative fallout that would accrue from the shooting. Unnecessary media attention, plus the fact of the casualties themselves.

Still, the motherfucked nature of the police calls for specialist treatment. This you have to weigh against the fact that you would be leaving telltale evidence behind in the shape of lead in victims. Not very many people have access to the kind of ammunition you plan to go in with.

You look at the choices at your disposal. The hollow-point projectile designed to expand on impact, ensuring high-energy transfer in human tissue. But the jackets on these are too weak. They could rupture even if they hit the chain around your neck or a brass button. There's also the semi-wad-cutter bullet, which cuts a core out of the flesh, rather than letting the wound channel close after it. In short, you bleed to death. But that's not your choice. What you are looking for is a slug that combines maximum speed of incapacitation with zero sneak-out capability. Of course, that assumes maximum body penetration, which gets a black mark in your standard police manual.

You have the luxury to go for fourth-generation Special Forces ammo. The high-energy dump, reliable, no ricochet, no shoot-through projectile. You could choose the Glaser safety slug. Fired at nineteen hundred feet per second, its cap ruptures, releasing spheres in your body, causing systematic shock and immediate liquidation. The thing with this bullet is that you get no chance to walk up to the guy and say, "Sorry, buddy. I was actually aiming at the guy next to you." At eight dollars a round, it's also costly, but that's the least of your worries.

Another option is to use an accelerated-energy-transfer slug. The German Gecko action or the British Equally. Gecko's a hollow bullet with a plastic core. The core's displaced as you fire the bullet, and once it hits the target, its construction causes it to tumble through. But it cannot penetrate angled cover. Equally, on the other hand, has a specialist anti-hijack role, but it can be fired only from a revolver. The advantage of this slug is that you can stop it in four inches of Lux soap.

But what you load is French THV rounds. The reverse-ogive ballistics make it the closest to the perfect CQC round ever made. With a forward protrusion and a velocity of 2,700 feet per second, it has an AET profile in a ninety-degree arc throughout the bullet's path. It causes hydrostatic damage of grave dimensions.

You also pack a Remington 870 shotgun. The advantage of twelve-gauge is that you can shoot a variety of cartridges, from grenades to the Hatton to the CS gas Ferret. Gas, you think, could be your ace in the hole. Keeping that in mind, you have also packed a MARK-12C tear-gas-cum-fog generator that can pulse-jet fifty thousand cubic feet of gas in about ten seconds. An antiriot weapon that you presume Major Rodriguez uses to flush out Mossies from attics and under floor planks. If you take gas, you cannot but throw in three rubberized respirators for your rescue team.

Your main weapon in case Operation Flush Out goes sour is the Heckler & Koch MP5SD submachine gun. The silent version of the MP5, it has a laser-lock device, and its primary feature is that it lets off its slugs below the speed of sound, which prevents bullet boom. You also throw in a dozen E182 multiburst disorientation grenades with high decibel levels and half a dozen rapid-opening Dart cord-frame charges to blow precision holes through steel frameworks and concrete.

You pack all these in two Nike tennis bags. Though your hardware backup is of GSG9 quality, you are low on planning. You have had one of the 5 Kumaon lads nick a staff Gypsy from the motor pool at 16 Brigade headquarters, which is twenty minutes' driving time from the warehouse. One of the ones that have red flashers on the top and a siren. You plan to ride into police HQ with siren blazing and numb the DSP on duty with your audiovisual entrance. You wear a colonel's army uniform, and Gulab Chand and Indramani dress in NSG regalia. An army officer flanked with two black cats, siren on and lights flashing, with some kind of funky music emanating from the Gypsy, which you discover has a stereo system—that's your plan to disable police brainpower and introduce a high compliance factor.

You have typed an impressive release order on regular army stationery and signed it with a bogus name, stamping it with a very authoritative-looking seal. You could have also forged a bail release order from the court of a night magistrate in New Delhi, but that would have looked even more dubious. You have a backup team of two following you in a stolen Maruti. They've been assigned just one primary task: to speed off with the impounded truck, which is still parked outside on the main street, instead of in the police garage.

Yes, you have dark glasses on and a fake mustache.

You couldn't pull off anything with a cuckoo plan like this at Scotland Yard, say, but Delhi police HQ is a softer proposition, a mazeland of Jats who might take your MARK-12C gas generator as some kind of fancy television apparatus. Besides, you also have a basic reason why you want to push with the plan fast, instead of waiting for the imminent arrival of Major Rodriguez, who would be more adept at thinking these things out. So far, he has come out superior on every gig the two of you have slung. Operation Flush Out you plan as your own spunk, a leadership gambit to draw level.

And as Gulab Chand hits the porch of police HQ, running with his motherfucker gear on, and you get off the Gypsy with the air of one who is used to such things, the sleepy police personnel in the complaints area look at it as a moment of beauty, the likes of which they haven't seen in their lifetimes. Indramani covers you from the rear, and you walk with crisp steps to the desk of the inspector on duty, who gets up and salutes you. You hand over the impressive-looking envelope. Half a dozen civilian stragglers hang about the reception area, absorbing the scene. You ignore them.

"Yes, sir," he says. He handles the envelope like a piece of porcelain, afraid it might fall from his hands.

"Release orders for Major Joseph," you say. "From the prime minister's office."

"Yes, sir," he says again. You notice his pants are falling because his belt is unbuckled. His feet were way up on the counter when you came bursting in on him, displacing the cool of the place. But his eyes are riveted by the MP5SD that is hanging loosely from Gulab Chand's left shoulder. From his right is suspended the Nike bag.

"Where is he?" you ask. You nod at Gulab Chand and he zips open the Nike bag, revealing the barrel of the MARK-12C. Next, he and Indramani slip on their rubberized gas respirators. "There's very little time."

You plan to get the inspector from every direction. Give him no time to get his faculties in place. Already, his eyes have switched to the MARK-12C's barrel. He looks at it with awe. Gulab Chand lets off a squirt of gas, a quarter-of-a-second squeeze. About three feet of gas whooshes into the media briefing room. The civilians squatting on the bench in the reception area get up in panic.

"What's that?" asks the inspector. He hauls up his pants, tightens his belt. The letter is tucked under his chin. Sleepy police constables gather in a knot.

"DDT," says a civilian, trying to be helpful. You glare at him.

"Who's the seniormost officer here?" you ask. Your voice is tinged with impatience.

"The deputy commissioner of police has left for home. You can talk to me," he says.

You move behind the counter, put your arms around his shoulder, take the letter from his fingers, and tear open the envelope.

"This is the release order for Major Joseph, whose truck hit a wireless police van early this morning," you say in a whisper. "The truck was carrying radioactive material. You understand we have to decontaminate the place."

The inspector looks at you blankly. Evidently, the search engine in his brain is drawing a big neurotransmitter failure with words like *radioactive* and *decontaminate*.

"Nuclear material," you say, nodding. His eyes widen. He's heard of nuclear.

"The army man is downstairs in the basement lockup," he says.

"Good," you say. "Let him out."

He understands the order. The thing with all forces is to keep telling personnel what to do, since things crack up if they have time to think. He pulls a drawer to get out a bunch of keys, then walks downstairs rapidly. You follow him. So does your two-man crew.

"How many people got hurt?" you ask. You attempt to show the considerate face of the army. And yourself. The tough officer with a heart warm enough to care for the health of minor minions.

"Three," he says.

"How did it happen?" you ask.

"Nobody saw it. There was a big bang. The van got smashed," says the inspector.

"How are the men?"

"Leg and chest injuries," he says.

"Nobody in a coma, I hope," you say.

"No," he says.

"That's good. Where's the truck?" you ask, though you have seen it outside.

"It's parked on the road," he says.

"*On the road.* Shit," you say. "Indramani, go secure the truck."

The inspector watches Indramani go.

"Not to worry. We have guards there," he says. "I saw the crates inside the truck after the accident and put on a guard."

"I hope you didn't touch the truck," you say.

The inspector falters. He exhibits traits of neurotransmitter failure once again.

"I don't remember," he says.

"Just stand here," you say. You take your rubberized respirator from your pocket and pull it over his head. You push him face-first into the stair walls, knock his legs apart, and spread his hands. "We are going to decontaminate you. Just stand still."

The inspector is shivering. "What are you doing, sir?" he asks.

Gulab Chand is also slow to pick up on this. But you grab the barrel yourself and press the pulse trigger from ten feet away. The inspector disappears in a cloud of smoke.

"You can walk down now," you tell him. "This smoke is special. It kills all the radioactivity. You don't want to get cancer, do you?"

You see Major Kohli pacing in the lockup. He looks at you with considerable surprise. The inspector hands the keys over to the constable on duty. He unlocks the steel cage. It takes three keys. You slip the mask off the inspector and hand it to Kohli. The inspector sneezes.

"Captain Joseph, stand by for decontamination," you say. Kohli, who has watched the whole game from his cell, looks distinctly uncomfortable, but you repeat your orders.

"Captain Joseph, stand by for immediate decontamination," you say.

Kohli pulls on the respirator reluctantly, and then you whoosh him with a dose, too. You're beginning to enjoy this.

You walk up. Everything under control. But then a bit of leftover smoke drifts toward you and you borrow Gulab Chand's respirator. It is when you are taking the mask off, about to impress on the inspector the necessity of keeping all this under wraps for the next hour at least, that your mustache comes off with the rubber. What you have also failed to do for about three minutes since the release of Kohli is subject the inspector to constant sensory confusion. You have given him time to get his breathing rhythm back. You smile at the inspector. For the first time, you glance at the name tag on his uniform. RUKNAM SINGH, it reads.

Ruknam's face hardens. His instinct tells him there's something funny going on here. You can almost feel the whirring and clicking going on his head, the jingling of alarm bells. You stick the mustache back even as he looks at you, giving him time to make his play.

"I will have to consult with my superiors first," says Ruknam. You notice that the air of obeisance has disappeared. Logic is making a comeback. He reads the letter for the first time. It has an army HQ logo. "We are not supposed to take orders from the army. You said PMO. We will be delivering him at the court of the metropolitan magistrate in the morning. We have booked him for reckless driving."

Outside, Indramani has already backed the Gypsy up to the porch. You look at Gulab Chand. Kohli relieves him of the Nike bag. Indramani switches on the light and the siren. Ruknam stiffens. The cops start smelling the tension in the air.

"I think it's time we decontaminated the place," says Major Kohli.

But you want a very quiet exit. You move behind the counter once again. You put an arm around Inspector Ruknam Singh. Ruknam shrugs it off. But he's listening.

"We are officers on special duty," you say. "OSD. Heard of that?" Ruknam nods. "We have to use disguises so that people don't recognize us."

"But I just want to check with my superiors first," he says. "It will take two minutes." He picks up the receiver of his push-button BelTel.

"We can't stay," you tell him. You walk to the door. Gulab Chand and Kohli follow you.

"*Hello,*" says the inspector. "Ay, hello." He's not talking into the phone. He's shouting after you. You try not to hear.

"Hello, hands up," he shouts when you are two feet away from the main entrance. Three constables come hustling by. They block your exit. Ruknam is leveling his revolver straight at Major Kohli's chest.

"Cool it, will you," says Kohli. But Ruknam is in his Jat element. The scene, you figure, is getting more fucked by the minute. Gulab Chand is leveling his SMG at Ruknam, who still can't see it because Major Kohli is in the way, but then he moves, gives Gulab Chand a clear shot at Ruknam. You are thinking, Hell, this wasn't part of the plan; maybe he won't go for the heart. He doesn't. There's a small pop, like a cork falling limply off a champagne bottle, and the inspector's right wrist blows away. The revolver clatters to the floor. A triple-hammer precision maiming blow with THV rounds. Ruknam's stump starts bubbling blood. He is staring in shock at his wrist. He clutches the tip with his spare hand. He starts howling. A few sleeping cops in magenta boxer shorts come rushing out from an adjacent room. They walk right into a river of smoke.

Kohli has taken out the three constables blocking your way. They are still unsure about what happened when he put the MARK-12C on full release. He turns the barrel on the new arrivals. Even a savory dose for the civvies on the bench, all of whom scramble downstairs. You rush to the Gypsy. In ten seconds, police HQ looks like the place is on fire. Only there are no flames. Gulab Chand discourages any pursuers by dropping a few stun grenades. *Boom, boom, boom*, they go. Lightning flashes, 1-million-candela intensity. Gas billows out of the building.

You provide your own touch to the party. With your Remington 870, you knock out a tire each from the four police jeeps standing by the porch. Then all of you get into the Gypsy and get the hell out of there.

"Fuck," you say to no one in particular. "Why did my mustache have to come off?" You rip it off and chuck it out of the window. "Where's the truck?" you ask Indramani.

"They should be halfway to the warehouse by now," he says.

"Thanks, MM," says Major Kohli. He grins at you, then slaps Gulab Chand's back. You are happy to have done a good turn for Major Kohli. In the days ahead, you know, the time will come to reel in your favors.

At home, you find Karnam sleeping on your settee. You are surprised. One arm rests on her forehead; the other hangs down. In sleep, many things swim to the face that lie moored deep down during moments of consciousness. You see in the contours of her face an innocence that reminds you of another face, another time. Or maybe you put the innocence there. Sometimes you see what you want to see.

Lately, the woman in the one dream that you have has metamorphosed into Karnam. For the first time since Shomali went her way, you have begun to see some hope for yourself.

The highway you are on leads to doom sooner or later. What started you on it was your own sense of melodrama and the defeat and rejection you felt when Shomali left, leaving you with a void, a waiting, which you filled in with the chemical demands your body made, natural or artificial. You began to see life as a movie, in which your thing was to get a bang out of the play. Squeeze the juice out of the moves.

But always, even in that, there was also a sense of waiting for something that would bring an end to it all, a tether line stretching taut, putting brakes on your soaring. You think Karnam could be that tether. You haven't known her long, but in such things, it's the lava flow that matters.

You let her sleep. You slip out of uniform. You go to the kitchen and make some coffee. You are pouring the brew in a cup when you feel her hands encircle your waist, a body press against your own. A voice asks, "Nothing for me?"

"Honey, all of mine is yours," you say. You kiss her. Your lips brush her forehead. "How did you get in?"

"I came here late at night. Your door was open. I waited for you. I fell asleep," says Karnam.

"Lucky me," you say. You begin fixing another cup.

"Where were you?" she asks.

"Me? I am a night bird. I hunt for fun," you say.

"So, where's your prey? Should I be jealous?"

But you are moved from kissing her and aren't really listening. Incredibly, your eyes get wet and you catch a burst of sunshine through the sink window.

"Is something bothering you?" A hand rests on your shoulders.

"Lots of things," you say. But your weakness is a passing spasm, a bit of dust in the eyes. You regain control. "Sugar?" you ask.

"Let me finish it," she says. You let her take over. A woman in your kitchen. You go to the hammock that stretches on your balcony. You swing in soft rhythms of memory. Karnam comes and sits at your feet. With one hand, she sips her coffee; with the other, she halts your swinging.

"You remind me of someone I once knew," you say.

"Someone close?"

"Very."

"What happened?"

"Who can tell? It's over."

"Then why does it keep coming back?" she asks.

"Memory is something you cannot kill," you say. "What brought you here?"

"I thought maybe we could go somewhere."

"Your father must be worried to see you mixed up with someone like me."

"I doubt whether he's even noticed my absence," says Karnam.

"What happened between him and your mother?" Karnam's eyes falter for an instant and she avoids your gaze. There is something in this movement that warns you, but you can't get it right, and when you do, many days later, it's too late. "It's okay if you don't want to answer."

"No, it's not that. It's only that nobody ever asked before. They just assumed I wouldn't want to talk," says Karnam. "He developed this drinking problem, and with that came a lot of other things. You know what I mean. When we were here together and I was in school, I didn't understand, but I think my mother did the right thing by leaving. My grandfather was in the States. My mother went to him."

"How did they meet at all?" you ask.

"Oh, it was an arranged marriage. Lots of dowry and stuff. That's the money that started off Father's printing press and his publishing business," says Karnam.

"Your mother married again?" you ask.

"No. But she had her flings after Grandfather passed away," says Karnam.

"Around the same time that you met the Syrian?" you ask.

"Yes. Why did you ask about Yakub?"

"Strange fucking guy. You didn't make that one up, did you?" Karnam looks hurt. "I'm just asking."

"Why would I make it up?" asks Karnam.

"Women have their reasons," you say.

"Not death."

"You got a photograph of the guy?" you ask.

"Not here. I mean not in India. It was a painful episode," says Karnam. "But what's that snap of yours there in uniform?"

"National Defense Academy, 1985," you say.

"You were in the army?"

"Training to be there," you say.

"Tell me about yourself. Why did you leave?"

"Nobody leaves the army. I got sacked."

"What for?"

"It's part of a long story. It begins way back. I don't think you would have the patience," you say.

"Try me," pleads Karnam.

So you tell her the crazy fucking story of your life. Not the *whole* story, but very close to it. In your life, rebellious patterns emerged at the age of thirteen. One fine day, you boated all the way from Allahabad to Benares on the Ganges with four other buddies, a physical jamboree that took you all of five days. While your friends were part of the National Cadets Corp rowing team and earned valuable credits for their actions, your presence had more to do with the spirit of expedition. In the holy city, you split and embarked upon a project of self-discovery.

One of the good things about life is that you never can tell what is going to come next, and when one day you sat next to a Dutch plumber who was on a six-month trip to India, things suddenly changed. You sat watching the boats slip by on the river and the wrestlers doing their evening routine, when he suddenly turned to you and revealed why he liked the ghats so much. "This is the only place in the world," he said, "where you can have a conversation and a goat can come and sit next to you. No problem." His name was Juster. You couldn't get the pronunciation right, but he liked you well enough to invite you back to the seedy hotel he was staying in to meet his wife, Patricia. Your own accommodations were a matter of chance and convenience. Strangely, the couple didn't mind you bunking with them for the remaining five days that you planned to stay in town. It was Patricia who gave your impulsiveness a new direction altogether.

And it all began in a quirky sort of way. She sat sketching the fishermen on the river, and when she finished, she showed you the sketches she had done over the past four months. Of the rains in Gauhati, the tea gardens at Darjeeling, the tigers at Corbett, the Gypsies on the trail in Rajasthan. In the desert, two camels mating under the sun.

"They couldn't do it by themselves," said Patricia mischievously. "They had to be helped by the people. They were too clumsy." You looked at her with all the seductive hope of a thirteen-year-old and asked, "Are you?" The first time you did it was the same afternoon when Juster went to Bodh Gaya alone because you and Patricia, with tacit connivance, dropped out of the cultural trip. You were about the same height as she was, and her breasts made a perfect fit in your palms. You couldn't come that first time, but she did, and you remember this with pride even today. You also remember her scent that first time; it was somehow different from the other times that you did it with her over the next two months. It was a mix of jasmine and lavender; that's the closest you can come to describing it.

Over the next four days in Benares, Patricia, besides keeping you tubed, was the first person to introduce you to the thrill of risks. You discovered that sex in itself was great but that it somehow became greater if you did it while Juster was having his bath or had gone to the local shop to get some mosquito repellent. The risk of discovery and all that followed with it spurred the pleasure factor to unimaginable heights. And soon, when the time came to say good-bye, Patricia invited you to accompany her to Cochin. She was splitting with Juster for the remaining part of the trip, he going to Sikkim and Patricia longing for the greens of Kerala.

Of course, you had school. You argued that sex and tourism for two months was a better choice than sharpening your trigonometry. The kind of school you were in didn't bust you on attendance. They just asked you to pay a fine of fifty bucks for every day your name drew a blank at roll call. Also, your old man gave you a reason to go when you landed at home with Patricia in tow and made your intentions open. He got depressed and sulky and then threatened to chuck you out of the house. Your mother wasn't in that evening, and even though she wouldn't have been able to stop your father, he might have been more considerate with her around. Your father seemed to have given up on you. Of course, you didn't know then how troubling your juvenile escapades were to your father.

So you split for the south. Though Patricia was exactly double your age, it didn't put any noticeable crimp in your relationship. Sex, you discovered, was a universal language. It didn't need a cultural unipolarity to get itself going, nor did the Dutch do it in places where any enterprising couple anywhere wouldn't, given opportunity and a feeling of privacy. Sometimes, when need was great, you felt that privacy itself was a discountable commodity. For instance, on the train trip to Kerala, the loo often wasn't the best place to satisfy your urges. Balance was difficult and the smell and sights were mood suppressors. So one night, the two of you said fuck it and huddled together on a second-class air-conditioned upper berth. You drew the blanket around you and innovated an angle that could do without the luxury of space. There was a thrill here, too. In the berth facing you, an old man in his sixties snored. His closed eyes faced you, and your moments of decadence were punctuated by anxious looks in his direction.

The next morning, there was the strong smell of spunk in your cubicle, and the young mother on the lower berth looked at the two of you with great disgust and refused to be drawn into your unfinished conversation from the day before. But, then as now, social casualties didn't ruffle your feathers.

Patricia checked in to a small hotel in Cochin, and the first thing the two of you did was go on a backwater cruise to Alleppey and then all the way down to Trivandrum. The tourists hadn't discovered the ride yet. The two of you rode alone in a thatched grain boat with a crew of two, who cooked you rice and curry and kept Patricia high on local toddy.

At Cochin, you became friendly with Nicky, who ran an antique furniture shop in the Jewish area of Matanacheri. Nicky soon warmed to your bantering skills and asked you to help out in his shop for a few weeks, since his deputy had gone on leave. You sold beds, desks, chairs, drawers with fancy mirrors, pillars, tables—anything. Two-hundred-year-old Malabar teak was a great selling point with foreigners, who had the stuff shipped out to Europe and the Americas. Nicky bought the stuff at dirt-cheap prices from ancestral houses in villages, had his carpenters spruce up the piece bought, then arranged for the shipping.

Your part in the scam was to provide a historical perspective on the wooden pieces, sell them as an exalted heritage. It was at Nicky's that you first learned the art of bullshitting. You took a 5 percent cut on each piece you sold. Your style of operation was simple.

This is how you would spin your yarn: "The term *antique* is very loosely focused these days, sir. What most dealers might pass off as an antique will not be more than forty years old. But if you look in the dictionary, sir, it is described as a work of art or handicraft that is more than a hundred years old. It's not that they want to cheat you, but history, except in a very superficial sense, is not one of their strong points. There's a trend these days, sir, to buy furniture not because of its good quality or for the love of it but as an investment or as a means to show off. But you don't look that type, sir. We don't encourage this kind of buyer.

"Now, I don't know the reason you are looking for a heavily carved piece. Restorers like us don't like those kind of pieces. It's the dealers who love them. They make easy money on them. But we call them 'dust-gatherers.' We like the pieces we sell to be well cared for, and bulky and impractical constructions, our research shows, are the most neglected in people's homes. Besides, with space becoming a constraint these days, simple designs that take very little space and are easy to maintain are what most people look for. But I guess, sir, if you are insisting on a heavily carved writing bureau, it must be because you want to make it the central aspect of your living room or study. That is usually recommended, for then the furniture complements the living space, and because of having a function, it doesn't look stressful to the eyes. Now, this piece here, sir, is what I would suggest you take a good look at. It's a rosewood construction with, as you can see, ten side drawers. The legs are carved in a floral motif, and on the sides, you can notice delicate brass inlay. It's a very heavy piece. We like to show all our buyers the raw pieces before we restore them, so that you can judge for yourself whether it is genuine. You can estimate the age of this piece by a look at the joinery, sir, and the age of the bolts and the hinges. This is from the Wadiyar period, sir. My great-grandfather was a minor functionary in their state. You can see, sir, this is seasoned wood and at least a hundred and fifty years old. The wood isn't bent or cracked. While restoring it, we take care not to alter the original proportions, since that violates the basic design principle of the antique. We also don't believe in painting or varnishing furniture. That's not part of our philosophy. We like to highlight the natural grain in the wood, and that comes out best if we give a sandpaper finish and then wax the wood. But the piece is expensive, sir. It will cost you one hundred thousand rupees, plus cartage.

"If you want a reproduction, we have another branch that deals exclusively in that, sir. We are fortunate enough to have an excellent team of duplicators who make some of the most elegant reproductions of all styles, even Western. But even that would be about half the price. You see, sir, we don't compromise on the quality of wood we use. There are some dealers around here who would try to pass off red *paduk* wood as teak and you wouldn't know the difference. But you will in five years, when your piece cracks right down the middle. What we use here is white cedar, not even rosewood. And white cedar has so many knots on the surface that you have to go right down to get a smooth surface. It takes a lot of work. Also, we don't ever reproduce furniture on the basis of photographs. South Indian furniture is so structurally correct that unless you have an authentic life-size piece, it's a fallacy to think that you could reproduce the design.

"Of course, you can do it with the French, Portuguese, and Dutch colonial furniture, because that's well documented. What I would like to tip you off with, sir, is that the real antiques are selling in the market like hotcakes. There are so few of them around these days. If you came again next year, there might not be any left. Most of the things you see here have already been sold. That hat stand, for instance, is going to a London connoisseur. He's crazy about hats and where you put them. And camphor chests with the strong fragrance are so rare, you have buyers killing each other to get hold of one of them. Then you have these interior decorators from Bombay coming here with these aesthetic ideas. They would sell their mother for these Vasco da Gama teak barrels that we have. They are willing to pay any price to convert about five of them into a bar counter. My brother Nicky told them to get lost. He considers them family heirlooms. You see, sir, Vasco da Gama was this Portuguese guy. You will see his grave in a church right down the road. It's a tourist spot. He came here in the sixteenth century. Those barrels are from that period. My family has this special secret of keeping wood intact. It's like an invisible paint. It's a combination of formaldehyde and secret herbs that only we know about. My brother Nicky goes and collects them once a year from the Nilgiri Hills. He is supposed to pass on the secret to his son, but he isn't married yet. He has a girlfriend, though. We are hoping something will happen soon. You see, sir, ours is a very traditional family. For us, furniture is a passion, sir. We make a living out of it, and when you make a living out of something in India, it becomes a religious kind of thing. You wouldn't believe it, sir, but we have things laid down by our ancestors. For example, the kind of bed my brother Nicky has to sleep in on the first night of his wedding. It's a Chettinad-style bed. It has inserts for old ceramic tiles. An Austrian was here a couple of months back, and my brother invited him over for lunch. We took him around the house and he came upon the bed. He offered us fifty thousand dollars for the bed straightaway, Visa card. We told him no. Dealers around here, they consider us crazy for holding on to principles like that. But my brother Nicky says if a guy doesn't respect what his family told him, he is like a straw in the wind. He is going to be tossed all over the place. He's going to have no peace."

You could hardly believe it when people fell for this kind of spiel. Nicky himself couldn't. He made me write down my speeches once so he could have a go. It was his bad luck to run into Maj. Ed Friske of Edwards Air Force Base. Friske was a test pilot, and he flew jets at twice the speed of sound over the Mojave Desert to see if all the nuts and bolts in the aircraft would remain tight if he pointed the nose of his flying bird down at the ground and pressed the throttle. These test pilots, you learned at the age of fourteen, were a special breed of men. What brought him to Cochin was his girlfriend, who was Jewish and doing her doctorate on the Jews of Cochin. There were about three hundred of them around, and their ancestors had come to India at the time of the Crusades. All Friske was interested in was shipping a chaise longue back home to Edwards Air Force Base, but Nicky opened up on him with your speech, which he had gotten down by rote. This one was about adapting antiques into pieces of furniture for everyday use. Nicky was tearing into Friske. "You could, for instance, turn this wooden nineteenth-century bucket into an umbrella stand." Friske stared at him the way he might have stared at a Lockheed aerodynamics engineer who had just sent him up on a plane with a faulty left wing.

But Nicky went on. "We could turn these carved legs from the Queen Anne–style four-poster bed into table lamps."

Friske shivered. "Will you shut the fuck up," he said. "All I want is a chaise longue. I want to use it like a love seat. What the fuck would I do with lamps?" But Nicky couldn't take hints even of this magnitude. He pressed on. "We could take the headboards of this Victorian-style bed and craft a crockery case for you. No problem. Or, see this low Burma teak trunk? We could turn it into a drum seat for your bar."

By now, you could see that Friske had had about enough of it all. "You see this palm of mine," he said, "I can turn it into a Stone Age nutcracker." Then he grabbed Nicky by the balls and set him up on a wooden elephant with ivory work from the Warrangal period. That was the end of Nicky polishing up on your speeches. But you got friendly with Major Friske and traveled with him around Cochin in your spare time. He instilled in you the desire to fly supersonic jets.

And now three months of selling antiques had netted you enough dough to put you through university in style. You didn't stretch it long with Nicky, though, after Patricia split for home. She discovered that she was pregnant. That was the end of your relationship. She freaked out. Even you got scared. She didn't want to have an abortion in India. She didn't trust Indian medical facilities. She flew home. That was the last time you saw her, and when you try to remember her face, it doesn't come to you in one piece, but like a fragmented negative that you have to piece together, a visual jigsaw puzzle. That was the end of a period in your life.

You went back home, and things had changed between you and your parents. You swam in a deluge of space. You caught your father on a couple of occasions brushing up on a childrearing book. One day, he even called you over in a gruff voice and told you about the facts of life, while you listened with proper decorum. Life, he told you, was about rules and following them. He wanted you to focus on the days and years ahead. For some strange reason, he wanted you to join the armed forces. Like father, like son. Over the last many months, you had given him cause for too much hypertension. You loved your old man. Even more so your mother.

And in 1985, at the behest of both, you took the Academy exams and passed them. Only the air force guys busted you in the medicals for the lack of stress-bearing capabilities in your spinal column. They said your vertebra were stuck so close together, ejection would be a problem. You tried some humor. You said you had been ejecting since thirteen, with hardly any mechanical problems at all, but they cold-shouldered you and shunted you to the army, which you had given as a second preference. You weren't really keen on joining the army, but your father prevailed. This was the second stage of your learning process.

It was at the NDA that you first fell in love. You met Shomali. She was Lt. Col. Ravi Kumar's thirty-year-old wife. You were eighteen. The way you met was when Colonel Kumar requested you to chauffeur Shomali to Bombay and back one weekend. Shomali's mother was in bad shape—severe asthma. She was stuck up in an oxygen tent at Jaslok Hospital. Your deportment was the very best. You drove considerately, offered the right kind of commiseration, brought medicines, and spent time with her mother. That made Shomali start off with a special feeling toward you, the kind that comes your way when you help people in need.

But gratitude is not what you look for when you fall for a woman, though it does help in sneaking an entry through the perimeter fences. You soon discovered that Shomali was a very lonely woman. Colonel Kumar was a fitness freak. One of the things that he introduced at the Academy was archery. But for all his flowing deltoids, he couldn't swing it in bed. This is where you came in. Shomali was the best thing that happened to you after Patricia. Even better. You felt a torrent of passion sweeping you, and she developed in you her need for a confidant.

One of the things she showed you after the first few weeks was the handkerchief she had embroidered with the initials of men she had been with. Yours were the eighth and last. She got you by your initials, MM. There were no initials that you recognized except Colonel Kumar's, and that made it a little less painful for you. But she volunteered the information that Sammy was the best she'd ever had. He was sixth on the list. She never told you who he was, and you never asked.

The way you would work out your timings was that she would phone you by the mess hall and pretend to be your mother calling long-distance. But she couldn't always do that with the colonel around, especially after he took to setting up a sixty-five-foot archery range in the backyard of his house. He would insist she help him out and try out the sport herself. Then, when he got out of the way, you wouldn't always be around the mess hall. You worked around this in a highly ingenious way. You got Cadet Mohan, a fresh batcher, to swing a flare packet out of the rafting and hiking club. The flares went up 3,250 feet and fell under a parachute half the size of a ladies' umbrella. They took about one minute to come down and were visible three miles away. The Academy was half that distance.

On weekends, when the colonel tried his hand on the golf course, things were a little smoother. You had time, and because the colonel went in the evening and stuck around there close to three hours, polishing his drive under the lights, you often took Shomali out for a drive to a hill point near Lonovala, one hour away. For you, Shomali was everything you had ever wanted in life. Your dreams fired on all cylinders. You probed the possibility of a serious alliance, but she laughed it off.

"This is it," she would say after a toss on the bed. "MM, learn to live *now*. I am here and so are you, and that's what there is to it." That was how she lived, and that's what is left in you of her after these many years. But even she crossed into the future, and that one transgression gave destiny the opening it was looking for.

"MM, I want your child," she said one fine day. You were combing your hair. The colonel was sterile. He fired blanks, and not even that lately.

"Why me?" you asked.

"Because I want my child to grow up like you," she said. That's how her moods were.

"Me. I am a born scumbag. What about Sammy?" you asked.

"No, not Sammy. You are wild, but it's a wildness I like. Sammy, he's *too* wild. And dangerous," she said. Then she laughed. "Sammy as father.

Ravi will kill me even if it's you, but maybe not as fast as with Sammy. You see, they are close. Sammy is Ravi's nephew on his sister's side."

"You serious?" you asked. You finished combing your hair and looked in her eyes.

"Very," she said.

"Better sort out the colonel first," you said.

"We will see when the time comes," she said. That's how she planned things. But you didn't see things that way. You saw in this an opportunity to make her your own. That's when you reassessed your priorities in life. You were getting sick of the Academy, and now Shomali was giving you a reason to move on. The thing about getting out of the Academy is to make them chuck you out, for though you can leave of your own free will, they make you fork out a pile of money to be able to do that. And right then, you were having cozy little dreams of setting up an antique store in Bombay with Nicky's help. Cash in on the leftover liquidity from three years back. That's when you recognized the opportunity that the shit-kicking of Cadet Mohan would present to facilitate your plans. Cadet Mohan was the favorite punching bag of cadets in the senior dorm. Was Cadet Mohan really as dumb as he looked, or could you provoke from him some deed that would outshine his previous misdemeanors, like asking a senior cadet to pass the salt at the mess table?

That was early on, and the first time that Cadet Mohan got an introduction to the Academy's predator-prey balance. Cadet Mohan was designated as the cadet in charge of salt, and for a fortnight his energies were channeled into fetching salt for any senior who felt the need to sprinkle some sodium chloride in his soup or lentils.

"Hey, you motherfucker, the salt's all stuck up in here."

"You asshole, can't you see whether the cap's screwed on tight before you tap the dumb thing over my soup? Now drink this fucking soup yourself."

"You got a problem with my face, asshole? You take two fucking minutes to come to my table with salt."

"You, Mohan. Sister-fucker. Stand up when you pass me the salt."

Cadet Mohan never got to eat that fortnight. The mileage he logged in fifteen days at the mess hall could have taken him all the way to Madras. You interceded on his behalf and got him off the hook, and after that, Cadet Mohan's gaze alighted upon you with great gratitude. But there was nothing you could do about the genetic dumbness in Cadet Mohan. His legend grew by leaps and bounds. He could dismantle and reassemble the Indian SLR in no time flat, but he couldn't hit a TV at forty yards. In drill, he passed out three times in a week. He got caught out by the warden about half a dozen times for keeping smokes and rubbers in his room. Cadet Mohan didn't smoke, but he took no security measures to disallow his room being used as a contraband storage dump. Cadet Mohan didn't fuck, either, and from the way he looked at girls, you knew that he was as fresh as they come.

You were around when the warden busted him for the rubbers. "What do you do with so many of them, three fucking dozen?" asked the warden.

Cadet Mohan squeezed the packing. Maybe he thought it was chewing gum inside the squeezable plastic with the slinky woman-on-the-beach photo. He gave the warden a dumb look. But the warden marked him out as a slimy deal, an operator he had to keep under constant surveillance. On top of that, Cadet Mohan came and confided to you one day that he had a heart condition. Angina strikes the young, too, sometimes, and he almost managed to give the doctors the slip at selection.

You tried to smooth things out for Cadet Mohan by taking him on as assistant cameraman for your amateur movie assignment. That way, he could duck evening games for a month, a compulsory for all cadets, and give his heart a break. One of the philosophies at the Academy was to splatter money at the cadets to sharpen their minds and bring out leadership qualities. One of the ways and means of doing that, the Academy thought, was handing over a video camera to a cadet and asking him to have a crack at celluloid. You had duly submitted your documentary proposal and Colonel Kumar had approved it. You wanted to replace the existing sixty-minute video on life at the Academy—which was all a bore—with an updated version, one that would film faculty activities, too, especially something as interesting as the colonel's archery range in the backyard of his house. That was what got the colonel hooked to your proposal among a dozen others.

You made Cadet Mohan do all the shit work. You taught him the camera basics and discovered that his special powers lay in things mechanical, gadgets that whirred and purred and that you could set up on tripods. Within a week, you even felt confident enough to send Cadet Mohan to Shomali's place to shoot the colonel twanging his bowstring.

That was when things started to go out of keel. You, however, came to know this only a couple of days later, when you sneaked Shomali's embroidered handkerchief out of the handbag she kept it in to have one of your periodical checks. You read a ninth set of initials. The initials were the same as yours, and it took you a little time to place things in perspective. You realized that Cadet Milind Mohan had notched his first score in life.

"The guy kept looking at my bra strap," said Shomali. "I felt sorry for him." That's how she was. She felt sorry for Cadet Mohan because he hadn't gotten to use his dick for anything other than pissing. She even got Cadet Mohan to put the whole thing on tape, and she played it for you on the colonel's Sony VCR. Cadet Mohan's ineptitude in the whole matter made you feel embarrassed for the Academy. Among the many blunders that you got to see on tape, the first one stood out. Cadet Mohan got so jerky in his movements as his excitement levels compounded that he went on cruise without taking off his trousers and, in the process, because of the series of complicated maneuvers that he involved himself in, he bruised his dick on the zipper of his pants.

"How could you do it with a guy like him?" you asked, hurt.

"It didn't mean anything, sweetie," said Shomali.

"It does to me," you said.

Of late, you had been harboring a delusion that there wouldn't ever be any ninth set of initials and that you could put a lid on her promiscuity with the evident zealousness of your love. The insight you drew was that maybe promiscuity was as genetic a factor as complexion. Also, for you to be happy with her, all you needed to have were enough moments to tip the scale on your side. For Shomali, you realized life consisted of a series of moments, and she had to drain each one dry. To think you could be there in all of them was an idea you had to get rid of.

"I want your child, remember," said Shomali.

And you went to work on that. You had been working on that the past three weeks. For you, it was the building of a complex emotional web that would help you entrap her. For her, it was one of the things she felt her womanhood was incomplete without. And one day, the paper turned pink. Life had taken root. You were happy. She was delirious for the first week, but then her fear index started rising to the red mark.

In the meantime, you put your plans to leave the Academy in active mode. You keyed up Cadet Mohan to take a confrontational stance with the seniors. Cadet Mohan was swimming in new confidence after his pathbreaking tryst, and you found it easy to harden his resolve. Cadet Mohan simply waited for an opportunity to defy a senior. He chose a particularly nasty specimen.

"Hey, you asshole, bring down the cricket kit from the gym," ordered Cadet Gaurav Bhanot.

Cadet Mohan swung around, gave his chin a military bearing, and said, "Asshole yourself, asshole. And get your own fucking kit." Then he walked out of the net area, where Cadet Bhanot was nailing down the spikes to anchor the matting.

Cadet Mohan showed considerable initiative to get out of spike-throwing range. After this suicidal show of aggression, his life at the Academy became a living hell. He was shunned by all and sundry, and one night they boxed him in a wooden crate and nailed it shut. You were the one who crowbarred him loose the next morning. At this point in the game, you decided to play your hand. You crafted a letter of complaint, addressed to the general in command, and took up cudgels on behalf of Cadet Mohan. This is how it went:

Sir, this is with special reference to the treatment of Cadet Mohan at the hands of senior cadets in the Academy, which happens to fall directly under your command. Cadet Mohan is an exceptionally sincere cadet and joined the Academy with every intention of subsequently being commissioned in the army, to be posted wherever he might be taken in the line of duty. As you might be aware of the rough initiation process that every new cadet has to endure at the Academy, I need not take it upon myself to brief you on that subject. But what has happened, sir, with respect to Cadet Mohan is that his initiation period seems to have been unnecessarily extended by certain misguided elements at the Academy. While I wouldn't have bothered to apprise you of the case if the ragging had been within bounds, in Cadet Mohan's case, it has exceeded all traditionally accepted parameters. Cadet Mohan is in grave physical danger. The other day, he was locked up in a wooden crate, and if I hadn't come upon the scene, he might have suffocated to death, leading to an inquiry that would have brought great ignominy upon our great Academy. I beseech that you seize upon the matter immediately and establish a fact-finding mission of your own that will help you identify the mischievous cadets and issue necessary warnings. You might also, sir, once and for all, issue Academy warnings on this pernicious practice of ragging, which is the only blemish in this world-standard Academy we Indians are proud to have.

You posted copies of the letter up in the mess hall and left one at Colonel Kumar's office. You became a new point of hostility at the Academy. But fresh cadets with little brainpower came up to you from the shadows and shook your hand to compliment you on your brave stand.

Your classmates looked at you like the rivets in your head were coming loose at one shot. Stage two in your plan was to increase hostility levels to a boiling point and divide the Academy into two clear factions.

But events moved beyond your control at this stage.

Shomali started harboring these big doubts that the baby might be Cadet Mohan's after all. Which eventuality was not something that even a broad-minded soul like yourself was willing to swallow. Fighting wars for Cadet Mohan on two fronts was not something you were keen to do. And even though there were dim statistical probabilities in Cadet Mohan's favor, the two of you decided it was better to nip such a possibility in the bud and start afresh. With this in mind, you arranged for an abortion at an upmarket clinic located near the Hotel Blue Diamond in Pune. The clinic catered to the demands and needs of Bhagwan Rajneesh's many thousands of disciples, who congregated in the city from all over the world. The doc you chose confided in you that nearly fifteen international couples came to him in a knocked-up condition every fortnight.

Perhaps the series of coincidences that eventually took place started from your choice of clinic, because Bhagwan Rajneesh's ashram was a stone's throw away, and three months back you had introduced Colonel Kumar to the Korean Zen archer Myung Mong, who taught his craft at the ashram. You had read about the archer in a local paper and it became your strategy to have the colonel interested in him, too. Not only was it a power-packed career move on your part, but it performed the excellent function of hauling the colonel away from home and providing you with many adulterous moments.

Events, however, become a matter of conjecture for you after the point you dropped Shomali off at the clinic over a weekend when the colonel was supposed to take off to Bombay with Mong, who had invited him to attend a series of his lectures on Zen and the Art of Archery.

That was the last time you saw Shomali, but you never knew that it would be so. She asked you whether there was a phone she could use in case she felt like calling you. You told her there was one down the hall.

You left a couple of coins with her. The last image you carry of her is the one where she was flipping through the latest issue of *India Today*. You kissed her on the forehead and promised to return that evening, when the doctor had scheduled her in the operating room. And then as you were leaving, she called you and gave you the best moment of your life. She took a case out from under her pillow. Her fingers eased a gold ring out of the case. "I was planning to give it to you later today, in the evening. But wear it now," she said. That was the first time you saw tears roll down her cheeks. "I am scared."

Those were her last words to you: "I am scared." You slipped the ring onto your finger. You still have it. But strangely, the way you remember her in the last few scenes is how she flipped through the magazine, rather than when she gave you the ring.

You doubt she ever made it to the OR. This is what you think happened, from the bits and pieces that you heard and what came out in the papers. Nobody bothered to ask you the important questions, and you didn't volunteer to give leading answers. The colonel, you know for a fact, in his newfound enthusiasm, intended to tape archer Mong's lectures at the YMCA in Bombay. He had come and collected the video camera from you for that very purpose. Though relations between you and the colonel had become a little frosty after your letter to the general, it didn't stop him from commissioning the services of Cadet Mohan for handling the camera in Bombay.

You suspect that sometime during the day, after the colonel had collected the camera and before Cadet Mohan was supposed to join the colonel at his place, from where they were to proceed to the hotel Mong put up in and leave in the bus he had hired, the colonel checked Shomali's drawers for a blank videocassette. And that led him unsuspectingly to the tape that recorded in explicit detail the sexual bungling of Cadet Mohan. You figure it was foolish of Shomali not to have erased it or kept it in a discreet place, but her whole personality was one big self-destruct button. That was the way she was wired. The colonel lost it after that. But he maintained his outward composure.

You don't think the colonel really planned out the violent things that happened at this stage. That is, before Cadet Mohan dropped in on him. But Cadet Mohan's immediate presence might have put too much pressure on the colonel's disturbed sensibilities. It must have pressed some trigger in him somewhere, a secret spring that set a vendetta in motion. Then again, it might have been limited to Cadet Mohan, if not for another evil coincidence. You suspect that when the colonel dropped by Mong's hotel, which was right across from the clinic you had brought Shomali to, he spotted her across the road, standing in the hallway where the pay phone was. You infer that Cadet Mohan also must have seen her, and since he was too dumb to put two and two together and take precautionary skin-saving measures, he might have been the first person to go across and say hello right under the colonel's nose, thus sealing his own fate.

The next bit you know from Mong's statement to the police. He said, "The colonel told me to proceed without him. He said he would catch up with me in Bombay the next day. He said he wanted to film something very interesting that I could show in one of my archery lectures."

So maybe the colonel swung some filming number and took Shomali and Cadet Mohan back home. You don't know what story Shomali invented about her being there. She was ingenious in these matters. She couldn't have known that the colonel's gunpowder was dry and the cannonballs were on their way.

At this point, you have the colonel's statement to aid you. He said, "I wanted to shoot an apple off Cadet Mohan's head. I wanted to surprise Myung Mong with the proficiency I had reached under his guidance. Only, as luck would have it, the arrow slipped from my hands and it went through Cadet Mohan's chest."

The tip went through the other side. It split the ventricles in Cadet

Mohan's heart from thirty feet. You don't know how long death took in coming for Cadet Mohan, but he got no medical attention.

Of course, Cadet Mohan's death was no mournful matter for anybody but his parents, and you used it to twist the Academy's arm to gain you a swift release. You hinted that maybe there was a link between Cadet Mohan's death and what you had warned the authorities about. You didn't do it to fuck Col. Ravi Kumar. You had no need to. He blew his own head off two days later with a Browning. And you figured that with him gone, you could use even his death to help your case.

You claimed you feared for your life. The army bigwigs, already swimming in a lot of mud from the episode involving the colonel, thought it prudent to cut your lines, for fear you might talk to the press, give the media some gibberish that would skewer them some more over the coals. It had become a national media event. The colonel's archery range became a coveted visual on Doordarshan.

You aren't quite sure why the colonel whacked his brains out. He couldn't have become sorrowful over the killing of Cadet Mohan. That must have been the one big pleasant memory he carried to his cremation pyre. Maybe it was Shomali's lack of fidelity. You don't know what transpired between the colonel and Shomali after Cadet Mohan's departure from earthly life. Maybe she told him about her impregnation. Maybe he'd guessed it already. Maybe she told him about her plans with you. Or maybe just the shock of seeing somebody as fucked-up as Cadet Mohan doing his wife was the last straw.

Shomali learned about her husband's death while the MPs were questioning her about Cadet Mohan. They were considerate enough to understand the fucked-up dimensions in the case and let her go home to attend to Colonel Kumar's limp anatomy before they took it away for an autopsy. Cadet Rodriguez and Cadet Kohli escorted her home in the company of MPs. Sometime in the night, Shomali overdosed on four thousand milligrams of Amytal. They had to break open the doors to the house in the morning.

Why, you might ask, didn't you make an effort to meet Shomali in those crucial two days? The answer is simple. You didn't want to give the army or police a reason to step on you, fuck your chances of walking through the exit door at the Academy. You decided to wait out the storm. Besides, Colonel Kumar's death was a bonus to your future plans, and you didn't for a moment think it would rattle Shomali in the way that it apparently did.

You break your narration for Karnam here. There were many other things that happened in the episode with Shomali and also later with RAW. But those are your own memories. You don't tell Karnam about the posted note that you received from Shomali the day of her funeral: "Hi, sweetheart, what a mess. But I guess we could go ahead with the baby now. Let's take a leap of faith. Rest later. Love, S."

That threw you out of the daze of incomprehension you were dwelling in after you got news of her overdose. Things fell into place for you when the priest performed the last rites and you heard Cadet Kohli consoling Cadet Rodriguez. "Come on, Sammy," he said in a whisper, "you did what you had to do." That was the first time you got wind of Cadet Rodriguez's first name. It explained a lot of things to you, and life after this piece of intelligence was never the same for you. You hadn't known Cadet Rodriguez or Cadet Kohli personally. But a week later, a few days before you left the Academy for good, you walked into the room that Cadet Kohli shared with Cadet Rodriguez with your video camera. Cadet Kohli sat alone in the room. He was polishing his marching boots.

"I hear you have some interest in amateur filming. I was wondering if you could finish this documentary that I was working on. You know I am leaving the Academy," you said.

"Me, filming? You must be crazy."

"It's easy. All I want is someone who knows the difference between a video camera and a MILAN antitank system," you said. "Point and fire is not the only thing that there is to go by."

"My Minolta fits in my palms. All I have to do is press the shutter. It's auto everything. Does all your focusing for you. This thing looks like a rhino's ass to me," said Cadet Kohli.

"It's the same principle. All you have to use is common sense. If Cadet Mohan could figure it out, so can you," you said.

But before Cadet Kohli could answer, Rodriguez coughed from the doorway. He'd been listening for some time.

"How much have you shot already?" asked Cadet Rodriguez.

"Almost all of it. Just needed a few more shots of the colonel ripping his arrows to cap it all up, but now, I guess, someone will have to think of something else," you said. "Funny, why the colonel's hand slipped. I have seen him do better than knock apples off people's heads. He could nail a lizard at forty yards, upwind."

"You have shots of his archery range?" asked Cadet Rodriguez.

"Yeah. Cadet Mohan got them. That's what must have given him the balls to go ahead with the colonel's suggestion. You see, he was there with me when the colonel split the lizard," you said. "The colonel, I felt sorry for him. I mean, doing Mohan like that. It obviously broke his heart. I guess, when you feel like that, all you can do is knock yourself off. What do you think?"

Cadet Rodriguez eyed you coldly. "This camera of yours, can you lend it for a while? I have to check a couple of videos," he said.

"Man, why do you want to borrow it? You can keep it is what I'm saying. All you have to do is take a couple more shots and knock thirty minutes in shape," you said.

"Okay," said Cadet Rodriguez.

"Thanks, buddy. This thing was hanging around my neck," you said.

Of course, you knew which videos Rodriguez wanted to check out. What you couldn't understand was how he'd figured the whole thing out without seeing the video. Maybe, you thought, the colonel told him. Or he happened to see a portion of it with Shomali that crucial night when he escorted her home. And in a flush of anger he decided to snuff

Shomali out with the Amatyl that the colonel kept to tranquilize himself before archery competitions. There were a lot of maybes.

"All you have to know is a couple of things with this shit out here. This takes the lenses forward and this backward. After you get a grab on focus, you get the thing rolling with this button here. Remember, when you pan the camera, you have to do it without any jerks. And flick on the mike switch when you are doing a talking shot. Another thing you guys will have to figure out is the background score."

"That's more up my street," said Cadet Kohli.

You zoomed the camera at Cadet Rodriguez's section of the room, your eyes glued to the eyepiece. You looked for something that could incriminate Cadet Rodriguez a bit more in your eyes.

"This zoom allows you to take a close-up shot from far away. If you don't want the subject to know you are filming him, this is the way to do it," you said. You sat on Cadet Rodriguez's bunk. Rodriguez pulled his pillow out of the way to give you more space. What you saw through the lenses got the blood rushing to your face. You saw Shomali's embroidered handkerchief on Cadet Rodriguez's bunk. Cadet Rodriguez pocketed it with one fluid movement of his right hand.

"That's it. It's all yours, guys. Just remember to put me in the credits," you said, leaving the camera.

"Hey, MM," said Cadet Rodriguez as you were leaving. "I never did know what your initials stood for."

"Minty Mehta," you said. Cadet Rodriguez had a very crude way of checking on facts.

"Very unlucky initials to have around these parts," said Rodriguez.

"Why do you think I am moving my ass," you said. "Milind Mohan gets knocked by an arrow through his chest. That guy Mong, I heard, slipped in Bombay and broke his fucking leg."

Cadet Rodriguez blinked. He looked like he had just solved a crossword puzzle. "Why, what was Mong's first name?"

"Myung," you said. "Fancy having a name like that. But he was a deadly shot. I have seen him take out a flying pigeon fifty yards at the colonel's place."

"He went there often?" asked Rodriguez. His voice shook with some kind of inner turmoil.

"The colonel and he were like this," you said, entwining two fingers. "He canceled his lecture tour in Bombay after he heard the news. Even the colonel's wife took to archery because of Mong. She didn't like it at the start."

"Yeah," said Rodriguez.

"Fancy her going like this. She had so much life left in her," you said. You watched Cadet Rodriguez closely. But you saw nothing. Cadet Rodriguez could gum his emotions successfully from the start of his motherfucking career.

"Here, MM," he said, handing you a joint. "Keep me posted wherever you are."

Even in those early days, Rodriguez was a big fan of grass. You were, too, and on a few occasions you rolled some joints together. That was the extent of your interaction.

That was the last you saw of him for more than a decade, but you didn't forget him. You kept a constant update on his whereabouts, waiting for something to come along that would allow you to even up the score. A simple hit wasn't what you were looking at. You wanted something theatrical.

Then one day, a month after you broke the nuclear submarine deal at *News Today*, you got a call from the RAW chief. You went and met him. He didn't beat around the bush.

"MM, would you like to work with us?" he asked.

Of course, that didn't mean that you started at the top of the heap. They had you examined by a psychiatrist and gave you detailed questionnaires to fill out. They asked you everything possible, from your attitude toward killing someone for your country to what you thought about democracy. You had to take three months' leave without pay just to let them be able to pick and poke at your brain every four days. You went through four lie-detector tests and had a two-month training session, a condensed version of the one they unplugged on their own regulars.

One of the first lessons you learned of the trade was that paranoia is a plus in the spying business.

You learned to construct covers. You learned how to follow in groups and individually in "busy" and "slow" areas. You had to inculcate the strategic concept of space and time. Learn to estimate the distance the subject you were following could cover in a certain period of time. You could lose sight of your subject at a street corner, and by the time you arrived at the same spot, he or she could have disappeared. You would then have to calculate whether, in the time that you didn't have sight of your subject, he or she could or could not have made it to the next crossing. If not, you would examine the bus stops and the buildings on the street, or simply wait for the subject to come out of one of the buildings.

Of course, once you had grasped the basics of following, you were initiated into the technique of being able to tell when you yourself were being followed. It's a method the RAW calls "road routine."

You were assigned a particular route, and at a fixed time of day, you left to do the route. At the end of it, you were to write a report stating whether you had been followed or not, and if so, by how many people and what they looked like.

You learned that in the business of espionage, it's as important to know that you haven't been followed as it is to know that you have been. In the paranoid profession you were embarking on, it is dangerous to know you are being followed, for it then raises questions of who, why, and where. One golden maxim you also learned is the thing never to do if you are being followed. You can't afford to lose your pursuer, for if you do, you won't be able to verify whether indeed you are being followed and by whom and for what purpose.

You were also given to understand that in spite of the RAW chief's keenness to recruit you, it wasn't a fait accompli. You had to pass the tests and the training session. You remember one particularly torrid week—one in which they tried measuring your confidence levels and your presence of mind. Your instructor took you to Connaught Place and signaled the DLF building for you. "There," he said, pointing at the glass front of the third floor, which housed the British Airways ticket office, "I want you in that room with all the blinds drawn and standing next to a person in a suit for five minutes. I want you holding a glass of water."

What you did was go to the business center of the Park Hotel, which was opposite the DLF building. From there, you made a telephone call to the corporate communications department of British Airways. You talked to a lady called Diana Patrao. You told her that you were from the Special Protection Group attached to the prime minister's security and that the prime minister was due for a personal visit to the Park Hotel the next day. You therefore had to scout the neighboring buildings and place some men for surveillance in one of them. You told her that you would need to look around the British Airways office for a site that served your purpose.

You were there within five minutes. She gave you a tour of the premises and you reached the area your instructor had designated. She was hospitable enough to provide you with a glass of Coke to slake your summer thirst. The problem of a man with a suit remained. You therefore asked specifically for one such specimen, as the area in question was full of women doing teleticketing. Diana's eyebrows shot up in curiosity. You explained. You said that there was equipment in place in the Park Hotel that was even then, as the person in a light blue suit came and stood beside you, measuring the refractive index of the colored glass of the building so that it could tell you what color of suits the security men placed in the British Airways office would have to wear. They were suitably impressed. You told them to keep the entire thing hush-hush.

Of course, the next day you called to say that the prime minister's visit

had been canceled. You thanked them, nevertheless, for their cooperation.

Incidentally, you failed this particular test in the RAW manuals, as
your instructor for the day said that you were supposed to have had water, not Coke. And that you were supposed to have stood next to a person
with a suit only and not a woman as well.

In another such session, you were told by your handler to stop all traffic at the ring road near the Hyatt Regency Hotel for fifteen minutes. You
stole a Maruti 800 from the hotel's parking lot and crashed it into the side
of a Blue Line bus. You then got out groggily and lay convulsing on the
tarmac, your mouth frothing. The driver of the bus got the thrashing of
his life. The toughest part for you was keeping a record of the minutes
even as you lay there shaking, hot tarmac burning your skin. Eventually,
you got up. The crowd that had gathered around you cheered, and a police van came around to transport you to the emergency ward of the All
India Institute of Medical Sciences. From there, you disappeared within
five minutes.

You also learned special methods of communication and underwent a
weapons-training program.

That was the start of your career at RAW. You joined for the fun of it.
But the fun didn't last long. You were the first one to clue them in about
Dinesh Patel after he babbled to you the story about the Stingers during
a drunken weekend at his Antwerp home. Patel was running a scam so
simple and stupendous, he had the Americans eating out of his hand.

"How many Stingers do you think the United States pumped into
Afghanistan?" he asked you out of the blue. That was the way it started.

"Ronald Reagan didn't tell me," you said. You were on your second
Campari.

"Nearly two thousand. Now they want to buy them back," said Patel.
Typical American ass-backwardness. "You know what the going price for
a Stinger is?" You looked blankly at him.

"A hundred and fifty thousand U.S. That's if you take one to the American consulate at Delhi. In the beginning, you could even take a picture of a dismantled and destroyed system and claim your money, but the Americans have stopped that now," said Patel, winking at you. The softest route for getting Stingers out of Afghanistan was, in the words of Patel, through the Kashmir border. "It's too hot at the Iran border. They want the Stingers badly but don't pay as much as the Americans. Same with the central Asian republics."

This was hot news for you. Patel had so far gotten five dozen Stingers through to Delhi.

"What if one of them falls into the hands of the bad guys?" you asked him.

"Bad guys," said Patel, laughing. "Those are the guys I buy from. The Americans don't deal directly with them."

"What about the Indians?" you asked Patel.

He laughed again. "They sail right through at the border. U.S. dollars can buy you passages anywhere," he said.

"What about you?" you asked.

Patel's eyes widened. "Yeah, what about me?"

"Nobody wised up?"

"I sail between the raindrops, partner. Dollars are the best raincoat you can have."

It was Patel, incidentally, who put you on to 5 Kumaon a month after your Stinger conversation. He wanted you to check out the unit.

"Some officer called Major Rodriguez," he said, "contacted my man in Srinagar. They are talking big. Could you go and poke around?"

Ah, me, you thought, ah, me.

It didn't take long for RAW to understand the importance of the intelligence, and you became their chief field officer in Operation Kalashnikov. It didn't take you long, either, to figure out that the guys who ran RAW were no better than the border Mossies the army went toe-to-toe with. They saw Operation Kalashnikov not as a chance to entrap and nail the army sons of bitches but as a way to skim some liquid funds for the agency.

"We are facing a resource crunch," said the colonel. "How much do you think you can net us?"

The dictum you gathered at RAW was that conscience doesn't have a place in intelligence agencies. "It's the best thing that's happened to us in a decade," the colonel said, confiding in you one day. "Mossie arms moving out of the country and the money coming to RAW." The Wing, you figured, was still at loggerheads with the army after the Indian Peacekeeping Force debacle in Sri Lanka.

"What about the army? Personnel quality is going down the drain," you said. "The next you know, they might let the Mossies smuggle in a nuke to south block, punch the code under the PM's chair."

"We skim first," said the colonel. "We will nab the bastards after we are sitting on the bucks. You see, MM, arms remain in a region long after the conflict they were meant for. These are moving out. That's a plus. That they could be moving to Bosnia or Chechnya or wherever is also a plus. Any shit that happens elsewhere because of these arms is also a plus."

You couldn't deny RAW's logic. The officially captured inventory of arms was sitting in ordnance armories, netting no foreign exchange and fucking no region. And RAW couldn't use it. You had good vibes about RAW philosophy. It gave you an opening to make your own pile, unload some H on the world scene. It also let you have your little game with Major Rodriguez.

You have been silent for too long, musing over these things.

"It's a crazy story," says Karnam finally. Even she had to mull over in solitude the little you'd told her.

"We live in crazy times." Suddenly, you are sleepy, but you want to be awake for her, this island of sanity in the madness of your life. You lead her into your bedroom.

"I want you," you say, "like I have never wanted another woman." Which is strictly a lie, because there was Shomali, but she is dead and gone. In your mind, she seems to have come again to you in Karnam. A second innings.

"I know. I can see," says Karnam.

"No you can't," you say. "Unless you have felt that way yourself." You both lie on the bed. You draw her close to you. "I want to only if you do, too."

"Is there a choice?" she asks, and laughs.

Karnam is made for you. She is woolly, and you like women who are that way. The blackness of her hair stands out against the high cream of her skin and swarms you with desire. The sweat and grime from your sunup blitz envelops you in a strange aroma.

"I am dirty," you say.

"It's okay," she says. "This way is better."

A woman with a taste for salt. Her tongue moves over you. It checks the hollows of your armpits, first the left, then the other. It rolls in circles over the aureoles of your nipples. She lingers there. And it's the first time you feel aroused through your nipples. She snakes down, and your rod is like a mast, tall and full of direction. Her mouth goes down on you, and for a long while it's as if you exist just there, as if the rest of you is fossilized. You note the skill with which she takes all of you and you know that she's done it before, and instead of dampening your desire, it works the other way.

Her fingers clamp on to the base and her mouth goes up and down in soft, slippery movements, and the only noises are your own sighs of delight. Your hands are holding the sides of her head, slowing her down when your cock feels as if it could explode in a million fragments. Then she runs her teeth over it slightly, first on one side, then the other, like pinpricks. You also take it as curtains for act one. You pull her toward you, tilt her on her back. It's your turn now. You work on her nipples first.

Her breasts are small, shapely, and compact. As you suckle on her nipples, she giggles, but once you move down, her body tenses; she is electric with anticipation. You eat her as you have never eaten anything before, as if she were your last meal before doomsday.

"Oh, my," she says. She is curving with pleasure. Her spine arches upward. Her breath comes in short gasps. Your tongue roves her clitoris, and she's so oiled up, the sheets go damp. Her hands encircle your neck. She can't take it anymore. She wants you inside. She wants to be on top. Even you favor this beginning to the agenda. For you, the fuck that is best is the one that has you most at rest.

She's aching for you to enter, and she can't manipulate your cock fast enough. She feeds it into herself and it slides like a car piston. You place your hands on her hips. This way, you can monitor her speed, keep the game from going beyond you. You are a perfect fit. You lift your hands off her hips and fold them behind your head, then watch her work. You observe every movement she makes: the way she lifts up, the passion in her eyes, the hairs failing in front of her face, the ripples her breasts make at each sinking, the spread of her crotch hair, and the angle she likes it best in. You pace yourself like a middle-distance runner. Your observation acts like so many brakes on your neurotransmitters; you delay going the final lap.

As you feel your temperature going into the red band, you lift her off you. It's time to try the dog now. This is your speciality. You can fuck so hard in this posture, a woman's eyes could pop out. But you go gentle on Karnam. Soft thrusts that pump your dick into far-ranging crevices. You cup her breasts. You want to squeeze them till they burst. Karnam disengages from the clutter of limbs. She wants it on her back now. You usually have some entry hiccups in the missionary. You place a pillow below her hips, get the right gradient, and she guides you in. Karnam wraps her legs around your back. Your legs stretch out behind you. You sweep the hair from her eyes. On the final stretch, you like to look straight into the eyes, get obstacles out of the way. Your spunk shoots above the red band, and as you come in the furnace of her vagina, you look deep into her eyes. Whatever else you might do, you can never get closer than this.

She keeps you locked in after you have shot and the party's over. Even you like it this way.

"I love you," you say, and as thought becomes words and the words roll over your tongue, you realize that you may have spoken the truth.

"Maybe you think you love me."

"Maybe the sky isn't blue."

"More than Shomali?"

"That was a long time back."

"Why can't you answer straight?" she says.

"I don't know," you say, and that's as honest as you can get.

"What you are seeing is maybe what I am not," she says.

"That could go for me, too," you say.

And then you lock your palms behind her head and lift it till her eyes can't be any nearer to yours.

"Will you be mine? Will you marry me?" you ask.

Your doorbell rings at precisely this moment. It's strange. You rarely give people reason to come your way. You slip into your shorts. The door's unlatched. You open it, only to stare down the muzzle of a pistol.

You are familiar with the P7M8. The barrel has polygonal rifling, which reduces deformation of the bullet, and with its eight-round magazine almost vertical to the barrel feed, it reduces the chances of jamming. But the unique feature of the pistol is its cocking action, which can be achieved by squeezing the cocking lever, which runs on the front side of the pistol grip. Another distinctive selling point is its sighting system, which consists of three white dots and can be picked up in all light conditions for a quick-reaction shot. In short, it's an ideal personal weapon.

"Do I know you?" you ask. You face a Sikh in uniform; his two nervous sidekicks stand in the background, acting like a contingency reserve force.

"You know this?" asks the Sikh, waving the P7 in front of your face. That is as nice a way as any to begin on a strong note.

"Maybe you have the wrong house," you suggest. Too much of your time these days is being taken up by pistol-waving military types.

"Maybe if you don't invite us in, we might feel like putting a hole in your head and making the place our own."

You step aside, a graceful host, letting the execution squad in. You see the futility of an aggressive stand.

"What's this shit you have on the floor? Bamboo matting. A guy like you sitting on millions of dollars doesn't need bamboo to fuck up a place. These things burn like petrol, MM," he says.

"You have a name?" you ask. You feel like you have seen him somewhere, but you can't place him. "Who sent you, asshole? Whose chickenshit agenda are you carrying out?" you ask slowly, deliberately. He lines the P7 at your head. Your experience with fringe players is that they like to run the show on their own terms, and the best way to baffle their radar is to derail them. A seasoned player like Rodriguez might, on the other hand, like to convey an impression of weakness till he gets the chance to twist the screws on you.

But the Sikh goes red in the face, and you think you might have taken a wrong read on the situation. You know he's going to press the trigger, and you tense up, but he angles out at the last moment and takes out your ten-thousand-buck crystal vase on the sideboard. The glass shatters in a million fragments, some of the shards catching his sidekicks at the waist. The bullet goes clean through the wood.

"Jesus Christ," you say, ducking involuntarily. "You nuts?"

Karnam comes running out of the bedroom, a scenario you have been dreading. You had been hoping to settle the issue before it got out of hand or, alternatively, to raise your voice enough for Karnam to figure out that all was not well and exit out the back. With her in, you feel the odds tilt irrevocably.

"What happened? Is everything okay?" Karnam asks.

A saving grace, you feel, is that she has had time to get dressed.

"Ah, my, what do we have here? Miss Universe herself," says the Sikh officer.

"Leave her out of this," you say.

"Now, let me guess. Thirty-four, twenty-six, thirty-six. Am I right, beauty? You shack up with this cunt here. I could give you twenty big reasons I am better," he says. He pokes her shoulders with the P7 barrel and starts tracing a line down her sides.

Karnam jerks his arm away. "Keep your hands away from me," she says.

You tense for any opening you can get. The sidekicks are busy pinching out small shards from their uniform. They aren't bleeding, a bad sign, as far as you are concerned.

"What do you want?" you ask.

"I can see your vocabulary's improved," he says.

You feel you have a chance against him one-on-one, but his backup is behind you.

"You pulling this shit in uniform? The army's got this place wired. They don't like me very much. Your shot probably hooked some military police to come by, check out the new nutcase in my house."

"The way I see it, if I sort you out, they are going to roll the president's medal my way."

"You have it all wrong. I have my arm so deep in their asshole, getting me out of the picture isn't going to take it out. What is it you want? Or is the best way you socialize by blowing holes in people's homes?"

"You have something that belongs to us. Some white powder that the 5 Kumaon stole from us. You know what it is, MM. All we want is what is ours. You do a friendly and we won't collect on interest."

"I don't know what you're talking about." But it's clear to you now whose agenda he is pulling. "The 7 Sikh is barking up the wrong tree."

"Bark. I haven't started barking yet, my friend. I am here to refresh your memory. I can see you believe in investing in quality. How much did this Hewlett-Packard Vectra set you back? Is this the shit they advertise that has all these latest add-ons chipped in? Fax card, video interface, Internet-ready, CD-ROM. Does this wash your ass, too? Or you didn't sell enough of our stuff to go for that kind of superior model?"

"I think there's some tremendous misunderstanding. I think you are way off the mark," you say. He nods at his men. They start the search by opening the drawers to your sideboard, emptying the contents on the floor.

"Where have you stashed the stuff? Or have you sold it already? In which case, your time is at hand. All we will give you is a one-minute break to mumble your prayers."

"You are wasting your time."

"Not at all. It's giving me great pleasure fucking your place up. What's this? A dressing table in walnut wood. What kind of furniture you pick up, MM? A bachelor and all. Or did you buy it for our lady here to hook up her straps?"

"Keep her out of this. She just dropped by."

"More bad luck for her. Going with a guy like you can cause a girl great harm. You should be more judicious, lady. Pick us sane types. This guy, Interpol's got a file on him a mile thick."

A drawer's not opening. One of the men turns around.

"You have a key for this?" the Sikh asks.

"The stuff in there won't interest you."

"Now I have to see it," he says. "Are you getting the key for it, or do you want me to engage in some precision firing?" He aims the P7 at the drawer.

"I will get the key," you say a little too fast. It's an opportunity for you to get the Glock, which is in the drawer of the study table in your bedroom. You walk to your bedroom. His footsteps ring behind you. One of the men stands behind Karnam and pushes her forward. You keep your body between the drawer and the Sikh. Your hands reach out to pull the knob.

"Now there, MM. Not so fast. You are making me nervous. I am the guy who does any opening and closing that goes on here," he says. He presses the barrel point against your neck. You back off. He pulls the drawer. "Now, now, now. What do we have here? A Glock."

He picks it up, checks the magazine. "This piece is something I have always wanted to own. You have put me in a very bad mood, MM. Very bad mood. You were going to pull this on me?" He weighs the piece in his hand. He looks at Karnam. "This is some heavy artillery your boyfriend has here. Did he tell you how he got it?"

Karnam looks at you. You shrug. "I will explain," you tell her weakly.

"I can explain better," he says. He latches the magazine out, springs the bullets on his palms, and hands the empty box to Karnam. "If you look inside, lady, you will see a name scratched out. Could you read it for me, please?"

Karnam angles it against the light. You don't know where the thing's heading.

"Captain Prakash," says Karnam, and your blood runs cold.

"Ah. As I had thought. You are a lousy player, MM. You can't even switch the magazines of the guns you steal."

"I didn't steal it."

"Prakash gifted it to you? Or did you sneak up to his room after you pushed him from the Cessna?"

"You know better than that," you say. Rodriguez, you think, is either dumb in certain ways or an even bigger motherfucker than you thought.

"All I know is that Captain Prakash was a buddy of mine. And now you happen to have a thing he was too fond of to give to a pimp like you."

"Somebody presented it to me."

"Who, Rodriguez? How a guy like you got mixed up with that asshole is what I cannot understand. Tell me, how did the two of you work Prakash in? I just want to know. I am curious."

"His chute timer malfunctioned and pulled him out of the door."

"Now, MM. Even we know that. I was hoping you would tell me the real story. Earn yourself some points to make me go easy on your place."

"If there was something else, I am as much in the dark as you."

"You chose the wrong side, MM. Rodriguez is going to dump you as soon as you've sprung the deal for him. Team with us and you might still have a future outside the crematorium."

"Go fuck yourself."

The men boot the drawer open.

"What do we have here? Floppies. What do you do with all these three-inchers? High-density Sony. What kind of data you store in here that makes you lock the drawer?"

"That's the entire *Britannica* in twenty floppies. You don't need to buy those big volumes," you say.

"The way I see it, I don't believe shit. I plan to have them checked out. There're more floppies in here than I have ever seen in my life. This kind of thing is way over my head," he says.

The men come up with your shooting kit, which was in the back of your wardrobe.

"What's this? You keep this shooter without any real stuff around? What do you shoot? Distilled water? The least you can do is get disposables for yourself, instead of flushing your works with bleach. You better check with your local hospital to see whether this shooter of yours is boilproof. Some of these needles collapse in the heat, and you might crack them in a vein," he says.

"Thanks for the advice."

"The thing I have difficulty figuring out is how a grafter like you who doesn't want to spend a few rupees on throwaways has the mentality to buy this fashion stuff," he says. He is fingering the trousers in your wardrobe. And the jackets. "Armani. Gucci. Pierre Cardin. Versace. What is this Girodin? Never heard of it. But it doesn't stop me from getting jealous. The only way guys like us get to see this stuff is in the magazines. And even the stupid magazines have become too expensive to buy. All you can do these days is flip through the pages till the newsstand guy tells you to fuck off. And here you are rolling in it. Man, just feel the stuff. It's better than what a woman could give. You could fuck these things and not know the difference."

"You are sick. You need some counseling," you say.

He ignores you. He takes out a pair of your trousers and hangs them from his waist. "Where did you get your height from, MM? This thing could hug a fucking giraffe," he says. He tries on your jackets. "What's this material your uppers are made of? They feel like fucking raincoats. Life sucks."

He takes out a switchblade from his pocket and goes about making incisions in your pants at crotch level. "Thing is, with the kind of screwing you do in this room, you should wear something that allows you to launch a quick shot. All these things with buttons, they jam the action."

"You can take them if you want, instead of doing it this way," you say. You are pained to see your wardrobe hit the dust. "You mind leaving a few? I can't go to the office in shorts."

"Shit. What's this in here? This looks like what the Eskimos must wear," he says. It's your Everest kit he's discovered. You are grateful that your main equipment lies someplace else. He throws the thermals on your bed. "These things could fit a grizzly. What do you do with this stuff in Delhi? Hatch eggs?"

"Altitude gear. This is for the Himalayas. It's not mine, either. It's David Breashear's, the American climber. He stores his kit with me," you say. "His name's stitched on the collar, in case you don't believe me."

"The only David Breashear I heard of is this guy who hosts the breakfast show on Sky. For all I know, this is a brand name. You might be packing some of the heroin in here. Always wanted to see what down looked like. I have this English sister-in-law who keeps these down pillows. They are so soft, you could fold them in your pockets. Well, nearly," he says. He rips a sleeve of the Gore-Tex jacket. "Man, this is like fridge packing. It smells like shit, too. How can you sleep in this stuff? Jesus, what's this drum in here?"

"That's ice equipment."

"I have to see it," he says. "Our mountain division doesn't get half this quality." He rolls out your plastic barrel, pulls the lid out, and hangs the drum in the air, letting your gear fall and scatter in a big heap on the floor.

"This is one hell of an ice ax. Look at the grip. Hell, adjustable glare, snow goggles. This is like James Bond. You could even wear this to the Jazz Bar," he says. He puts on the snow goggles and lifts the ice ax with his right hand. One of his men is holding the P7 for him. "You look like shit from in here," he tells you. "And you, lady, you look like you don't belong to this guy."

Karnam's absorbing the whole thing with a cool head. You have been trying to make eye contact, but she's following the Sikh.

Then he swings the ice ax as far as it can go and brings it down on the door of your wardrobe. It splits the door in two. "Swell, man. Did you see that? This is one hell of a thing to haul around." He throws the ax on your floor and it crashes against the side of your bed, hitting a hollow note. "Jesus, what's this? You got a box bed. I thought that went out in the seventies. This kind of tank design—what do you pack in here?"

"Why don't you see for yourself?" you say. You have given up.

He opens the side to one of them. "Shit, shoes. What kind of place is this to keep your leg gear in? You will get fungus on them. You have so much leather in here, you could rig up a platoon. But what's your fucking size, MM? Looks like both my legs could fit in one and leave space for a bull to shit in."

He looks out of your back window. There's an open drain hugging the houses on your side of the road. He picks up your shoes and throws them in the drain one by one. He clears the backyard of your ground-floor neighbors with thirty-odd throws. "Phew," he says. "You had some heavy soles in there. Didn't know Woodlands were like fucking dumbbells."

Next, he crashes open the top of your other bed. That stores your booze. There's an array of Johnnie Walker, Bailey's, Drambuie, Jamaican rum, Smirnoff, and some others. You haven't accessed your bar for a long time. You use the bottles to keep your sources in good humor.

"Man, you have enough alcohol in here to launch a polar satellite vehicle," he says. "Johnnie Walker Blue label! The only time I've seen the bottle is in a Star TV ad, the one with that slinky blonde in it who blows her skirt in the ventilator. You seen that ad, MM?"

"I have better things to do."

"This is amazing," he says.

His men eye the bottles with considerable interest. "Looks like this is the only interesting thing we can carry off from all your lousy stuff," he says. "You got some packing?"

"There are some plastic bags in the kitchen," you say.

"This is what I hate about yuppie bastards. You guys are such stingy creatures. I can see those Samsonites stacked there on top of your cupboard, and all you can offer me is some lousy cellulose. The thing would probably tear before we got to base," he says.

The men pull down the suitcases. They are empty. They place the bottles in neat rows, leaving you four bottles of Bailey's. "This stuff tastes like cold coffee," says the Sikh, and he opens the door to your bathroom to pour the Bailey's into the shit pot. "What's this fancy shank you have in here, MM? How do you get the water going?"

You keep quiet. He kicks it on the side. "The lever's on the side," you say.

"What's inside? This is the first water pot I've seen that's screwed on top. Maybe you have some stuff in there in waterproof," he says. He comes back to your bedroom, picks up the ice ax, whacks it on the shank. It bursts like bloated plastic and the water runs all over the place.

"If I had anything, I wouldn't be stupid enough to keep it here," you say. "I am going to get you for all this, asshole. Aggravated assault. The army's going to cook your goose within an hour of you getting out from this place. Your ass is going to be mine."

"Well then, I guess I have to make most of the time when your ass is mine," he says, grinning.

"Can I leave now?" asks Karnam.

"Ah, lady. I just figured a new plan. I think you are going to make excellent collateral," he says. "What do you say, MM? Put yourself in my shoes." The P7 is back in his hands, and he's swinging it around with his forefinger in the trigger guard.

"You do that and I will kill you," you say. And what you discover is that you mean it. "I will talk to the army chief."

There's a change in the Sikh's demeanor. His prancing goes. The lines on his face become taut and he steps up an inch from your face, the P7 hurting your ribs. "You still haven't figured it, have you, MM? I am the army. This here is what the generals send me to do. How do you think the 7 Sikh shunted me into temporary military police duty? With the help of the generals? The generals don't know that I have two agendas. You can bomb your questionnaire on Delhi, for all I care, but we want the heroin and whatever else that thug Rodriguez has scrounged for you."

It's now that you realize the deepness of the shit you are in. And this spark of reality ignites in you a memory that places the eyes of the intruder in another locale. You recognize the eyes. It was the turban putting you off all this while. You remember the locale now. The 7 Sikh officer at Kupwara on the day Capt. Satish Warrier got eighty-sixed. That day, he had no turban in place. Today, he is a Sikh with a turban.

"Major Raunaq Singh," you say.

"You brain works slow, MM. You wouldn't last two weeks at the border," says Raunaq. "We will give you twenty-four hours. We want the one hundred kilos that 5 Kumaon stole from us if you want to see your beauty again."

With that, he walks away with his two honchos and Karnam.

You don't bother to clear the mess after the departure of Maj. Raunaq Singh. Events are moving out of orbit and you need time to dodge the debris coming your way, get your navigation racing full-time. It's also time, you think, to set your own shit in motion. To slip in momentum now would be to lose your status as a player, let the likes of Singh and Rodriguez run the show. And right now, you have to use one to get the other. Somehow plan to bounce Karnam back into circulation. The nature of your profession has trained you for all manner of contingencies. But the consequences of interwining your romantic life with the business of espionage is something that no manual has answers to. Before pursuing Karnam, however, high on your immediate itinerary is to pick up some breathing space, boogie the army off your back. It's an opportune moment, you think, to use the tape.

You have had the foresight to prepare things in advance. You have taken the photographs from Jolly, the ones about the frolicking air marshals. You have also drafted a bogus VMA test report on a fake letterhead, faxed it to a friend in Phoenix, Arizona, who faxed it back to you. It confirms the voice on the tape as belonging to the defense minister. The original tape completes your blackmail kit, along with a copy of an analysis of the questionnaire. All these you kept in an envelope taped at the bottom of the gas cylinder in your kitchen, a precaution that came in handy in the face of Major Singh's armed intrusion. You remove the envelope from the bottom, pop two purple hearts, and hunt for something to wear that has escaped Singh's blade. You locate an Allen Solly. Then you hop in your Defender and drive to south block.

You have direct access to the defense minister, Suresh Yadav. He is from your hometown, Allahabad. The way you met him was when he made his debut in Parliament, having won his seat by the biggest margin in the history of the Indian electoral system, and you were assistant editor at *Honey Bee*, your school magazine. Those were days just before you joined the Academy and took an interest in things literary and academic.

You went to interview Suresh Yadav, and he indulged a schoolboy for ninety minutes. The encounter served you in good stead in later years, for the parliamentarian leapt ahead in his career because of emerging caste equations in Uttar Pradesh state politics, and he learned to play the formula to boost his ministerial ambitions in New Delhi. At suitable points along the route, you got the opportunity to write up some goodwill stories, favors he remembered. The last time you cashed in on them was using his influence with the Haryana state government to allot you some prime real estate where Jumbo's and your entertainment complex now stands.

But dealing with the army is different. For all his political savvy, Yadav is a little in awe of the brass button and stripe species that he has to deal with daily from the forces. The first time he became defense minister, the story runs, he thought protocol demanded he pay a visit to the three force chiefs to get himself a briefing. But his personal secretary tipped him on convention and he avoided a faux pas. With great consternation, he learned that in a democracy, the armed wing is subservient to the executive and that all he had to do was pick up some fancy hot line and the generals and admirals and air chiefs would come wagging their tails, give him a blow job.

You bump into the army chiefs ADC, Maj. Rishi Bhatnagar, in the minister's anteroom. You haven't met him since you submitted your application to train with the paras. He is surprised to see you.

"What are you doing here?" asks Major Bhatnagar.

Given the present state of affairs, the question assumes the proportions of a physical assault.

"Can't see that it's any of your business," you say.

"It already is. We are cracking into you after the minister signs this," he says, waving a file. "We have filed a First Information Report with the Delhi police and are having the case transferred to the Central Bureau of Investigation."

"What's this, a frame-up?" you ask. With this one, you feel, the generals could be caught in overreach. "This morning, I get a bunch of goons smashing up my place, and now you tell me the army's cranking a case up my ass. Even a setup doesn't have to look like one."

"I guess they are pissed about the poll you pulled on the troops."

Bhatnagar, you judge, doesn't know from black. It was not like generals to get so worked up over a questionnaire. A whole regiment on the move with arms for export could, however, work them into a heavy sweat, commit them to an indiscretion. What you wonder is how they got the stink. You look afresh at Bhatnagar. There is no need to lose your cool with a duty boy. Bhatnagar, you remember, is an ex-para. Someone who once mentioned to you that he hates not owning a parachute himself. That would provide him the opportunity to do a bit of sports jumping. A free-fall top from Pioneer costs in excess of eight thousand dollars. You have one to spare. You diversify your conversation.

"Thanks for the help in getting me through to the Pathfinders. The jumps were good. I loved them. Thanks. I got a spare chute, in case you want to keep it," you say.

Bhatnagar's eyes light up. "I would love to."

"You are lucky those assholes didn't come across it today. They would have ripped the webbing."

"Now, who would do that?"

"You bump into this military police asshole yet? Goes by the name of Major Raunaq Singh. He was in 7 Sikh. How come he's on MP duty?"

"Yeah," he says. "Normal infantry doesn't ever go MP. He got floated in from above ten days back. Temporary assignment."

The 7 Sikh, you deduct, is on a dangerous squealing mission. It's important for you to sing a melody that warms Bhatnagar's heart, sets him up on a kindred pitch. He's tuning to your megahertz.

"All this is nothing personal, buddy," he says. "I heard you did real well up in basic course. For me, you are para. And I never made it to the Pathfinders. I heard they took you up for a while."

"Yeah. It was tough. I dropped out. It was a motherfucker."

"So it is."

"Listen, you better tell me what's in that file. They get me here, they might move to confiscate my property. Seal my flat, and some MP asshole might disappear with my spare chute," you say. "Know what I mean?" You wink.

"I tell you what. You go in there before me. All I have in here is a copy of the FIR that army HQ has filed against you and your editor, Ashok Mehra. There's also a copy of the notification transferring your case to the CBI. The chief, he wants to hide his ass behind the minister," says Bhatnagar. "He's worried about something. I don't quite know what."

The army chief, Gen. Subhas Rampal, has reason to worry about his goose getting cooked. Corruption makes banner headlines, and the kind that you are helping personnel from the 5 Kumaon practice would roll many heads should it become public knowledge.

"He surely should have more things to worry about than me," you say.

"Right now, it's you. He rang me up at eight in the morning to get copies of all this and have them delivered to the minister. I didn't meet you, right?"

"Right."

You walk the hallway to the minister's room. You don't plan to let Yadav's secretary, Yashpal Ande, buzz you in. The minister might avoid you or slot you for later in the day.

But you can't bypass Ande. He chooses this moment to step out of his room. He has a cigarette clamped between his lips and you have no doorway to slouch in.

"MM," he says. He's lighting the end, but the lighter slips from his hands and clatters to the ground. You pick it up and light his Wills for him.

"The minister in?" you ask.

Ande blows some smoke in your face. Yadav is asthmatic. He's into smoke-free zones. Ande, therefore, has to indulge in his vice outside his office, since the minister often comes by with personal instructions, instead of buzzing on the phone and calling him. Ande isn't part of the government steno force. He's Yadav's trusted aide, his go-between and henchman. It was he who ironed out the kinks when you were trying to push through your documentary on Siachen. In return, you remembered to get him a carton of Rothman kings, his favorite brand, the next time you passed through the duty-free. That, and a Toshiba laptop for his son, paid for by selling part of the Siachen footage to a French television company. Clearly, the Toshiba has regressed into dim memory.

"He's in a meeting," says Ande.

"It's an emergency."

"I will have to check."

Ande has taken four puffs so far, and you wait patiently for him to run through his stick.

"We have to discuss things," you tell him. "I might have something to buy from your nephew." To dial Ande right, you have to keep up his expectation levels. Ande's nephew has an interior decoration outfit. Ande wants him to spruce up your Gurgaon drug retreat.

"Not here," says Ande. "What are you up to, anyway? The army chiefs been calling the minister about you."

"Yeah? When?"

"Four days back."

"The chief is paranoid. He's cracking."

"What's in that envelope?"

"Heroin," you say. "The minister needs it for his asthma."

Ande chews your answer over. He is having a hard time digesting the intelligence you seem to have provided him. You can almost hear him shifting it backward and forward and sideways in the various compartments of his brain. Yadav has tried many remedies to contain his asthma. Once, he swallowed live fish.

"You can go in," Ande says. "He's having his juice."

Yadav has an elaborate morning routine involving carrot and orange juice. Orange for his calories and carrot for his weak eye muscles. Both for his late-morning shit, which is vital to his mental equilibrium. Then he does his eye exercises. If you didn't know about them, you'd be in for a shock. He'll drop off right in the middle of a sentence and squint at the tip of his nose or rotate his pupils clockwise and then the other way. He finishes off by drawing one finger slowly toward his face, till he sees it double, and keeping it there for a count of ten seconds.

You know his habits in detail because you have traveled with him on campaign trails, watching his personal assistants lug carrots and oranges over the countryside and pack a battery juicer in the car. Once, when the juicer's battery died, the Exide battery pack under the car's hood was pressed into service. It burned the juicer's coil, and Yadav canceled his speeches till late afternoon.

Yadav looks at you over his spectacles as you enter his office, the corner of his lips wet with carrot juice. He smiles and waves you in from the door, belching. "Aghm. I have been wanting to get in touch with you, MM. What trouble are you up to?"

"Sir," you say, "things are not looking good."

Yadav muses over this. He takes a sip from his glass. "The army chief's been ringing me about you. He's saying your magazine is about to publish an illegal poll on troops in Kashmir. That you conducted that poll. They have also registered an FIR under the Official Secrets Act and the NSA. Then two hours back, he rang me up again to say that you assaulted an army officer in the morning at your house. It's troubling. What is all this?" asks Yadav. Part of how you went to Kashmir was by getting Ande to call the army chief's office. The chief was now attempting to smear responsibility on Yadav, too, make a merry party if his ship were to spring a leak. He has precedent to warn him. One of his predecessors nearly got yanked out of his chief generalship by giving an interview to a paper that called a neighboring country a nation of "bandicoots." The then chief had great problems wriggling out of that one. He got away by muddling the reporter and later sacking the defense PRO who had liaised the interview.

"Sir, I think you should know what really happened. That's why I am here. It's General Rampal who's having all this done to me."

"What?"

"He sent over three MPs to my place. They tore my clothes, broke my desks and cupboards, and took my liquor away in suitcases. Next, I'll be charged with bribery."

"MPs?" says Yadav.

"Military police, sir. Not member of Parliament."

"Yes."

"They left this packet with me. They know about our relations and knew I would come straight to you. I think you should have a look at what's inside," you say. "They are trying to get at you through me. They are framing you. You have to be careful."

There's nothing that spikes Yadav's antenna into hyperactivity more than the mention of trouble headed his way. You tear open the envelope and heap the contents next to the teapot that holds his orange juice. Yadav stares. When he concentrates on things at hand, his specs slip on his nose. He has to keep pushing them up.

"How?" he asks. He buzzes Ande on the intercom. "No calls. No visitors." He motions you to sit next to him.

In the murky politics that Yadav is used to dwelling in, the easiest thing to sell is a conspiracy theory. That said, Yadav is unusually paranoid.

"The Intelligence Bureau and military intelligence have had you under surveillance for six months. They gave me a tape," you say. You place the tape in your pocket-size Sony recorder and play it for him.

"We regret the mistake," the Korean says. "We confuse between bank. I get information you call, I call you immediately. We rectify mistake tomorrow. We will pay you the whole amount. Okay, sir. *Gam sa nida.*"

A short lull.

"Yes, yes," says Yadav. "Could you repeat the number, please?"

"Seven eight nine one oh one two three," says the Korean.

"That's right. Please do the needful. I need two million dollars immediately," instructs Yadav.

"Okay, sir. *Gam sa nida,*" says the Korean, and the line goes dead.

"*What is this?*" asks Yadav. He has some trouble placing the context, but memory sweeps his eyes for one brief second, and that's your confirmation.

"They are saying it's you and a representative from Korea Power," you say. "They faxed me a copy of the report of a voice-match analysis. It's a hundred percent identification." You hand him over your fabrication, and though he takes it from your fingers, he doesn't read it. Of course, while you are on your game, you have to provide Yadav a hole to save face. "I think what they have done, sir, is patch together the tape from your conversations. It's very easy."

Yadav nods. "But why?"

"Sir, your juice will go sour," you say.

"Huh," says Yadav.

"The three chiefs are after you, sir," you say. "You see, our magazine is on to the MiG-21 upgrade scam. The air force is worried that once the story breaks, you might go for a scrub at the top. The army is—"

"What's the MiG-21 scam?" interrupts Yadav.

You look at Yadav with shock. "I thought intelligence would have briefed you by now." You hand over the pictures to Yadav. "These are Indian air force officers in Russia while they were striking a deal with the Mikhsoyan design bureau, the agency that designed and developed the MiGs."

"How do you know?" asks Yadav. Of the dozen-odd snaps, he's riveted most by the one of the air marshal giving it to a woman. Her palms clench a bike's handlebars and her knees rest on the single padded seat. So enthralled is he by the snap, he places it apart from the rest. It sticks out in between you like a third presence.

"We know. A few officers squealed."

"And the army?"

"You wouldn't believe what they are up to, sir. First, there's the IED detectors. . . ."

"IED?"

"Improvised explosive devices. What the Kashmir militants use. Remote-controlled things that can blow your shit out from six hundred feet away. On paper, the army owns several million dollars' worth of IED detectors and jammers to block the frequency of these things. Shipped in from Germany, Belgium, and Canada. But the equipment, except for a few samples, never came in. All the IED detection team does is give demos to journalists about the sophisticated stuff they have," you say.

This all comes from Major Rodriguez. Army command, in its foolish-ness, kept passing the nonexistent equipment to 5 Kumaon for trial and evaluation, and 5 Kumaon duly reported high attrition levels, equipment breakages, and losses to militants, and inventoried the phantom gear out of stock. Colonel Sangma and Major Rodriguez were only too happy to oblige. This is part of the discomfiture burdening the army chief: the top brass in a regiment going solo and having the gunpowder to blow the lid on the IED deal. Robber against robber.

"Who told you about this?"

"Army sources," you say. There's a spare glass on the table. You pour yourself some orange juice. "This is not all. What the chief is worried about right now is the 7 Sikh. He is planning to swap the blame, put it on you."

"*What blame?*"

"The regiment is exporting the arms it captured from militants. To terrorists. It's not only AK-47s. They have detonators, explosives, walkie-talkies, the works. Even a few of the IED detectors. I think the chief's involved, too. And they know that I know. They plan to get at you through me."

"How?" asks Yadav. He is functioning on basic vocabulary.

The orange juice tastes good. The problem with politicians like Yadav is that you have to spell everything out for them, number each piece like on the back of a jigsaw box. And since you are inventing most of the cutouts, you have to make sure they fit snugly.

"They are creating a smoke screen." Yadav has trouble with big words. They make him acutely aware of his small-town upbringing. (And Bahraich, his ancestral town, is as small as they come.)

"Smoke screen?"

"Diversion, sir," you say. "They are setting 5 Kumaon up. They are going to claim that I am the conduit and I am acting under *your* instructions. They will shovel all the blame on 5 Kumaon, and since Yashpal Ande helped organize my stay with the 5 Kumaon when I was filming this border documentary a few weeks back, fingers are going to be pointed at you. Big numbers are involved, sir. The chief, he was the commanding officer of the 7 Sikh twenty years back. That's how he has his finger in the pie."

"How big is the consignment?" asks Yadav.

This is a sign that you are at last beginning to align him on the field. A big bastard like Yadav sees the implications of the tangle first in terms of greenbacks and then national security, if at all. That is how he got this far.

"Forty million dollars. Maybe more." You sit on the sofa. You make him an offer.

"They told me to make you an offer, sir," you say. "Actually, they made me the offer so I could work on you. They said it came straight from the general."

Yadav is squinting. He wants to work on his vision as he listens to you. A two-in-one approach. Debutants witnessing the phenomenon might think he was about to faint, but you know better.

"How much?" he asks. At least Yadav always takes the shortest distance between two points.

"Twenty percent," you say. You're acting out of authority here, speaking on behalf of the 5 Kumaon brotherhood. It might make Rodriguez, Kohli, and Sangma squirm, but with the 7 Sikh and the army chief on your ass, you have to buy some cover, go for some overheads, instead of filing for bankruptcy.

"What does that mean?" asks Yadav.

You have cut deals for Yadav before. The last one involved container loads of rotten cashew nuts that you had shipped to Antwerp, overinvoicing them heavily. The cashews were incinerated at destination, the commission came in laundered, and you used one of Jumbo's many front companies to siphon cash to Yadav's constituents.

"Payment for neutrality. Passage money."

"What do you say?" asks Yadav.

"We could play along," you say.

"No problems with your magazine?"

"Even if there are, I will take care of them."

"The chief?"

"He's an amateur. We will outflank him," you say. "But I need you to sit on him for a while. Get him off my chest. Also, call the CBI director and tell him to go slow. Tell him I am on a special mission."

"Why is that?" asks Yadav.

"General Rampal might call the CBI director and feed him some bullshit. He's itching to smoke me out. Tell him I have special clearance, that I am your mole in the hole."

"If they jump the gun?"

"We will jump it before them. We have enough dirt on them to blow their shit out of army HQ."

Of course, your main purpose is to buy time. If you go under, Karnam goes under. If you are afloat and fighting, she has a chance. The last thing you want is the CBI to crack a nonbailable arrest warrant for you, fuck up your hectic schedule.

Events are coming to a head, and for you now, speed is the essence of war.

Your next stop is the office. The time will come when you will clear your head and concentrate on your love life, but before that, certain logistics have to be smoothed out.

You have to whittle the MiG story to size, lash together a pager on the IED scoop, keep the Yadav tape in readiness, and write, in record time, your fabrication of the doings of border regiments. This should be your lead piece if you use them all at one shot.

As things are, you don't stand to gain a lot by letting these stories through the gate right now, but in the event that you have to use them, you have to keep them in the system like loaded and cocked weaponry.

It's when you are scanning the pictures that you have a brush with Digs. His antennae have sensed your presence. He catches you alone in the design alcove.

"Where's Karnam?" he barks.

You shrug. "I don't know," you say. And, for once, there's some truth to what you say.

"Her car's parked over at your place," says Digs.

"She spent the night with me," you explain.

"Damn you," he hisses. For a moment, you think he's about to hit you. But he's delivering a warning. "Stay clear of my daughter, MM."

"She has her own mind."

"See me in my office," says Digs, and walks off. Unfortunately, you need him: The magazine is one of your most important tools of war. Today, while coming up the stairs, you stuck your head through the door to the mezzanine floor, but Gulab Chand wasn't there manning the ducts. Though he could have stepped out momentarily for a cup of tea, you have forbidden him to do so. One of the dangers inherent in that act, which would give the game away, would be if he was spotted by some 7 Sikh asshole keeping tabs on you.

You enter Digs's office with great apprehension. Others, too, have collected there. What's this, you think, a public sacking? But Mukherjee has a wire printout in his hands. You come to understand that your dawn raid on Delhi police HQ has been picked up and flashed by the Press Trust of India.

There's a transformation in Digs. Like a good CEO, he has put his personal problems behind him. He's also putting into application Robert Fritz's creative curriculum. A few weeks back, he spent ten thousand per head to herd the editorial staff into one of Fritz's seminars, where you were told over two days that creativity is a skill to be mastered the way you learn to drive a car. It's Digs's philosophy that creativity should be an inherent factor in a journalist's makeup. It makes him write better copy, apply the right syntax while editing. Part of Digs's enhanced creativity after applying Fritz's formula has resulted in him clubbing some yoga relaxation techniques with Fritz's step-by-step goal-realization scheme. What has become disconcerting are Digs's attempts to introduce Fritz's formula in editorial meetings, which is what this gathering seems to be.

"When dealing with the unknown, any thought about it is pure speculation," says Digs. "Your starting point always has to be current reality." It was Mukherjee's good fortune to be on sick leave during Fritz's seminar, but now he has to contend with Digs's version of Fritz without adequate background.

"What we know is that there was a successful commando type of operation and an inspector got injured because of shots fired by military personnel," says Mukherjee. "These army-police skirmishes always make interesting reading. I think we should slip a pager in. We still have time before the issue closes for the week."

"There's more to the story than that," says Digs. "The army has officially denied any involvement. For all we know, the raiders could have been civilians disguised in uniform. Assuming the person rescued by the raiders was from the army, we don't know why it was so important to rescue him."

With Digs speaking your mind, you don't feel the need to join the fray. You avoid looking at Mukherjee. You feel it best not to pick up any imploring eye signals. In normal circumstances, you might have thought his case had some merit.

"We will be the first magazine with the news," argues Mukherjee.

But Digs is wallowing in vintage Fritz. "It's important, Mukherjee," he says, "to distinguish between what can be known and what you cannot possibly know within the time frame you have. If you can answer the unknowable within the next hour, you are welcome to do the story." Out of the corner of your eye, you can see Mukherjee look at you with some bewilderment. Leslie chips in with a weak "I will tell Photo to click police HQ and the injured inspector just in case."

Digs treats the matter as dismissed. He swivels his chair around to face you. You are the only person who can see the lipstick imprint underneath his shirt collar on the right side of his neck. Nonita, you feel, is leaving her signature in rather conspicuous ways.

"MM," begins Digs. "I want to carry your para story this issue. I don't want the issue after the anniversary issue to be a total letdown. But I want you to add a box to that. The human-interest angle. The death of the jumper you told us about."

You nod. This, you can see, is the beginning of Digs's fucking with you. He isn't finished, either. "I would also like to see the edited version of your border documentary by next week. It's to be forwarded to the army for screening before Doordarshan can telecast it."

You nod once again. A week is a long time in your current plight. Even to tuck in a journalistic human-interest obit on Captain Prakash is going to put a strain on your energies. But annoying Digs is out of the question. He dismisses the others. He motions you to stay on. You know what's coming.

"I don't want you socializing with Karnam," he says.

You listen quietly. Under an artillery barrage, it's better to wait things out in a bunker.

"She's impressionable, and I don't trust you."

You cough. "It's not what you are thinking, Mr. Mehra," you say.

"Don't even begin to think what I am thinking or you will shit in your pants," he says. "I have seen climbers like you, MM. All you can see are footholds on the way to the top. I don't want my daughter to end up as a foothold."

If Digs keeps holding you from business at hand, you think, Karnam might end up being worse than a foothold. But what you say is what you want Digs to believe. "I think, Mr. Mehra, in being harsh on me, you are being harsh on your daughter. All she wants to do is surprise you with this investigative story she is working on. She wanted a little help from me because she was afraid of the kind of people she was having to mingle with. I was just her bodyguard."

Digs is starting to look confused. "What do you mean?" he asks.

"Karnam is on to the hottest story this magazine will ever have. She is her dad's girl. She wanted to prove herself to you, to make you proud," you say. You slow down. You don't want to lay on the poetry too thick.

"What story?" Digs asks suspiciously.

"She told me to leave it for her to tell you."

"Where is she?"

"I wish I knew."

"She is not in any danger, MM, is she?"

"I hope not."

Digs appraises you with a new look. "I hope you haven't gotten her into some jam, MM."

"Not me, Mr. Mehra. I admire your daughter," you say. There's truth in that, too.

Digs mellows a bit. He seems to be coming to a decision. "I hope you are coming for the anniversary party I am throwing at my house tonight. I have invited five hundred people. The politicians are going to be there, and some bureaucrats. Some cabinet ministers might also turn up."

"Certainly, Mr. Mehra. Wouldn't miss it for all the world," you say. "Now I think I had better work on the human-interest box, Mr. Mehra, if you want the story to run in this issue." You have half a mind to scare him with the FIR the army has filed, but you don't want to raise his temperature too much.

"Yes," says Digs. He throws another peculiar look at you. And it floats in your brain as you give Captain Prakash some evocative treatment. This is how you begin in your cube:

> Captain Prakash was a friend. He was part of the elite force in the Indian army: the Pathfinders. A force so elite, it has just a hundred men on its rolls. They specialize in jumping from aircraft at heights upward of thirty thousand feet and gliding toward their target. They are the advance party that secures the landing zone of paratroop forces behind enemy lines. They jump from high up and open their parachutes low. This so they can avoid enemy fire for as long as possible. In February of this year, as he was going on a practice run, Captain Prakash . . .

The rest is easy. While you're on the job, you also write up your lead piece. Mixing truths with half-truths, you plan to sling a few convoy loads of mud onto the 7 Sikh and the army top brass. This is how you start with your coup de grâce:

It's possibly the most ominous development India has seen since independence in 1947. Evidence available to The Post *incriminates an army unit in Kashmir for arms dealing and heroin smuggling over a period of two years. Though the army top brass haven't yet launched thorough investigations of their own, well-placed army sources indicate that it would be highly optimistic to believe that the rot would be limited to one unit.*

The rogue army battalion in question happens to be the 7 Sikh. Based in Kashmir for the last two years and led by its commanding officer, Col. Heminder Sikka, who is in detention, the unit reportedly amassed a huge fortune for its officers and select men by selling arms and ammunition confiscated from militants. Over a two-year period, the unit, according to conservative estimates, amassed a sum close to $10 million. The sum also included profit from selling heroin at market prices. Says a top Defense Ministry official, "We can no longer say that the army is the one institution in the country that's by and large been able to remain untainted."

What is even more alarming is that most of the arms and ammunition made their way to anti-India terrorist outfits. For instance, the NSCN in Nagaland, the LTTE, and BODO and ULFA activists. Sources indicate that the recent spurt in railway track bombings in the North East could owe a lot to the sophisticated arms and ammunition sold to the outfits by 7 Sikh. Apart from state-of-the-art assault rifles, big quantities of RDX, Semtex, detonators, IEDs, and walkie-talkie sets were also sold. It is not yet known whether training was imparted by army personnel.

What's ironic is that the same unit or any of its sister outfits could be posted in the North East to face the same militant organizations they sold the arms to.

Cause for even more alarm, however, are reports from highly placed sources that the army chief, Gen. Subhas Rampal, himself may be involved (General Rampal's parent unit is the 7 Sikh, and he is the brother-in-law of the 7 Sikh commanding officer, Heminder Sikka). Though it's still too preliminary to know the exact extent of his complicity in the selling of arms, what's beyond doubt is his involvement in the improved explosive devices (IED) deal, which he signed one year ago. Worth $5 million, it involved the purchase of detectors, jammers, and other related equipment to detect and disable IEDs, which have emerged as the second-largest casualty factor of Indian armed forces involved in counterinsurgency operations.

What has also been intriguing is the manner in which the army and air force top brass have combined to falsely incriminate the defense minister, Suresh Yadav, in this matter. According to sources in the preliminary investigation by the Central Vigilance Commission, the entire blame has fallen on Yadav. . . .

You continue in this vein. You entangle Rampal and the 7 Sikh in webs so complex, no press conference could unravel them. Then you crown your effort with a stroke of genius. You attach Digs's byline to the story. You figure it will be tough for the bastard to get out of this one. You then access systems with Jain's password. You don't want a trail leading right to you.

You retrieve Jolly's MiG story from Digs's file Q. You give it some sheen and direction. Next, to add greater luster and background to the whole package, you retrieve your sizzler, the ace in the hole, the questionnaire. This completes the package. Your first spread is all photo and headline. You go for DANGEROUS EXPOSURES. The lead photograph is of the 7 Sikh's CO, Heminder Sikka, addressing his men. You punch the caption—"Heminder with his men: How many rotten apples?"

After you have chopped and fitted copy to size for the ten pages in your package, you convert your Quark file into a Postscript (PS) file. The way the publishing and printing mechanics of *The Post* work is that the magazine files are sent by telephone lines directly to the Data Printing Press in Mumbai. The PS file that carries the data cannot be opened or seen. The file can be downloaded only by the shitheads at Data onto an image setter and seen on the screen as positives.

To cross-check whether the positives are coming properly or not, a PDF file is sent. It has low memory bites and you can chuck it along as E-mail. You can open and print a PDF file, but you cannot edit it. Its primary function is to serve as a quality meter of the PS file.

What you have already done, unknown to Dilip, the Systems guy at *The Post*, is install a software program in the server to intercept all *The Posts's* outgoing PS and PDF files for you, if you so wish. By a few strokes of the keyboard, you can delete the regular PS file and piggyback your package onto it. Along with this, of course, you have to delete all the relevant PDF files and manufacture your own.

To cut down on costs, Digs has stopped the policy of checking last-minute proofs of what's going in the magazine. You intend to exploit this single loophole to your advantage should you feel the need to. What this means is that you could even substitute the sex survey's cover photo with your own defense special for the upcoming issue. Replace the current cover shot of a supine model with a shot of the army and air force chiefs at Hindon Air Base. You can see in the background a row of six MiG-21s lined up.

In what you are planning to do, as in other things in life, it is good policy to have your weaponry greased at all times. For what good is a weapon if it's not a breath away from flashing its venom?

There's an art to drawing a gun. The way you have learned it at RAW is always to twist and bend down at the same time to make yourself a smaller target. You leave your jacket open: The time taken to unbutton it might cost you a hole in your heart. You pack a Beretta because it's small. Your other colleagues at RAW prefer the Browning, the favorite of Scotland Yard.

Your weapons training took place in Manesar, where the National Security Guards have their training base. You checked in as police personnel. You learned to shoot in "extreme static," the term RAW has for impossible circumstances. You would be walking in the galley and cardboard targets would spring up all around you. You have also put in time shooting targets with strobe lights flashing. Someday, your instructor told you, you might have to plug a Lashkar-e-Toiba Mossie in a discotheque.

You learned that survival is an end in itself. To live is to fight another day. You were told in plain language that in a shooting melee, there is no such thing as an innocent civilian. Your responsibility, RAW explained, is to protect the assets of RAW—that is, you.

You learned how to pull a gun when sitting in a restaurant. You were told to fall back in your chair and kick the table over while doing so, or just fall back and take aim from under the table. All this in one fluid motion. They also told you to lift your head as you are hitting the ground, so that you take the weight of the fall on your shoulders. What they didn't sort out for you in their manual is the fact that often in a disjointed fall like this, you have your head up your ass, and the real danger in shooting your piece in such a situation is saying good-bye to your balls.

For all of Maj. Raunaq Singh's bluster in your house, you have him listed in the amateur book. Your kitchen cupboard has a false back, an inch and a half from the wall. You've stashed behind it the Beretta and five kilos of heroin, a cut to cover your overhead expenses for the 5 Kumaon deal.

Your dealings with Akramov have reached combustion phase. In a few days, you are airlifting your container loads of heroin to Moscow in the cargo hold of a Russian charter plane, concealed within several thousand pounds of furniture: a dismantled oak sitting room (part of an executive ranch house), cowboy-style. A rage among Moscow outfitters, office furniture is always easy to unload in Russia, where businesses start and disappear daily. This background of instability has made the Russian citizen hesitant to do business with any company that looks down-at-the-heels. People like Jumbo have made a killing selling the con man's show of prosperity.

Of course, you yourself aren't turning Chippendale. Most of your furniture pieces have secret cavities, little hollows you will soon be filling with heroin. To throw the dogs off, you spray concentrated lacquer on the wood. Lacquer throws a wrench in the canine sense of smell. There is a neat pile of money to be made even in the furniture, and since you overinvoiced it, part of Akramov's payment is to be overboard. The rest

you plan to take in old hundred-dollar bills when you prime the furniture and shut the container in the presence of Akramov's lieutenants.

What Akramov does at his end is his business. But you know of the
stateless nations employed by Akramov and his kind. The Ibo and Ogoni
of Nigeria, the Kosovan Albanians, the Kurds in Turkey and Iraq, the
Chechens in Russia, and your very own Tamils in Sri Lanka. The politi-
cally fucked of the world make excellent narcotics runners. They carry
the mob's powder in one direction and return with its dollar stash from
the other. In the late eighties, you have learned, 90 percent of the heroin
in Spain was carried by Liberation Tamil Tigers for Eelam guerrillas
working with Pakistanis in Barcelona, Madrid, and Seville. After the cops
destroyed the network, they were soon replaced by Kurds. At the end of
the century, it's the Kosovans and the Africans who run the show. The
desperation of the Kosovan Albanians makes them ideal recruits for the
mafiosi. Till NATO wrought havoc, the nerve center of deal making was
the lounge of the Grand Hotel in Pristina, where you could sell napalm,
grenades, detonators, missiles, or assault rifles for shipment to all corners
of the globe. Discretion in a place like the Grand was pointless.

The bulk of Akramov's narcotics goes in plastic sachets at the bottom
of his gasoline trucks. Very early during the Yeltsin years, the suppliers
learned the supply-and-demand mechanics of state-subsidized gasoline.
Tanked up at sixty-five cents a gallon, the trucks are driven to the Polish
border, where a network of contacts ushers them into Poland and then to
Germany, where a sixty-five-cent gallon of Russian gasoline trades for up
to six dollars. In this manner and with similar margins, the Russian Mafia
has drained coal in millions of tons, Uzbekistan cotton in wagonloads,
gasoline from Kazakhstan and Chechnya by the lakeful, and acres of
Siberian timber—none of the money going to the various government
treasuries involved.

You know all this because in one of your trips to Moscow, when you
went on behalf of RAW to recruit Russian naval engineers for the Indian

navy's nuclear-submarine project, you had to tap the Mafia resources for quality personnel. It was then that you heard of Akramov. You had a brush with his henchmen, but at that stage in the breakup of the Soviet Union, it was too unimportant for him to notice personally, since his underlings were doing the job. But you have remembered. It was only as a safety measure that, for your current transaction, you contacted him through the help of Patel.

Your search for personnel took you far and wide. It involved locating former employees of the Central Design Bureau for Marine Engineering Rubin and ballistic missile experts. The Indian navy, you learned, was having problems launching a ballistic missile from submarines. The main trouble was the effect of water in the nozzle on motor ignition. The U.S. Trident 11 system faced similar setbacks. What you also learned was that the submarine-launched Sagarika was not a cruise missile, as reported, but the "big one," with a range of three thousand miles.

Since then, you have kept close tabs on the Advanced Technology Vehicle Program—navy jargon for a nuclear-powered submarine. You know, for instance, that even though the diplomatic line is deterrence against China, what is perceived as the main threat is the U.S. military presence in the Indian Ocean. The job of your employers in RAW has been to acquire, steal, or buy, whatever has been essential to the ATV project. The mission has also been to spread disinformation. This was where you came in handy. You planted stories about problems in the development of the 190-MW power reactor. You were trying to con not only the media but foreign intelligence agencies as well. This necessitated some time and expense, too. It led to the purchase of low-enriched uranium from China, essentially to suggest that the capability to separate large amounts of highly enriched uranium didn't quite exist in the country.

You know, although you shouldn't, that of the five nuclear-powered submarines planned, two have already been tested and are operational: The people you recruited for the project have gotten back to you time and again. Although that's something RAW wouldn't have you indulge in, you firmly believe that in the theater you have chosen for yourself, battlefield awareness is a vital tool for your own survival and that of those who depend on you.

Digs has strung up helium balloons on the roof for *The Post's* first anniversary, which, thanks to you, might turn out to be its last. You spot your gang of Dravid, Karim, Dilip, Jolly, and Matthew. You tap out a Marlboro and try to put Karnam out of your mind. But there is the need to watch your back. Though you have been more than useful to RAW, you aren't an insider, so to speak. You don't exist in the personnel files, and loyalty in intelligence outfits, your own experience tells you, largely boils down to the principle of immediate exigency. In the upcoming maneuvers, you are going to be playing for high stakes, and the fallout involved could make you an ideal candidate for numero uno fall guy—the Lee Harvey Oswald kind of situation. Eventually, that will lead to you being worth more dead than alive.

Since morning, you have thought it best not to dwell on what the 7 Sikh could be doing to Karnam. There are other pressing matters to attend to. So long as you have the white powder, the controlling lever is in your hands. And when the time comes, you have what it takes to bring them to the table, or so you think.

You spot a triumvirate of defense correspondents. You will soon have need of them. Ashish Massey of the *Nation*, Vikas Khanduja of the *Times of India*, and Brajesh Gupta of the *Indian Express*. You decide that the time is propitious to do a little advanced public-relations drill with the defense caucus. You insinuate yourself into the group. You know them well and have traveled with them on many occasions. You come in when Khanduja, arms waving like copter blades, is directing his artillery fire at army policy.

"They said in 1987 during the war in Siachen that they would raise an

alpine division. After the victory, it went on the back burner," says Khanduja.

Gupta chews Khanduja's salvo left and right, up and down.

"Costs, costs," mutters Gupta. "Seventy percent of the budget is going
in wages. Some artillery officers were telling me the last time they fired
their guns was two years back. Half the units have netted their field guns
to conserve on ammunition and spares."

What you would like to know is which ones. But Massey is opening
his mouth.

"I shouldn't be talking about it, guys. It doesn't go beyond here,
right?" implores Massey. His itch to be the first with the information mil-
itates and wins against his desire to be prudent.

"The MiG-21s," Massey begins.

You tense involuntarily. Sensing that Massey is on the brink of some
big news, Gupta and Khanduja bank toward him, drinks forgotten.
Massey is whispering now.

"Ninety percent of them were grounded till two weeks back. Engine
problems. Best-kept secret in the fucking air force since God knows
when," adds Massey.

It's your turn to chew on something. This, you admit to yourself, is
news to you as well. Gupta recovers. His tongue swipes his lips. A predator eyeing a tip.

"Yeah, I had heard of something like that. But I doubt it was on this
scale. I think it was some routine maintenance snags. A little more than
usual," says Gupta.

Massey's face contorts with agony: his master scoop of the evening dismissed as "routine maintenance snags." "What do you mean, 'routine'?
Half your force goes into a coma and you call it *routine*?"

You give more credence to Massey, for it plugs with your own assess-
ment of what you think could have happened. The Russians blowing up
the MiG-21 upgrade scheme. But the problem, you figure, could have

been more on the avionics side of things. Khanduja looks for an opening to regain the momentum.

"The Mirage 2000, man, it flies with no bombs," says Khanduja. He looks around at the three of you, scanning your faces for effect. "It's a gun with no bullets. The French delivery schedule is all screwed up."

"This is scary, boys. An air force with planes that can't fly and no bombs to chuck," you say.

"And a navy with a submarine that doesn't sink," says Gupta. His ace in the hole for the evening.

"You are joking," says Massey.

"Serious," says Gupta. "I heard the Mazagon docks just made an on-scale prototype for their ATV, minus the power reactor, and it wouldn't sink off Vizagapatnam."

This you recognize as a bit of propaganda from your own outfit. You decide to add some fuel to it.

"Yeah, it's true," you say. "The hull also leaked at a depth of a thousand feet. It was designed to go more than twice that deep. Turns out they have some major complications with the HY-80 steel they are using in the hull."

"Yeah?" says Massey.

"That's incredible," says Khanduja. "They should have the entire ATV project audited. It's a scam."

You decide it's time to go into battle with your hooks and tackle.

"Are you guys free for the whole of July?" you ask.

"Why?" asks Gupta. You figure he's the key for the two others also to say yes.

"There's a project coming of the Indian Defense Initiative. It's an NGO with Carnegie Foundation links. It wants some research work done in Russia and the central Asian republics. Map out the Indian army's supply line, the T-72 assembly in the Ukraine, the MiG factories, the works. It's part of a long-term project. They don't want academics.

They want solid investigative guys. All of you would be on a fellowship," you say. You take a pause, let the hooks settle in. Then reel it all in. "They are willing to dish a per diem of three hundred dollars. That's about ten thousand for the month, plus research and travel costs of two thousand. Any of you guys interested? I have to tell them by next week."

Gupta's lips are going dry. Khanduja draws closer to you, his body language that of a supplicant. Massey's pupils are dilating.

"I have been to Moscow," says Khanduja, laying the foundation for his credentials. "They have whores falling at you from the hotel walls."

"I know this army colonel; he was the Soviet defense attaché in France. Met him in Paris on an airbus trip," Gupta squeaks, throwing his jack of clubs.

"I think you need the Mafia pitching in on this. You can't take a leak there without a Chechen asking for his cut. My brother, he works with IBM Moscow. His job is to know which Mafia to send the monthly to," says Massey.

You throw some competition in to quicken the pulse.

"They might just go with two," you say. "But let's see. I might be able to work out something." It's been your policy now and then to grease up the defense correspondents at RAW's expense. But here you are playing solo, lubricating the media with your own hard-earned cash.

Khanduja feels his gambit hasn't been quite as decisive. He makes amends. "I was on this Aeroflot flight to New York and got spooked in Moscow for a week. No flights. Fucking airline strike. They didn't even put us up in a decent hotel. But I used the time to do a few interviews. I met Zhirinovsky, that nationalist guy. He said if he was in power, he would swing a couple of dozen nukes India's way, instead of putting them in the grinder because of these SALT treaties. That's your ICBM problem solved right there," he says.

Gupta senses the temperature variations. He goes for the kill. "This colonel I told you about. He retired. He went into defense consultancy. He's been to India about a dozen times. His mind, it's like a computer.

He could reel you the dimensions of the T-72 turret. Every time he meets me, he wants me to do some liaison work for him. I told him no. The guy ultimately went for this retired deputy naval chief. But he's got a dacha outside Moscow the size of a football field. He's sent me about a dozen invitations to spend time there."

You are in the mood to check out any prospects of interference at the starting block itself. Get your early-warning system in the air to detect any circuitry quandaries.

"By the way," you begin, "I might be cruising some hard news by your noses in the next few days. I will make sure to send you an advance press release of the scoop we will be carrying in our magazine."

"On what?" asks Gupta. His antenna's on full alert.

"You will know when you see," you say.

"Will the shit hit the ceiling?" asks Massey.

"And more. We will need a six-column front-page preview on that. We need to get some power under our hood. A steroid boost to circulation. Give the competition a scare," you say.

"It won't cost us our jobs, will it?" asks Gupta.

"The thing I like about you, Brajesh, is that you come to the crux of the matter," you say. "I think you will be chasing the story for the rest of your goddamn career."

"Can't you give us a hint?" asks Khanduja.

To give a hint now, you think, would be inappropriate. If things leaked, it might put a snarl in your kismet.

"Well, let's say that people will be going down. There will be carnage and mayhem. It will be happy times for our breed," you say.

Looking across the lawn, you see Digs heading your way. A cruise missile with a purpose. You are not in the mood to take him on without your mental supplementaries. Your Marlboros, too, have run out. With his heart condition, he doesn't like smoke wafting his way. You look for background you can disappear in. You say bye to your peers and disappear behind the bar. It's a saloon construction, complete with American Western motifs and guys with leather boots and cowboy hats. One of Digs's literary heroes is Oliver Strange. You, too, have grown up on Jim Green, alias Sudden. Times, you muse, haven't changed much since the days when being the fastest draw made you king of the dung pile. In the age of atoms, you figure, it doesn't make much difference who pulls the rod first. Now, whether you score first or later, it's immaterial, since you still end up not being in the frame.

As you walk behind and past the bar, your radar scope on battlefield alert, you spot intrusion.

Col. Ray Chowdhary eyes you with carnivorous appetite. You have spent a big part of yesterday afternoon planning the Akramov end of the operation at the RAW HQ off Lodi Road. You are rarely invited to HQ: They don't want you bumping into anyone you might know.

But rules were given a detour in this case, as the chiefs in RAW were salivating at the prospect of netting close to $40 million, money they wouldn't have to account for even in internal audits. Money, some of it at least, that could line their own pockets. You are hot property at the moment, a fucking pioneer. A Vasco da Gama establishing the Asian spice route.

"I didn't know you were coming," you say.

"It's best to keep the cavalry on the hoof."

You notice he sticks close to the hum of one of the many lawn fans Digs has sprayed over his property to keep the breeze circulating. A creature of habit, Chowdhary is making it as hard as possible for any potential eavesdroppers. He was on temporary assignment to the Indo-Tibet Border Police, having cut his teeth going toe-to-toe with the Chinese in Tibet. You know for a fact that he masterminded SSB forces, Tibetan irregulars, to blueprint the Chinese nuclear capability stationed in Tibet. It was courtesy of the SSB that the rest of the world came to know of the three nuclear sites in Da Qaidam, Delingha, and Xiao Qaidam. The Chinese house their Dong Fieng ICBMs there. They have a range of some four thousand miles. The Chinese are also developing a fourth site in Nagchuka, 125 miles north of Lhasa. It was largely the Chowdhary investigation that forced the Indian government to go for its three nuclear tests in Pokhaan in 1998. But ballooning over the Himalayas hasn't really spiffed Chowdhary up enough to meet the demands of urban espionage.

"There was some trouble at police HQ. Were you involved?" Chowdhary asks.

"A piece of cake. Nothing that we didn't have the enzymes for," you say. You wonder too late whether Chowdhary might mistake enzymes for a new kind of assault rifle.

"We don't want any incidents. The press starts making some links and we are dead," says Chowdhary.

"The press will think what you lead them to think. They are sheep you can lead to slaughter," you say. You believe it. You have an insider's view. Chowdhary, despite all his Chinese experience, is less equipped to operate at your level of subtlety.

"What's getting me worried is whose slaughter you are planning," says Chowdhary. "Ours, yours, or some people we don't know about? We are getting nervous, MM," adds the colonel.

For all his Chinese CV, you admit to yourself, Chowdhary isn't totally without weight. You hadn't quite made the whole of your plans legible to Chowdhary and company. Also, the 7 Sikh escapades of the morning and your meeting with the defense minister have made it clear that for you to survive, the first salvo has to be fired at the army. Somebody there has to go down. The bigger the better. These aren't plans that you are anxious to get approved by RAW.

One, they might get nervous at your audacity and forbid it. That would complicate your life. You might still have to go through with your plan, for want of any better, and earn their disapproval. Censure in the intelligence-agency lexicon often means a bullet in your head. Two, and this is your premise, once the shit started, it would be difficult for RAW to back down, as that would only encourage the cycle of shit to get bigger. So to step on the shit would be, ironically, your best bet of pulling off your scams. Of course, with Karnam in the frame, something that RAW isn't tuned in to yet, you figure, the complications and, therefore, the shit would amplify in proportion.

"Nervous at this chickenshit operation? Save your fuel for bigger contingencies, sir," you say. Normally, you are not obsequious with the likes of Chowdhary, but you don't want to raise his hackles, give him cause for alarm, get the RAW artillery on your case. That would mean the opening of another front, a stretching of your resources.

"I think your paranoia is derailing you, sir," you say. There's no point in omitting your flattery after giving him a taste of it. That would be another glitch. "Things are in control."

"They had better be," says the colonel.

You savor an ominous echo in his parting words. But, in your game, if you are jostled by the likes of Chowdhary, it means it's time for you to go AWOL. It would be more dangerous to tell him your plans than to act and draw him in, whether he likes it or not.

Chowdhary takes off when he sees Digs head your way. Digs is in a rugby charge, a Tomahawk on lock. You have no option but to weather the storm. Your life, you feel, is a dossier on tangling with the Digses and Chowdharys of the planet.

"The party's going great," you say. "Is the prime minister coming?"

Digs glares at you. He's not frothing at the mouth, but he's pretty close.

"Listen, where's my daughter? You better tell me before I file a complaint with the police."

You take Digs aside. His posture is rigid. He's eyeing you as if you are about to drizzle him with your spit. You have to buy some time. Think of some outlandish bull extempore. Plausibility, you have always felt, has to have in it elements of the truth.

"Mr. Mehra, this is no way to lose your cool. You remember, after the nuclear blasts, there was this big talk about some of India's retaliatory nukes being mobile on the rails? Karnam's working on an exclusive about that. A contact's taking her right to the secret depot. We are getting the works, photos, everything but a test firing."

"What?" says Digs.

"I didn't want to load you on it from the start. If she scores a zero, it would mean we'd booted you up for nothing. She told me not to tell you. I am sorry. I think in something this important, we should have pulled you in from the start," you say.

Digs is sweating. He is pulling up his trousers. His mouth is opening and closing. "Huh," he says. "Are you monitoring the whole thing? Is she safe?"

"I think once we get the story, we will have to think in terms of a print overrun of at least thirty thousand copies. We could look to sell an advertising logo for the pages. Give News Today some ulcers," you say. The logo, you feel, could be a clincher. "Some defense companies might give it a bite. Bofors, for instance. They are looking to mend their fences with the Indian setup. Even these German wagon makers. I believe the Indians blew the top off to fit the missiles in. Next time around, they might send some that fit the Agni 3 just perfectly."

You don't know whether Digs has bought your story. Either he is a very good actor or plain dumb. As you await his comeback to your brain wave about an advertising logo, you are joined by Tapash Mitra, editor of News Today.

"Congratulations," says Mitra. "But you have a lot of catching up to do." Mitra, of course, is rubbing in the fact that his magazine has a superior circulation. A prig in office and a prig out, Mitra, you cannot but believe, is vying with Digs for the crown of the gilt-edged asshole. There's a transformation in Digs. He's back to his garrulous self. The perfect host. He starts summoning his waiters, and Mitra gets inundated with scotch.

"We sure do," says Digs. "But I believe there's a place for both. Ultimately, it's to the reader's benefit. Previously there was one; now he gets two."

"It's good for the information highway," you say. Mitra now deigns to notice you.

"Hello, MM," he says. "Read your piece on the Narmada agitation. The business behind antidam agitations. Good stuff."

"That was Jain," you say.

"Yeah, sorry, I always get confused between the two of you," says Mitra.

That, you think, is highly illogical. But you let Digs come to his rescue.

"Let me introduce you to our designer, Leslie," says Digs, sweeping Mitra away. "He's got some fancy ideas."

You take a breather. You notice Karim signaling you from the first floor of Digs's house. You trespass in Digs's house. In your absence, your fraternity has been venturesome. Dravid's fiddling around in Digs's study, going through the book titles on the shelves.

"Look here, what I found, *Camp 6*. The book has been out of print for sixty years. Shall I ask Digs for a read?" says Dravid.

"I doubt he knows he has it. Keep what you see. It's on the house," you say.

"What's with Digs's wife? Are they divorced or what?" asks Jolly.

"Who's surprised?" says Dilip. "Look what I have here. A *Playboy* collector's edition. It was in this drawer here."

There's a scramble. Karim, Dravid, Siddy, and Matthew make their way to Dilip's electric haul. There's *Hustler* as well, and a French porn magazine that has a lengthy photo feature of women doing dogs.

"This is sick," says Jolly.

"It's fucking art," says Karim. "Look at the layouts. We should get Leslie to copy one of these."

"Where do these women come from, man?" Siddy asks of no one in particular. "The only time you get to see this quality is in hotel lobbies and fashion shows."

"Consider yourself lucky you don't have any of them in your life," you say.

"Why's that?" asks Karim.

"Women like them, they skin off a man's defenses. First, they suck your romantic side in about two days. Another half a day perhaps for your masculine self. And then you will be left all exposed, like a peeled banana. You will soon discover she's cut up your cock in her cornflakes," you say.

Everybody laughs.

It's at this moment that Digs enters the study, a look of maximum alarm on his face.

"MM," he says. "We have a murder in the office. Somebody killed this electrician on the mezzanine."

The Beretta digging into your flesh is alive once again.

Gulab Chand has a tiny bullet hole above his heart. The exit hole in his back is the size of a rhino's head. You and others notice this after the rope tying him up to his chair is unwound and they lean him on the table for a few minutes. There is blood splattered on the walls, on the floor, and on the ceiling. On Chand's work table lies a copy of *Debonair*, and a take-out container, undamaged, with the dinner uneaten. Chand obviously slipped in his sentinel routine, left the mezzanine door unlocked, and made it easy for 7 Sikh powder-explorers to punch him a one-way ticket ahead of the millennium. You look for signs of torture. You notice the toes are quashed, the nails turned, and there are burn marks on the chest. Chand, you realize, didn't give his secrets easily.

The guards didn't hear any gunshots. But Chand had two visitors at 8:00 P.M. They made a few trips with duffel bags to a parked jeep. You know why. But you hope. The guards got nervous during the duo's last trip to the jeep and asked to look in the bag. One of them got a bullet in the shin for his challenge. That alerted the neighborhood, but the damage had been done.

There's also the lettering on the wall in Chand's blood: "Ha-ha-ha, we found out." That's intended for you. Only one part of the scene remains to be checked out further. But you reached the mezzanine about the same time as the local police. Digs was too nervous to be able to take the drive. A Delhi police DCP is poking his forefinger in and around the scene of the crime.

You don't want to stay longer than necessary. The forensics don't interest you. You just want to confirm your worst fears. You look closely at the grille that covered the air-conditioning vent, searching for signs of an entry. You find scratches all around the frame and the top end is bent, as if pried with a crowbar. The vent wasn't a good idea after all.

The photographer has come now. You notice that Chand's Glock is missing, a valuable addition to the 7 Sikh's armament acquisitions. Chand, you know, didn't carry around his army ID, specifically to avoid trouble for his 5 Kumaon brotherhood in case of disasters like this.

You go to your office on the first floor. You draw the blinds on the glass windows and the door. You lock the door and switch off the lights, so nobody knows you are inside.

You take off your shoes, jacket, shirt, and trousers. You lock the Beretta in your drawer. You stand only in your VIP briefs for your commando assignment.

You push your table till it's underneath the vent, remove the grille, and pull yourself up into the aluminum tunnel. Your legs thrash under you, hitting thin air for a second, as you heave your torso through. Once inside, you navigate your way, using light from your wristwatch, its glow pattern as powerful as a penlight. The duct leads to the library. There, another duct will take you to the mezzanine.

In the dark of the library, you work hastily on the grille. You don't want somebody taking it into his head to include the library in the investigation. Discovery would involve more than a little explanation on your part.

You work your way into the mezzanine, dragging yourself as softly as you can, for part of the way takes you over the landing, where dozens of police personnel jab and peck at would-be evidence. Your watch has a metallic strap, and you don't want any metal-to-metal clank. Progress is slow: It takes you close to fifteen minutes to reach the turn that gives you a clear look at the mezzanine vent where you had stashed the heroin. The light in your watch has been faltering for the last two minutes. It's flickering on and off, the battery packing it in. The vents are empty, as you knew they would be.

You have come up here to look for any telltale signs the bastards might have inadvertently left behind. Signs that you could use to zipper down on their tracks. Scraps of paper, or maybe even a button that had come loose.

You have to return fast, for your light is nearly gone and the way back slower, since you have no place to turn around. But you feel you have to go forward one more yard to get a look at the mezzanine grille, the hole directly over Chand's desk, fifteen feet away. Your light flickers off and on, then stays off. Your eyes adjust to the darkness, which is illuminated only by the spill from the vent hole. But it's not bright enough for you to see anything that might be hidden there.

You know what's coming, though, when you hear the special rattle that, in your ears, can only be the sound of death spinning your way. Your right hand is stretched in front to probe for the grenade you now know is there. It's too dark for you to see. You realize they've used a trip wire—a mechanism with a difference. Instead of blowing up the grenade directly, it has loosened the grenade inside the vent, allowing it to roll down the incline to where you are squeezed in aluminum, a coffin in the making.

All at once, the light in your watch comes back to life and bounces off the grenade, allowing you to make the catch of your life. You hurl the grenade toward the vent. You know you have four seconds before the chemicals mix and match, and you hope the grenade will hit the vent, where its energy would be directed downward instead of at you. You bury your face in your arms.

The explosion fills your hole with light and smoke. Even as the acrid smoke fills your nostrils, you realize it's just a stun grenade, a light and sound show to unnerve the enemy. The 7 Sikh assholes, you figure, have a sense of humor.

You take your own sweet time going back, making all the racket you want. You can hear the stampede that clears the building.

In the silence and dark of your office, you get back into your clothes. Though your heartbeat has slowed, your central nervous system is still disorderly, the neural pathways clogged with traffic. You feel the need for a hit to improve the aerodynamics of your mind.

You keep enough for a couple of lines in your drawer. Within a couple of minutes of snorting them, your belly warms up and calm flows through your veins. You return to what it must have felt like when you were in your mother's womb. Today, you take more than your normal dose.

The world, you feel, owes more than it thinks to the Germans. Perhaps even the Renaissance. It was during that period in the sixteenth century that the Swiss-German physician Bombastus von Hohenheim accomplished the pharmacological breakthrough of producing a tincture of opium by mixing it with alcohol, a preparation he called laudanum. The concoction saturated Europe, and civilization was on track for sedation on a mass scale. The proceeding generations fiddled with Hohenheim's pharmacological forerunner, which became the indispensable tool of medicine in the eighteenth century.

In 1805, however, it was left to another German, Frederick Serturner, to isolate the alkaloid of morphine from opium. This separation of the principal ingredient from the parent compound was a dazzling feat. It unleashed into the market a drug ten times more powerful than opium.

There was another first for Germany when the Bayer Company started the commercial production of heroin in 1898.

Heroin wasn't Germany's only area of chemical triumph. In 1855, the German physicist Friedrich Gaedcke isolated the "active principle" of cocaine. World War II also saw the German invention of methadone as a substitute for heroin.

A half an hour later, your system at peak efficiency, you make a call to Major Kohli.

You are in battle gear for the second day in succession. Major Kohli's army networking has gotten him the intelligence all of you need. You have the precise location of the 7 Sikh hideout, where Karnam, in all probability, is, too. It's a farmhouse in Chattarpur, on the outskirts of Delhi.

To your surprise, you receive a call from Maj. Raunaq Singh on your mobile. You don't normally like to carry one, for in your business, the instrument could be pinpointed and your location given away by Airtel software. But in predicaments like the one you find yourself in, it becomes a sterling device.

"Asshole," says Major Singh, "are you feeling a little less cocky?"

You recognize the voice. That he was able to trace your number increases your estimate of his ingenuity, since your office doesn't list your digits.

"Maybe," you say.

"How about we do some business?"

"Depends on what you want."

"What I want is what I already have and more. Your balls are here, too. They are worth maybe something extra," he says.

It's easy to digest the general theme of proceedings if you are at the butt end of things. In the overall blueprint, Major Singh is aiming for a wholesale conquest. The 5 Kumaon's arsenal of weapons, though loose change compared to the haul in heroin, is still a tempting acquisition. But you feel a little combativeness is in order.

"Maybe we are already drying our gunpowder. Getting ready to fry your nuts," you say.

"That would be a mistake," says Major Singh. "We have already drilled a hole in one of your heroes. If we have to do that to you and some of your other friends from 5 Kumaon, it would put me into a depression. Besides, in case you are forgetting, we hold the cards. You try something funny and your whore might end up as our evening recreation."

You grimace. Your life, you feel, is getting too entangled with all the fucked-up majors of the world.

"Keep her out of this," you say. "It's not her fight."

"That may be, but she stays. You see, I have gotten used to her presence. It takes a while to break a habit."

"What do you want?"

"Ah. The thing I admire about you, MM, is that you have brains enough to see that the shortest distance between two points is a straight line," says Major Singh.

"That's also the way of a bullet."

The major ignores you. "How about letting us lift your booty from your warehouse?" he asks. "I will see that you get a cut and the army gives you a certificate of merit."

"It isn't mine."

"All the better. That way, you wouldn't lose sleep over it, would you?" says Major Singh.

"I haven't seen the place."

"Aha, MM. You disappoint me. All I want is an address."

"All you need is a bullet up your ass, Major. You are a thief and a murderer," you say.

"So are you, MM. We are quits now. Captain Prakash can feel easy in his next life."

"How about a partnership? That would be more up my street. I could get a price for you guys that would double whatever you're selling at," you offer.

There's a moment of quiet at the other end.

"Interesting," says Major Singh.

"Let's meet," you suggest. "The Jazz Bar in the Maurya at five. If you want a change of plans, you have my mobile number and I yours. And please, no grenades this time. I don't want you strapping one to my chair."

The major laughs. "That was a present to bring you up to date with reality. I didn't think you would fall for it, though, MM."

The line goes dead.

Major Singh has accepted your enticement. The major, you feel, would chime an SOS if he knew you were taking his call outside his burrow. He isn't up to date with cellular technology. With Dilip, your resident computer expert who has access to Airtel software, you confirm the location of the major's call. You are on the right track. Your plan is to wait till the major leaves for his appointment with you. You have a feeling he will leave with a few of his gang members, insurance in case you are pulling a fraud. That would leave the 7 Sikh with a major personnel depletion.

In your reconnaissance, you have taken Polaroids of the building from as many sides as possible. It's a sprawling double-story structure, with a swimming pool thrown in. At a corner and attached to the main house is a huge garage—likely the 7 Sikh's armament warehouse. Though you have no way of knowing for sure where the heroin is, the only way to find out is to get in the game. The same goes for Karnam.

It's your belief that your opposition has between eight and ten hardcore members of the 7 Sikh. There are three of you. But you have roped in Jumbo as your ace-in-waiting. Wearing dark glasses, he sits a hundred yards away in a white Sierra. His job is to drive the getaway car if you have the 7 Sikh chasing you in vehicles they have hidden away from your prying eyes. Had you located any such vehicles, Kohli's planning included smashing their distributor caps. Since you didn't discover any, you would now be concentrating on the wheels, which would be less messy and it wouldn't involve opening the hood.

Ideally, you would have waited for Major Rodriguez to come and boost your manpower. But you have no time. If the current section splits, you can say good-bye to your heroin, and that would create an obstacle course for you that you are in no mood to attempt. And for you to tap into RAW's resources would make them privy to the picture, which eventuality, too, you want to detour.

Besides, you take comfort in Kohli's antecedents. You know he has been assigned to the National Security Guards for three years. He has also trained with the Gourmet d'Intervention de la Gendarmerie Nationale, the low-profile French antiterrorist outfit, where soldiers learn to hit a moving target at a range of eighty feet within two seconds and, subsequently, graduate to hitting the "vital" spots on six moving targets at the same distance within five seconds. You have been in courses like these yourself and know what it takes. Hence, your confidence in Major Kohli's abilities. Indramani is hard-core infantry and stable.

Your raid arsenal is formidable. All three of you have MP5 machine guns with silencers. Indramani's weapon of choice is the AK-47, but you have forbidden it because you don't trust anybody with it on auto. The major oscillates to your viewpoint. Besides, your inventory doesn't include a silencer for the AK.

The three of you sit in an Ashok Leyland truck. This you have brought along to haul the 7 Sikh arsenal. Major Kohli is at the wheel. You sit beside him, while Indramani lines up the 7 Sikh's bungalow in his binoculars from the back. Major Kohli has already identified your team's approach route once Major Singh leaves. The truck sits on top of a manhole cover, which, in fact, is the main service outlet for the drainage channel that empties the swimming pool in the 7 Sikh's compound. The three of you plan to follow the channel to the swimming pool, which is nearly empty, at the back of the house. From there, you will split three ways. Major Kohli will take the ground floor from the east side and you the balcony route from the roof, while Indramani will remain your principal reserve, cutting off exit routes from the rear of the house. Though you stand the chance of getting your legs wet, it's less risky than a frontal entry through the main gates or over the boundary walls.

Jumbo has lined up your local pizza boy to go and ring the bell two minutes after Major Singh's exit.

You have planned this diversion to allow you the minute you will need to get out of the swimming pool and rush for the roof and for Major Kohli to make a breach through one of the bedrooms. The pizza ploy will draw at least two of Major Singh's thugs out into the open. It will also give you a clue to the numbers you will have to deal with. Your pizza boy is under instructions to say, "Sorry, wrong address," then beat it the hell out of there.

You have a long wait ahead before Major Singh leaves for the Jazz Bar. You listen to Major Kohli's tale of how it first started out with 7 Sikh on the border.

"Rodriguez came up with the idea of LRRPs, long-range reconnaissance patrols. Four guys slogging it for a week or more. We used to cross the line of control and make underground shelters right under the nose of their border outposts. Sometimes as close as a hundred and fifty feet," says Major Kohli.

"You were allowed to do that? Cross the line of control?" you ask, incredulous.

"The fuck we were. We never let on. At first, we didn't even tell the boys. Didn't want to make them nervous. We did it to gather intelligence. Check out the Mossie movement. The moment we spotted them preparing to go across, we would alert our boys on the other side by radio. Sometimes we would even radio down mortar fire on them when they were near the border but on their side of the hill. This way, it was less messy. They would ditch their equipment and heroin, and if it was a big catch, we would pick it up and return. That saved us some firefights.

We rarely called for artillery fire, since then the news would get to brigade HQ and they would start poking their noses into it," says Major Kohli.

He unwraps a pack of Wrigley's and cuts himself half a stick. You take the other half.

"The first time we did a hide, we didn't know what we were getting into. It was Rodriguez, me, and two of the men. We wanted to check out the concept. It gets incredibly boring. You are sitting here in this underground six-by-four thing, if you are lucky, waiting. That's the worst part. Not even the shitting is that bad. You shit in polyethylene. The first time, we mixed our shit and piss together and the packet burst. We had to stay two more days in that because some fifteen Mossies came and parked themselves a hundred and thirty feet from us. We couldn't even call for some shelling, as we were too damn close. We used to take turns sleeping. One sleeping bag for four people. Every time a patrol returned, they would smell like pigs.

"We would move in the dark only if we needed to; otherwise, we had fashioned our bionics into periscopes. We had night-vision equipment. Sometimes, in daylight, we even took potshots with a sniper rifle we had captured from four mujahideen. A Barrett M82A2. It's a 12.7-millimeter thing. It's a fucking monster. It weighs twenty-five pounds, and the best part is that it cuts a guy in two even if he's got steel plates on. That way, they never got to know where the shots were coming from. We used silencers and flash suppressors. Things got bad when one of our LRRPs bumped into a 7 Sikh patrol in the night as they were returning from a mission. They bumped off three of our men. One escaped to tell the tale."

"Can't say I blame them. How were they to know you weren't Mossies?"

"Funny thing is, they were waiting for us. How they came to know about our patrols is anybody's guess. But they wanted a piece of the cake. And the guy who was leading the 7 Sikh patrol that night was Captain Prakash," says Major Kohli.

"Hmm," you say, things beginning to fall in place. "No inquiry?"

"They never claimed any kills, and we wrote our three off in a terrorist encounter. Nobody did a postmortem to check on the slugs," says Major Kohli.

You figure it's time to put a brake on the major's monologue. You know about his not-too-recent attachment to an elite unit, and you don't think he knows you know.

"What if you were captured? What uniform did you have on?" you ask.

"We always wore our own. That way, we could say we'd strayed and maybe return as POWs. But luckily, nothing like that ever happened," says Major Kohli.

"There's some talk about mining the passes with TNMs," you say. "You guys try any long-range patrols after that and it's going to be ta-ta, good-bye. Your balls will land on the moon."

"TNMs?"

"Tactical nuclear mines. Fifteen-hundred-foot total-kill radius. No radiation detected after one hour," you say.

"Where did you get that?"

You can almost hear Major Kohli's mental machinery oiling into fifth gear.

"Ministry. Top secret," you say. You tap out a Marlboro and offer the major one. Of course, you are indulging in your speciality here—the MM gas discharge.

"You know what? That cannot be," says Major Kohli. There's a sly look in his eyes.

"And why not?" you ask. You can see the climax coming.

"We have this Mahatma Gandhi syndrome munching on our system. Fucking politicians want to go for a second strike option. Want the Mossies to vaporize our own nuts before launching the *big* ones. The TNMs would be first strike," explains Major Kohli.

"If at all. I doubt they've armed," you say.

Despite the cigarette smoke, you can see the major smile.

"I was wondering when you would come to that, MM. It took you a long time, didn't it? Rodriguez fucking warned me," says Major Kohli. He lets loose a string of smoke rings on your face. Tracer bullets hitting your nose.

You freeze at first, but then you think, What the hell. Can't win all the psy ops.

"Rodriguez is a motherfucker," you say, smiling.

"Well, MM, he isn't the only one," says Major Kohli.

The major is holding the cigarette with his thumb and forefinger. You don't see any mirth in his eyes. But the thing that keeps your spirits up is the fact that you don't see any hostility, either.

"Never lose sight of that fact. I was just wondering what kind of rail system they have going to keep our nukes ready," you say. You are referring to the 16 Agni 2 missiles that you know are, temporarily, the responsibility of the NSG till the army raises two battalions of its own on line with the Special Forces. You have known for a while, courtesy of RAW, that Major Kohli is part of the initial deployment, will be until his term with the NSG expires and he reverts to his parent unit, 5 Kumaon. Technically, that is. Because you know the major is squeezing all the sick and study leave he can take from the NSG these days to be with his parent unit. He doesn't want the riches to bypass him.

"They put us on dummy runs for a month, trying to identify the security kinks. It's a fourteen-wagon train, eight for the missiles and the rest for the troops to bunk in. The missiles are in these special wagons. They dip in the middle to get more clearance at the top. The command wagon, from where you can launch the lot, is right in the middle. It has about twenty different kinds of radio sets. I went in just once," says Major Kohli. He drops his cigarette stub on the truck floor and crushes it with his black sneakers.

You promptly offer the major another and light it for him. It's in your interest to keep his train of thought going.

"Because of the special wagons, the train can't go faster than forty-five miles an hour. But the average speed is just fifteen miles an hour. That used to give all of us a lot of sleepless nights. At those speeds, even bloody dogs can jump on and off."

"Traffic?" you say. Your own Marlboro has run out. You spin it outside the window.

"The bloody Indian railway's got eighty percent of its traffic on twenty percent of its tracks. In the Delhi-Mumbai sector, you have fifty trains going up and down each way. Your freight-train priority shunts you to the bottom of the list. You have to watch every son of a bitch on wheels overtake you. Every time the shit halts, your blood pressure goes up. It takes about three minutes for the thing to stop, even if it's going twenty-five miles an hour. I don't know whose dumb idea it was to stick it up in the Indian railways. Twenty guys could take the shit down and roll with the rockets."

You register what the major has just told you.

"Say, Major, will six men do?" you ask. You have a twisted smile on your face. You don't know which way it will play. A leap of faith is what you are taking. If things go bad, the major will have to be taken out, and fast.

But the major has a big grin on his face.

"Why go for six when you can raise all the men you want? Policy of my entire life. Where you can grab chocolate fudge, who wants a Diet Coke?" says Major Kohli.

The 5 Kumaon, you feel, had its wisdom all cut out and dried to keep the airwaves free from chaos. You are smiling, too. But the major's smile is thinning out. There's more coming.

"Of course, it depends on whose funeral you are planning," he says.

"Nobody's," you say. For a change, you mean it. "Some missile doctors just want to glue their ears to the end of their stethoscopes. Find out the kind of circuitry our chips have going in the cone. Your folks on the train can have the gadgetry back once the surgeons are through."

"What's this? Hire purchase? You play for keeps in this business, MM.

Also, what species of diagnosticians are you playing out the rope for?" asks Major Kohli.

"Well, let's say from the developed world," you say.

"We are having no Mossies," says Major Kohli.

"Who wants them?" you reply.

"It all depends on what Rodriguez thinks," says Major Kohli.

"Of course," you say. But you don't quite want Rodriguez to hop on to this if you can avoid it. Major Rodriguez brings with him his own set of complexities that drive your blood pressure up. Besides, you want to drive a wedge between the two 5 Kumaon gunslingers. You want to start by giving Major Kohli some food for thought. "There are a lot of zeros in there for you, Major, if you can pull it off. But the more lads you get in on this, by the time your turn comes to lift your bag of cash, you would find it quite a bit lighter. There's the security aspect as well."

"What you are telling me, MM, is that you don't want Rodriguez in on this," says Major Kohli.

"That's not what I said," you say. You don't want any misunderstandings with a beast like Rodriguez at this stage.

"Now you are telling me I don't know my English," says Major Kohli.

Major Kohli is a difficult customer.

"No. What I am telling you is that Major Singh's Gypsy is just moving out of the gates," you say. The major, however, is moving alone. But that doesn't make your team change its operational plan.

Surprise, as always, is the key factor. As you elbow your way in through the channel to the swimming pool, you convey last-minute reminders to Kohli.

"Nothing happens to the girl," you say. "Or you are dead meat." You have already described Karnam in detail to your team.

In the end, that doesn't prove to be necessary. Even before the pizza boy has left, you have found Karnam in an upstairs bedroom. The windows have been pasted with brown paper and the curtains are all drawn, but the door is open. It's the second door you check. She is lying on the bed, wearing the same clothes that you last saw her in. She is surprised to see you. You raise your finger to your lips. She motions to the end of the hallway, quick to the game.

"How many?" you ask her softly.

"Four," says Karnam.

With Major Singh gone, that's three your team has to face. The 7 Sikh, contrary to your expectation, is impoverished in the employees department. With nearly a one-on-one situation, the battle, you feel, is going to be a cakewalk. You signal Karnam to get under the bed.

You can hear the engine of a Honda starting and picking up power. That, you infer, would be the pizza boy leaving. Time for you to step on your artillery. Your upstairs approach gives you an advantage over any 7 Sikh gentry breaking ground to come after Karnam. Your weapon is at your shoulder and you are seeing things through your sights. Your training has taken over.

Already, from downstairs, you can hear the soft spits of an MP5 riding a silencer. But some of the bullets are hitting glass, furniture, whatever, and now, to any professional on the first floor, things would be unmistakable. The first shouts and yells follow.

The door at the end of the hallway bursts open and you eye a soldier in your sights. He has on the trousers of his uniform. His upper body is bare. He, you figure, has just been roused from his sleep. You go for some precision shots here. You aim for the left shin. You hear the bone crack and the man scream. Like your team below, you don't want to take any chances. You don't want to go for any "Hands up" routine. You have only inflicted an injury that will make your man incapable of any surprises, but it will heal eventually. Your man is down on the ground, holding his shin.

You check out the two other rooms on your floor. Quick visual sweeps, with your weapon on alert. Your floor is clear, and the shooting downstairs has also stopped. But your training won't let you relax. At the

NSG "killer range," where you have honed your bag of tricks, they had electrodes attached to your various muscle groups for measuring your relaxation levels. If your adrenaline dipped, gun barrels would whiz up on hydraulics thirty yards from you and riddle you with air-gun pellets. They wouldn't draw blood, but they had a sting you wouldn't forget in a hurry.

Major Kohli and Indramani race up the steps, taking them two at a time. The major's giving you a thumbs-up sign. Your own thumb is up as well, and your weapon falls at your side.

"How many?" you ask Major Kohli.

"Two," he says.

"There's one here. I picked his shin," you say. Upon seeing Indramani, though, the man's groans have abruptly ceased. There's panic in his eyes. And before you can quite read the situation, Indramani has leveled the barrel four inches from the man's face and pulled the trigger. His head bounces twice against the floor. His mouth opens, oozing a dribble of blood down his chin, and his eyes roll to the back of his head. His hands have already released his shin, and now they lie by his side as a low whistle of air escapes from his mouth. A spray of blood follows.

"Payback time," explains Major Kohli.

"What the fuck for?" you say, aghast. "It wasn't essential."

"You found your girl?" asks Major Kohli.

"Yes," you say. You indicate the room she is in. Indramani has taken an amulet hanging from his breast. He is kissing it and kneeling down in prayer now. Elaborate 5 Kumaon postmurder ritual, you think. But the major explains.

"You see, MM, Indramani was the sole survivor from that LRRP that ran into the 7 Sikh. These three here were part of Captain Prakash's patrol. They killed his mates. He has waited a long time for this."

On your way to keep your appointment with Major Singh, you drop off Karnam and change clothes at Jumbo's place. You have two reasons for keeping your date. One, you want to hold the major there long enough for your team to clean out his warehouse. Second, you need to know who his buyers are and avoid them, or word will also get back to Major Singh about who was floating around the 7 Sikh inventory. They might try to get it back. Also, right now, though you and 5 Kumaon will naturally be suspected of the mayhem and the rip-off, you will have a partial alibi in the major himself. As a diversionary tactic, you have told Major Kohli to take out the 7 Sikh hideout with a few antitank missiles. Get the police working overtime. You have also told him to leave some of the hardware in the garage for the police to recover. Among it, a MILAN antitank system and a few crates of RDX. Not counting, of course, the trail of bodies, along with their IDs.

You spot Major Singh at the corner, near the entrance to the Jazz Bar at Hotel Maurya Sheraton. He has half an eye on an escape route.

"Hello, Major," you say. "I hope I haven't kept you waiting too long. The traffic's a killer at this time of day." The major, you notice, doesn't shake your proffered hand. You smile at him. "How come you're alone? Your goons have abandoned you?"

"For you, I am enough. Two more minutes and I would have been gone."

You think the major's been nursing a Bacardi. You order more of the same for yourself.

"How's Karnam?" you ask.

"Well, I haven't come here for some social chitchat, MM. If you have things on your mind, spell them out."

"I have some contacts. Together, we could go places with this," you say. "In this game, if you don't know the right people, you could end up taking a hit. All your sweat on the border while chasing the Mossies could go down the drain."

"What I am wondering is why you should be so helpful."

"You hold my girl. You have the powder. I already have overheads. I figure I have to make good on my investment," you say. "Besides, in my line of business, we stick with the players. You seem to be holding the aces right now." You offer a Marlboro to Major Singh. He refuses it. You light one up yourself. The waiter comes with your Bacardi. "You need another drink, Major? Try a pineapple colada; it will smooth your wrinkles. Stop your hair from graying."

"Black or gray, my hair's taking me nowhere. I got a turban to pack it all in. But you, MM, with your kind of lifestyle, you need all the black you can keep. You have this fancy girl lined up. She might ditch you for some other asshole if your hair turns gray," says Major Singh.

You tap the ash after your first three drags. You need to pump the major a bit more.

"I know these Italians. They will give you door-to-door service. Cash at your doorstep, and you don't need to bother about packing your stuff. That's a turnkey approach," you say.

"I am happy shaking a leg or two. Keeps my muscles in shape," says Major Singh.

"That's not the point. The Italians will take your hardware as well. They will dump it on the Kosovans. Save you the bother of looking up the Red Brigade's number for selling your MILANs. They have all their works under one roof. It's a clearinghouse," you say. You can hear the major's mind whirring and buzzing, a killer bee on a race flight. You can see the 7 Sikh is having problems selling its goods. In about ten more minutes, it won't have any more goods left to sell. The powder, too, shall be yours.

"We don't want to hold our stuff too long. The boys have to go back to their units," says Major Singh. "We also have these 5 Kumaon dogs sniffing at our asses."

"No problem. I could have your shit lifted out in two weeks. In fifteen days, you could be sitting in Lausanne, looking at the boats sailing in the lake."

"Lausanne. Where's that?" asks the major.

"You come with me, Major, and I will give you a world geography tour free of cost. Lausanne is in Switzerland. That's where Bill Gates has his flat."

"My problem is the LTTE's already paid me an advance. The last thing I want are some Tamil assholes chasing me with bombs strapped on their chest," says Major Singh.

You hadn't thought the major would reveal his card so easily. "That can be taken care of, Major. I can pay them back with interest. All you have to do is give a nod and I can start things rolling. Of course, I would want you to free Karnam first, and it would be great if you could take the generals off my case. Tell them nobody is going to squeal," you say. You have the major in your sonar, no obstruction. You look at your watch. By now, you estimate, you could start a zoo in the 7 Sikh warehouse.

Digs is in observation at the Escorts Heart Institute. The attendant publicity that Gulab Chand's murder in *The Post's* premises brought has freaked his metabolism. His heartbeat has gone irregular. The newspapers are doing their bit to aggravate Digs's condition.

Major Singh's prank with the stun grenade has widely been interpreted as an unsuccessful bomb attack. Your normal stun grenade contains a mixture of magnesium powder and mercury fulminate. The fulminate is a percussion explosive and detonates with near eardrum-shattering intensity, igniting the magnesium, which generates a 60,000-candlepower flash, disorienting a room's occupants for up to sixty seconds.

In the library, the magnesium set a blaze going, which consumed all the buildings' fire extinguishers before gasping its last breath. You were in your own office, snorting on heaven, while everybody was panicking downstairs. Then you simply went up to the roof, crossed over to another building, and walked down the stairwell to the street.

Naturally, you added your own spin to the incident when crime reporters called you on your mobile for inside dope. You spoke reluctantly and off the record. You referred to it as an "attack on democracy" and a "sinister government conspiracy." You let it be known to selected reporters that you suspected the attack was meant for one of the *Post* journalists working late on a hot story but that the assassins "goofed." They were so happy about your precious comments, since Digs was unreachable and the other staffers too scared to open their mouths, that even though you offered no facts supporting your theory, they ran with the story.

The murder has knocked your assault on police HQ right off the front page.

It's also fortunate for you that the office network has emerged undamaged in the fire. It's late in the evening when you reach the office. You are on the soot-blackened correspondents' floor when you bump into Leslie.

"Hi, MM," says Leslie. "You heard the news?"

It has been a hectic day and you have had no time to scan the wire. "Why?" you ask.

"The MiGs thing," he says.

You freeze. What could Leslie have found out? you wonder. "Yes, what about them?"

"Oh, you don't know? The Mossies picked two of ours from the skies. Boom. Boom. Missile hits. One pilot's in their custody. The other's got a ticket to Abracadabra," says Leslie. "Buddy, we have war on our hands with Pakistan. What fun."

You stop in your tracks. You have known the push was imminent. Since early May, reports have been trickling in from the border. But you were expecting the fun to begin a few weeks hence.

The fresh dimension calls for some emergency stocktaking. Your sex survey was put to bed this morning. Your plan was to run your spurious defense cover story the following week, but by then, it will be too late. You figure that, as war escalates, nationalistic sentiments won't take kindly to an anti–defense forces piece. It will have to be now or never. You check the printing schedule, which gives you an idea of how to juggle the pagination of the issue. You give your questionnaire a new slant. First among the many questions you raise is the capability of the Indian armed forces to fight a war with Pakistan in light of the findings of your survey. A war that is imminent. You also find some space for the reported cache discovered at a "destroyed" 7 Sikh armament warehouse and give hints about a battle that seemed to have taken place before the building was blown up. A call to Major Kohli gives you the names of the three dead 7 Sikh soldiers. Even though crime reporters will have reached the site of your battle in Chattarpur, information will leak in dribs and drabs while the rubble is sorted out and the police decide on a course of action. As a magazine man, you want to be on the ball with your story when it hits the stands on Monday. There is some risk that the police might decide to hold back the identity of the deceased and might give a different spin to the incident altogether, but you're prepared to take such risks. What you have done, however, is plaster the story with Jain's byline. It will buy you time.

You then access the PS and PDF files on the sex survey from the system. They haven't been sent yet. You substitute your bumper issue with the contents of the sex survey and flash the whole thing on its way using Jain's system ID. He is in the office, too, the asshole. Thursdays, there's always a heavy workload for the people putting together the Business section.

Next, you prepare your press release on the cover story, which, however, will be sent special delivery to your three select defense correspondents only on Sunday. This on Digs's letterhead and with his fake signature. You don't want the shit to break a day earlier, when magazines usually allow newspapers a sneak preview. On Sunday, you'll have other pressing matters to attend to. Most significantly, getting your container loads to Akramov. Major Rodriguez will be arriving early that morning with the rest of the heroin, just a day before the transaction. From then on, Jumbo, along with the rest of your men, will be busy packing the heroin in the furniture. Though the 5 Kumaon have their marching orders from Kashmir, they haven't packed their bags yet. With war looming, you feel, their peace posting could be delayed by Northern Command HQ.

A few unsolved blips remain on your radar. But you have those figured out, too. Digs has planned a blitz of advertising for the issue with the sex survey, labeling it "The Anniversary Special." Leslie has designed the layouts to be released to newspaper offices directly on Monday. They would then run on Tuesday, a day after the issue hits the stands. It would be a goof of major proportions if the issue itself was the one with the defense cover and the advertising for the sex survey.

You design your own layout in the same size. Nothing fancy. You simply substitute the picture with new text. IS INDIA PREPARED FOR WAR? is your headline. Under a second headline, WRONG TIMING, you run four strap lines: "CVC report nails Defense Minister Suresh Yadav"; "The India air force in the dock for MiG upgrade scheme"; "Army Chief Subhas Rampal under cloud because of suspicious IED deal"; and "Is there a link between the Chattarpur incident and Pakistani 151?"

You get the negatives developed outside the office. What you plan to do is substitute the packets for the newspaper offices with your own. In the whole operation, just one uncontrolled factor remains. On Monday, when Digs comes to know about the fiasco, he could order a recall of the copies from the stands. But that's easier said than done. The damage will have been done. Packing a genie back into a bottle is not as easy as letting it out.

Later, you catch up with Karnam. Digs being in the hospital gives you a free run of his place. You are tired.

"Hello," you say.

"Hello, sweetheart," says Karnam.

She kisses you on the lips, then leads you to her room, where a leather couch awaits. You slump in it. She adjusts your posture. You now lie with your head on her lap. You kick off your shoes. Your Beretta is digging into your flesh. You take it out and put it on a side table. Your jacket, you hang on a chair.

"You still haven't answered me," you say.

"About what?" asks Karnam.

"Well, what was it that I last asked you about?" You look hurt.

"Oh, marriage. MM, you are really weird. Bringing up marriage in the midst of all this. I was a nervous wreck with them," she says.

"This is nothing. This is routine," you say.

"Maybe for you. But not for me. Being kidnapped, then shoot-outs. What happened to them, anyway? I didn't see any of them coming out."

Major Kohli and Indramani dragged the bodies of the 7 Sikh soldiers

to adjacent rooms before letting Karnam out. You shepherded her outside the house as quickly as possible.

"You don't see dead people," you say. A silence hangs over both of you.

"MM, I don't understand. I am not used to this," she says.

"It's a phase," you say, consoling her. "It will soon be over. Trust me."
You nestle your nose against her belly. Her smell is setting you off. She
unbuttons your shirt and you help her take it off.

"You haven't told me about this," she says. She traces an eight-inch-
long suture on the side of your ribs. "What story does it have?" Her fingers softly knead your neck and shoulders.

It's a long story, and you set about telling her.

It all began when the then USSR withdrew from circulation fifty- and
one-hundred-ruble notes in January 1991. You were stranded in Poland
after crossing over at Brest-Terespol. Along with you were four Russian
scientists you had hired for the submarine project from Jupiter Z, a scientific institute in Saint Petersburg that was part of the Russian Academy
of Natural Sciences. Apart from individual contracts that you had negotiated with each of the scientists, who were to lend their expertise in the
area of submarine communications at ocean depths of two thousand feet
and more, you had to pay off the Russian "defense Mafia" for having located the personnel you wanted and helping you arrange their passage to
Poland, where you waited with Canadian passports for them to aid their
onward zigzag travel to India.

In short, you owed five million rubles to Akramov's men. You were not
part of the main negotiation, which was conducted by a RAW agent,
Sishir Datta. Datta had been one of your instructors in your training
interludes with RAW. With the ruble notes being outlawed—an unforeseen hitch—the Russian Mafia was trading in its currency stash at dis-
counts of up to 25 percent. Caught in no-man's-land, the two of you
suddenly found that you were short 500,000 rubles of your facilitators'
fee. You asked for credit, which was denied. So you went for the next step
you were trained for. You decided to jump the Mafia. You and Datta sped

with your scientists to Germany, instead of boarding a plane from Warsaw.

Though you could have waited for money to arrive, Datta was harried by the fact that the Pakistani ISI was hot on your trail. Colluding with the CIA, it had already sabotaged two personnel deals—in one case, having a scientist liquidated. Two of your present catch were known authorities in the blue-green laser field, whose further development was vital for the ATV's communication setup. The Laser Communication Laboratory at the Indian Institute of Technology (IIT) in Madras was producing laser beams that couldn't penetrate the ocean waves. With hired brains, they hoped to rectify this.

The 267-mile-long Oder-Neisse line separating Germany from Poland was hardly anything that could be called a frontier in 1991. You crossed the border at Frankfurt an der Oder, the chief German checkpoint (the Polish one wasn't manned at all), and fled to Frankfurt, where Indian embassy people waited for you with papers for your Russian friends. They made it out safely. They, of course, didn't know anything was the matter.

Datta and you stayed in Frankfurt. You were working on a deal to get blueprints of the acoustic system used in the top-of-the-line Russian Lada-class nuclear submarines. A Ukrainian naval officer was helping you.

But Datta was spotted one fine morning by the Russians. They had an alert out for him. They didn't know about you. They trailed him to the apartment you were using and followed him in. Among other things that they did to him was nail his scrotum to the planks of his bed and cut the skin of his legs, peeling it off like stockings down to his knees. The killers were on the way out when you abruptly entered the slaughterhouse. There was blood everywhere, and you had a tough time keeping your feet on the floor. Even now, when you remember the way you fought for your life, a shudder passes through your spine. The first of the *vorovskoy mir* killers swung his serrated knife at you, opening a long gash at your ribs. You butted his face with your head, using all your strength. It broke his nose. His knife clattered to the floor, and the best luck you had was getting hold of it even as the second Russian was on you and you grappled on the floor for your life.

Among the techniques that you'd learned at RAW, the one that saved your life was pushing the knife through the killer's eye, penetrating into his brain. Least resistance, maximum effect, you'd been told at RAW. You can still see the shock on his face, hear the yell of pain that suffocated as soon as it came up, and see the fading of life from his left eye. The long-distance look that glazed over his other pupil. That, and the soft quivering of the limbs even after his breathing stopped.

The other killer ran. To this day, you don't know why. The contact was too violent, sudden, and short for him to have carried memories of how you looked. Hence your studied risk in walking unprotected into Akramov's lair. But you have planned on getting even with Akramov for a long time, and Sunday will give you that opportunity. Datta taught you many things, and even though loyalty to him or RAW doesn't fit in with your larger agenda, it's a luxury that you are permitting yourself, a small game within the many big ones.

Karnam's mouth is still open when you halt your story. You have clearly been around and seen a lot. This, no one would begrudge you. But your life has strung you up like a bow for too long. It is time for you to fire your last few arrows and drop out of the scene. In your calling, things catch up with everyone without exception. The trick is to know when to retire. Too early and you won't have learned anything. Too late and you die a dog's death.

You don't know what moment of weakness makes you confide your RAW background to Karnam, but in the insanity that you swim in, you want to tell her everything.

Karnam's lips are finding yours. Her hair is falling over your face like a shield. She jerks her hair back and brings the bundle back again with a toss. You find it superhumanly sensual. You get up and lead her to the bed. She does the hard work of undressing you. Your cock is still not straight and high like Mount Everest. It needs some work along the fault lines, the crevices where desire rests.

She's taking off her blouse. It's on the floor. Her breasts are placards for the endomorphically endowed. In spite of yourself, a soft whistle escapes your lips. She's taking off her slacks now. They lie in a heap on the floor. Her panties are white and translucent. You can see the dark hair sticking to them inside. There's a design as well. You gasp.

"What's that?" you ask. You see a designer pussy—hair shaved and ordered in the shape of a swastika. The Aryan denominator.

"I did it for you," she says. "A treat for rescuing me. It took me a full hour."

You smile. Every day you live and learn, you think. Today, you learned the ways of a girl feeling indebted. But the motif has done wonders for your arousal, especially the thought behind it—a lover's special stencil. As your hands roam her back and breasts and trace the swastika on her mound, you start feeling like an ancient Aryan warlord yourself. A chieftain in communion with his power source.

You are kissing her now—her cheeks, her ears, her neck, her cleavage, her breasts themselves, and the nipples, which stand like two twin peaks of pink. She is arching her back with pleasure. She climbs on top of you. She starts with your nipples. It tickles you. She moves to the base of your mountain, her tongue tasting your sac. She looks at it with the fascination and desire of the newly initiated.

She sandwiches your nozzle between her tits, massaging it with a slow rhythm. A trailer to bookmark the events ahead. For now, she has taken you in her lovely mouth. Your palms are holding her neck and your thumbs are at her ears, regulating the speed of her head as she swallows and then sucks up your machinery.

She is topping up your engine oil for the cross-country event to come. Your rpm are hitting a new high. To wait any longer would be to lose prime time.

"Yes," you say. And she mounts you. The first insertion, you can say from experience, has always been your most delightful. You try a novelty here. You protect three-fourths of your cock with a closed fist. You limit your area of operations for the time being to the tip of your cone. You let her raise her steam to a new desperation level. You can see droplets of sweat beading on her forehead. She pleads with her eyes and then moans for you to relent. But you wait. You exercise an iron restraint, building your own cubic feet of pressure, till you can hold on no longer and she slides all the way down to the base of your cock. You feel the heat, the viciousness of molten metal.

She picks up a Bugatti's momentum. You want her more at a Volkswagen's steady trot. Squeeze the maximum mileage out of your gallon of gas. But she's eating up the road with all cylinders blazing. You lift her out. You want to try different kinds of fusion.

You turn her around. You are looking at her back now.

"What's this?" she asks.

You don't need to explain, or she is inducted easily. She starts lowering herself onto your cock as she looks at the ceiling, your hands pressing on her breasts. This way, somehow, you feel closer.

"I didn't know you could do it this way," she says.

But you tire of the oddity. For your final moments, you return to tried and trusted postures.

The missionary position, for all its drawbacks, still works for you. In it alone you get the melting feeling when you are nearing apogee and your eyes are padlocked with one whom you wish to possess and own. You look at each other during moments that burst in your brain and down below, and you at least, after a long time, feel this is heaven and the rest is but waiting.

You lie on her for a long time, breathing her breath and inhaling the air she inhaled. Then you break up and lie alongside her. Things are quiet till you hear a rush of footsteps coming to the door of your room. There is something abnormal here, you feel. Your Beretta is still on the table, many yards away. The door opens and in bursts Digs. His mouth opens in surprise. The ambush is the other way around. His face is turning red. He is taking too long to register this spectacle, you feel. But you can almost see him gather his reserves. He straightens his spine.

"Out, you two," he says. "*Now.*" He then stalks out.

Karnam is jolted with embarrassment. Though you recognize the feeling, you are beyond that sentiment yourself. You wonder with amusement whether Digs had enough time to take in the swastika that his daughter had tooled with such care.

It's dawn. Sunday. And one of the amusements that you are still savoring from the day before is the knowledge that Akramov's man in India is Col. Anatoly Grupov, defense attaché at the Russian embassy. Such Mafia-state collaboration is not unknown to you. Hence your amusement, rather than surprise.

You arc planning a con so simple in nature as to be almost childish. You have rented a warehouse in the Gurgaon Export Promotion Zone on Haryana Urban Development Authority Land, twelve miles from the Indira Gandhi International Airport. It has a high security wall all around it and fifteen concrete sheds of considerable dimension. They stand in a single line. For a decent pile of money, you have rented the entire premises for two weeks. You don't need all that huge space or that much time. For you, two sheds and three days will do, but you don't want to bump into other civilian traffic at the site. Besides, with the array of numbered sheds, you plan a little confusion for Colonel Grupov and his band of chemists with their portable laboratory to test your H.

For purposes central to your deception, you have rented eight empty containers that meet aircraft specifications and had them unloaded at your shed. In work that has taken a full month, a team of twenty carpenters, working round the clock under Jumbo's supervision, has scraped, hammered, peeled, and varnished two identical sets of furniture, possession of one of which Colonel Grupov will be taking later in the day. In the presence of Colonel Grupov and his lieutenants, Jumbo's men will pack the hollows of the special furniture with heroin and then load the furniture in four containers. Then Jumbo will seal them in his own very special and irrevocable way. You have discussed all this with Colonel Grupov in minute detail.

Then you will use the locks that Colonel Grupov will provide to secure the shed. The containers will stay at the site overnight. Early the next morning, the Russians will come with their handlers and truck the load to Aeroflot.

Here's where your special execution plans will fall into shape. You are not going to tamper with the locks. That would be amateurish. Instead, fresh numbers will be painted on the doors. In the shed, everything will be organized the same way and the four other identical containers placed in precise locations. Obviously, these will contain the matching set of furniture, packed and sealed in a similar fashion. You have divided your load of empty containers in both sheds for background effect, to make the whole thing look realistic.

To cook Akramov's goose in full measure, you are filling the hollows with white distemper. Provide them with the arsenal to freshen their setup, whitewash their dreary Moscow abode. In the morning, the Russians will be led to the dummy consignment.

Needless to say, you have exempted 5 Kumaon from this bit of chess play on your part. You have, however, taken a calculated risk by opening a channel with the LTTE. You have the numbers of one-eyed Srinivasan, who is the LTTE's point man in Delhi, their liaison with Mafia don Dawood Ibrahim. You have met him in the past in Singapore and discussed matters of mutual interest. You have conveyed to Srinivasan that his advance to 7 Sikh would be honored by you as well. You also convey to him the enormous volume of arms you are seeking to unload. Over a cup of coffee and a sandwich at Kovil Restaurant in Connaught Place, you have sung an exquisite melody to him, a 15 percent discount over the prevailing market rates. The Stingers, you feel, have clinched the deal.

The LTTE's mode of payment, however, will not be cash. This much you knew before you initiated contact. It will be a barter with heroin. The Tamil troupe will be delivering you a metric ton of heroin. You know where that will come from. It will come to you from the Malwa-Mewar region of Madhya Pradesh and Rajasthan, an area that has over sixty thousand acres of land devoted to the legal cultivation of opium. The districts of Ratlam, Mandsaur, and Neemuch in western Madhya Pradesh account for 50 percent of the world's pharmaceutical demand for morphine. Its creamy yellow powder is higher in quality than the neon pink variety that comes out of Pakistan and Afghanistan.

You have nothing against the swap. In the long run, it increases your profitability. You intend to dispose of the heroin without too many intermediaries in the lucrative markets of Europe and America.

The way you are going to do it is dissolve the heroin in bottles of solvent. It's going to take one million bottles of solvent to dissolve this much heroin. The solvent will then be vaporized to get back the heroin. This process will be carried out in temporary laboratories set up for this very purpose and spread over many countries. The way you and your Sicilian contacts—you have sought Dinesh Patel's help here, for whose efforts you have set aside 2 percent of the net profits—have planned the shipments is for the containers to be shipped to Amsterdam from India.

The Dutch, you think, are among the most civilized of modern states. While marijuana is outlawed in all EC countries, it's a commercial crop in the Netherlands, worth $200 million and distributed legally through four hundred licensed Dutch coffee shops. The Dutch policy of dissuasion rather than prohibition has paid rich dividends in the controlled consumption of soft drugs by its own civilian population. Its laws are also custom-made for the goons of the planet. Holland doesn't believe in sending anybody to jail for more than six years. And those who escape are not tailed, on the grounds that "wanting to regain freedom is a natural tendency in human beings." As a result, drugs in transit through the Netherlands are "not a priority for the Dutch police." Forty thousand ships docking in Rotterdam annually off-load 7,500 containers every single day. The Dutch have allocated ten customs agents to go through the manifests of all the ships. You have it on Mafia authority that, on average, the agents manage to check just twenty containers a day.

From the Netherlands, your containers will move on Transport International Routier trucks to various ultimate destinations. The Customs Convention on the International Transport of Goods under the cover of TIR is customized for the Cosa Nostra. The EC now saves half a trillion dollars a year just by cutting the time a truck needs to cross its territory, the time and expense of checking cars and baggage at the dozen internal borders. TIR is an essential component of the narcotics trade. It eliminates the necessity of customs examination of road vehicles as well as containers carried on road vehicles at each international border. Containers that have been approved for transport under customs seal are inspected again only at the end of the journey. You observe, cynically, that with the formation of the EC, the twelve inner borders have gone down for the thieves united but not for the cops.

Part of your consignment will also move within traps built in the TIR trucks themselves. Traps built into the gas tanks are favorite areas to conceal contraband.

Your defrauding of Akramov and cuts from the arms consignment will garner RAW a profit of $40 million. You are stashing this away in many different forms. It has been your practice to spread your illicit gains around. A significant percentage of your money is going to Austrian banks. The Swiss no longer offer ideal protection for laundered funds. The crown now belongs to Austria, Western Europe's number one laundry state. The Austrian enclave of Oberstdorf has a network of banks where you can open an account simply by flashing the color of your passport.

The bulk of your greenbacks will, however, be deposited in the Com-

mercial Bank of Aruba. After gaining independence from the Dutch An-
tilles in 1986, Aruba has blossomed in financial skulduggery. The beauty
of the operation is that you are not an account holder in the bank. You
own the bank. You have bought the fully chartered private international
bank with no assets or liabilities, with a Class A license, bearer shares,
and a professional management service thrown in, all for twenty thousand dollars. The hard part, as is well known in banking circles, is to get
the suspect cash into the banking system. Once it's in, you can transfer
millions of dollars by wire anywhere you want, a concept that goes by the
term *layering*. After a dozen-odd transactions, the cash is untraceable.

Aruba also offers you the facility of establishing AECs, or Aruban exempt corporations, which can be controlled through anonymous bearer
shares and are exempt from taxation of all kinds. You will form these corporations to deposit money into your own bank and then loan them
more of your laundered money. These loans, now legitimate, you will
never pay back. Instead, you will use the money to invest through further
dummy corporations wherever your fancy takes you.

The 5 Kumaon that Colonel Grupov will be disseminating later in the
day, you plan to get converted through the havala route. Not all of it, but
a big chunk. For officers Rodriguez, Kohli, Sangma, and others, you
have offered a financial consultancy in the Caribbean free of cost. For
the soldiers, you are opening many chit-fund companies in India, where,
gradually, their share of the hard work at the border will be made available to them in currency that they will understand.

Things, however, rarely work according to plan. Colonel Grupov has
come to your den with his own set of ideas. He is also flanked by four
plainclothes Russians, from the embassy or elsewhere—you don't know
and don't ask. The various bulges in their suits speak of concealed
weapons. Akramov's bewildering crew has come well prepared.

"Shall we take them on, MM?" Major Rodriguez asks you.

You smile. Major Rodriguez has joined you on that very day. He drove
nonstop in an army *jonga*, followed by a Shaktiman with the remaining

two hundred kilograms of heroin in their custody from Kupwara. The 5 Kumaon, you learn, is under orders to proceed to Kargil from the valley to take on the six-hundred-odd Pakistani intruders atop different heights. And the deal with Akramov has come at the right time for the unit to jettison its extra load and become fighting-fit. Major Rodriguez and his men have to return as fast as possible to begin their height acclimatization at Drass, which stands at 10,500 feet, before fanning out in the Mushkoh valley to take on the Mossies. You plan on joining the major and his unit soon. You have reasons for covering the war as a journalist. But first, you have a few more scores to settle.

"Major, they are giving us only fifty percent of the money right now. The rest, they will release in our numbered accounts abroad tomorrow, after I deliver the relevant banking papers to them. Of course, if you want to give them a fifty percent discount, we can kill the Russians now," you say. You forget to add that your background check on Colonel Grupov has disclosed to you his Spesnatz—the elite Russian force—breeding. That is an added complication.

Major Rodriguez smiles back. "Just nervous," he says.

The major, you reckon, has reason to be. His own share is coming to a couple million dollars. In a few days' time, he is also going to be fighting a war. You send the major to the office you have set up at the back of the sheds to organize a power point for a currency-counting machine and some laser equipment to do random checks for counterfeit notes. Better to keep the major busy than have him come up to you with bizarre whims.

Colonel Grupov's gang is doing a lot of random sampling from the containers. They have brought their test tubes and burners. The purity of your cargo is too high to lend to analysis by snorting. That would require an elephant. It takes Grupov's crew two hours to assess the integrity of your operation. Jumbo seals the containers. He nods. And then Grupov drops his bombshell.

"My men will be sleeping here in the shed for the night," says Colonel Grupov.

You haven't been prepared for this. This uncalled-for eventuality could burn your pocket of many millions of dollars. There is the possibility of bribing the men, but you discount it as too remote to work.

"Of course, Colonel. With pleasure. Anything you say goes," you say. You can see Jumbo raising his eyebrows. "But first, let us celebrate, Colonel. I have a case of champagne ready for just this moment." It's imperative that you lead the colonel and his men outside the shed. You take them to your office, where Major Rodriguez does the honors. You can see everybody relaxing. Colonel Grupov has handed over to you three trunks filled with cash. You have started the process of counting the greenbacks.

Elsewhere, you can hear the double-siding cranes start up. You'll need something to cover the noise of Jumbo's operation. The container forks are busy switching containers.

You lead your group to the main gate, where Major Kohli keeps vigil with a platoon of 5 Kumaon men. You can discount the 7 Sikh only at your own peril. You are huddling with Colonel Grupov.

"Colonel," you are saying, "I want your opinion." You take the INSAS from one of the soldiers. "This is the new Indian infantry rifle. Could you give us an opinion? The Pakis up in the mountains have the AK. Will the INSAS hold?" You collect ten magazines from the soldiers, two each for the Russians, and lead your group to the edge of the boundary fencing. For the next fifteen minutes, you intend to convert it into a firing range.

Jumbo comes to your shooting party at the end of ten minutes. Fast work, you think. You lead the colonel back to the shed. He is spraying you with his opinion on the INSAS, but you have other things on your mind.

"Colonel, do your men have sleeping bags, or should I send some over?" you ask.

You are with Major Kohli at Khachar, two stops from Buxar, which is forty miles as the crow flies from Mughal Sarai, the biggest railway junction in India. Kohli has taken your bait. Your experience in human affairs has taught you that once you have the key to a guy, only the price remains to be negotiated. The key to Kohli is his desire to become rich. You have already, unknown to Rodriguez, passed Kohli a sum of $250,000 as advance incentive to help you make off with the Indian nuclear warheads moving on the rails. Kohli is a dog on a leash, as far as you are concerned.

The price you offered him is chicken feed compared to what you stand to make. You could have a bidding war going among the Americans, the Pakistanis, and the Chinese.

You might also consider keeping some of the warheads as a memento. Part of the reason you are in this, after all, is to test your own motherfucker potential, apart from earning bonus points from your handlers if you pull off a coup of this magnitude. That will ensure your making the leap from triple agent to legend.

Of course, if RAW got wind of where you are or what you are planning to do, the game would be up.

But you are planning this to be your swan song. Not only does the size of your retirement kitty hinge on this operation, but you have dreams that your many days of hard work might in due course form a case study in the annals of espionage. Maybe someday a professor at Harvard University will lecture about your work in the subcontinent and you will listen to his words of wisdom as you sit in the audience. There would be an aura of mystery about your real identity, which, in more ways than one, would be equally confusing for you.

You have roped Karnam into the operation. You trust her. Or hope that in showing this trust, you will make her more a part of you than she was. You have prepared the logistics of it with Kohli. Though Karnam doesn't know what the operation is about, she helps you hire Dauphin helicopters from the Oil and Natural Gas Commission. The Dauphin AS 365 has a range of 515 miles, a maximum speed of 175 miles per hour, and a carrying capacity of eight people. You and your crew are wearing freshly starched Strategic Forces Command uniforms, those of the newly created unit that has been given the weighty task of guarding the Indian second-strike capability.

You have learned from Major Kohli that in exercises to check the state of alertness of the company guarding the rail line, inspection parties from the nuclear arsenal headquarters have flown themselves, without notice, to the train in Dauphins.

To exploit this accepted tradition is your main game plan. You intend to fly to your target with six battle-hardened 5 Kumaon veterans, including Major Kohli and a captured scientist whose expertise may be called upon. You yourself are dressed in the uniform of a lieutenant colonel from the SFC.

Of course, you are not taking Karnam to the battlefield. But you have also utilized her services to organize ground transport at Khachar, possibly in Tata Mercedes trucks parked near the expected rendezvous point. You have that explained to her that it is an Indian government exercise to check the security apparatus in charge of the nuclear arsenal.

And how are you going to ensure that the train stops at Khachar? You might think that elaborate planning would be required to manage the Indian railway signaling system. Blinking certain red and green lights at crucial points to fool the engine driver and make him switch tracks, but that would have required a company-level engagement, besides the co-opting of railway personnel. And no way are you planning a commando-type operation on a moving train. It would be suicidal to take on the skills of the NSG whose job it is to take care of the nukes till the SFC raises its own cadres. You see those riveting engagements only on celluloid. You have trained with the NSG and have made sure that the detachment under Colonel Kothari, the CO of the nuke train, is not one you trained with. Nor, for that matter, have you bumped into Kothari.

But Major Kohli works under his command now, since his temporary assignment to the NSG from 5 Kumaon. He has knowledge of the communication codes that the SFC has formulated—the highly secure communication setup that is lodged in the central car of the nuke train. He has the authority to access the setup through the SFC's temporary offices at Manesar, which also headquarters the NSG. And he has accessed the network for you.

You know, for instance, that Khachar is one of only three places that the SFC uses to rotate its staff on the train. They avoid the big stations, for they want to keep their movements under wraps. And their staff is flown in on Dauphins from the SFC's support base at Lucknow.

Like all things Indian, the Ministry of Defense has left scope for confusion. While the SFC's writ runs in the central communication railcar housed in the middle of the nuke train and in the cars that hold the Agni missiles, elsewhere on the train the NSG rules.

You learn through Major Kohli that there has already been huge friction between the staff of the two agencies over the rotation policy of the staff on the train. While the SFC rotates its communication experts and the missile-maintenance personnel by choppers once a week at Khachar, the NSG sharpshooters and officers have to hike it by road to Bamrauli Station, near Allahabad, where the Central Air Command is based. There, they relieve their staffers once in ten days. Ten days on rail can be quite a desultory and perhaps a shaking experience even for the Special Forces.

There is also the question of daily hardship allowance. The SFC has sanctioned a five-hundred-rupee per diem for its noncommissioned staff for the time they spend shitting on railway tracks, while the NSG has budgeted a measly one-hundred-rupee per diem. Such five-star treatment of the SFC has given the NSG gunslingers cause for bellyaching.

Though Major Kohli's chumming up with you had little to do with this disparity in allowance structure, it opened up avenues for information to be gathered through disaffected personnel. You learned of passwords, missile drills, and other such tidbits of information. But you are still unhappy with your planning. Then a piece of luck heads your way.

You learn that a missile crane on one of the railcars has malfunctioned and damaged the fins of a pair of missiles. Needless to say, this provides you a window of opportunity for a rather ingenious intervention. The warheads have already been separated from the missiles by the maintenance crew on the train, and while the missiles themselves will be unloaded at Khachar into waiting army trucks, among which your civilian trucks will wait, courtesy of Karnam, the warheads are going to be flown by helicopter to the SFC headquarters at Manesar.

Flying in warheads for repairs on choppers is a rather unusual and dangerous procedure, but you assume that the border skirmish at Kargil has something to do with the haste.

Your trucks waiting at Khachar are also carrying three platoons of the 5 Kumaon, your contingency plan in case the SFC decides to abandon the chopper option and relies on wheels on the road to see the warheads through to DRDO labs. That will shift the theater of war to the Grand Trunk Road or National Highway 24 and necessarily force you to engage in a firefight with the NSG, a scenario you don't relish. While you rate the skills of the 5 Kumaon high, the NSG is a pain in the ass. You might have given yourself some healthy odds, seeing that the element of surprise is on your side, but you realize that you lack leadership. Keeping Major Rodriguez out of the picture has meant avoiding any risk with other officers of the errant Indian unit. If your sonar hit an officer at a deep end, it would alert Rodriguez.

Even Major Kohli will not be on the road. He's going to relieve Colonel Kothari's second in command and stay on the nuke train, just long enough to give your Dauphin time to reach Delhi. Then, before the shit hits the ceiling, Kohli will slip off the train and go AWOL. You have provided him with the necessary papers to get into Europe, where you will take care of him in peace. Part of your plan is to break up the bastard team of Rodriguez and Kohli. Together, they are a nuisance that you can do without.

Your plan is simple. Almost too simple. You will be impersonating the SFC crew that is supposed to get the warheads back to base. A simple matter of loading the cones into lead containers and flying them back to Delhi. This time, you won't be returning to the Manesar helipad but will detour instead to the Safdarjung Airport in New Delhi, where your army of helpers is waiting to protect and escort you to your munitions warehouse. Jumbo is oiling the logistics at this end.

At Manesar, Kohli and his gang of mercenaries have taken out the SFC missile crew—four scientists from the Bhaba Atomic Research Center at Mumbai and two from the Defense Research Development Organization. All six are on deputation to the SFC. The substitution involved a complex maneuver. It was facilitated by the fact that the SFC still hasn't managed to raise a captive fleet of choppers for its use. Although the helicopters have been sanctioned by the Ministry of Defense, Bell and Dauphin haven't delivered the initial lot of ten helicopters.

The SFC, therefore, has had to make do with hiring the spare capacity of the ONGC fleet and, of course, occasional SOS calls to the army and air force. The SFC's favored helicopter, because of its night-vision capability and reliability, is the Dauphin. Which is where Major Kohli tells you to pitch in. Using your contacts and Karnam, you had to hire, for miscellaneous purposes, all the available Dauphins in the ONGC fleet for a whole week. There are four of them. You used the good services of an aviation correspondent at the *Times of India*. You paid money in advance through one of Jumbo's front companies.

You have gone through all this labor and paperwork in order to replace the ONGC pilots with your own. You have flown in four pilots from Mauritius. They aren't participating in the ruse, but they think they are making good money for a week's work. It would have been dangerous for you to have hired pilots from Europe. White skin for such an operation would be a risky proposition. You have made the jobs of the pilots easier by supplying them with an abundance of navigation data.

The original ONGC pilots, you have kept captive at a secret location in South Delhi, along with five of the scientists. Jumbo is moving them around in safe houses. They will be released two days after your operation.

The initial stages have gone off without a hitch. The SFC, as expected, has sent in an SOS to the ONGC, requisitioning two Dauphins. The ONGC, in panic, as expected, has called Jumbo's front company to cancel leasing arrangements for two of the four choppers. Since the helicopters are in your possession, their pilots have already been safely relieved of their duties. Your crew is in place. At Manesar, Major Kohli performs another sleight of hand. He has an NSG supply truck full of coal tar break an axle and veer into the helipad at full tilt. A stunt of high magnitude, it forces the SFC scientists to catch the choppers at Palam Airport. It is while they are on their way to Palam that Jumbo hijacks them.

You are flying one scientist in your party for any nuclear emergency that might develop. You foresee none, but you don't plan to get a dose of lethal radiation, either. The scientist has been blindfolded and his thigh then strapped with cakes of soap, which he has been told are plastic explosives. He's sweating and pleading with you. You calm him down periodically.

Colonel Kothari and his men have been expecting you. With Major Kohli in your flying party, you feel your bona fides will be apparent to Kothari. You are a little worried about the rest of your six-man crew passing themselves off as scientists, but they are in SFC uniforms and have fake IDs, and you will do your best to keep them in the background. They have borrowed equipment from the abducted scientists, so they look genuine, at least. That's how you convince yourself. For you to have roped in actual nuclear personnel would have been even riskier.

Besides, you traveled here in two choppers. It's late evening, and by the time the dust settles and the rotors stop their racket, night has set in and you feel more confident. More significantly, perhaps, the clinching point in your favor are the sonic booms coming your way by a pair of Mirage 2000 jets flying overhead. The slick flying machines are there to escort your choppers back unscathed to New Delhi.

You are walking the whole length of the train. Your main purpose has been to attach sensitive transmitters to the railcars. This is something that even Major Kohli doesn't know about. These are third-generation pulse transmitters that have a battery life of five years. Rust-colored and the size of pencil erasers, they attach themselves magnetically to targets. You are directing the beam of your flashlight ahead of you. And as you pass three cars that you know house the Agnis, you stoop, as if your boots are bothering you, and stick your gear in the undercarriage.

Of the six personnel accompanying you, you have instructed three to walk on ahead and have their flashlights on full beam. You want light in the eyes of the NSG personnel watching you walk up to the communications railcar. Your twin Dauphins, too, are illuminating the area with their landing lights. Behind you, toward the tail of the train, NSG personnel are walking German shepherds. Major Kohli has omitted telling you about the dogs. But, you figure, dogs or no dogs, the satellites will take over and program the transmitters.

Colonel Kothari meets you at the steps of the communications car. He cracks a smile at you. Your eyes crinkle. You nod. Major Kohli does the introductions.

"We have a situation here," says Colonel Kothari, gesticulating.

"What?" you ask. Your neck muscles tense.

"The Rajdhani to Calcutta is speeding up on this track. We can't stop long," he says.

"I am told it will take just ten to fifteen minutes," you say.

"We haven't done it before, so we don't know. But are your boys all prepared?" asks Colonel Kothari. He sizes up your contingent.

You feel the cold metal tucked away at the back of your waist. Your six-man crew, too, is all loaded and primed.

"Raring to go," you say.

"How come you got a deputation to the SFC, Colonel?" asks Colonel Kothari.

"The 2 Rajput Rifles didn't like my face," you say, smiling. "Besides, I wanted a posting to New Delhi. Also, I have a degree in nuclear physics. They figured it could come in handy, though I can't see how."

"Major, why don't you lead the men to car two. That's where the action is. I will show the colonel around," says Colonel Kothari.

While you are happy that Kohli has taken your six goons out of the way before Kothari's antenna started crackling with suspicion, it makes you nervous to see your party split up.

"Come let me show you our communications setup," offers Colonel Kothari.

"Shouldn't we oversee car two?" you suggest. You want to keep your crew together.

"Don't worry, Colonel. The guys are lining up the Caterpillar we have on car three. It will take the cranes some time to load the Caterpillar with the missiles. The trucks are three hundred feet away. We will join them once the carting starts," says Colonel Kothari. "The warheads are more important. We will oversee that personally."

You can't see how you could suggest having problems with that. What's worrying you is that your troops have moved out of your line of sight. Also, four NSG personnel have come in behind you. Presumably, Colonel Kothari's personal ensemble.

"You see that dish going up there? That can send a signal to Andromeda and back," boasts Colonel Kothari.

"What?" you ask. The jets drown out the colonel.

"Retractable housing. Israeli technology. We can track our babies right to the point of impact," explains Colonel Kothari, his hands moving like rotor blades till he smashes his right fist into his left palm.

"Deadly stuff," you agree.

The two of you enter the communications railcar. Cool air surrounds you. You see people sitting in front of computer screens with earphones. There's also the crackle of walkie-talkies.

"A bit like ATC," you comment dryly. Colonel Kothari looks blankly at you. You feel you have to expand on the initials. "Air traffic control."

"Yes." Colonel Kothari nods. "Come, let me show you the command center." Kothari punches codes on the door and then puts his five fingers on a fingerprint scanner. The door whirs and opens. The SFC, you surmise, has organized a five-star nuke train for itself.

As you follow the colonel, the door shuts on you. You balk. Colonel Kothari comes out. "No weapons allowed inside," he says. "The door has a built-in metal detector."

"Oh," you say. You would rather not go inside than part with your Beretta. But SFC sidekicks on the train join you, and you have little option but to deposit your weapon. You feel naked as you enter the room.

You realize too late that you have committed a blunder.

A chair swivels and you see the visage of Col. Ray Chowdhary, your RAW handler, as he rises to greet you.

"Hello, MM. Fancy seeing you here," he says. There is no mirth in his eyes. You realize the immense complications you are facing. You feel the barrels of two guns, one an MP5, poked against your ribs.

"The surprise is all mine. I didn't know they had recruited you as well for the STO," you say. You even manage a grin. You're busy figuring out who the mole in your crew is. To give yourself a chance in what you now know will happen, this piece of information is vital.

"You see, MM, you aren't the only smart guy around. And this isn't a standard training operation," explains Colonel Chowdhary.

Colonel Kothari is eyeing you like a viper.

"Good acting, Colonel," you say, complimenting Kothari. "What's next, Ray? I can explain. Things may not be what you think."

"Depends on what you think I am thinking, MM," responds the colonel. "Right now, you may be interested in seeing a little closed-circuit television."

Colonel Kothari flicks a switch and the television lights up. You know what's coming next. You see images of your six men lined up against car two, hands on their heads, knees on the gravel, searchlights on their faces. You begin to curse Major Kohli, but he, too, comes in the frame with three gun barrels pointing at his head. Two dogs are chasing your pilots out of the Dauphins. Even though you are sinking in shit, you can't help but smile at the plight that faces your Mauritian pilots.

"Ray, you are playing beyond your league. Cool down. This is coming straight from the office of the national security adviser," you say lamely. Anything to gain time while you think.

Col. Ray Chowdhary ignores you.

"I am disappointed I ever let you in the game. The question is, whose game are you playing, MM? This is as serious as it gets," he says.

"Ray, be a hero for a while. Tomorrow, your ass is mine. I am going to blow the shenanigans of RAW sky-high," you say.

"Let me take the smirk off your face, you piece of shit. You don't know what's headed your way," says Colonel Chowdhary. "Officer, could you enter now, please," he roars into the intercom.

The colonels are in a party mood in the command center, you figure. You hear steps coming in through the door.

"MM, I figure this officer might be after your own heart," says the colonel. "Meet Captain Rekha Satpathy, military intelligence. You may stand at ease, Captain."

Your head turns and you go numb. Whoever it was you thought had given you away, this was the one person you never doubted. But then you think of when you flipped through Digs's family album in his sitting room. Which contained no childhood snaps of Karnam, who doesn't resemble Digs's wife at all. The flaw in memorabilia that should have tipped you off.

You are trembling. Emotions are running through you. Your voice has deserted you. You know that after this, you may not have a ticket out.

"I loved you," you say.

"I love my country," says Karnam.

She doesn't look at you, though. You catch faint noises of a firefight. That would be the NSG mopping up your 5 Kumaon brothers waiting in the Tata Mercedes trucks.

"Well, Ray, since you seem to be flashing all the cards, you might educate me as to what's happening next," you say.

"The captain here has been our double ace, MM. You have been forgetting your training," explains the colonel.

You ignore him. You turn to Karnam. Your confidence is coming back. "What about the Syrian?" you ask.

"That was for real," says Karnam. "I joined the forces soon after."

"Well, baby, that was good work," you say. "I hope you maintain the swastika in my memory."

Karnam blushes.

Your body is suspended in a tank of slowly flowing water. Your head remains above, enclosed in a black mask. You can hear the monotonous rhythm of your breathing and sometimes the imperceptible sound of water gurgling in the pipes. You know the routine, and your only slim advantage lies in the fact that your interrogators may think you are unfamiliar with contemporary regression techniques.

They are depriving you of sensory stimuli and feeding in you a hunger for more. Isolation serves as a powerful stress factor for the mind, and deprived of its usual diet from the senses, it soon starts projecting its fears and memories outward. This is the theory, in any case. The final aim is to induce regression of your personality to a level that dissolves your resistance, breaks down the many interrogation roadblocks you are creating, and ultimately snaps your mental autonomy.

You are being interrogated by officials from military intelligence, though occasionally Col. Ray Chowdhary from RAW makes an appearance. The authorities have slapped the National Security Act on you, and even though your case would go to the CBI eventually, right now you are being given a combing-over in the premises that house the offices of the Directorate General of Military Operations. They have a basement set aside for cases like yours. You can sense their fight against time. A war with the Mossies is on and the Indian nuclear arsenal has nearly been compromised. Besides, there is the matter of the two deviant army units. There might also be other unknown threats. They want to crack you as quickly as possible to avoid future surprises. To know whom you really work for. They also want to keep you quiet.

What would also be important for RAW and co. would be to ensure that you don't damage them inordinately. For if you started speaking the truth, it would cause upheavals in the intelligence setup of the nation.

You know you cannot last indefinitely. Nobody can. But you will stretch the game as long as you can before you buckle. In the first few hours, you have already gone through the detention rigmarole. Your clothes were taken away and you were given prison garb. You know the psychological imperatives working behind those moves. The circumstances of detention are supposed to amplify your feelings of isolation. You have not been given a belt, and your pants are four sizes too large.

You know what is coming next. Even as the drug flows through your veins, you know from the initial creep in your arms that you have been injected with BZ, or quinuclidinyl benzilate. An LSD variant, its psychotic properties are more potent after an immersion in a sensory-deprivation chamber. You know monsters are soon going to fly in your brain. The BZ is a brain bomb. Though you don't have immunity, you have built up considerable resistance against the drug.

A large part of your training has been devoted to weathering coercive interrogation methods, especially chemical. That, in fact, has been your speciality. You have been injected with mind-boggling toxic concoctions to evolve your chemical safeguards. The mind, you have been told in training, is above the body. This much you knew. But they took you a step further.

They put you through an extended course in audiovisual desensitization. They gunned you with disturbing images till you became tired of them and your distress meter flickered at zero levels. Then they graduated you to more extreme images and repeated the process till your anxiety levels hit a new low. They started you off with films of heart surgery and then amputation before progressing to videos of people accidentally cutting limbs and severing toes, then capping it still further with films of torture. To make you overcome your initial nauseated responses, they clamped a device on your eyes to prevent blinking.

It was thought that the desensitization would work to your advantage when psychotic drugs started playing havoc with your mind.

You did, in fact, benefit enormously. You passed a test run with Haldol at a high dosage. This was a drug that nearly caused you to die from hypothermia when you took a low hit before your desensitization drill. Haldol first gained notoriety in Vietnam, where it was administered to unsuspecting troops as a cure for shell shock.

But BZ is a big bastard. During your course, a teammate was found pissing his pants and taking a shower in his uniform. These effects were considered mild.

They haul you to the interrogation chamber while you are still combating BZ. You consider this a big flaw in their routine. The interrogation drill should follow the SDC directly. The calculated provision of stimuli during interrogation makes the subject view the interrogator as a father figure and strengthens feelings of compliance. But with the BZ in your bloodstream, you have a license to act like a psychopath.

You stand up from your chair. Your pants fall to your ankles. You make no effort to pull them up. You start urinating in front of your interrogators. This is a high-degree provocation from your side. You intend to extract a violent response. One of your other specialties is to bear intense pain for long periods of time. Your strategy is to break up the interrogation assault into two modes, chemical and physical. That way, because of the time constraints faced by your interrogators, neither mode will gain enough momentum to make you talk.

But the physical response doesn't come your way. Your two interrogators react as if pissing is quite normal on your part. You are not rattled by this response, but impressed.

Your interrogators have been successful in disrupting your sense of time. There has been no light in your room, and the soundproof environment has been uncanny. Your meals and sleep periods have been highly irregular, and you can't tell with certainty how many hours or days have elapsed since the BZ first flowed in your veins.

The questions are coming at you through a haze.

"How did you come to know about the rail deployment?" asks the interrogator to your left. Though he is in uniform, he's sitting in shadow, so you can't make out his stripes. The other is in civvies. His armpits are damp with perspiration. Both bastards, you notice, have come in without wristwatches. Part of the plotting to give you permanent jet lag.

"There was an advertisement in the *Times of India*," you say.

"Who were your partners in this project, apart from Major Rodriguez and Major Kohli from 5 Kumaon?" asks your uniformed friend.

"There was ADC Bhatnagar from the office of the army chief. There was the PA to the defense minister. There was Colonel Antony Howard, defense attaché at the American embassy," you say. You want to delay the next round of chemical intervention as long as possible. Even though your interrogators are eyeing you with maximum skepticism, you have to keep up the routine. You have to think of new and complex admissions that will take them longer to disprove and discredit. You are exploiting one of the fatal flaws in counterintelligence interrogations—because your sessions are being conducted for the purpose of information and not for prosecuting reasons, as long as you talk, you will be less vulnerable to your second bout with chemicals.

"Could you describe Colonel Howard to us?" asks the guy in civvies.

"Tall guy. Black hair. Wears his uniform. Age forty or so. He's got a herpes situation," you say. "Can I get a smoke?" You are trying to figure out their routine. You aren't quite sure which one of the interrogators is planning to play the good cop. Or maybe the situation is so fluid, they'll decide along the way. They ignore your request.

"Have you any friends in 7 Sikh?" asks the guy in civvies.

"You don't believe me, do you? I mean, I was told there was a mock exercise on the rail arsenal and I could come along as a journalist. I didn't have any hand in planning or anything," you say.

"How long have you known Major Rodriguez?" asks your uniformed questioner.

"How long would you have me know him?" you say. "I really do need a smoke."

"What's your height?" asks the guy in civvies.

"You want to stitch me a coat?" you say.

"How many times have you been to Europe?" asks your uniformed interrogator.

"Did you have sex with Karnam?" asks the guy in civvies before you can answer the last question.

"How many bank accounts do you have?" asks the guy in uniform.

You are now wising up to the tactics. The Alice-in-Wonderland routine, part of the CIA manual. A confusion-inducing technique, its motive is to confound your conditioned responses. The questions, you notice, are following illogical patterns, and the pitch and tone are unrelated to the importance of the questions themselves.

Your interrogators are soon replaced by two others. It's a fucking relay they're throwing at you. They are systematically thwarting your attempts to establish a rapport. You are unfamiliar with this babble procedure and the logic behind it. But they soon move you to familiar territory.

You have been patched up with electrodes on your chest. You are getting an intramuscular shot of something. You don't yet know what it is. Then, as the ants start climbing up your spine, you get your first clue. Pro-

lixin. The beauty of this drug lies in the fact that your nerves don't remain your own. It grinds in your sinews and synapses till you ache with a
disquietude that you don't want to downgrade by calling it an advanced
form of restlessness. You get up and pace your cell, which is a ten-by-ten
proposition where you can't see your own hands. You think your vision is
blurring, but you can't really be sure, as there's no light to check. After
ten paces, you think you are increasing your pain by pacing, so you sit on
the floor, but then you think you are better off walking. So you get up
again, and this goes on in swift cycles. You are finding it difficult to locate
the source of your pain. It's everywhere and nowhere in particular. You
can hear yourself hitting the walls.

And then they come in and lead you to a different room, where they
poke something into you again. Your restlessness subsides a bit. You
think they have given you a tranquilizer, maybe Sinequan, to calm you
down, but you soon change your opinion. And in spite of a tranquilizer
coursing through your system, you are beginning to panic. The nerves in
your fingertips are dying. You feel the special panic that comes when you
start losing control over your eyes. You recognize the early-warning
system of the drug Anectine, a variant of the drug tubocurarine, which
raids your respiratory system within two minutes of being injected. You
feel the dosage is symbolic, since you are still breathing. But they have
been smart enough to place a lung machine alongside where they have
strapped you, and even though your vision is not normal, it's good
enough for you to identify it.

Anectine, you know, specializes in providing a sensation worse than
dying. In minute quantities, it can serve as a muscle relaxant, but at high
doses, it collapses your respiratory system by arresting your intercostal
muscles and diaphragm. Your heart rate nosedives to fifty beats a minute,
and your lungs could go anywhere from two to four minutes. In terms of
sheer torture, you rate the drug at the top of the horror list.

You have never been apportioned a combination of Prolixin and
Anectine. But as the chemicals attack from deep inside you, and before

your ability to concentrate is decimated, you realize their complementary nature. Prolixin is panicking you like never before and Anectine, because of the way it has relaxed your muscle groups, is denying you the mechanism to provide an outlet for your panic. You are in semiparalysis and the floodwaters are rising. You don't think you can hold out from a full dose of Anectine, if and when it eventually comes. You are in unchartered waters. Your training has never thrust you to such an edge of chemical endurance.

Some small feelings of guilt are beginning to rise in you. The people you work for trusted the potential you once showed, and now you are feeling you have let them down big-time in their hour of dire need. Your capture couldn't have come at a worse moment. You don't have much to give by way of spoils if you crack, for Jumbo will have taken the expected precautions. He will have moved the money around and covered other critical trails.

But you are the spearhead. The anointed leader of the Alkifa. You have a lot to give if the Indians know what to look for. For you, the victory is in not lending them the key to what you really are. What they think you are is none of your concern.

Even as you begin to slip into unconsciousness and see them monitoring your vital signs, you feel a big rumble and then a roar. You are thrown from the stretcher that holds you onto the floor. You are already hoping against hope. And as you fade out, there's a smile on your face.

our real name is Arbaz Khan. You are the new face of jihad. For you, Islam without jihad doesn't exist, and the best of all jihads is the word of truth in the presence of the unjust ruler. In the emancipation of the oppressed people of Kashmir lies your own deliverance. The Hindu Kafirs have to go or die. Such is Allah's will and so you have been taught.

For you, it's been a long journey, and it began just after you left the Academy and your father, Col. Om Mehta, was given a voluntary discharge from the Indian army for health reasons. As your family adjusted to civilian life after the orderliness of a cantonment, the two of you spent many days alone together. You sensed a preparation for something. One fine day, the waiting ended. He took you for a drive to the tomb of Nizamuddin Chisthi.

You were perplexed. The destination wasn't unusual, though. You had done this sort of thing with your father in more places and times than could have come about purely from secular dictates. In the past, you had put it down to his Sufi mind-set. As a child, you had been taken innumerable times to the shrine at Ajmer Shariff. You love the place. And you paid regular visits to the Baba Haider Sheikh shrine at Maler Kotla in the Punjab.

In the early years, these things inculcated in you a tolerance for all things religious. Later, to your father's chagrin, you devoted yourself to the pursuit of pleasure. Even in those days, as now, the Muslim call to prayers, the *adhan*, struck a chord in you that you were never able to explain rationally. It always calmed and enervated you.

Later, the drugs took over. But that day, there was something in his eyes warning you that whatever was coming was going to leave an indelible imprint upon your life. He held your hand, and with his eyes cast far away, he made you familiar with your roots.

He started with a bang. He told you in so many words that he wasn't your biological father. Even as you mulled over this piece of news, he spun a story so astounding that you immediately sensed it was too tangled for imagination to have played a part in its origin.

He told you that you were a child marked for the Alkifa, or struggle. That you were the firstborn of parents who had had the courage and the spirit of sacrifice to bequeath you to jihad. He himself didn't know who they were, for you had come bundled in the arms of a courier couple who flew in one night in December on Pakistan International Airlines and left you in his custody. They left a week later. You were a month old.

You learned that the man you knew as your father had come to India in 1965, at the age of seventeen. He enrolled at Allahabad University. New papers were provided and a Hindu identity assiduously built. He was one of an elite. One of an exclusive band of sixteen who had come to India with the single-minded purpose of infiltrating key areas of the Indian government.

You asked anxiously about your mother. You wanted to know whether she, too, was a part of this Cold War subterfuge. You remember hoping even at that moment that she was Indian, a Hindu. That would provide some reason to veto the existence that you saw coiling toward you. But you had no such luck. She was very much part and parcel of the operation. Smuggled into India in 1970, she was a bride carefully designated for your father. You were adopted only because, early on, your father suffered from impotence.

Your father told you that he had kept his part of the promise in the 1987 Indian army battlefield exercise Operation Brass Tack, under General Sunderji's command. The salient features of the armor show were documented in detail by your father. Apart from alerting Pakistan in case the exercise suddenly developed into an armor thrust into Sind, your father was able, later, to pinpoint the weaknesses of the Indian effort and relay to the ISI chief such engagement minutiae as the effects of sand attrition on the tracks of the T-72.

That was the apex of his career. At the point of his retirement, he realized he could travel no further in the army hierarchy and was advised not to compromise himself, for fear of endangering the future that you, MM, might harvest for Pakistan. Your family moments suddenly began to fall into place. How happy your father had been when you joined the Academy and how aghast he'd been—something you hadn't understand then—when you left.

That night, you couldn't sleep. Or, for that matter, many nights after that. Initially, you sought in your mother something that would oppose the perplexities your father had introduced to your life. But in her eyes was all the confirmation you would ever need. You desperately wanted an ally to strengthen your initial mutinous desire to sever ties with a past you'd had no hand in shaping. But to deny a future for their lifetime of work would be to reject them. Out of guilt grew a sense of duty. Theirs wasn't a story of three decades of deceit. It was, instead, a cocktail of duty, sacrifice, and competence. Above all, you simply loved your old man. After the rebellion of your teens, it wasn't in you to refuse him anything.

Your father hadn't met or seen his family since he'd come to India. For pragmatic purposes, his death was staged in a 1965 fire in Islamabad's

Gulshan enclave. Your mother was an orphan. Over the years, she tried her best to invent a Hindu motherhood for herself. You were reminded once again of the small routines that your family never had but which you observed in full flow in the lives of neighbors. Daily rituals for the gods were absent in your house. The deities were there in a symbolic concession to popular perception, but they often stood in layers of dust. On numerous occasions, you had felt the absence of aunts and uncles. Of the band of sixteen who came to India in 1965, your father knew just one.

You knew who that was before your father began to unravel the mystery. He was the head of the only extended family you ever had. Jumbo's father went on to join the Indian Railway Service. One might ask what good that would do for the Pakistani establishment. But he systematically rose, plotted, and gained for himself a position in Military Rail, the exclusive All India cell that coordinates all military traffic in India. He was the one the military approached to requisition railcars and locomotives to move their battalions. At any given point, he had with him the location of India's strike formations.

It comforted you to know that Jumbo, too, was in the same boat. You had an ally with whom to share your trials and tribulations.

But you didn't train together. For you, they arranged a fellowship in the UK. From there, you flew on a Singapore passport to Pakistan. You stayed there a year before you went back to England, and then you returned to the land you knew first but which now you must plot against. You have returned subsequently for more bouts of training. Your inventory of motherfucker skills has grown by leaps and bounds. Especially after your biggest coup, the infiltration of RAW, which you achieved in the early nineties. There, your annexation of talents grew. You are one of a rare breed, those who have been schooled by two intelligence agencies.

Now, of course, you stand exposed. The whole breach is not yet visible, but there will be questions. And with questions come suspicions.

As you make your way to Kargil, you are going with the full knowledge that the final chapter of your life is possibly unfolding. With Karnam, you might have had a reason to begin anew. But your antennae short-circuited there. You still believe that she really felt for you, but you don't know for sure. You can only laugh at your own indiscretion. The one saving grace is that your confidences never crossed the line where all would have been irrevocable.

In Kargil, you intend to bow out with a bang. You have not come with suicidal focus, but, as a professional, you understand the inherent risks. The task you have been assigned is to recover something of what is quickly turning out to be another embarrassment for your brothers from across the border.

Though you intended to be in the war zone from the start—under the pretext of covering the war—with the devaluation of your status, you have to sneak in as a civilian truck driver carrying relief material for the civilian population of Kargil. Jumbo is your cleaner. You are a month late, thanks to your nuclear expedition—which wasn't totally unsuccessful, since the direction finders you installed on two of the railcars are transmitting loud and clear—and to your brief capture and subsequent recovery period.

It was a simple operation to flush you out. The surprise was all on Jumbo's side. Your handlers in Islamabad assigned four personnel to Jumbo for the purpose. You were too valuable to spend more time than necessary under the MI's scalpel.

They parked a civilian vehicle right next to the DGMO building, and before the flimsy security could come and raise a few questions, the 440 pounds of Semtex it held had blown half the annex away. Of course, you weren't in the annex. In the resulting confusion, they extricated you from the basement without any opposition. Before departing, they blew up the basement as well, so for a time, at least, the Indians wouldn't know whether you were alive or dead. That gave you some space for a breather and time for a detoxification course.

You used it to catch up on events. Your manipulated issue of *The Post* taking on Defense Minister Yadav, General Rampal, the air force, and 7 Sikh, among others, had been a sellout the day it hit the stands. Jain the motherfucker, whose byline you'd plastered on big chunks of copy, disappeared. There was much talk about the questionnaire. And Digs, you learned, to your great amusement, had a mild stroke the day he saw it. After that, he remained under strict observation at the Escort Heart Institute's ICU ward. Your three defense-correspondent friends had previewed *The Post*'s story as front-page leads. Innumerable follow-ups ensued, and television chat shows devoted entire evenings to Digs's scoop.

With war at full tilt, criticism of the forces was muted. Patriotism swayed more in the media. Calls for heads to roll, especially those of Defense Minister Suresh Yadav and the army chief, Gen. Subhas Rampal, began in a small way but will pick up after the war reaches some sort of conclusion and the monsoon session of Parliament begins. But again, if the Indians win, all will be forgotten. The characters at the top might make the leap from the dung heap to the list of heroes. Expectedly, Gen. Subhas Rampal gave a clean chit to the 7 Sikh, his parent unit, now attached to the Drass brigade.

Interestingly, there was no mention in the media of the attempted heist of the nuke train. Though news leaked about your arrest, it had to do with a red herring: the questionnaire. After your escape from the DGMO HQ, you were declared dead in the bomb explosion. At first, you credited this to the genuine confusion and the profusion of unidentifiable bodies. Now you know they want you dead. Their blunder in declaring you dead has hindered their search for you. What reason could you possibly give to flash a dead man's picture on television with rewards leading to his capture?

For a while, you tinkered with the idea of an undercover press conference with a select few to embarrass the Indian army, but you know that wouldn't contribute to your overall scheme. Instead, it could provide them clues to your whereabouts. It has taken you many weeks to recover from their chemical barrage. Jumbo has nursed you back with great care and concern. The whole of June, you have been bedridden and building up your strength for the final lap.

You think about Karnam as little as possible. You are still baffled by Digs's cooperation with RAW, planting her on you. Fucking Ray Chowdhary, you think. You underestimated the bastard.

There have been reasons, though, to feel pleased with yourself. You are sitting on $80 million in your bank account in Europe, the bulk of which you will soon pass on to Pakistan's ISI, 60 percent of that money having come from Akramov, the rest from the heroin that the LTTE headed your way as payment for the arms and armament you channeled into Jaffna via Vedaranyam in Tamil Nadu. Jumbo has overseen the logistics of that during your recuperation. You are pleased that you have all but wiped Akramov out of business. You hear that he has taken out a contract on you. A worry for another day—if you survive what you have set out to do in Kargil.

If Shomali were around, you wouldn't think twice before splitting, but if Shomali were around, perhaps you wouldn't be what you are. Maybe if Karnam hadn't been what she turned out to be, you might have considered absconding, but you hope your sense of pride in what you do is too overwhelming to be overidden by romantic considerations.

What you know is that if you survive July, you can take jihad to new heights.

But June has seen many reverses for Pakistan.

Tololing Ridge fell on June 12. Peak 5100 fell on June 28, and 4700 fell a day later. Tiger Hill alone remains, and Point 4875, which rises from Mushkoh. There is hope as long as Tiger Hill remains. It will be possible then to rally troops and go for a fresh offensive. Your job in two days is to see that Tiger Hill remains in the hands of those engaged in jihad.

The iridium satellite phone that you and Jumbo carry can provide you with GPS data. Your immediate task is to get a fix on all the artillery positions on the Indian side, especially the Bofors batteries. The Indian success at Tololing had to do with the direct firing from the Bofors guns, something that artillery manuals don't teach you. You want to nullify that advantage when the Indian troops push for Tiger Hill.

In the gunnysacks of relief material that you are ostensibly carrying for the civilian population of Drass and Kargil, you have considerable quantities of explosives. You have come prepared for all eventualities. Opportunities, rather. Of the many acts of sabotage you could enact, blowing up a bridge or two on the Drass-Kargil highway is high on your list of priorities. Though the Drass ammunition dump was taken out by your brothers a few days into battle, you plan to get a fix on the new location. All this in addition to your general brief of placing IEDs at strategic checkpoints and unit camps.

Jumbo has already pulled off a coup. At Sonmarg, the first stop on the highway running from Srinagar to Leh, and the halt for the civilian truck convoys, Jumbo pushed IEDs into the gas tanks of some fifteen trucks. The explosives are wrapped in special polyethylene and timed to explode after forty-eight hours. The trucks will soon spread out on the highway. Who knows where they will be in two days' time? But they would certainly block out huge stretches of narrow, mountainous terrain.

Once you reach Kargil, you plan to switch to a Maruti Gypsy complete with army uniform and rank. You have one waiting there for you in army green, with identity marks of the 15th Corps, which is headquartered at Batwara Gate in Srinagar. Though the local population at Kargil are Shia Muslims, their sympathies are with their Sunni brothers in this conflict with the Hindu Kafirs, and it wasn't tough to organize the logistics of this conversion in Kargil. Besides, the network proved itself in the early days of the war. They radioed in exact positions of the TV tower at Kargil and the huge ammunition dump at Drass. Both are smoldering remains now.

At Sonmarg, they hold up all upgoing traffic till 1:00 P.M. to make way for the convoys coming down. They don't want the convoys to pass one another on the mountains, since that would slow them and create pile-ups, which Pakistani artillery spotters would be quick to exploit, particularly in the seven-mile stretch between Kharbu and Zero Point beyond Drass, where our hills look down on the Indian highway. Spotters have been told to give the green for shelling at the slightest bit of traffic movement, and the treacherous Indus riverbed skirting the highway holds many burned-out skeletal remains of Tata trucks.

The way up to Zojilla Pass, where the climb bottoms out, is muddy because of rain. No matter how many times you cross the Zojilla Pass, it never prepares you for the next time. At 10,500 feet, it's one of the highest drivable mountain passes in the world. And today, your crossing is met by the roar of the Bofors guns. At three hundred feet, nothing can prepare you for that, either.

It's a battery of four guns packed at the side of the mountains, where your shells would find it difficult to loop and zero in on unless the exact quadrants were known. It is your job to find out.

A press briefing is in progress. You see Major Purshottam, PRO of the 15th Corps, with a minibus full of journalists. You don't want to complicate matters at the outset by taking the risk of going yourself. You pull up and spring open the hood of your Tata truck. Jumbo goes with a jerrican to fill up on water from a nearby waterfall. Jumbo also has the iridium under his shirt to get a fix on the Bofors. You recognize a few of the journalists.

"Let's have some fun," says Jumbo once he gets back.

You know what he's up to, and you give your smile of approval. You move up fifteen hundred feet and park again, this time protected behind rocks. Jumbo dials the necessary numbers. The quadrants travel to Delhi and then by E-mail to a Web-based encryption service, which then forwards the information by fax to Karachi, and from there it travels to Skardu, the brigade HQ for the Pakistan Northern Light Infantry. It takes ten minutes for the information to reach Skardu. From there, the artillery units can have their music going in five minutes. You watch the briefing going on through your binoculars. Jumbo is waving the other trucks on.

The likelihood of a direct strike is slim because of the height of the hill that the shells will have to loop over. But they can definitely land 160 feet away and close in the perimeter by several feet every round. It's too risky to stay on and correct the fire. And you don't want some jagged lead flying your way.

You wait for the first few rounds to land just so you can watch the scattering of the assembly. You hear the whistles and then the thuds. If you hear the whistle and hit the ground, they say, you are probably safe. Of course, if it's an aerial burst, then you have the odds stacked against you.

The initial few land after twenty minutes. You are beginning to think your side isn't in the mood, but then the barrage finally comes. The first shell gets the bus. It explodes in a ball of fire. Some shells fall on army tents. But they perk up the assembly and send the journalists scrambling.

You move off with relish. Your first kill. The war is an adventure for you, though you are hopping on late. You travel at a leisurely pace, stopping off at various places to talk to the troops, finding the location of their units and mapping the quadrants off the artillery guns. At times, you even give lifts to stranded troops. They prove a valuable source of information. For instance, a 5 Para commando tells you of his Dhatak Company, which was operating behind the line of control, trying to cut the supply lines leading to the Mushkoh valley. They had suffered some losses at Kala Patthar.

Jumbo is dialing up a continuous relay of information. You don't call in the hits. That would be a sure giveaway. You are saving up the information for tomorrow, when, your network tells you, the Indians will be making a push for Tiger Hill.

You plan to reel in the strikes then. Hit the guns or whatever can be hit at one go. This will leave the 18 Grenadiers, the unit charged with leading the assault to the top of the 16,250-foot peak, with little artillery support. It would expose your friends at 7 Sikh as well, who have been charged with encircling Tiger Hill at the base. The western ridge is still in your hands and is the sole supply route to your men at the top. Lack of artillery support for the 7 Sikh will make it difficult for them to assault the western ridge and threaten your supply lines. Tiger Hill, incidentally, is your escape route as well.

The dragnet is closing around you: Using the airports would be suicidal. The choices for you are Kathmandu and Dhaka, both of which you have ruled out. Your minders across the border will be sending a detachment of the elite Special Guards to Tiger Hill to assist you in switching sides. That is the plan, anyway.

Of course, for that, you need to tune in Maj. Raunaq Singh, who no doubt is nursing his wounds in the combat zone. The 7 Sikh has been sucked into the war along with 5 Kumaon because they happened to be in Kashmir when the shit first hit the ceiling.

You hit Kharbu at eight in the evening. You are the fortieth truck in line. All of you are waiting for the convoy from Kargil to pass you. Kharbu to Zero Point is a high-risk area. Trucks drive at night with their headlights switched off. If the shells don't get you, the drop to the Indus will. The river roars and swirls 150 feet below the road.

Between these points, the drivers proceed with a fear that you can smell from afar. The convoy you are part of leaves in total darkness. Just yesterday, three trucks were knocked off, an Indian gas tanker taking a direct hit. The tanker burst and then rolled down the slope and into the river, disappearing.

All is silent till you reach the halfway mark, and then you hit a road jam. Five trucks ahead, a Sumo with a flat is holding up traffic. Drivers start honking. At Kharbu, there are stories of truck drivers bulldozing cars and knocking them into the Indus if they block their way in the shelling zone.

Jumbo's nervous. You are, too. Not so much for yourself as for your cargo. A stray splinter is enough to blow everybody within 150 feet to kingdom come. You climb down and watch the Sumo driver work his jack. He is feeling his way around the screws. There isn't enough light to work the wheels at normal speed.

And then with the pressure on him, he does something that nobody thinks he would ever be dumb enough to do. He dives into his glove compartment and pulls out a flashlight. His passenger in the front seat holds the beam in place as he attacks the wheel with renewed haste.

Everyone in the convoy is aghast. You can feel a wave of terror pass from the front to the back.

"Here it comes," says Jumbo.

"We have five minutes," you say. "Any chance of calling in a negative?" By the time your message reaches Skardu, the shelling will be over. You figure you will have to take it with the rest of them.

"No," says Jumbo.

He's already in the back of the truck, selecting stuff you can't afford to have destroyed—the MP5s and Glocks and some special flares, your pre-decided signature tunes for the Special Guards waiting to flush you out. The Sumo is right on the edge of the curb and falls short by a couple of inches of letting the rest of the traffic go by on the road.

In the darkness, you first see the green and yellow trails of light the shells make as they travel across the cold summer evening sky. The first few hit your side of the mountain 150 feet above you. It starts a gravel shower in your direction. You know the next few rounds will travel down systematically till the gunners figure the right trajectory to land the shells on the road. The Sumo driver is panicking. He hasn't had time to unwind all the screws in his flat tire. Three are still on. He decides to risk the mountain terrain on his hobbling wheel.

In your truck, Jumbo takes the wheel and shifts into gear. You have packed all your stuff, along with the satellite phone, into a waterproof army haversack. If you have to jump off your truck, you'd better have all your workings in one bag. You watch the Sumo career off into the first bend. "The son of a bitch," you mutter.

The drivers are going berserk now.

"Switch on the lights," you instruct Jumbo. You don't want the Indus to have you for dinner even if the shells miss you. You calculate the chances of a shell hitting you in the zone as one in a thousand, even if you are a dead giveaway because of your halogen headlights.

The others follow the same logic. Tonight, the shells have no luck. The gunners aren't getting the range right; within ten minutes, the quarry has cleared the danger zone.

You hit Kargil three hours behind schedule. On your previous trips, you have put up at Hotel Siachen, the designated media spot. But times have changed, and you push straight for the plateau, three miles from the main town and en route to Leh. There your Gypsy awaits you, and you get a briefing from the network. Tomorrow, you will have a climb ahead of you, and you are worried about Jumbo. Neither of you has time to acclimatize, and although your body has withstood such abuse in the past, Jumbo already has a headache.

You are up at six in the morning. The coffee brings with it a phone call. Your iridium shakes and shudders, its vibrator battery in overdrive. Both you and Jumbo freeze. You know it can't be glad tidings. You press the receive button with great trepidation.

"Arbaz Khan, your time is up. You Mossie piece of shit."

You recognize the voice. Major Rodriguez has sourced your number and he knows your name.

"You bastard. Why don't you go to the nearest checkpoint and surrender yourself. It would save all of us a lot of running around," says Major Rodriguez.

Jumbo is listening in on an improvised headphone.

"Aha, Major," you begin. "I am glad—"

"Glad my ass. You just listen now and listen hard. Your game's over. You can't come off the hills."

Major Rodriguez, you observe, is giving you more than he should. He is, for instance, implying that he knows you are in Kargil. Or he thinks you are and wants to confirm.

"Major, whose side are you on, anyway? I thought you were content with the money coming your way," you say.

"MM, you piece of shit. It never was the money, and you know that," says Major Rodriguez.

"Then what was it, Major?" you ask. You want to push him, to get to the bottom of the affair. You want to know the source of the leak.

"MM, you turd. Here, listen to your old man," says Major Rodriguez.

You stiffen. So does Jumbo. You aren't prepared for this. You hear the scratch of a chair and then the voice of your father.

"Sorry, son," he says. "They nearly killed your mother."

You want to ask him more. Find out about your mother. But Rodriguez isn't finished with his games.

"Happy, you Mossie asshole?" he asks. "Finished with your Allah talk. Now that you know who has your balls, will you do what you must?"

You are too numb to answer immediately. Jumbo's eyes are starting to go wet. You get a hold on yourself. You sense the anger rising in your blood.

"Major, you know what? You've done what you had to do. Now I have to play my part out," you say.

"Touché," says Major Rodriguez. "An asshole with a philosophy."

"Major, if your generals want me so badly, why don't you come and get me?" you say. Rodriguez goes silent. You know the idea appeals to him. Perhaps he gets a green from Col. Ray Chowdhary, who is, undoubtedly, listening in. A motherfuckers' final round.

"Where are you?" asks Major Rodriguez.

"Now, Major, I might be an asshole, but I'm not foolish," you say.

"MM, you bastard, we have this signal traced right to your ass. You can't fart without the 15th Corps waking up," he says.

"It's about time they did," you say. You want to make sure Rodriguez comes after you. "And now you listen, you goddamn toy soldier. You're still a cadet, aren't you? Cadet Rodriguez. You Goan piece of shit. Or should I say Portuguese? You think nobody knows who got Shomali. What was she? Your aunt. All I know is, she was the best lay in the whole wide world."

You hang up after that. You switch off your instrument. When the time comes, you'll switch it back on, but today, there's a lot to be done. This wasn't the way you had ever imagined you would use Shomali's name. But it was important that Rodriguez come after you. You can't split all the acts of your life into probability equations. Some things you do because it's in your nature. And before you cross the border, you have a score to settle with Rodriguez.

You regret that Jumbo's IEDs were on a forty-eight-hour fuse. You wish you could advance them by a day. You spread your bedsheet on the floor. The two of you have never prayed together, but there's always a first time. You face Mecca and say the Hadith.

You hit the road in the Gypsy, with Jumbo driving and in army fatigues. Though you, too, have the option of a uniform, you decide to forgo it for the time being. The Gypsy will give you swift access through checkpoints, and your cover story of being a *Times of India* journalist will provide passage to unit commanding officers in their camps.

In the back, you have your cargo, equipment, arms, and other paraphernalia. The Hindu Kafirs have obviously struck gold in their ploy of using a thief to catch another thief. You are sure both Major Rodriguez and Major Kohli will now be utilized by military intelligence and RAW to get at you. Or a spy, rather. You are not quite sure where to slot yourself. And now, of course, anger is fogging your brain.

Your first task is to do a recce in Drass. Look for telltale signs of the Indian timing for the Tiger Hill assault, and the route as well. There are three possible routes to the top from the Indian side. After the fall of Tololing to the Indians, all three sides are completely blind to your spotters. The Indians could spring a surprise or two, and it is your job not to let it be a surprise for your side.

It's a two-hour run from Kargil to the Drass brigade HQ. On the way, you see two Bofors guns being towed toward Drass. Ominous signs. You pass an artillery convoy. More important, two multibarrel-rocket-launching trucks. The Indians are gearing up their direct-fire artillery.

At Drass, you see other signs. Bunkers being beefed up and two 15th Corps top-brass staff vehicles parked at the local school. You know through your network that the commanding officer of brigade HQ, Brigadier Aul, isn't really in charge of the Tiger Hill operation. The operational brigade is the 17th of the 26th Division, with Brigad. Tejvir Singh as the officer in command. The HQ of the 17th is in the school where you saw the cars parked.

You then proceed to the camp of the 2 Rajputana Rifles. You have to return part of the way you came to get there. The 2nd Raj Rif was the spearhead Indian unit in its successful assault on Tololing Ridge on June 12. The unit took sixteen hits in all, eight of them officers on that single night. But it had performed its task. Now the men lie in a stupor at the spur of the ridge they fought on, mourning their losses and awaiting further orders.

You are escorted to the commanding officer, Col. Vinod Tewari. The colonel is courteous and accepts your media credentials at face value. He warms to you and orders breakfast. You are there ostensibly to do a Tololing reconstruction. Also, a piece on what moves men in battle. The colonel warms to your second stated objective.

"I have come to believe," Colonel Tewari begins, "that nobody can fight a war without having a belief in God." The colonel has arranged chairs for you in the open, and you have a panoramic view of Tololing Ridge.

You scribble furiously. The colonel goes on to enumerate instances in the Tololing battle that support his war theorem. You nod vigorously.

"An officer from our unit was three feet away from one of the militants. He was totally exposed. The AK-47 of the militant jammed. They had a hand-to-hand combat and the militant died. You see that rock there. My battle HQ was there. I sat there for ten hours on the night of the tenth. No shell landed within one hundred and fifty feet of where I was. That night, I got a message on the wireless and went to confirm the message at my radio tent. A shell landed bang in the middle of my battle HQ at that moment. Four of my men died. What would you call that? Luck? No, sir. It's not luck. It's the invisible hand of God. It was an aerial burst. My men turned into lumps of meat."

You take fifteen more minutes of Colonel Tewari's battlelogue. What you have come for would take possibly a minute, but you have to till the ground to sow bonhomie and trust.

"It must have been quite an experience, Colonel," you say, appearing as awestruck as possible.

"It was, son," he says.

"I have some friends at 18 Grenadiers. I hear they are taking Tiger Hill tonight," you mention casually.

"Yes," he says. "I just wished Thakur the best of luck. He's the commanding officer. We were together at IMA."

"It's going to be a steep climb," you say. "It's over sixteen thousand feet, isn't it? Won't they need oxygen?"

"No, not really. The high-altitude instructors are going to be laying the ropes," says Colonel Tewari.

You have gotten more than you expected. That the dolly was on for tonight, you already knew. More important, what the colonel has indirectly revealed to you because of his mention of the instructors from HAWS is that the Indians will be taking the steep side, the back of the Tiger route, the near-vertical east face, which is hardly protected at all.

You take your leave of the colonel after presenting him with a collection of airline liquor miniatures and a carton of Rothmans. He's overwhelmed.

"Leave me your number in Delhi so I can look you up when I'm next there. When will this article appear?" asks Colonel Tewari.

"Shortly," you say. You leave the colonel your number, for whatever it's worth. You have one last request.

"I have a friend in 7 Sikh. Could you patch me to him on your secure lines?" you ask.

"Sure as hell," says Colonel Tewari. He picks up the phone on his table and asks Drass exchange to put him through to Maj. Raunaq Singh. He hands over the headset to you.

Jumbo gets the colonel out of hearing range. "Would you like to check out some other brands, Colonel? There's Dunhill in there and some packs of Marlboro," says Jumbo. He hauls out a bag from the back.

There's a background hum in the headpiece and then the noise of artillery. Major Singh is obviously in the thick of things. "Colonel Tewari?" he asks twice.

"Hello, Major," you say. "MM here." There's a silence at the other end. "I have some news for you, Major."

"I am listening, MM," says Major Singh.

Obviously, the major is a bit stunned at your access to the secure line. You come straight to the point. "I heard you are having big fun at Tiger. Some of your friends want to join you. Would you like to play host to Rodriguez and Kohli?"

"Does a man want a million bucks?" replies Maj. Raunaq Singh.

You are driving down to the Drass helipad. You have to go through two checkpoints at Drass HQ, but with 15th Corps markings on your Gypsy, you have no problems.

Cramped in the back of your Gypsy, you have already managed to don the uniform of a major. There's been a sudden switch in your plans. When you dial out to your network through your iridium, the call instead gets transferred to Major Rodriguez. You can hear the whine of helicopter rotors as the major comes on the line.

"MM, you piece of shit, one hour and we have your Mossie ass," says Major Rodriguez.

This is an unexpected hindrance. The Indians have obviously worked Motorola Communications fast. You have no way of telling Skardu when they'll attack Tiger Hill or how.

This is when you think of taking the battle to Rodriguez very early in the game. Right when his chopper lands at Drass. The surprise element is too great an advantage to be ignored. You can then hijack the chopper to cross the line of control or fly somewhere near Tiger Hill. The risk is obvious. Without your having informed Skardu of your plans, your troops will have no way of knowing you are in the chopper. You'll have to brave missile fire from your side. That is a risk you will have to take. You thus abandon your earlier plan of a trek to Tiger Hill—the way, incidentally, Major Singh is expecting you to come. You will now provide a surprise to 7 Sikh.

The Drass helipad was a dangerous zone itself till Tololing was taken by the Indians. The choppers then gave up landing at Drass because of the shelling and fear of shoulder-fired Stingers from the top of Tololing Ridge. Nothing can put a crimp in a pilot's mental makeup faster than news that he could be chased around by infrared missiles.

You notice a detachment the size of a company at the helipad. You recognize troops from 5 Kumaon who you know are in the region. You also spot Colonel Sangma, the 5 Kumaon commanding officer, in the ATC hut. Major Rodriguez has obviously organized his dogs of war to come after you. His last ace in the hole to earn some brownie points for himself and the 5 Kumaon from the army's top brass. Earn some clemency where none should exist.

This introduces a snarl in your strategy. Though you are in uniform, there exists the possibility the troops might recognize you if you step out of the Gypsy before the chopper arrives. After it does, there will be the dust swirl and other distractions to capitalize on. You put on your dark glasses for added camouflage. Jumbo parks the Gypsy behind the ATC hut, out of the direct line of sight of the troops.

You hear the sound of the rotor blades after five minutes of waiting. You have already screwed silencers onto your weapons. As the MI-17 hovers above the runaway, you enter the aviation hut and take out the two radar controllers and Colonel Sangma. You don't bother to fall to the temptation of introducing yourself to Sangma, rekindling his memories. There is no time for a cat-and-mouse game. You go for their brains. You don't even have time to watch the blood oozing from their foreheads as they slump on their chairs. Sangma falls to the ground.

With Rodriguez, of course, it is going to be different.

Jumbo, meanwhile, is already walking to the chopper before the dust has settled. He walks unencumbered by the kit bag, which you carry slung on your shoulder, twenty paces behind. You can see Major Rodriguez unstrapping his seat belt. There's Major Kohli as well, the way you have anticipated. They are making it a party. The doors are opening, but Jumbo is through before they realize what is happening.

They recognize Jumbo too late. Rodriguez and Kohli are in the backseat, Kohli nearest to the door. Jumbo has already opened a gash on Kohli's right eyebrow with the back of the Glock. You, too, greet Major Rodriguez with a swing of your Glock. It takes out four of his front teeth.

"Hello, Major," you say. Then you swing around and take an MP5 out of your bag. You squeeze your trigger on the 5 Kumaon welcome committee advancing toward the chopper, as yet unsure about what really is happening. Now they know.

You get a dozen of them in the first volley. The others scatter for cover. Jumbo makes quick work of the copilot and throws his body onto the tarmac. At ten thousand feet, there is only so much freight that a chopper can take into the air.

Within two minutes, you are flying again. Jumbo sits in front, setting the course for the pilot, while you glare at Rodriguez and Kohli in the back.

"Welcome, Major," you say. Rodriguez's mouth is bleeding and he's pale, but he still manages to give you a toothless smile.

"Ha, MM," says Major Rodriguez. He spits out a tooth. It falls on his lap.

"A bit of a turnaround, ah, Rodriguez?" you say. You're keeping a close eye on Kohli. He's jukebox-solid, though he can hardly see through his right eye, swollen and bloody as it is.

You put the barrel of your Glock on Rodriguez's temple. The way you feel, you wouldn't mind firing. But that would be too smooth an end for a bastard like Rodriguez. You plan to turn him and Kohli over in one piece to the 7 Sikh. Let things take their natural course.

Rodriguez's composure is slowly returning to normal. There is one thing you can't call Rodriguez, and that is a sham.

"How long have you been in this game, MM?" he asks.

"Long enough," you say. "How are my parents?"

"The last I knew, MI was having another go at them," says Major Rodriguez.

You grimace. Jumbo looks back with concern.

"Sorry, MM," says Major Rodriguez. "I know how you feel, but that's the way it has to be. It was RAW's idea, anyway—some Colonel Ray Chowdhary who's in charge. He just missed getting onto this chopper. They got me in the game when they had cracked the whole thing."

"Thanks," you say. Rodriguez's gums are starting to bleed.

"Where are you planning to fly us, MM?" asks Major Rodriguez.

Jumbo is moving around the chopper on the Indian side, deciding the best way to go behind Tiger Hill without getting picked up by air defense units. Jumbo's done some fixed-wing flying and he can read the gauges. He flashes five fingers three times. You guess fifteen minutes of fuel is more than enough to get you where you want to be.

"Major Singh wants to hold a welcome party for you," you say.

Major Rodriguez pales. So does Kohli.

"You got your money, MM. And now you have a chopper. Why don't you just fly to Mossie country while your luck is holding? Seeing as you can't fly yourself, we will give you a lift. We will try our luck coming back. Dodge the missiles," suggests Major Rodriguez.

"It will suit me better if you try your luck with the 7 Sikh. Try dodging Major Singh and his men," you say.

"If we live to do it," says Major Rodriguez. He grins and points his hand westward.

Jumbo and the pilot are already panicking.

"Incoming," says Jumbo, and then you realize what's happening. A ground-to-air missile has locked on.

The pilot is discharging flares left and right, and he goes in a steep dive, skimming the valley floor. You are flying six feet above boulders in the valley behind peak 4875.

It's a near miss. You hear the explosion of the missile as it zeroes in on one of the flares. Next time, none of you may be that lucky.

The event has engrossed you and diverted your attention enough for Major Kohli to think he can take advantage. He spins on you, his torso picking up momentum. His right hand has grabbed your Glock and he's fisted you in the solar plexus with his left. You butt Kohli with your head, but as the helicopter banks sharply to the left, you get flushed out from your seat, as you don't have your safety belt strapped on. You have lost your balance and are now half kneeling on the floor. You haven't lost your grip on the Glock, though Kohli is twisting your wrist.

Jumbo, meanwhile, has taken a kick on the head from Major Rodriguez. The major has unbuckled his harness and launched himself on Jumbo, going over your head. You feel the pilot pull up on the throttle. He's hovering now, preparing to land. You feel your grip on the Glock beginning to loosen and nearing the point where if, in the next couple of seconds, you do nothing to retrieve your balance, you will surely end up as bug kill on the mat. You squeeze the trigger of your gun. The trajectory is lethal for everybody on board, but apart from the fact that Kohli's grip on your wrist allows few other angles, you have also taken into account the fact that you are probably just three feet or so above ground level, hovering, and with little gas on board to go up in flames on impact.

You see the pilot's head slump on his chest. You hear something snap above your head, where Jumbo is dealing with Rodriguez, or the other way around. And then, as the chopper veers to the ground, out of control, you hear the blades hit the rocks and you can feel the flying machine going head over heels. As it tumbles, your head hits the seat frame in front of you and you lose consciousness.

When you come back to your senses, you are lying twisted amid metal. There is smoke and the faint odor of gas in the air. There are splinters of glass embedded in your face and hands. You don't yet know whether all your bones are in place. There is a gash on your left forearm and blood is dripping from your nose. Major Kohli is slumped over you. You don't know whether he's alive. You are surprised you are. What you see of Jumbo is making you nauseated. A broken piece of rotor blade is sticking out from his chest. His neck is at an unnatural angle, and even though blood is clouding your vision, you detect no signs of life.

What matters most in the way you find yourself is that Major Rodriguez is not where you saw him last. You are finding it difficult to turn your head, but by slanting it a few degrees, you have him in your vision. You can see him outside. He's looking at you and smiling, even though it's a toothless smile. He's rummaging through your kit bag, or what's left of it. You surmise that the crash flung him outside. Your feet are suddenly cold. Water is making its way into the helicopter. It's crashed in a small rivulet. In desperation, you look around for your Glock.

"Looking for this?" asks Major Rodriguez from the outside.

He's palming your piece. Obviously, you have been unconscious for a long time and have slid into the category of the fucked. He's aiming at you now. The son of a bitch even squeezes the trigger. The bullet hits the twisted and charred cockpit controls, which have buckled and are hardly a foot from your face. It ricochets off behind you.

Unexpectedly, you don't flinch. For two reasons. You are suddenly weary and don't care to live any longer. Jumbo's death is getting at your yin and yang. Two, you don't think Rodriguez would relish writing your final chapter so early in the game. He is too much of a cat-and-mouse man to let this opportunity go.

You somehow manage to extricate yourself from under Major Kohli. Kohli copped it from the back. A strip of metal—part of what component, you don't know—entered his heart from between his ribs. His jacket is all soaked with blood, and you see the expression on his face for the first time. Not horrific or pained, but puzzled. You glance at his wrist-watch. Your own is broken. But Kohli's Timex ticks amid all the death and mayhem. The time tells you that it could be an hour since you crashed. You are surprised some troops haven't made it to the crash site yet. You figure distances take a long time in terrain such as this. The Indians will be eager to know the fate of their helicopter and the officers in it. Your own side will be determined to know it first themselves. Information such as this could be spun for huge propaganda, depending on which side of the line of control the machine went down on. The Indians will be aching for a CNN trip to the site, if indeed the wreckage is on their side of the border.

But first there is the looming problem of Major Rodriguez. He is lining you up in his sights once again.

"MM, your time has come. Say your prayers," he says.

"Hey, Rodriguez, what about your money? You don't want your cut anymore?" you ask. "Your money goes with me." Meanwhile, you have twisted and contracted your various muscles to check for injuries. You are badly bruised, but your bones seem to be holding. On what remains of the cockpit floor, in areas that are still dry, lie the flares that you were carrying in your kit bag. You sense an opportunity. They are special non-cartridge flares with brass toggles at the end of strings to set them off. The charge propels the flare four miles into the sky before setting it off. It comes down tied to a miniparachute, even as thick orange smoke emits from the canister, leaving a colorful trail in the daylight.

"You know what, MM? Why are we the only two guys coming out of this crash alive?" asks Major Rodriguez. The major is in a philosophical mood.

Your back is toward Rodriguez. You are shielding the flare with your forearm and the tattered remains of the sleeve of your uniform. Though you would like nothing better than to deliver Rodriguez to the 7 Sikh, you also realize that the flare offers you one slim chance to avoid such a dreary end yourself.

You pull the toggles as you turn, and the flare fires from between your ribs and elbow. You feet the shearing heat, the incandescent burst of red, and as you charge the major and butt his pelvis with your head, you can see the flare has embedded itself in his chest and his clothes are on fire. Shortly, you feel your own scalp burning. And soon you smell the burning flesh from Rodriguez's chest.

You have taken the major down with you in a roll, and though he has yelped in agony, he soon locks himself in a silent death struggle with you. You have taken two rolls in the stream, locked chest-to-chest with Major Rodriguez. The flare has burned you as well, and Rodriguez jabs you ferociously in the ribs and face and flings you loose.

Somewhere in the tussle, the Glock has slipped from his hand, and while he looks for it desperately, he's also lying in the stream to douse the fire engulfing his chest. Then there's the smoke from the flare. Billowing incessantly, it takes Rodriguez in and out of your rather groggy vision. But now you have a two-foot-long piece of jagged metal straddling your arms, and through the smoke and the hiss of steam, realizing the loathing that you have borne for Rodriguez for many years, you swing it in an arc and bring it down in lethal fashion over his chest. You think you have gone through his heart, for a spray of blood hits you. Your palms, too, are cut from where you held the metal.

And even as you lie panting from your exertions and watch life ebb from Rodriguez in shudders, the blood oozing from his mouth, what stays embedded in your memory is your brief glimpse of the fearless gaze in his eyes even as they glazed over.

Though you are glad that Rodriguez is no more, you feel you have lost a kindred spirit. In another time and age, and if the shadow of Shomali hadn't been there, you could have been brothers.

You are fading out yourself. The crash and the fight are getting to your brain. And as you slip into that zone where you don't know whether you are conscious or asleep, you can hear the boom of artillery echo through the hills. What you can also hear, magnified by the hills around you, are cries of *"Jo Bolo So Nihal, Sat Sri Akal."*

You pass out with the selfish knowledge that with the 7 Sikh going into battle at Tiger Hill, there will be no spare troops in the vicinity to come hunting for you. You also know that your Mossie brothers will be out looking for you, and you hope they will find you before all is lost as the battle wages through the night.

When you come to your senses, you are surrounded by soldiers. You recognize the uniform of the Special Services Group, the elite force of the Pakistani army.

Dawn, too, is breaking, and the guns are still booming. You sense from the somber mood that things haven't gone well for your people. It's a while before they notice you have regained consciousness. You feel intact and strong, except for the burn on your chest and some cuts on your forearms and palm. While they have kept you on IV for what you guess must be close to forty-eight hours, you get up in the bunker that you are in. You can hear a machine gun rattling from an adjacent area. You can hear shells flying across and exploding nearby. Near, very near.

"Huzoor kaise hain aap?" asks a voice. You can see he's the medic.

You ask questions and learn about the shit you were in. Of course, you knew this already, except you are now with a different cast of characters. You learn that a platoon strength of the SSG was flown in on two choppers on the west approach of Tiger Hill. Eighteen men were dropped off to locate and extricate you. Each of them had been shown photographs of you, and when they clambered to inspect the ruins of the downed Indian MI-17, which Jumbo had managed to crash about a mile and a half from Tiger Hill, they found you, tattered, bruised, burned, and unconscious.

They lost three men, two of them officers, in sniper fire from the

7 Sikh—who were packing the western approach to Tiger Hill—in just getting you to a fortified bunker two thousand yards from where all hell was breaking loose in the night.

You hear, as you knew two days back, that the Indians had launched an assault up the northeastern side of Tiger Hill, a sheer vertical face of rock, and the least protected side.

What you knew then is not intelligence now. Your army has already suffered from the lack of reliable data. Here, you might have been to blame. Even in dying, Major Rodriguez ensured his victory, albeit indirectly. Tiger Hill has been captured by the Indians—a speedy thrust up the vertical face, coupled with diversionary attacks on the western flank of the hill, which drew the bulk of your troops away from where the action was. The 7 Sikh apparently shouted their war cries on megaphones to convey the presence of large numbers. A very kindergarten-level deception, but very effective.

Followed, of course, by suicidal tendencies when they started radioing for artillery on positions close to them, their logic being that more of yours would be killed than their own. Having successfully dislodged the Northern Light Infantry from the peak, they are now engaged in mopping-up operations.

A window of a few hours remains, however, to launch a counterattack before the Indians consolidate the area with reinforcements to seal their victory over an army dedicated to jihad.

The SSG, which had been tasked to get you out ASAP, has, in light of the humiliating scenario, been retasked to lead the counterattack. You know it's a matter of great shame for an army to be dislodged from an entrenched position, especially one so prestigious and which gives a commanding view of Drass.

The SSG has already committed half a dozen men to lead you away to Skardu by foot. The rest prepare for battle.

But in a way, you have known what you were going to do before the plans for your flight were disclosed to you. You have had this premonition from the moment you hit the hills. You have known you won't get off them in one piece.

As the soft light of the dawn turns harsh, you take over the reins of the SSG. With its officers dead, this is easy. In fact, and you are faintly surprised by this, the top brass of the Pakistani army actively wants you to do so. Obviously, ground realities have been conveyed to them, and in you, perhaps, they see some hope of redeeming lost honor.

They even patch you through to army chief Gen. Pervez Musharraf. The general attempts to pump you up.

"I have wanted to talk to you for a long time, MM. I have read your file. You are a legend. What would we have done without you? The honor of Pakistan and its army rests in your hands. The international situation doesn't allow us to commit any more troops to Kargil. The Americans are pushing us to deescalate. If we can regain Tiger Hill, we will fight on, but if we lose, the Americans are going to push us to withdraw. You have trained with the officers of the SSG, and with you guiding them, I am sure we have a chance," he says.

You are amused. Now that the shit is about to hit the ceiling, the general is reluctant to commit elite forces to the field. Musharraf, you surmise, doesn't know from shit. He doesn't know, for instance, that you are worth more to Pakistan alive than dead. That if you live, Pakistan will live and fight another day, and possibly win. Of course, you won't be on the field anymore. You are too burned for that. But even that, why not? There is plastic surgery. You don't, however, enlighten the general about these thoughts of yours.

"General, I shall do my best," you say. "*Insh'Allah*, we shall drive them out."

It's not that you haven't pondered on what you have decided to do. You aren't about to attempt anything that you haven't been trained for in some measure or other. But in this thing, as in any situation of life, it's your state of mind on which things hinge.

And yours has, perhaps, undergone a paradigm shift. The Americans would call it "blowing a fuse." But the shift that has happened is basically technical in nature. Having been somebody who played the probability game, you are now embarking on something in which you are reducing probability to a sucker's pastime. And you aren't a sucker.

It's actually simple to explain, but the fact of the matter is that it can be understood only by the few of you in the world who belong to this trade. The best of you don't ply your trade for ideology, or pay, or women, or whatever else. That could be a reason for joining. You do it for the rush that comes from a job well done.

It's this philosophy that has permeated the various strands of your life.

Of course, there comes a point, as it has come to you, when you tire even of the rush. That's when the intelligent among you walk out, for the danger after this point is that you don't care anymore whether you score a ten or not. That, too, is a kind of rush—not caring. Actually, this expla-nation might be a trifle unfulfilling. You could be aching for one big rush, the mother of all rapids. A rush like this comes just once in a life-time, and it can come only when you don't care about the consequences.

Which is exactly the place you have reached. How you build up to that point is a matter of individual makeup and circumstance. In the case of yours truly, you are perhaps so meshed up with guys like Rodriguez and Kohli that maybe you are missing the bastards for the fun they gave you. Now, rather than suffer withdrawal symptoms, you want to have one final roller-coaster ride that ends up with the trolley car running out of rails. Besides, no umbilical cords remain for you. You know your adopted parents will soon be history.

You are with strangers now, but it's an outfit that belongs to Islam. There are twenty-seven of you, and all of you take turns to offer final prayers to Allah the Almighty. You have taken off your Indian army uni-form and slipped into a dead soldier's. Some of your men are apprehen-sive that it will bring bad luck, but you can't be bothered with such banalities. The job at hand requires you to function at optimum efficiency, and you want all the totems of military motivation to come to your aid. You are now Kamal Sher of Delta Company of the 12 Northern Light Infantry. The name is threaded on your khaki shirt. You have the stripes of a captain, and you are leading men of the SSG into battle.

At noon, you have gathered your men around you. You acquaint them with what awaits them. You brief them on the enemy. They are from the 7 Sikh, you tell them. What you omit is that in late April you polished off three of the 7 Sikh in your solo run away from Rodriguez's pack. That was your atonement for the incident when you went on patrol with Rodriguez and watched him slaughter five Mossies who had just crossed a stream. Your solo left Rodriguez bewildered. He didn't know the blood that flowed in your veins. That was your first taste of Sikh blood.

But you tell your men about the historic battle of Saragarhi in the nineteenth century, when twenty-two Sikhs fought till the last man and the last bullet against a superior force of Afghan tribesmen.

"You are going to face the same here. They are a brave people. But we are braver," you tell them. Though if someone asks you how a corrupt army unit can offer war that is so gallant, you would have no reasons to give. Except pride in their unit and race.

Somewhere behind the rocks in front is also Maj. Raunaq Singh. It will be a charming, lead-filled encounter, you muse.

You then go into your battle cry of "*Allahu o akbar*," and it resonates around the hills and the valley. The Sikhs go silent. Some last rites remain. You proceed into the bunker where you regained consciousness that morning. As you go inside, you see written in chalk across the entrance the number the NLI gave to this place of refuge from Indian shelling—Bunker 13. You smile at the coincidence. Maybe, you think, this was the way your Maker was giving you the green light—not that you were looking for one. You remember the same number from the place where Major Kohli initiated you into bunker politics.

In privacy, you tear your chemical kit from your underwear. You take your last infusion of heroin. With heroin, you have passed the stage where the chemical affects the clarity of your mind. This is to blunt the pain that you know will come your way as you launch into battle with the Sikhs. You are about to lead twenty-six men to their deaths. And the chances of success for your band depend on how long you are able to stay alive.

ACKNOWLEDGMENTS

Satya Pramod Shastriji for his prayers. Monu and Dwarkanathji for their well wishes and for suffering my numerous phone calls; Dada and Lakshmi for some big favors; the fish I have enjoyed feeding at the river that runs through the Sharada Peetham at Sringeri; Babaji; Dada in Allahabad; Livleen; and Dr. Kashyap.

My daughters, Rhea and Esha, for sitting on my lap on occasion as I worked my computer—Rhea being mesmerized by the screen and Esha by the keyboard; Reema, for her good-natured tolerance of the many hours I have been immersed in word machines over the years; Tarun and Vinod Mehta for sanctioning me two months' unpaid leave way back in 1996 when this novel started; Gillon Aitken and Antony Harwood, for seeing some promise—they have to now suffer this; Jonathan and Jon for some splendid editing; Anne Korin and Stephen Farrel for making some suggestions; the many dozens of books that I researched from and whose names I was too sloppy to take down for a proper mention; and Mita for egging me to complete it.

Also, to all the lawyers and others who have supported us at Tehelka over the last two years and more. I would have had no time, inclination, or peace of mind for any creative pursuit had it not been for their pro bono work and extraordinary support. In order of appearance (based on my chaotic memory) I profusely thank Viraj Dattar; Pravin Anand; Kavin Gulati, my schoolfriend whose general equanimity and common sense have seen us through many months of legal turmoil; Siddharth Dave; Nishith Desai; Ashni; John Holton; Medhanshu Tripathi—if law failed us he could double as our chief muscle man; Kapil Sibal, the nuke in our arsenal; Prashant Bhushan, who has a conscience few lawyers can equal; Vishal; Sidharth Luthra, who put in many dozens of hours of frenzied work and held the fort on days when the vandals were screeching at the gates; Pramod Dubey, for showering us with his precious Bihari insights; Dushyant Dave, who can dictate a twenty-page application in about fifteen minutes while listening to Mozart; Shanti Bhushan, whose mere presence gave us minions at Tehelka many million volts of confidence; Rani Jethmalani, who gave us much required moral support along with delicious sandwiches; Baldev Malik, Gitanjali; Ram Jethmalani—when you have him on your side it doesn't matter how many thugs the Union of India has arrayed against you, his voice is enough; Meet Malhotra—you can give him some task and forget about it; Satyanarain Vashisth; Amit Prasad; Madhukar Pandey; Kapoorji; Smriti; Vaibhav; Uttara; C. V. Nagesh, the genius from Bangalore; R. K. Anand, who could give Sherlock Holmes a run for his money; Rajiv Dhawan, who can untie a legal knot in real time but who isn't quite enamored of our tendency to disappear for weeks without notice; Gopal Chaturvedi, who can regale you with anecdotes all day; Anil Diwan, for moral support and agreeing to be our general in reserve; and Rakesh Dwivedi.

Of course, this list wouldn't be complete without mentioning some Tehelka staffers, former and current, who put in many hours of toil. Anu Nair, for her industry; Arun Bhanot—without him we would have been at sea; Sanjeev Kapur, for his meticulousness and reliability; Kumar Badal, a very special colleague and one who, realistically speaking, has shouldered the bulk of the government's vendetta against Tehelka—maybe someday there will be an inquiry against the CBI for his malicious prosecution; Arnab Pratim Datta, a tireless and most loyal colleague; Shamya Dasgupta, for being on call; Arun Nair, for staying on and helping us in the most crucial of phases; Brij, our one-man army; Neena, for her energy when she's around; Parsa Venkateshwar Rao, Jr., and Venkat Parsa for believing in Tehelka; Hemendra Singh; Ajay; Minty; Prabal; Matthew Samuel, without whose heroic deeds many of the above wouldn't have been employed;

Shoma Chaudhary, for being one of the few pleasant sights as I labored for a month on the witness stand; and Rakesh, for managing the cumbersome logistics of lunch.

Which brings me straight to put on the record my special thanks to Sir V. S. Naipaul, Lady Nadira Naipaul, Pradeep Kishan, Uma Shankar, Upendra Baxi, Anand Patwardhan, Madhu Kishwar, Mark Tully, Admiral Purohit, and Prem Shankar Jha, for speaking their minds without fear or favor.

It would also have been difficult for us at Tehelka to survive so far without friends like Madanjit Singh of the Rainbow Foundation, Carl Pope of the Sierra Foundation, Shenaz, H. S. Vedi, Satya Sheel, Arundhati Roy, Nilanjan Tolia, Manoj Prabhakar, Biswadeep Moitra, Manish Tiwari, Carin Fischer, Deven Verma, Mahim Mehra, Mahesh Jethmalani, Madhavan Kutty, Devanshu, Vijay Raman, Shekhar Bhatia, Billy Singh, the late Priya Tendulkar, Sudhir Varma (our number cruncher), and Pavan Sethi (may everybody have a landlord like him).

Last but not least, Shankar and Devina, for they have taught me the meaning of courage in the face of evil; and all my friends in the media.